# WESTERN

*Rugged men looking for love...*

## The Maverick's Resolution
### Brenda Harlen

## A Match For The Sheriff
### Lisa Childs

# MILLS & BOON

Brenda Harlen is acknowledged as the author of this work
THE MAVERICK'S RESOLUTION
© 2024 by Harlequin Enterprises ULC
Philippine Copyright 2024
Australian Copyright 2024
New Zealand Copyright 2024

First Published 2024
First Australian Paperback Edition 2024
ISBN 978 1 038 93907 4

A MATCH FOR THE SHERIFF
© 2024 by Lisa Childs
Philippine Copyright 2024
Australian Copyright 2024
New Zealand Copyright 2024

First Published 2024
First Australian Paperback Edition 2024
ISBN 978 1 038 93907 4

This is a work of fiction. Names, characters, places, and incidents are either the
product of the author's imagination or are used fictitiously, and any resemblance to
actual persons, living or dead, business establishments, events, or locales is entirely
coincidental.

MIX
Paper | Supporting
responsible forestry
FSC® C001695

Published by
Harlequin Mills & Boon
An imprint of Harlequin Enterprises (Australia) Pty Limited
(ABN 47 001 180 918), a subsidiary of HarperCollins
Publishers Australia Pty Limited
(ABN 36 009 913 517)
Level 19, 201 Elizabeth Street
SYDNEY NSW 2000 AUSTRALIA

Cover art used by arrangement with Harlequin Books S.A.. All rights reserved.

Printed and bound in Australia by McPherson's Printing Group

# The Maverick's Resolution

## Brenda Harlen

MILLS & BOON

**Brenda Harlen** is a former attorney who once had the privilege of appearing before the Supreme Court of Canada. The practice of law taught her a lot about the world and reinforced her determination to become a writer—because in fiction, she ould promise a happy ending! Now she is an award-winning, RITA® Award—nominated, nationally bestselling author of more than sixty titles for Harlequin. You can keep up-to-date with Brenda on Facebook and Twitter, or through her website, brendaharlen.com.

## Books by Brenda Harlen

### *Montana Mavericks: The Trail to Tenacity*

*The Maverick's Resolution*

### *Match Made in Haven*

*The Sheriff's Nine-Month Surprise*
*Her Seven-Day Fiancé*
*Six Weeks to Catch a Cowboy*
*Claiming the Cowboy's Heart*
*Double Duty for the Cowboy*
*One Night with the Cowboy*
*A Chance for the Rancher*
*The Marine's Road Home*
*Meet Me Under the Mistletoe*
*The Rancher's Promise*
*The Chef's Surprise Baby*
*Captivated by the Cowgirl*
*Countdown to Christmas*
*Her Not-So-Little Secret*
*The Rancher's Christmas Reunion*
*Snowed In with a Stranger*
*Her Favorite Mistake*

Visit the Author Profile page
at millsandboon.com.au for more titles.

Dear Reader,

When the clock strikes twelve, Ruby McKinley has one resolution for the New Year: to be the best mom she can be to her four-year-old daughter. Shortly thereafter, an unexpected phone call leads to her amending that resolution to include a three-month-old baby boy.

Julian Sanchez can picture what he wants for his future, and Ruby and her kids are part of that picture. Of course, it's going to take some doing to convince the wary single mom to give him a chance—a task further complicated by the fact she used to be married to his best friend.

Love isn't always easy, and Ruby and Julian's fledgling relationship will face its share of challenges, including leaky dishwashers, spontaneous social worker visits, well-meaning but interfering family members and even an octogenarian uncle in search of his missing bride.

It's been a big year for the Montana Mavericks series as it marks thirty years of happily-ever-afters, and I'm thrilled to bring you Ruby and Julian's story as part of the celebration.

I hope you enjoy visiting Tenacity, Montana...and perhaps you'll see a long-awaited happy ending for Winona Cobbs and Stanley Sanchez, too!

xo *Brenda*

For foster parents everywhere, with appreciation for everything you do and the boundless love you share.

And especially my sister and brother-in-law, aka "Mimi and Papa" to their Emy.

# *CHAPTER ONE*

*Tenacity, Montana*

RUBY MCKINLEY DIDN'T mind having to work New Year's Eve. Besides, it wasn't as if she had any better offers for the evening. Unlike her babysitter, who bailed at the eleventh hour when her sometimes-boyfriend invited her to go out, forcing Ruby to take her daughter to work with her. Thankfully, four-year-old Emery never complained about going to the inn with her mom, though that didn't make Ruby feel much better about it as she settled her little girl on the sofa in the manager's office with her iPad while she worked the front desk.

Though the hardscrabble town wasn't anyone's idea of a holiday hot spot, one of the event rooms at the inn had been booked for a party tonight. Ruby had seen the musical entertainment— the Row House Four, according to the placards posted on either side of the doors—come in earlier to set up for the party and had recognized one of them as Marisa Sanchez.

Marisa was a local piano teacher who'd become an internet superstar after a video of her multicultural, offbeat spin on the holidays had gone viral the previous Christmas. Ruby didn't know Marisa well, but the pianist's brother, Julian, was a good friend of Ruby's ex-husband. Her bandmates were apparently Marisa's roommates from her college days in Boston.

Ruby tapped her foot to the beat of the music emanating from behind closed doors and wondered what it would be like to have friends like Marisa had—friends who would travel halfway across the country to perform with her, just because she asked. Ruby was still in touch with some of her friends from high school and college in Wyoming, via the exchange of holiday cards and occasional text messages, but she honestly couldn't remember the last time that she'd met Lucy for lunch or had coffee with Shanice or even chatted on the phone with Caitlin. Of course, her friends were all married now and busy with their own families, and since Ruby's parents had moved to Florida, she had no reason to make the trip back to Wyoming.

Sure, she'd made new friends in Tenacity—including Megan Grant, the manager of the Tenacity Inn; Chrissy Hastings-Parker, who did catering for the hotel; and Lynda Slater, who'd selflessly offered both friendship and free legal advice when Ruby's marriage was falling apart. And while she enjoyed spending time with her friends when their schedules allowed, most of her hours outside of work were occupied by her daughter.

Suddenly, the music faded and the revelers in the party room began to count down to midnight. A quick peek into the office confirmed that Emery had fallen asleep watching her favorite Disney movie. Her wispy blond hair was splayed out on the throw pillow behind her head, and her hand was curled into a pudgy fist, her thumb resting against the lower lip of her Cupid's bow mouth.

Emery had never taken to a pacifier, but she did love to suck her thumb. And while Ruby liked to think she'd been making some progress in her efforts to break her daughter of the habit, there were occasional lapses—most often when the little girl wasn't in her bed at home, as was the case tonight.

The sound of noisemakers emanating from the party room confirmed that the new year had arrived, and Ruby lifted her can of 7UP in a silent toast to her daughter.

*Happy New Year, my baby—the very best part of my life. I've never been big on resolutions, but this year, I'm going to do better for both of us.*

The celebratory din began to fade, only to be immediately

followed by another round of cheers. Before Ruby had a chance to speculate on the potential cause, Marisa Sanchez and Dawson John burst through the doors. The sound of cheers, whoops and a distinct *pop* of a champagne bottle could be heard in the event room.

Marisa waved her left hand in the air, the diamond on her third finger flashing in the overhead lights. "Dawson asked me to marry him—and I said *yes*." Then she turned to her fiancé and gave him a smacking kiss. "I feel like I'm the luckiest person in the world."

"Second luckiest," Dawson countered. "Because *I'm* the luckiest."

"Well, congratulations to you both," Ruby said sincerely.

And she was truly happy for the couple, who were obviously in love and excited about their future together. At the same time, she couldn't help but feel a little sad, because it didn't seem like so very long ago that she'd been the one showing off her engagement ring. That she'd been the one full of hopes and dreams for her life with the handsome and charming Owen McKinley—a life that had quickly fallen apart.

As she watched Marisa and Dawson, now surrounded by family and friends who'd spilled out of the party room into the lobby to offer their best wishes to the happy couple, Ruby found herself wondering if she'd ever experience love again…

Or maybe she should wonder if she'd ever know the joy of truly loving and being loved—because she'd recently found herself questioning if she'd really been in love with the man she'd married or just wanted to believe herself in love. Because at the time she'd met Owen, several of her friends back home in Wyoming had been planning weddings and preparing to have babies and Ruby, newly arrived in Tenacity, Montana, had been feeling alone and lonely.

And wasn't that a sad commentary on her marriage?

And perhaps proof that Owen had been right to blame her for its failure.

She pushed aside the unhappy thoughts, reminding herself that her marriage was in the past and she was looking forward to the future, especially now, at the beginning of a brand new year.

And then every last thought slipped from her mind as her gaze landed on Julian Sanchez and registered the fact that Marisa's brother was making his way toward the front desk.

Julian had gone to high school with Owen, and he'd spent a fair amount of time hanging out with her husband when she and Owen were married, which was how she'd gotten to know the local ranch hand. He'd always been polite and respectful—albeit a little distant, until Emery's birth had breached that distance.

From the first minute, the little girl had him wrapped around her finger, and watching him respond to her daughter with such openness and warmth—a contrast to Owen's cautious disinterest—had filled Ruby's heart with joy. He'd been a doting and favorite "uncle" throughout the entire first year of her daughter's life, until Ruby learned about her husband's cheating and kicked him out of the house, resulting in Emery losing not only her father but also her honorary uncle.

Of course, Owen was entitled to visitation, and Ruby had been more than reasonable there. The fact that he rarely chose to spend time with his daughter was entirely on him. Thankfully Caroline and Mark McKinley—Emery's paternal grandparents—doted on their granddaughter and stepped in to fill at least some of the void resulting from her father's abandonment.

Ruby suspected that Julian's absence had left an even bigger void back then, but of course her daughter had been too young to have retained any memories of him.

But Ruby remembered him, and while he was obviously at the inn for the party, she had to wonder—why was he coming toward her?

And why was her heart suddenly beating a little too fast inside her chest?

It was possible that her physical reaction had something to do with the fact that Julian Sanchez was a seriously good-looking guy.

He was about six feet tall, she guessed—similar in height to her ex-husband. But that was where the similarities ended. Owen McKinley was smooth and polished and always immaculately dressed—his designer shirts neatly pressed (by the local dry cleaner, of course, because he couldn't trust his wife to do it right) and his ties perfectly knotted.

No one would describe Julian Sanchez as smooth and polished. He was usually unshaven, his hair seemingly always in need of a trim, his broad shoulders straining the seams of his Western-style shirts. But it was his eyes—dark and intense and full of wicked promise—that caused a woman's blood to heat inside her veins when they were focused on her. And his mouth—exquisitely shaped and quick to curve—that made a woman's knees quiver when he smiled at her.

Of course, she meant any *other* woman's blood and any *other* woman's knees, because his friendship with her ex-husband had made her immune to Julian Sanchez.

But he looked *really* good tonight, his usual rancher attire upgraded to include dark jeans and a shirt that looked more L.L.Bean than C.C. Filson, plus dress boots and a leather jacket.

Still, that was no reason for her blood to suddenly be humming in her veins.

And that was *before* he smiled at her.

As his lips curved, an unexpected warmth spread through her veins.

Or maybe she was having a hot flash.

Was twenty-nine too young for menopause?

Probably.

But she was reluctant to consider any other explanation for her physiological reaction to the rancher's presence.

"Hello, Ruby."

She managed to smile back. Even better, she didn't stammer as she replied, "Happy New Year, Julian."

"And to you," he said. "Though I'm sure it would be off to a better start if you hadn't had to work tonight."

"I didn't mind," she said. "It's not as if I had other plans, anyway."

"No other plans?" He sounded incredulous. "A beautiful woman like you? I find that hard to believe."

Beautiful? Did he really think so?

Or was he toying with her?

Either way, she felt her cheeks grow warm in response to his words.

"Trust me," she said. "There aren't too many men who want to ring in the New Year with a single mom and her four-year-old daughter."

"I think you'd be surprised," he said. "But speaking of—where is Emery tonight?"

She nodded toward the partially closed door behind her. "In the office."

"Eating caviar and sipping champagne?"

He was obviously teasing, but it had been so long since she'd exchanged playful banter with a handsome man that she'd evidently forgotten how.

"Sleeping."

Julian grinned at her lame response, anyway, and her knees melted.

Seriously, the man's smile should be registered as a lethal weapon.

Or maybe her visceral reaction was a sign that something was wrong with her.

This man was a friend—a *good* friend—of her ex-husband. And while that didn't necessarily make him her enemy, it certainly gave her cause to be wary.

Even if Julian had always been kind to her.

But she didn't think he was only being kind now.

In fact, it almost seemed as if he was flirting with her.

Or maybe that was wishful thinking on her part.

Because more than a year after her divorce—and three years after the breakdown of her marriage, she hadn't been on a single date. Which meant that she hadn't kissed a man—never mind anything more intimate than that—in more than three years.

In fact, it had been so long since she'd experienced anything like sexual desire, she'd been certain that her hormones had gone dormant, like flowering bulbs in the cold of winter. Except that winter had lasted three long years for Ruby, and though it was still winter now—and bitterly cold outside—those hormones seemed to be stirring to life again.

Her unexpected reaction to Julian's presence was so unnerving that she was almost relieved when her cellphone rang, intruding on their conversation.

She glanced at the unfamiliar number displayed on the screen.

It was just after midnight on New Year's Day, and as she'd exchanged text messages with her parents and each of her siblings earlier in the evening, she suspected this was probably a wrong number.

"Excuse me," she said to Julian.

"Of course."

She swiped to connect the call. "Hello?"

"Ruby McKinley?"

"Yes," she confirmed warily.

"It's Hazel Browning from Family Services."

The caller's identification only exacerbated Ruby's confusion.

Why would Family Services be calling her at this time of night?

Unless...

Her heart skipped a beat as cautious hope unfurled inside her.

"What can I do for you, Ms. Browning?"

"I'm hoping you can foster a baby boy."

Ruby was stunned.

Overjoyed.

And maybe just the teensiest bit apprehensive.

When she was interviewed after applying to be a foster parent, she'd been warned that she might never get a call. That her interest in being a foster parent was appreciated, but that single parents weren't able to provide the optimal environment for a child in need of a family.

She'd been disappointed, of course, but not really surprised.

If she'd had a choice, she wouldn't be raising her daughter as a single parent, either. But all things considered, it was preferable to raising Emery in a home where her dad's infidelities weren't a secret to anyone.

"Ms. McKinley? Are you there?"

"Yes," she said. "And yes, I'd be happy to take the baby, just tell me when."

"Now."

"*Now?*" she echoed, stunned.

"Or in about two hours," Ms. Browning clarified. "Which is how long it will take me to get the baby and all his stuff packed up and make the trip from Bronco."

"Two hours." She glanced at her watch.

"Is that a problem?"

"It's just that I'm at work right now. At the Tenacity Inn."

She heard papers rustling over the line before Ms. Browning spoke again. "There was nothing in your file indicating that you work nights."

"I don't usually," she explained. "I'm just covering for someone tonight."

"Well, you've got two hours to get someone to cover for you," Ms. Browning told her. "But if you don't think that's possible, I can call the next name on my list."

"No!" Ruby protested.

Her vehement response caused Chrissy Hastings-Parker to pause on her way past the desk.

"I'll figure something out," Ruby continued at a more normal volume. "Please don't call anyone else."

"Okay," Ms. Browning relented. And after verifying Ruby's address, she promised that she'd be on her way as soon as possible.

"Is everything okay?" Chrissy asked, when Ruby ended her call.

"That was Family Services."

Chrissy immediately went on the defensive. "Why would they be hassling you?" she demanded to know. "You're a wonderful mother to Emery."

"They're not hassling me," Ruby hastened to assure her friend. "I'm going to be a foster parent."

"Oh. Wow."

"Yeah, that's exactly how I'm feeling."

"So they have a child for you?"

She nodded. "A baby boy."

"I guess that's good news then," Chrissy said.

"Except that Ms. Browning is on her way from Bronco with

the baby right now, and she expects me to be home to take custody of him in two hours and I'm scheduled to be here for another five."

"I can cover the desk for you," Julian said.

Ruby blinked.

In her excitement about the call, she'd forgotten that he was there.

*Why was he still there?*

"Thanks," she said. "But I can't just abandon my responsibilities to someone who has absolutely no hotel experience."

"How do you know I don't have any hotel experience?" he challenged.

"Just a wild guess," she said. "Am I wrong?"

"No," he admitted. "Unless checking in from the other side of the desk counts."

"It doesn't," she told him.

"But I have hotel experience," Chrissy chimed in. "I can hang out here until the day clerk arrives."

"I couldn't ask that of you," Ruby protested.

"You didn't ask, I offered," her friend reminded her. "And what other option do you have?"

"I was hoping Aihan might be willing to come in early."

"If she is and she can, great," Chrissy said. "If she isn't or can't, I'll be here until she shows up for her usual shift."

Ruby was torn. "I really would like to get Emery home and settled into bed before Ms. Browning arrives. And I should tidy up a little, because I'm sure she'll want to do a quick inspection of the house before she leaves the baby."

"So go," Chrissy urged. "And don't worry about the desk. I can't imagine anyone is going to be checking in during the wee hours of the morning of New Year's Day."

"I'm going," Ruby promised. "But before I do—would you know if there's anyone working in maintenance tonight?"

"What do you need?" Julian asked.

"If I've got time before the baby arrives, I might be able to put Emery's old crib together so he has somewhere to sleep."

"I can help with that," he said.

"Do you have more experience assembling cribs than you do behind a hotel desk?"

"As a matter of fact, I do. And while it's admittedly limited experience, it was assembling your daughter's crib."

"You put Emery's crib together?"

"Have you ever seen Owen assemble anything more complicated than an Ikea bookcase?"

"No," she admitted. "And even that wasn't completed without a lot of cursing."

"There's a surprise," Chrissy muttered under her breath.

"But I'm sure you have better things to be doing at—" she glanced at the watch on her wrist "—half past midnight on New Year's Eve."

"Isn't it technically New Year's Day now?"

"I guess it is," she agreed.

"And no," he said. "I don't have anything better to be doing."

"How about sleeping?" she suggested. "Doesn't morning come early when you work on a ranch?"

"It does," he acknowledged. "But what kind of a cowboy would walk away from a woman in distress?"

"I'm not in distress," she felt compelled to point out.

Chrissy elbowed her in the ribs. "Ruby, the man's offering to do you a favor."

"And I appreciate it, but—"

"The correct response is, 'that would be helpful—thank you, Julian,'" her friend interjected.

Ruby felt her cheeks grow warm. "Is that the correct response?" she asked Julian.

He shrugged. "Only if you think it would be helpful."

"I do. I mean, it would. If you happen to have a screwdriver on you. My neighbor borrowed my toolbox on the weekend and hasn't yet returned it."

"I've got a whole set of screwdrivers in the toolbox in my truck."

"Then that would be helpful," she acknowledged. "Thank you, Julian."

He responded with a nod and a smile, and she nearly melted into a puddle at his feet.

"Now that wasn't so hard, was it?" Chrissy teased.

Ruby rolled her eyes at her friend, who grinned, unrepentant.

"I'll follow you home," Julian said.

Now Ruby nodded. "Okay. I just need a few minutes to pack up Emery and her things."

To her surprise, he followed her into the office and began gathering up the books and toys that her daughter had left scattered around.

"Just dump everything into that bag," she said, gesturing to the bright pink-and-orange backpack that Emery insisted on taking with her everywhere.

While he did so, she wrestled her sleeping child into her puffy coat and snow boots.

Emery stirred as she tugged the second boot into place. "Mommy?"

"It's time to go home, Em."

Her daughter blinked sleepily. "Is it the New Year?"

"It is," she confirmed. "Happy New Year."

"Happy New Year," Emery echoed, yawning. Then, having caught sight of Julian, she said to him, "Who are you?"

"That's Mr. Sanchez," Ruby said.

"Julian," he chimed in.

But the little girl's interest in the stranger wasn't any match for her sleepiness, and her eyes drifted shut again.

Ruby retrieved her coat and purse from the rack by the door and buttoned herself up against the cold outside before reaching to lift her daughter into her arms.

"Let me carry her," Julian suggested.

"I can manage," Ruby assured him.

"I'm sure you can," he said. "But I'm offering to help."

Her friend's recent admonishment echoing in her head, she said, "That would be helpful—thank you, Julian."

He grinned and took the sleeping child from her arms.

Ruby picked up the backpack and her purse and led the way out of the office, pausing at the desk to thank Chrissy again and finagle her promise to call if she had any questions.

"The Honda SUV," she told Julian, gesturing with the key fob as they exited the building.

As she hit the unlock button, the lights flashed. She hurried to open the back door, so that he could put Emery in her car seat.

"I'm going to let you buckle her up. That way you know it's done right," Julian said, stepping back so that she could lean in to secure the five-point harness.

She started the engine and turned the defroster on high, then stepped out again with her snow brush in hand.

"Get in," Julian said, giving her a gentle nudge. "I'll clear the snow off."

"Shouldn't you be dealing with your own vehicle?"

"It had stopped snowing by the time I got here. My truck's fine."

With a shrug, she slid into the driver's seat and watched through the defrosting windshield as he brushed the snow away. When he was finished, he opened the passenger-side door and set the brush on the floor mat.

"I'll be right behind you," he promised.

"22 Pine Street," she said. "In case you lose me in traffic."

He chuckled at the unlikelihood of that happening and hurried to his truck.

She waited until she saw him pulling out of his spot, then made her way to the exit of the parking lot.

It was a short drive to her house from the inn—of course, most everything in Tenacity was a short drive from everything else—and less than ten minutes later, she was pulling into the driveway of the simple two-story Colonial that was now her home with Emery.

True to his word, Julian was right behind her.

She grabbed her purse and her daughter's backpack and unbuckled Emery's harness, then stepped back to allow him to pick up the still-sleeping child.

Her boot slipped on the bottom step and she wobbled a little. Even with his arms full of little girl, he managed to reach out and steady her.

"You alright?"

She nodded. "The steps are a little bit slippery. As soon as I get Emery settled in bed, I'll come back out to shovel them off. Or at least throw some salt down."

"You take care of your daughter," he said. "I'll take care of the steps."

She decided there was no point in arguing.

And why would she protest when the idea of venturing out into the cold again in the early hours of morning held little appeal?

He waited patiently in the foyer while she removed her boots and coat and put them away in the closet, and he continued to hold Emery while she took off her daughter's outerwear.

"S'eepy," the little girl said, her eyelids flickering.

"I know, baby," Ruby said, her voice a gentle whisper. "I'm going to take you up to bed right now."

"And I'll be back to deal with the crib as soon as I get those steps taken care of," Julian promised, matching her tone.

"You haven't asked where I keep my shovel," she noted.

"I don't need your shovel," he said. "I have one in the back of my truck. And a bag of salt, too."

"You must have been a Scout."

"I wasn't," he said. "But I did grow up in Montana, so I know the importance of traveling with the basic requirements for survival in winter."

"Then I'll let you get to it," she said. "Thank you."

But she stayed where she was for a few more seconds, watching as he walked out the door and thinking that it had been a long time since she'd had a man around her house—and certain she'd never had a man like Julian Sanchez.

## *CHAPTER TWO*

HE SHOULD HAVE walked away.

Back at the inn, when Ruby excused herself to answer her phone, Julian should have turned around and gone back to the party.

But he'd been curious to know who might be calling her at such an hour, and that curiosity compelled him to linger.

Of course, being New Year's Eve, it could have been any number of people wanting to wish her a Happy New Year. A family member or friend. Possibly even a boyfriend.

Though he didn't think she had a boyfriend. He likely would have heard through the grapevine if she was dating anyone, but it wasn't outside the realm of possibility. Ruby McKinley was a beautiful woman and she'd been divorced for more than a year now.

The divorce—especially the reason for it—was further proof to Julian that Owen McKinley was a fool. Because he'd had an amazing woman like Ruby as his wife—and an adorable daughter like Emery—and he'd thrown it all away.

Of course, to hear Owen tell it, he was the injured party. He didn't want the divorce, but Ruby had kicked him out. The fact that he'd been cheating on her—and with more than one woman—wasn't any reason for her to abandon the vows he'd already broken. Besides, he'd continued to argue in his defense to his buddies at the Grizzly Bar, she'd let herself go when she got pregnant.

And then, after the baby was born, she barely had two minutes for him. Any time Emery made a sound, she jumped up to see what the kid needed. And the kid got a lot more boob time than he did. (Yes, those were Owen's actual words!)

Was it any wonder, he'd argued, that he'd found himself looking outside of the home for comfort and companionship?

As Julian sprinkled salt over the now cleared steps, the burn of his residual anger at his former friend ensured that he wasn't overly bothered by the cold temperature, despite the clouds that appeared with each breath he exhaled.

Sometimes he found himself wondering how he'd ever become friends with Owen McKinley. Of course, the absence of any kind of moral compass in his friend hadn't been as readily apparent to Julian back in high school, which was when Owen had sought him out. Even then, he'd known the most popular kid in school had ulterior motives for his apparent offer of friendship. But Julian hadn't cared, because hanging out with Owen immediately made him part of the "in" crowd, which afforded him a certain amount of deference and respect—and increased attention from the female element of the student body.

But while they'd both graduated from high school a lot of years earlier, it seemed that Owen had never really grown up. He still seemed to think he was the biggest man on campus and expected everyone else to defer to his wishes.

And why wouldn't he?

Owen had always gotten everything he wanted—including all the prettiest girls. Even Laura Bell, though Owen hadn't looked at Laura twice until Julian started dating her.

But that was a long time ago.

Water under the bridge—his mother would say.

After high school, Owen had immediately gone to work with his father at McKinley Insurance Brokers and Julian had been promoted to full-time ranch hand at Blue Sky Beef. With many of their former classmates off at college, Owen and Julian had spent a lot of their free time together.

Working a nine-to-five office job, Owen had a lot more free

time, but Julian didn't envy him that. He'd much rather ride the range than sit behind a desk.

No, Julian didn't envy Owen at all until Ruby Jensen moved to town and Owen immediately moved in on her.

Less than six months later, they were engaged.

Six months after that, they were married.

Julian had stood up for his friend at the wedding, his heart aching with the certainty that Owen was marrying the woman meant for *him*.

Not that he would have ever let her know how he felt, because Owen had met her first, and there was no way he would ever make a move on his friend's girl.

But she wasn't Owen's girlfriend or fiancée or wife anymore.

She was his ex-wife.

A single woman.

And Julian had never stopped wanting her.

He'd spent a fair amount of time at their house when Owen and Ruby were married. After they separated, he had no excuse to stop by to see her or her daughter, who had taken hold of his heart as quickly and completely as Ruby had done.

But he'd knocked on her door once—after he'd heard that Owen was celebrating the finalization of his divorce in the Grizzly Bar—to make sure that she was okay.

She'd been wary.

Understandably, he supposed, as she'd only ever known him as Owen's friend.

But more than a year had passed since then—proof of which was most evident in her little girl. Emery had been a toddler the last time he saw her; now she was a preschooler. And every bit as irresistible as her mom.

He returned the shovel and salt to his truck and walked up to Ruby's front door with his toolbox in hand.

She opened the door before he had a chance to knock and offered him a smile.

And just like always, that smile landed like a fist to his solar plexus and stole all the air from his lungs.

She stepped back to allow him entry.

"Emery all tucked into bed?" he asked, when he'd managed to catch his breath and could speak again.

"Tucked in and fast asleep."

"To be a kid again," he mused.

"Tell me about it."

She hung up his coat while he took off his boots.

He noticed that she'd taken the time to change out of her work attire while he was outside, trading her black pants and blazer for a pair of navy leggings and a lighter blue sweater with a big sparkly snowflake on the front. Her hair was still loose, the blonde tresses spilling over her shoulders.

"Where's the crib?" he asked, picking up the toolbox again.

"Upstairs. In the spare bedroom."

She started up the stairs, and he followed—admiring the subtle sway of her hips and the shapely curve of her bottom.

"I almost got rid of it, when I was packing up for the move," she confided. "The way my marriage ended, I couldn't imagine that I'd ever have another child. But I guess I wasn't ready to give up the dream entirely, because I held on to all of Emy's baby furniture."

"A good thing," he noted.

She nodded.

"So this is where the baby's going to sleep?"

"Actually, it might be a better idea to put the crib in my room," she said. "I think he's only a few months old, which means he'll be up a few times in the night, and if he's all the way across the hall, he might wake up Emy before I can get to him."

"You *think* he's a few months old? They didn't give you any specific information about the child?"

She shrugged. "I was so surprised to get the call, I didn't think to ask."

"Why were you surprised?" he asked her now.

"When I was interviewed by Family Services, I was bluntly advised not to get my hopes up, because single parents are always at the bottom of the list when it comes to placing a child."

"Apparently whoever told you that was wrong," he noted.

"More likely, being it was New Year's Eve, they couldn't

get in touch with any of the other foster parents on the list and eventually made their way down to my name at the bottom."

"Even if that's true, I'd say the baby coming here lucked out."

"I hope he thinks so, too," she said, picking up one of the pieces of the disassembled crib leaning against one wall and carrying it across the hall.

He followed her with a couple more pieces, then made one more trip across the hall and he had all the pieces to begin assembly.

"Is it too much to hope that you have the instructions?" he asked.

She retrieved the manual from the other room. "Right here."

"Thanks."

She perched on the edge of the bed—neatly made with what looked like a handstitched quilt in various shades of blue and a couple of matching throw pillows—which wreaked havoc with his efforts to not think about the fact that he was in her bedroom, only a few feet away from the bed in which she slept.

*No good deed goes unpunished.*

He glanced at the instructions, wondering about the origin of the subtle scent that teased his nostrils. Her perfume? Shampoo? Or maybe the trio of chunky candles on her dresser?

"Can I help or do you want me out of your way?"

Ruby's question yanked his attention back to the task at hand.

"Actually, an extra set of hands would be good," he said. "You can hold the pieces in position while I secure them with the hardware."

"I can do that," she agreed. "Probably."

At his questioning look, she shrugged.

"Owen always said I was useless at household tasks."

"Well, your ex-husband always was an ass."

She seemed taken aback by his remark. "I thought you and Owen were good friends."

"We were," he said. "And then I realized that he was an ass. And an idiot."

A glimmer of amusement shone in the depths of her blue eyes. "And what made you come to that realization?"

"I saw the way he treated you."

The amusement vanished and she quickly looked away, a slight flush of color infusing her cheeks. "You know he cheated on me."

"I'm sorry. I shouldn't have said anything."

"No." She shook her head. "It's okay. I mean, it's *not* okay, but I'm sure, by the time I finally got around to kicking him out, everyone in town knew that he was tomcatting around."

"Which had absolutely nothing to do with you and everything to do with him," he assured her.

She laughed softly, though there was no humor in the sound. "It had everything to do with me, because I was his wife. If I'd been able to keep him satisfied, he wouldn't have gone looking elsewhere."

"I'm sure that's what he told you, to make you feel responsible," Julian said. "But you're smart enough to know it isn't true."

"So why do *you* think he cheated?" she asked him.

"Because marriage has specific rules, and Owen was never good at playing by the rules."

She breathed out a soft sigh. "I wish someone had told me that before we exchanged our vows."

"Would you have listened?"

"Probably not," she admitted.

"Because you were head over heels in love."

"Or thought I was, anyway," she said. "But even now, knowing what I know, I wouldn't go back in time and change anything if I could, because then I wouldn't have Emery."

"All things considered, you are a lucky woman," he said. "And she's a very lucky girl."

Ruby smiled again, a faint hint of blush coloring her cheeks.

For the next several minutes, their attention was focused on the assembly of the crib—which apparently didn't require his toolbox at all but only the Allen wrench that he'd found in the baggie with the dowel pins and screws and washers.

As he was attempting to tighten one of the screws, he drew in a breath and inhaled that tantalizing scent again. The Allen wrench slipped out of his grasp.

"I've got it," Ruby said, leaning forward to grab it.

As she did, her hair brushed against his cheek, tantalizing him with its silky texture and scent.

Yeah, it was definitely her shampoo—and how pathetic was it that he was turned on by whatever she used to wash her hair?

"Here you go." She held out her hand, showing him the tool.

His fingertips brushed against her open palm as he retrieved the wrench, and suddenly the air was crackling with electricity. He was pretty sure she felt it, too, because when Ruby's blue eyes lifted to his, he saw surprise and a hint of wariness in their depths.

"Thanks."

She cleared her throat. "No problem."

He set the last two screws in place.

"All done?" she asked.

"Now I have to go around and tighten all the connections, to ensure it stays together," he said. "But I can take it from here, if you've got other things to do."

"Oh. Okay. I'll, um, go get the crib sheet out of the dryer."

He was finishing up when Ruby returned with a pale yellow sheet dotted with Winnie the Pooh characters. He helped her cover the mattress, then dropped it into the crib.

A wistful smile curved her lips as she smoothed a hand over an imaginary wrinkle in the crib sheet. "Emery's so big now, it's hard to believe that she used to sleep in this."

"How do you think she's going to feel about someone else sleeping in her crib?"

"She's going to be thrilled," Ruby said confidently. "Ever since she started preschool, she's been asking when she's going to get a baby brother or sister, like so many of her friends have."

"Kids never ask easy questions, do they?"

"Aside from 'what's for dinner?'—no," she agreed. "And although I tried to explain to her, when I filled out the application, that a foster sibling was like a temporary sibling, I'm not sure she's old enough to understand what 'temporary' means."

"You're worried that she's going to get too attached."

"I'm pretty confident we're both going to get too attached," she confided. "But even knowing that, I didn't withdraw my application, because I knew that if we were ever lucky enough to have a child placed with us, it would be because that child needed us—and I could never refuse a child in need."

"You're an amazing woman, Ruby McKinley."

She offered a small smile. "I don't know about that, but I do try to be a good example for my daughter. And—to tell you the truth—as excited as I am about this baby coming, I'm also a little apprehensive."

"Why would you be apprehensive?" he asked, surprised by her confession. "Emery is pretty solid proof that you know what you're doing when it comes to raising kids."

"Emery's a girl. This baby's a boy. I don't know anything about baby boys."

"I'm not sure there's very much difference when they're babies—they cry, they eat, they poop, they sleep. And the next day, they do it all again."

She laughed softly. "How much experience do you have with babies?"

"Not very much at all," he admitted. "Though I expect that will change in the future, when my siblings get married and have kids."

"You don't plan to have any of your own?" Ruby asked.

He shrugged. "If my life had gone according to plan, I'd already be married with a couple rug rats running around the Sanchez ranch."

Her eyes widened with surprise. "You've got your own ranch now? When did that happen?"

"It hasn't happened yet," he admitted. "But I'm hopeful that things will start moving in that direction very soon."

"Well, good for you," she said. "And maybe the wife and kids will follow soon after?"

"Maybe."

They finally left the bedroom and made their way down the stairs again. She turned at the bottom, and he followed her into the kitchen. He glanced around, admiring the bright, cheery room with glossy white shaker-style cabinets, blue countertops and checkerboard blue-and-white tiles on the floor. He guessed that the wide window over the double sink looked into the backyard, though it was pitch dark outside now. The appliances looked moderately new, and the refrigerator even had a water and ice dispenser built into the door. To one side of the kitchen was a breakfast nook, with built-in seating and blue cushions that matched the countertop and floor tiles.

"Can I offer you something to drink?" Ruby asked him.

He was tempted by the offer—enticed by the opportunity to spend a little more time with her. But he thought they'd made some progress tonight in reestablishing a tentative bond of friendship and he didn't want to push for too much too soon.

He understood that his connection to Owen gave her cause to be wary, so he was determined to take things slow, to ensure that she knew his interest in her had absolutely nothing to do with her ex-husband and everything to do with the fact that, even after watching her exchange vows with said ex-husband, he'd never quite managed to shake the feeling that she was meant to be with *him*. Though he suspected it was going to take some time to convince her of the fact.

"Thanks," he said. "But I should be heading out. You don't want to have to explain the presence of a strange man in your home when the lady from Family Services arrives."

"You're not all *that* strange," she said.

She was teasing—a sign, he hoped, that she was already starting to feel more comfortable around him.

"Rain check?" he asked.

"Of course."

He headed out.

IT WAS ALMOST 3:00 a.m. before Hazel Browning arrived with the baby, and while Ruby could have—and should have—napped while she waited, she was too excited to sleep. And too worried that the social worker's inspection of her home might find it lacking in some way, so Ruby spent the time polishing away every last speck of dirt and sweeping up every hidden dust bunny to ensure Ms. Browning would have no reason not to leave the baby with her.

But notwithstanding her excitement over their imminent arrival, as she'd wiped fingerprint smudges off the refrigerator and polished the mirror in the bathroom, Ruby had found her thoughts wandering in an unexpected direction—to Julian Sanchez!

She didn't know what had compelled him to offer his help with the crib, but she was sincerely grateful—and a little bit uneasy to acknowledge, if only to herself, her response to his nearness.

It had been so long since she'd felt the first stirrings of attraction to a man, and the fact that it was Julian—a friend of her ex-husband's—was more than a little unnerving.

The tap on the door jolted her back to the present and caused her heart to leap inside her chest.

They were here.

*He* was here.

She hurried to open the door.

"Take him," Hazel Browning said, shoving the infant car seat at Ruby. "I've got a bunch of other stuff to bring in."

Before Ruby had a chance to respond, the social worker was gone again.

"Okay," she said, lifting the car seat higher to peer at the baby securely buckled inside. "I guess it's just you and me for the moment."

His big blue eyes, with ridiculously long lashes, stared back at her. His chubby cheeks were pink, no doubt from his brief exposure to the cold, and his expression was solemn.

"Well, having your life upended is serious business," she noted, moving into the living room to set the carrier on the coffee table. "I've had some experience with that, so I can empathize." She knelt in front of the baby to unfasten his harness. "But wherever you came from, you're going to be staying here with me and my daughter, Emery, for a little while. Or maybe a long while. I really have no idea at this point, but I promise that we will take very good care of you for as long as you're with us."

Suddenly and unexpectedly, the baby's adorable Cupid's bow mouth curved, and Ruby's heart completely melted.

The same thing had happened the first time she'd felt movement inside her womb when she was pregnant with Emery. In that moment, she'd known that she would do anything to protect her child. And she felt exactly the same about this one.

It didn't matter that she didn't share the same biological connection to him. It only mattered that he was a child—an innocent, helpless baby—who needed someone in his corner.

"My name's Ruby." She lifted him out of the seat and snuggled him close to her body, breathing in his sweet baby scent. "And hopefully I'll learn your name when Ms. Browning comes back."

"It's Jay," the social worker said, returning with a case of formula balanced on top of a box of diapers in one arm and a clear garbage bag full of baby clothes clutched in her other fist.

"Jay," Ruby echoed. "Is that short for Jason? Or Jack? Or something else?"

"Nope, it's just the long version of the letter." She deposited the items she carried on the floor inside the living room. "Dottie named him."

"Dottie?"

"His first foster mom," Hazel explained. "He didn't have a name when he came to us, so Dottie suggested J—because j is the tenth letter of the alphabet and he was her tenth foster child."

"Why did Dottie give him up?" Ruby asked curiously.

"She didn't give him up—she had a heart attack."

She was immediately concerned. "Is she going to be okay?"

"The doctors expect her to make a full recovery, eventually. But right now, she's obviously unable to care for a baby, which is why we called you."

"Or several other applicants before me," Ruby guessed.

"It wouldn't have been my first choice to drive a hundred miles to a new placement," the social worker acknowledged. "But I wouldn't be here if I didn't trust you can provide the care he needs."

"I can. And I will," Ruby promised, already fiercely protective of the baby in her arms.

Hazel nodded. "I'm just going to take a quick look around, and then I'll leave the two of you to get better acquainted."

"Of course," Ruby agreed, understanding that it was the only acceptable answer. "Although I'd think this little guy is probably more interested in sleep than anything else after the busy day he's had."

"You'd think," the other woman agreed.

They were both wrong.

## CHAPTER THREE

RUBY HAD BEEN right about morning coming early for a rancher. And for some reason, bitterly cold winter mornings seemed to come even earlier than most.

As Julian traversed the open fields on the ATV, icy snowflakes stinging his cheeks, he considered—not for the first time—why he wasn't moving south to pursue his goal of owning his own ranch. Texas, for example, was renowned for its cattle—and a much more hospitable climate.

But the answer to that question was simple: he couldn't leave Montana because his family was here. His parents and his siblings were the reason his boots remained firmly planted in northwestern soil.

Well, his family *and* Ruby.

He was, of course, familiar with all the Ten Commandments, and of the fact that he was guilty of coveting his friend's wife—even if he'd never acted on those feelings.

The first time he met Ruby, she was already Owen's girlfriend. But his friend had never been the type to date any one woman for long, and he'd felt confident that Ruby would soon be Owen's *ex*-girlfriend.

Six months later he'd been proven wrong when, instead of ending his relationship with Ruby, Owen put a ring on her finger.

Julian had toasted the happy couple at their engagement

party—because what else was he going to do? And when they set a date for their wedding, he felt certain that their impending nuptials were the incentive he needed to finally get over his secret crush on his friend's bride-to-be.

As he watched them exchange their vows, he sincerely hoped their marriage would last, because it was obvious that Owen made Ruby happy, and he wanted nothing more than for her to be happy.

And she was—for a while.

During the course of their short-lived marriage, Julian had been a regular visitor to their home, because he believed that spending time with Owen and Ruby—painful though it might be—would force him to accept that any illusions he had about a future with his friend's wife weren't anything more than that. And when Emery was born, he'd immediately become "Uncle" Julian to their infant daughter.

But Ruby was no longer Owen's wife, and Julian no longer believed that his feelings for her would fade.

In fact, spending just a few hours with Ruby the previous evening had proved the exact opposite. And then, when he'd finally gone back to the house he rented for its proximity to Blue Sky rather than its dubious charm and crawled into his empty bed, he'd dreamed about her.

Yeah, there was no doubt that he had it bad.

The question now was—what was he going to do about it?

It was, he decided, a question better pondered indoors, because the air temperature was cold enough to freeze the balls off a pool table.

His breath made puffy clouds in the air as he broke up the ice that had formed on the surface of the watering troughs overnight. Having completed his task, he climbed onto the ATV again and turned back to the barn.

He didn't think he'd mind the bone-chilling cold so much if he was ensuring the water supply for his own cattle, if the fields in which they foraged were his own land. But the fact that he was out here while Colin Hanrahan was most likely cozy and warm in his big fancy house with his wife and kids scraped like the raw wind.

*Algún día.*
*Someday.*

Someday he'd have his own spread, his own home, his own family.

But he'd been saving for as long as he'd been working and had started to question whether his "someday" would ever come.

Spending time with Ruby the previous evening had renewed his commitment to his goals and inspired him to turn his dreams into reality. Not "someday" but "soon."

And Ruby was an essential element of that dream. Not only because she was smart and sexy, but because she was one of the warmest and kindest people he'd ever met. Despite having her hands full with her house and her job and her own daughter, she was nevertheless willing to open her heart and her home to a child who needed love and shelter.

Julian could only hope that he'd be able to convince her to open her heart to him, too.

Until then, he'd be satisfied with her opening her door again.

RUBY LIFTED THE pot of freshly brewed coffee to refill her mug, desperate for the caffeine to kick her brain into gear.

"I wanna juice box, Mommy."

Her daughter's impatient demand yanked Ruby's attention back to the present.

"We don't have any juice boxes," she said, pouring milk into a cup.

Emery looked at the cup with suspicion when Ruby put it on the table beside her plate of cheesy scrambled eggs.

"Where's your breakfast, Mommy?"

She held up her mug of coffee. "Right here."

"Mimi says breakfast is the most 'portant meal of the day."

"Mimi" was Emery's name for her paternal grandmother, and while Ruby might despair that her ex-husband was the very definition of an absentee father, she found some solace in the fact that Owen's parents were wonderful grandparents.

"Mimi's right," Ruby said. "Which is why you need to eat up all of your eggs."

In fact, the eggs she'd made for her daughter were actually

a second breakfast, aka lunch, as she'd given Emery a bowl of cold cereal when she first woke up. But the little girl considered eggs breakfast, whether she was eating them for breakfast, lunch or dinner, and Ruby didn't bother to dispute her characterization now.

"I said I wanted waffles for breakfast."

"And I heard you, but we don't have any waffles."

Another item on her grocery list.

"Mimi makes waffles in a pan, not the toaster."

"That's because Mimi has more than two minutes to put breakfast in front of you before she has to hustle you out the door to preschool and herself to work."

Emy poked at her eggs with her fork. "Do I go to preschool today?"

"No. We're both on holidays until Monday."

"Is Jay on holidays, too?"

Emery had been overjoyed to see the baby sleeping in the crib in her mom's bedroom when she woke up that morning and had been full of questions about him ever since.

"He is," Ruby confirmed.

"Is that why he's still sleeping?"

"He's still sleeping because he was up very late last night."

"Past his bedtime?"

"Way past his bedtime—and mine, too."

"When is he gonna wake up?"

"Probably when he gets hungry."

"I wanna play with him."

"I know you do," Ruby said. "But Jay is just a baby, and babies can't really do much."

"What can they do?" Emy pressed.

"They cry, they eat, they poop and they sleep," she said, echoing what Julian had said the night before.

Emy giggled. "I can do all those things, too."

"That's true. But you can also walk and talk and eat scrambled eggs with a fork."

The little girl dutifully moved a forkful of eggs from her plate to her mouth. "What does Jay eat?"

"Right now, he only has formula."

"What's that?"

"It's a special milk that gives him all the good stuff he needs to grow big and strong."

"Can he have cookies with his milk?"

"No. He definitely cannot have cookies," she said firmly.

"But *I* can have cookies," Emy said, just in case her mom needed a reminder. "Because I'm a big girl."

"You are a big girl," Ruby agreed. "But you're not going to grow any bigger if you don't eat your breakfast."

"I want juice."

"You have milk," she told her daughter.

"I want juice," Emery said again.

"We'll get more juice boxes tomorrow, when the grocery store is open. Today, you'll have to drink milk."

Emery responded to that by pushing her cup off the table.

Thankfully, it was a sippy cup with a no-spill lid.

"And now you don't have anything to drink," Ruby said, picking up the cup and setting it on the counter.

"Drink! Drink!" The little girl punctuated her demand by banging her fork on the table.

"Emery, please be quiet so you don't wake the baby."

But the caution came too late and was immediately followed by the sound of a muffled cry through the baby monitor.

And then her phone rang.

"Finish your breakfast," she instructed her daughter, grabbing her phone as she headed toward the stairs.

Could it be Ms. Browning checking up on her already?

She didn't recognize the number—and it obviously wasn't anyone in her list of contacts or the name would have shown up on the screen—and answered warily.

"Hello?"

"Good morning, Ruby."

A warm and distinctly masculine voice.

Definitely *not* Ms. Browning.

And while there was something familiar about the voice, she couldn't immediately put a name to it, though the sudden warmth that flooded her veins should have been a clue.

She glanced at her watch. "It's after noon."

"It is," he acknowledged. "But considering your late night, I thought you might have slept in today."

Now the pieces clicked together. "Julian?"

"I probably should have led with that," he noted.

"Or you could just tell me why you're calling," she said, wedging the phone between her ear and her shoulder so her hands were free to pick up the baby.

"I just wanted to make sure the crib held up through the night."

"I never had any doubt that it would." She nuzzled Jay's cheek, and he responded with a gummy smile. "And the baby slept like a baby—when he finally got to sleep."

She carried the infant down the stairs to check on her daughter, who was finger-painting the table with the remnants of her scrambled egg.

Because that's what happened when you left a four-year-old unattended for thirty seconds.

She bit back a sigh as she settled Jay in his reclining high chair and secured the belt around his middle.

"Do you need me to bring coffee?" Julian asked.

She moistened the cloth under the faucet. "Actually, I'm only about halfway through the pot that I made this morning."

She usually only made half a pot, but today she'd filled the water reservoir to the max, then, after measuring the grounds into the filter, added an extra scoop.

"In that case, maybe I could cash in that rain check you gave me last night?"

"You want to come over? For coffee?"

Butterflies fluttered in her tummy.

"Only if I wouldn't be interrupting anything," he said.

"Yes," she said. "I mean, no. You wouldn't be interrupting. I'll even put on a fresh pot."

"There's no need for that," he said.

"I don't mind," she assured him. "But if you want cream, you're out of luck."

"Do you usually use cream?"

"Yeah, but I didn't make it to the grocery store yesterday."

"I want juice, Mommy."

She pulled the phone away from her face before responding to her daughter. "I told you, we'll get juice boxes when the grocery store opens tomorrow."

Emery kicked the leg of the table. "I want juice *now*."

This time Ruby didn't quite manage to hold back the sigh.

"I can be there around two, if that's okay," Julian said.

"Two o'clock is good," she said, relieved that she'd have time to put on something more suitable for company than the oversize nightshirt with a cartoon bear yawning on the front with the words "Mornings Are Unbearable" beneath his bunny-slipper-clad feet.

JULIAN HAD PLANNED to play it cool.

Considering how reluctant Ruby had been to accept his offer of help the night before, he'd decided to give her some time before he made their paths cross again. But after he'd finished his morning chores on the ranch, he decided that he'd waited long enough.

After all, it was a new year, and he had goals.

Ruby opened the door in response to his knock, a weary smile on her face and a little girl cautiously peeking out from behind her.

"I heard someone say they wanted juice boxes," he said, holding up a bag from the local convenience store.

"Me! Me!" Emery said, her initial shyness pushed aside by her excitement.

"What do you like—apple or grape?"

"I like apple *and* grape."

"Then I guess it's a good thing I got some of each," he said.

Ruby eyed him warily. "How did you know?"

"I heard Emery when we were on the phone. And I saw the grocery list on your fridge last night, so I knew what kind to buy."

"Well, aren't you observant," she mused. "And thoughtful."

"I brought something for you, too," he said.

"What's that?"

"Cream for your coffee. And doughnuts—just because."

"And there goes my New Year's resolution to cut out junk food," she said.

"Do you want me to take them back?"

She snatched the bag out of his hand. "Don't even think about it."

He chuckled as he followed her into the kitchen, where the coffee was just finishing brewing.

"I told you not to worry about making a fresh pot."

"No way I was going to serve stale coffee to company."

"Am I company?"

She looked at him warily, as if it was a trick question. "Aren't you company?"

He shrugged. "I thought—I hoped—we were friends."

She didn't seem to know how to respond to that, so he granted her a reprieve by turning his attention to the wide-eyed baby reclined in the high chair.

"So you're the little guy that all the big fuss is about, huh?"

"He can't talk to you, cuz he's just a baby," Emery said, climbing into her booster seat at the table.

"Is that why?"

She nodded. "I was hoping we'd get a girl baby, but we got a boy baby instead."

"Does the boy baby have a name?" he asked her.

"Jay," she said. "It's a name *and* a letter in the alphabet. Just like my name."

"I thought your name was Emery."

She nodded. "But sometimes Mommy calls me 'Em.'"

"And sometimes Emy," Ruby chimed in.

"And sometimes Emery Rose McKinley." She fisted her hands on her hips, as if imitating her mother, and deepened her voice as she continued, "'I said *right now*, Emery Rose McKinley.'"

Julian covered his laugh with a fake cough.

"Thank you for that, Emery Rose McKinley," Ruby said dryly.

The little girl responded with a grin.

Ruby finished unpacking the contents of the grocery bag,

then poked a straw in the top of one of the juice boxes and set it on the table in front of her daughter.

"Thank you," she said politely.

"You should say *thank you* to Mr. Sanchez," Ruby told her. "He brought the juice boxes for you."

"Julian," he corrected her again.

"Maybe Uncle Julian?" she suggested, as an alternative.

He nodded, pleased to have his honorary title restored.

"Thank you, Unca Julian," Emery dutifully intoned.

"You're welcome, Emery."

Ruby filled the two mugs with fresh coffee and handed him one.

"Thank you."

"You're welcome, Unca Julian," she said, with a smile that told him she was teasing.

Ruby added a splash of cream to her coffee, then arranged some of the doughnuts on a plate before carrying both to the table.

She took the seat across from him and beside her daughter, who was studying Julian as she sipped her juice. The baby, he noted, had tracked Ruby's movements, and he kicked his legs when she sat down near him.

Ruby obviously noticed, too, because she smiled and tweaked his toes. The infant responded with another kick and a toothless grin.

Julian sipped his coffee. "Did you say the social worker brought the baby from Bronco?"

"Yeah." Ruby tapped a doughnut on the edge of the plate to knock off the excess sugar. "Why?"

"I wonder if Jay might be the baby that Marisa told us about—the one who was found at the church when she was in Bronco working on the holiday pageant."

"Ms. Browning did say that the baby had been abandoned at a church," Ruby acknowledged, offering the doughnut to Emery.

The little girl eagerly accepted the treat and immediately took a big bite.

"It's hard to believe that a mother could just walk away from her newborn baby," he mused.

"You're assuming it was the mother who abandoned him," Ruby pointed out.

"Who else could it be?"

"That's a good question," she admitted. "And one with countless possible answers. The father, a boyfriend of the mom who wasn't the father, a grandparent of the child, a neighbor or friend who believed the child wasn't being adequately cared for—or someone else with less benevolent motives."

"You seem to have given the matter some thought," he noted.

"Because my initial reaction was the same as yours," she admitted. "But the fact is, no one knows. And until the mom or dad or another family member is found, we won't."

"Can I go play now, Mommy?"

"Not until we clean all that powdered sugar off your hands and face," Ruby said, pushing away from the table.

The little girl dutifully stayed put while her mom moistened a washcloth and cleaned her up.

"And now I'm wondering about something else," Julian said, after Emery had scampered off.

"What's that?"

"Why a woman—a single mom—who works full-time and has a busy child of her own to care for would apply to be a foster parent."

Ruby brought the coffeepot to the table to refill both their mugs. "I've always wanted a big family, so that Emy could grow up with brothers and sisters, like I did. But my marriage falling apart kind of nixed that plan."

After setting the pot back on the warmer, she returned to her seat at the table. "And then I read an article about fostering and it seemed like a good opportunity to give a home to a child who needed one and give my daughter the experience of being a sibling."

He was hesitant to ask the next question but forged ahead, anyway. "You don't think you'll ever marry again?"

"I haven't completely written off the possibility," she said. "But I don't exactly have men lining up at the door to go out with me."

"Does that mean you're not seeing anyone right now?"

She shook her head. "I haven't been on a date since...well, it's been a long time."

Julian wasn't really surprised by the admission, because he imagined being a single mom took precedence over all else. But this confirmation that she was unattached threatened to wreak havoc on his efforts to keep his distance from his ex-best friend's ex.

"Look, Mommy! It's snowing."

Ruby turned her head to glance out the window behind her and confirm her daughter's proclamation.

"Santa brought Em a new sled for Christmas," she told Julian, explaining her daughter's enthusiasm for the weather. "Now every time it snows, she wants to go tobogganing."

"What was Santa thinking?" he asked, tongue-in-cheek.

"Obviously he wasn't thinking that Emery's mom would have to trek over to the park after every snowfall—or that winter seems to last forever in Montana."

Julian chuckled.

Ruby lifted her mug to her lips, attempting to hide her yawn.

"You're tired," he realized, and immediately felt guilty that he'd invited himself over when he knew she'd had a late night the night before.

"It was almost 3:00 a.m. before Ms. Browning arrived," she confided.

He winced. "That late?"

She nodded. "And after Jay slept in the car the whole way from Bronco, he was wide awake. Every time I tried to put him down, he started to cry, which led to me picking him up again so that he wouldn't wake up Emery. So we spent the next few hours playing pat-a-cake and peek-a-boo. I swear the sun was starting to rise by the time he finally fell asleep, which meant that I could finally get some sleep, too.

"And then Emery was awake about two hours later—hence the need for coffee," she said, lifting her mug to her lips. "Lots of coffee."

"I think what you need more than coffee is a nap."

"Unfortunately, that's not going to happen."

"Why not?"

"Because it's time to feed the baby again." She rose from the table to mix the powdered formula.

"And after you feed him, he's probably going to have a nap, right?" he asked, looking at the baby, whose eyes were already starting to look heavy.

"The odds are very good," she confirmed, pouring the formula into a bottle.

"So why don't you sleep when he does?"

"Because I've got company. And a four-year-old."

"I'm not company, I'm a friend."

She nodded, acknowledging the point. "But my daughter still needs adult supervision, and I suspect that she's only going to be distracted from the idea of tobogganing by the promise of fort building in the living room."

"Well then, this is your lucky day," Julian said. "Because it just so happens that I have serious fort-building skills."

# CHAPTER FOUR

RUBY WAS EXHAUSTED enough to let Julian put his fort-building skills to the test. And apparently Emery was satisfied with his efforts, because she didn't interrupt her mom's nap even once. It was only when Jay started to stir in his crib, waking from his slumber, that Ruby was awakened from hers.

A quick glance at the clock on her bedside table told her that she'd been out for almost two hours—and if she didn't exactly feel well-rested, she at least felt a lot better than she had when she'd laid down.

And a little unnerved, because her sleep had not been without dreams, and those dreams had starred Julian! She didn't clearly remember the details, and maybe that was a good thing, because the bits that she did remember—warm lips moving against hers, callused hands exploring her naked skin—made her feel hot and achy all over.

Pushing those alluring memories aside along with the covers, Ruby rose to deal with the baby. After changing Jay's diaper, she carried him downstairs, where she found her daughter set up at the kitchen table with a coloring book and crayons and Julian standing in front of the stove.

"I think I must still be dreaming," Ruby mused aloud from the doorway. And this image was almost as tantalizing as her erotic dream.

Julian glanced over his shoulder and smiled at her. "How are you feeling?"

"So much better."

"Hungry?"

"A little." She dropped a kiss on her daughter's head before settling Jay into his high chair so that she could make him a bottle.

She blinked when Julian handed her a bottle of formula.

"I mixed it up when I heard you moving around upstairs."

"Oh. Um. Thank you."

He looked amused. "Are you surprised that I was able to read the can and follow the instructions?"

She flushed. "No. Of course not. I'm just…surprised…that you would think to do so."

Because her ex-husband certainly wouldn't have.

Even when she'd asked for his help, Owen often feigned ignorance to get out of lending a hand with childcare duties.

"And you're making dinner, too," she realized.

"I hope you don't mind that I made myself at home in your kitchen."

"I definitely don't mind," she said. "But I really didn't expect this."

"I had an ulterior motive," Julian said, with a playful wink. "Which was hoping that you'd invite me to stay and have dinner with you."

"Consider yourself invited," she said, moving closer to look at the contents of the pan.

"It's sweet-and-spicy chicken. One of my mom's recipes."

"It looks—and smells—delicious," she said. "But I don't know if Emery will eat it."

"I wondered about that myself," he told her. "Which is why I made chicken fingers for her."

"I didn't think I had any chicken fingers." It was yet one more thing on her grocery list.

"You didn't, but you had chicken."

"Are you telling me that you *made* chicken fingers?"

"Actually, Emery and I made them together."

In response to her name, the little girl looked up and grinned.

"How did she help?" Ruby wondered.

"She crushed the cornflakes and cracked the eggs."

Ruby settled into a chair beside her daughter and tucked the baby into the crook of her arm before offering him the bottle. "Emery does like to break things."

Julian chuckled. "She was very helpful."

"Still, I can't believe you made chicken fingers."

"I would have thought you'd be more impressed with the sweet-and-spicy chicken."

"I am," she assured him. "And even more impressed that you were able to find all the ingredients you needed in my poorly stocked kitchen."

He chuckled. "This is where I have to confess that I made a couple of substitutions, but it looks pretty much as it should."

Emery abandoned her coloring and slid out of her seat to move closer to her mom.

"Can I help, Mommy?"

"Sure you can help," Ruby agreed, guiding her daughter's hand to the bottle. "Just make sure you hold it at an angle—like this—so he's sucking down formula and not air."

"Why not air?"

"Because air will make his tummy hurt." She brushed her free hand over the little girl's hair. "And you know how uncomfortable it is when your tummy hurts, don't you?"

Emery nodded, her attention focused on the baby.

Ruby was happy to see her helping out, because giving Emery the experience of being a big sister was one of her goals when she signed up to become a foster parent.

"Dinner will be ready in twenty minutes if I put the rice on now," Julian said. "Does that work?"

"That's perfect," Ruby agreed, ignoring the pang of regret that tugged at her heart.

This was what she'd imagined married life would be like: a couple working together to take care of their children and put a meal on the table. And though she and Julian weren't a couple and Emery and Jay weren't his responsibility, sometimes it was nice to dream.

JULIAN FELT PRETTY good about the fact that he'd managed to put a meal together for Ruby and Emery—especially considering the limited contents of the refrigerator and pantry. Or he did, until Emery looked at the chicken fingers and rice on her plate and asked, "Where's the veggies?"

"Um…" He glanced at Ruby questioningly.

"We have a rule about including veggies with dinner," she explained.

"Well, the breading on the chicken fingers is made from cornflakes," he reminded the little girl. "And cornflakes are made from corn."

"Does that count?" Emery asked her mom.

"We'll let it count tonight," she said. "But there are carrot sticks and cucumber wheels in the fridge, if you want some."

Emy shook her head.

"There are peppers in the sweet-and-spicy chicken," he told Ruby.

"I'm not judging," she assured him. "But I am eager to try it."

He set a plate in front of her and took a seat across the table. The baby, his belly already full, was strapped into something that Ruby called a bouncy chair, contentedly looking at the soft toys dangling from the handle.

"What's that?" Emy asked, eyeing the contents of her mother's plate with interest.

"This is chicken and rice, too," she said. "Just cooked a different way. Do you want to try it?"

The little girl considered a minute, then nodded.

Ruby transferred a piece of chicken, a chunk of pepper and a little bit of sauce to her daughter's plate.

Emery stabbed the chicken with her fork.

"It might be hot," Ruby cautioned.

Em puckered up and huffed out a breath as if she was blowing out birthday candles.

After a few more huffs, Ruby said, "I think it's probably good now."

She opened her mouth and tentatively bit into the chicken.

Almost immediately, her face scrunched up and she dropped her fork. "Yuck."

"That's not going to translate to a very good Yelp review," Julian remarked.

"No," Ruby agreed, digging into her meal again. "But I would rate your sweet-and-spicy chicken five stars."

"Only because you haven't had my mother's tamales," he said. "Now those are worthy of five stars."

"I'm still sticking with my five-star rating for this chicken."

"I guess my mother should get credit for it, too," he acknowledged. "She made sure that each of her kids was capable of putting a meal on the table. Because as much as she's always on me about finding a nice girl to settle down with, she does not believe it's a woman's job to cook for her husband. Or make his bed or do his laundry."

Ruby smiled at that. "I think I'd like your mom."

"I know she likes you."

She seemed taken aback by his response. "When did I ever meet your mom?"

"Both my parents were at your wedding," he said. "And now I'm wishing I'd kept my mouth shut."

"Why?"

"I don't want to be responsible for stirring up unhappy memories."

"My memories of that day are happy," she told him. "But I met and talked to so many people, they all blurred together in my mind."

"That's understandable," he said. "At least I know you liked their wedding gift."

"All done, Mommy," Emery said, pushing her mostly empty plate toward her mom. "Can I watch TV?"

Ruby pushed away from the table to get a cloth to wipe her daughter's face and hands. "What do you want to watch?"

"*Paw Patrol*!"

"One episode," her mom said.

Emery skipped out of the kitchen.

"Now might be a good time to tell you that we didn't break down the fort before we decided to make dinner," Julian said.

"I saw it when I came down the stairs," Ruby admitted. "I thought maybe you'd deliberately left it intact to show off your fort-building skills."

"That might have been a factor."

She picked up her fork again. "Anyway, back to the wedding gift from your parents—do you mean the hand-painted mugs from Mexico?"

He nodded. "They were made in the mountains of Michoacán, where my mom's family came from. The capulin design celebrates the Mexican cherry flower."

"I love those mugs. In fact, I specifically asked for them when the lawyers were divvying up our possessions during the divorce negotiations."

"Well, they certainly go well with your kitchen."

"When I was looking to buy a new house—for me and Emery—this kitchen tipped the scales for me."

"It is a nice kitchen."

"It's blue."

"More white than blue, but okay," Julian said.

"The house on Mountain Drive—the house that Owen picked out for us—was beige. Inside and out. I hated that house."

"It's simple enough to paint over beige."

"Owen wouldn't let me paint. He wouldn't let me put colorful throw cushions on the beige sofa. I bought a glass bowl for the coffee table—blown glass in shades of red and orange and gold. He threw it out."

"I didn't know he had an aversion to color."

"I didn't, either, until we were married."

"He must have really hated those coffee mugs," Julian mused.

"So much so that they were tucked away in the back of the cupboard above the refrigerator," she confided. "And when I stood in the middle of this kitchen, I actually thought 'my mugs belong here.' And that's when I knew that Emy and I belonged here, too."

"And if they'd given you orange mugs instead of blue?"

She pushed away from the table to carry their empty plates to the counter. "I would have bought the house on Juniper Lane."

He chuckled and followed her to the kitchen.

"Looks like you've got leftovers for lunch tomorrow," Julian noted, as she dished the remaining rice and chicken into a plastic container.

"Lucky me," she said. "Em might be happy with PB&J every day, but I like some variety. And I really like this chicken."

"I'd give you the recipe," he said. "But I'm afraid that you'll be a lot less impressed when you realize how simple it is to make."

"You made dinner for me—I will forever be impressed by that," she promised.

He put the stopper in the bottom of the sink and turned on the faucet.

"What are you doing?" Ruby demanded.

"I was just going to wash the pots and pans."

"No, you are *not*," she said. "You cooked. I'll deal with the cleanup."

"Who does the dishes after you cook?" he asked her.

Her cheeks colored. "That's different."

"Why?" he challenged.

"Because it's my house. My child. My responsibility."

"You don't ever let anyone help you out?"

"Of course, I do." She squirted liquid soap into the stream of water. "But you've already helped a lot. After a two-hour nap and that delicious meal, I almost feel human again."

"I'm glad." He frowned as she lowered the stack of plates into the sudsy water. "Why don't you use the dishwasher?"

"It's on the fritz," she admitted.

"Is that the technical term?" he couldn't resist teasing.

She responded with a smile and a shrug. "I don't actually know the technical term for the fact that water pours into the adjacent cupboard."

"Sounds like a connection issue," he said. "Or possibly a damaged hose."

"Either way, to me it sounded like a costly and unnecessary repair," she countered. "And I really don't mind doing a few dishes every night."

"I could take a look," he said.

"Or you could sit down and relax," she suggested. "I think you've earned it."

He sat, because it seemed important to her.

As soon as he did, the baby started to fuss.

Ruby sighed and lifted her hands out of the soapy water.

"I've got him," Julian said, lifting the bouncy chair up to set it on the table in front of him.

The baby looked at him for a minute with big, solemn eyes—and then rewarded him with a smile.

"This is a seriously cute kid," he remarked.

"You're telling me," she agreed, as she resumed washing.

"I bet he's already got you wrapped around his little finger."

"More tightly than he's holding on to yours right now," she admitted.

"So what are you going to do with this little guy when you have to work?" Julian asked.

"Thankfully, I don't work again until Monday," she told him. "I booked holidays so that I could spend more time with Emery during her school break."

"I can't believe she's in school."

"Preschool," she clarified.

"Still." It was hard to believe that the child he'd known since she was younger than this one was already spending some of her days in a classroom.

Ruby nodded. "They grow up fast."

"Too fast." Or maybe it wasn't too fast and just that he'd stayed away for too long. And though he wasn't entirely certain he should be here right now, when he saw Ruby working at the inn the night before, he knew he couldn't stay away any longer.

"As for Jay," Ruby continued, "I guess I'll take him to work with me."

"Your boss won't mind?" he asked.

"It's what I used to do with Emery, before I got her into Little Cowpokes Daycare, so I don't anticipate there being a problem." She glanced at the clock on the wall again as she rinsed the last plate before setting it in the drying rack. "But speaking of Emery, I need to get her ready for bed."

"Is that your polite way of asking me to leave so that you can carry on with your usual routines?"

"I don't mind if you stay," she said, drying her hands on a towel. "I mean, if you want to stay."

He did want to stay. Maybe too much.

Now his gaze shifted to the clock. "I've actually got plans with my brother tonight," he admitted, sincerely regretful. "But I can hang out with this little guy while you get Emery settled."

"That would be great." She touched a hand to his arm. "Thank you."

He knew the touch had been nothing more than a casual gesture meant to reinforce her words, but something electric passed between them during that brief contact.

Something that caused her eyes to widen as they locked with his, for just a moment, as the air fairly crackled with static.

Then the baby blew a raspberry, and the moment was over.

"You're cute," Julian said to the baby, when Ruby was gone. "But your timing sucks."

The little guy looked at him, all wide-eyed innocence—and then his mouth curved.

And Julian couldn't help but smile back.

# CHAPTER FIVE

*Bronco, Montana*

*"¡MUY FELIZ AÑO nuevo, Tío!"* Denise Sanchez said, opening the door wide to welcome him into her home—the setting of almost every family gathering and holiday celebration that Uncle Stanley had been part of since he'd moved to Bronco three years earlier.

"Bah, humbug."

His nephew's pretty wife smiled indulgently as she leaned in to kiss his weathered cheek. "I'd say that you're a week late expressing that sentiment, except that I heard plenty of the same at Christmas. And at Thanksgiving, too."

"I shouldn't have come," Stanley said, feeling a little guilty to know that his unhappiness would likely put a pall on the festivities. "I'm not really in a celebratory mood."

"I know." Denise hung his coat on a hook by the door, then hugged him tight. "But holidays are about *la familia* and we're not about to let you spend them alone."

And that was the true crux of the situation.

He *was* alone now, without the companionship of the woman he'd fallen in love with three years ago, the woman with whom he'd planned to exchange vows over five months ago.

He'd been so happy then. So full of hope for their future.

Until, on the day of their wedding, Winona disappeared without a word.

"Runaway bride," he'd heard one of the deputies say when they'd reported her missing.

That conclusion was followed by the snickers of his colleagues.

They'd tried to cover their laughter with fake coughs when they'd realized that Stanley had overheard their remarks, but he wasn't fooled.

Nor did he believe for a minute that his Winona had run.

She'd been as excited about their impending nuptials as he'd been—thrilled to finally be a bride.

Sure, there'd been a few bumps in the road leading up to the big day, but they'd successfully navigated those together.

"I'm going to be a nonagenarian bride," she'd said with a laugh. "And since it's my first trip down the aisle, I might even wear white." She'd considered that possibility for only a brief moment before shaking her head. "Though probably not, because why would I forgo all the colors I love on the most important day of my life?"

It was a good point, he acknowledged. And while he'd always been a rule follower, his bride-to-be believed in making her own rules—it was only one of the many things he loved about her.

"People will talk no matter what I wear," she'd noted. "Because people have always talked about me. But I don't care. I've had my share of trials and tribulations, but I've also been blessed with an amazing daughter and granddaughter and grandchildren…and now with you." She'd looked at him then, her heart in her eyes. "I didn't think I'd ever fall in love again. And then you walked into my life and I couldn't imagine—didn't want to imagine—living even one of the rest of my days without you."

He'd felt exactly the same way, and their courtship had proceeded at a whirlwind pace.

If anyone had asked, he would have said that the years passed too fast to take things slow. But no one asked.

His family—his beautiful, wonderful family—had immediately loved Winona because he did.

His nephew and wife had always believed in sharing with

others, and the first time he'd taken Winona to one of their wonderfully chaotic family dinners, neither Aaron nor Denise had blinked an eye. They'd embraced her person and her presence, simply shifting the place settings around to make room for one more and squeezing in another chair at the already crowded table.

He'd admittedly had some concerns about how they might respond to a new woman in his life. But they understood that he'd loved his wife with his whole heart for more than sixty years, and when Celia passed, he'd mourned deeply.

He hadn't been looking to fall in love again. In fact, he'd been certain that he never would. But he'd never imagined that he'd meet a woman like Winona Cobbs at Doug's bar.

*Love always finds a way.*

The echo of her voice in his mind made his heart ache.

She was right about that.

She was right about most things.

He knew there were some people who thought Winona was more than a little eccentric—and others who claimed she was cracked as a cracker—but he knew the truth. She was a gentle and generous spirit—though feisty when the occasion warranted—with a gift for seeing what others either couldn't or didn't want to see. In fact, they'd met at a "Free Psychic Reading" event at Doug's. And, only a few days later, they'd had their first official date at Pastabilities in Bronco Heights, where he'd fallen in love with her over fettucine and garlic bread.

Less than two months later, they were firmly established as a couple. And when he said grace before the Thanksgiving meal in this very house, he'd looked at all the familiar faces gathered around the table—his new love among them—and said a special thanks to the Lord for bringing Winona into his life.

This year, he'd railed at God for taking her away again.

Because how was Stanley supposed to go on without her?

The truth was, he couldn't imagine his life without Winona in it, and he was going to do whatever it took to find her.

# CHAPTER SIX

*Tenacity, Montana*

"YOU'RE LATE," LUCA SANCHEZ said when his oldest brother settled on the vacant barstool beside him at Castillo's, a favorite local Mexican restaurant.

"And I'm not going to apologize for it," Julian told him.

"You were with a woman," Luca immediately guessed.

"Also not going to talk about it."

"Who?" his brother pressed.

Julian ignored the question, nodding to the bartender who wandered over. "*¡Hola!* Rafael."

"*¡Hola!*" The bartender returned the greeting. "What are you drinking tonight?"

"I'll have a pint of Modelo."

Rafael looked at Luca's nearly empty glass. "You ready for another?"

"Yeah," Luca replied. "Give us an order of *sopecitos* and some chile con queso, too."

"I already had dinner," Julian told him.

"Which won't stop you picking off my plate," his brother noted as Rafael set their drinks in front of them.

"What did you eat?" Luca asked when the bartender moved away again.

"Sweet-and-spicy chicken."

"Where'd you have that?"

"I made it."

His brother's gaze narrowed thoughtfully. "Which isn't a direct answer to my question."

"Well, it's the only answer you're getting," Julian told him.

"It's not like you to be so tight-lipped about a woman," Luca mused. "Or maybe I just don't remember because it's been so long since you've had a woman in your life."

"You're the only one who mentioned a woman."

"If you weren't with a woman, you would have told me where you were."

"Okay, I confess—I was with your girlfriend."

"Ha ha."

"That's right—you don't have a girlfriend," Julian noted.

"I'm too young—and far too popular with the ladies—to want to be tied down," Luca said immodestly.

"So why do you spend most of your free time here, hoping to catch a glimpse of Rafael's cousin?"

The bartender glanced over, a furrow etched between his brows. "You got your eye on one of my *primas*?" he challenged.

"No," Luca hastened to assure him, giving his brother a kick in the shins.

Rafael didn't look convinced. "It'll end up black if you start sniffing too close."

"I'm not eyeing or sniffing."

The bartender folded his beefy arms across his chest. "Why not? You don't think they're *bastante bonita*?"

"Are you comfortable there, between the rock and the hard place?" Julian asked his brother.

Luca glared at him.

"I'm sure they're *mucha hermosa*," he said, attempting to placate Rafael. "I'm just not looking for a relationship right now."

"The only thing he's hungry for are the *sopecitos*," Julian said, coming to his brother's rescue.

After a moment's hesitation, the bartender nodded. "I'll check on your order."

*"Dios, mano,"* Luca grumbled once Rafael had disappeared

into the kitchen. "I'm not looking to tangle with a bartender who's also the bouncer in this place."

"Then you shouldn't be looking at Winter," Julian cautioned.

"I'm not looking at her. She's got a husband for that."

He snorted. "Her husband is good for nothing."

"Obviously she felt differently, or she wouldn't have married him." Luca nodded his thanks to Rafael for delivering their food. "But she should have ditched him at the altar, like *Tío* Stanley's fiancée did to him."

*Tío* Stanley was their great-uncle who'd moved to nearby Bronco a few years earlier, after the death of *Tia* Celia, his wife of sixty years. He'd adjusted remarkably well to the change in circumstances and had soon met and fallen in love with an older woman he'd planned to marry. Unfortunately his bride-to-be had gone AWOL before their wedding.

"Do you really think Winona just took off?" Julian asked, dipping a chip into queso.

"It's the only explanation that makes any sense."

"*Tío* Stanley doesn't believe it."

"He's hurting," Luca said, not unsympathetically, as he selected a *sopecito* from the plate. "But once he's had some time to think about it, he'll realize being single is better than being with the wrong woman."

Julian couldn't disagree with that, but he wondered how long he was supposed to wait for the right woman to realize that he was the right man for her.

WHEN RUBY WOKE up the following morning, she had no expectations about when she might see Julian again. Sure, it was possible that their paths might cross in town one day, but considering that had only happened a few times in the last three years, she wasn't going to hold her breath.

And she certainly wasn't going to admit that she wanted to see him again. Because a single mom with two kids—an idea she was still getting used to!—keeping her busy every waking minute of the day had no business daydreaming about romance. Especially not with a man who was a friend of her ex-husband.

Even—or maybe especially—if being around him reminded

her that she was a woman who'd ignored her own needs for far too long.

But when she responded to the knock on her door early the following afternoon, he was there.

This time, the bag in his hand bore the logo of the local hardware store. In his other hand was a toolbox.

"A new installation kit for your dishwasher," he said.

"Don't you have a ranch to run?" she asked, wishing that she'd taken an extra two minutes to put on some makeup that morning.

But between the baby and Emery, she'd felt lucky to steal ten minutes for a shower. And though she might wish she looked nicer, at least she was wearing clean clothes, aside from the little bit of baby spit on her sweater that dribbled past the edge of the burp cloth she'd put over her shoulder to avoid such mishaps.

"I'm hardly responsible for running it," Julian said. "I'm just a ranch hand."

"Still, my dad worked on a ranch, so I know very well that there are always things to do."

He shrugged, neither a denial nor an acknowledgment of her point. "It turned out that I had some time on my hands."

"And you want to spend it fixing my dishwasher?" she said dubiously.

"I figured you'd need it now that you have baby bottles to be sterilized."

Well, she could hardly deny that. "In that case, why don't you come in?"

As soon as he stepped over the threshold, Emery came running. "Hi, Mr. Julian."

"It's Uncle Julian," Ruby reminded her daughter.

"Did you bring doughnuts today, Unca Julian?" Emery asked.

"I didn't," he said apologetically. "Did you eat all the doughnuts I brought yesterday?"

She shook her head. "But I like choc'ate ones best."

"I'll remember that for next time," he promised.

Emery nodded and headed back into the living room.

As Ruby preceded Julian into the kitchen, his words echoed in her head.

*Next time* certainly suggested that he anticipated stopping by again.

So maybe she hadn't imagined the crackle in the air between them the previous evening. Or the sparks that danced over her skin when he touched her the night before that. Or—

"Mommy, Jay's stinky again."

And just like that, Ruby was yanked back to reality.

"I guess we'd better take him upstairs to change him," she responded to Emery.

"Uh-uh," Emy said, scrunching up her face and pinching her nose. "You do it."

"Alright," she agreed, before turning to Julian to say, "I trust you don't need my help in here?"

"I think I can figure things out," he said.

She nodded.

"You stay out of Uncle Julian's way, okay?" she instructed her daughter.

"Okay," Emy agreed.

But when Ruby returned to the kitchen with a freshly bathed baby in her arms (because diaper blowout!), she found her dishwasher pulled out, Julian reclined on the floor with his upper torso somewhere inside her cupboard and Emery crouched beside him, holding a flashlight.

She felt a quiver low in her belly as her gaze skimmed over the man—noting with appreciation the long, muscular legs clad in well-worn denim and flat, taut belly covered in soft flannel. She'd grown up around cowboys, so there was no reason that she should suddenly be feeling weak-kneed around this one.

Or maybe she had secret handyman fantasies. After having been married to a man who didn't know how to change a lightbulb, perhaps it wasn't surprising that she'd find herself attracted to one who could not only identify a problem but knew how—and took the initiative—to fix it.

Whatever the reason for the sudden tingles in her veins, she was determined to ignore them.

"So much for staying out of Uncle Julian's way," she remarked dryly.

Emery immediately swiveled her head to look at her mom, a smile spreading across her face. "I'm helping Unca Julian."

"Helping or hindering?" Ruby wondered aloud.

"Helping," her daughter insisted.

"You are helping," Julian confirmed. "But you have to hold the light steady, remember?"

"I 'member," she said, turning her full attention back to the task at hand.

"I found the problem," Julian said, speaking to Ruby now. "You had a cracked drain hose."

"Can you fix it?" she asked.

"That's what I'm doing."

She settled Jay in his bouncy chair and moved to the sink to get a dishcloth to wipe Emery's breakfast crumbs from the table. But when she turned on the faucet to moisten the cloth, she got...nothing.

"Water's off," Julian told her.

"Oh. Of course." She felt foolish for not realizing that he'd have to cut the water supply to replace the hose.

She made do with the barely damp cloth, shook the crumbs into the sink. "I'm starting to realize that I've been letting my daughter coast," she said. "But now that I know she can help with meal prep and household repairs, that's going to change."

"Letting kids help is how they learn to do things. At least, that was the excuse my dad always gave when he put me to work as his apprentice."

"Is there anything I can do to help?" she asked.

"Nope." He slid out of the cupboard. "It's all done."

"Already?"

"I told you it was likely a quick job." He took the flashlight from Emery and turned it off. "Thanks for your help."

"You're welcome." She turned to her mom then. "Can I watch *Paw Patrol*?"

"If you watch TV now, you won't get any screen time later," Ruby reminded her.

Emery hesitated. "Can I read stories to Jay?"

"You can absolutely read stories to Jay," Ruby agreed. "And thank you for thinking of him."

Emery smiled as she skipped off to get some books.

Julian's brows lifted. "She can read? At four?"

"She won't actually read the books," she explained to him. "She does recognize some words, but she'll make up a story for him based on the pictures."

"Ah."

"I really can't thank you enough for the dishwasher repair," Ruby said.

"You could offer me a cup of coffee," he said.

"Do you want some day-old doughnuts with your java?" she asked.

"Why not?" he agreed.

She retrieved the carafe from her coffee maker and made her way to the sink. "Do I have water again?"

He nodded. "It will probably sputter a bit at first, but it will be fine after it runs for a minute."

She turned on the tap—and took a quick step back from the sink when the water did indeed sputter and spit coming out of the faucet. When it was flowing smoothly, she filled the carafe and set up the coffee maker.

Emery returned with a stack of books in her hands. She set them down on the table beside Jay's bouncy chair then climbed into her booster seat and picked up the book from the top of the pile. "This one is about a very hungry caterpillar," she said, showing him the cover. "The caterpillar eats lots of different things and turns into a butterfly."

"Spoiler alert," Julian said under his breath, making Ruby smile.

He smiled back.

"I'd almost forgotten that," he mused thoughtfully.

"That the caterpillar turns into a butterfly?"

"No," he said. "That your smile can light up a room."

An awkward silence grew between them, the only sound in the room coming from the drip of the coffee maker and Emery's storytelling.

Then Ruby glanced at the ceiling. "I don't think you're giving enough credit to the track lights over your head," she said lightly.

"I made you uncomfortable," Julian noted. "And that wasn't my intention."

"What was your intention?" she ventured to ask.

He shrugged. "I don't know that I'd consciously formed an intention—I just said what I was thinking." He hesitated another beat before adding, "Though I held back from adding how much I've missed seeing your smile over the past three years."

Her cheeks flushed—though her face wasn't the only part of her body that heated in response to his comment.

Desperate to defuse the tension that had suddenly arisen, Ruby glanced at Emery, preoccupied with her storytelling, and Jay, captivated by the sound of her voice. She cleared her throat. "It's sad, isn't it, how divorce affects so many other relationships?"

"It certainly can," he agreed.

"Coffee's ready," she said, when the machine stopped gurgling.

Julian reached into the cupboard for the mugs while she put the doughnuts on a plate.

She poured a splash of cream into her mug and stirred, at the same time wondering if putting more caffeine into her system was a good idea when just being near Julian already made her feel jittery inside.

She didn't understand what had changed between them.

She'd known him for years and always felt completely at ease in his presence.

But that was when he was Owen's friend and she was Owen's wife.

Now the status of both those relationships had changed, which meant that Owen was no longer between them.

Instead, there was an inexplicable tension that made her feel…not uncomfortable, she realized, but aware.

Aware of the fact that he was a very attractive man.

Aware of the fact that she was a woman who hadn't been with a man in a very long time.

And suddenly wondering what might happen if she breached the distance between them and touched her lips to his.

"Do you want to test it?" Julian asked.

Her startled gaze flew to his.

Because for just a second, she'd been certain that he was somehow privy to her inner thoughts and was suggesting that they test the chemistry sizzling between them.

Then she saw that he was pointing to the dishwasher with the half-eaten doughnut in his hand.

And she wasn't sure if she was relieved or disappointed.

"Should I run a test cycle?" she asked. "Are you not confident in the quality of your work?"

"I'm so confident, I'll offer you a warranty," he said.

"Let me guess, if I run the dishwasher and end up with water all over my kitchen, you'll give me back every dollar that I paid for the repair?"

"That sounds fair, don't you think?"

"I'll let you know."

He swallowed another bite of doughnut. "How long have you been washing dishes by hand?"

"Since Emery's birthday."

"That was almost four months ago."

She was surprised by his reply. "You remember her birthday?"

"Easy to do since it's three days before mine."

It was also exactly a month before Owen's, but Ruby wasn't sure her daughter's father would remember if his mom didn't remind him.

And she didn't want to discuss her ex-husband with Julian, so instead she said, "Well, thanks for the fix. Sincerely. I've set a strict household budget for myself to ensure I can put money in Emery's college fund every month, so I'm not sure how long it would have taken me to save up to call for a repair."

"My parents taught all their kids to be as self-sufficient as possible, so I'm pretty handy around the house," Julian said. "If you've ever got a leaky faucet that needs fixing or a light fixture that needs replacing, just give me a call."

"Or a Kelly doll stuck in the toilet?"

"I'm not sure that's something I've had to tackle before," he admitted. "Was it Emery's Kelly doll?"

She shook her head. "My sister's, way back when. But it was my brother who decided to let it swim in the toilet."

"Did your sister get her doll back?" he asked, amusement crinkling the corners of his warm brown eyes.

"My dad got out his drain snake and the doll was retrieved—and disposed of," she said. "Because Scarlett didn't want it back once she understood what else went down that drain. And my dad made Garnet buy her a new one with his allowance."

"I'll bet that was the last time he flushed one of her toys down the toilet."

"It was," she confirmed. "Though he came up with other creative ways to torment his sisters."

"As brothers are born to do," he agreed.

"Speaking of little boys," she said, as Jay started to fuss, "I think this one is almost ready for a bottle and an afternoon nap."

"And that's my cue to get out of your way."

"Oh. Okay." She refused to acknowledge the twinge of disappointment his words evoked. Of course, he wanted to make an escape—he had a life of his own and he'd already given her a substantial amount of his time over the past forty-eight hours. It was silly to feel disappointed that he was leaving when she hadn't even expected to see him today. "Well, thanks again."

Emery closed the book in her hands and shifted her attention to the adults in the room. "Unca Julian, will you play Candy Land with me?"

"Uncle Julian has to go now," Ruby told her daughter.

The little girl's bottom lip pushed forward.

"I don't *have* to go," Julian said. "I mean, it's not as if I've got anything on my schedule more tempting than Candy Land."

Emy's pout immediately turned into a smile. "I'll go get it!"

"You don't have to indulge her every whim, you know," Ruby said to Julian when her daughter had dashed off.

"Is it okay that I said I'd play with her?"

"Of course, it's okay. I just feel like we've monopolized your free time over the past couple of days."

"I can't think of anywhere else that I'd rather spend my free time," he said.

"In that case, you better be prepared for some fierce competition, because Emy won't hesitate to push you into the Chocolate Swamp if you get between her and the Candy Castle."

"Got it!" Emery said, returning to the kitchen with her board game.

Julian linked his hands together and turned them over to flex his fingers. "Game on."

"THAT SPINNER THING is rigged," Julian announced, when Ruby returned after settling Jay down for his nap. "Every time I got close to the finish, I landed on the peppermint candy and had to go back."

"How many times did she beat you?"

"I don't want to talk about it."

Ruby couldn't help but laugh at his petulant tone—and again when a grinning Emy held up her hand showing four fingers.

"Four times, huh?"

"I don't want to talk about it," he repeated.

"Do you want Mommy to play?" Ruby asked. "Give you some competition?"

Emy shook her head. "I wanna go 'bogganin' now."

"We can't go tobogganing just yet," Ruby said. "We have to wait until Jay wakes up from his nap."

"Is Jay gonna go 'bogganin', too?"

"I think he's going to have to wait a few more years before he tackles the hill."

"If Jay can't go down the hill, why do I hafta wait?"

"Because he won't be happy if we wake him up, and we can't leave him at home by himself."

"Maybe Unca Julian could stay?" Emery said, turning to look at him with a hopeful expression.

"You can't volunteer other people to do a job," Ruby admonished her daughter.

"I'm happy to help in any way that I can," Julian said.

"Except that I can't, in good conscience, leave my foster child in someone else's care."

"I understand," he said.

"It's not that I don't trust you," she hastened to assure him. "It's just that you haven't been vetted by Family Services."

"Have I been adequately vetted by you?"

"Unfortunately, that's not how it works."

"I was only going to suggest that I could take Emery to the park to go tobogganing," he said.

"Yay!" Emery clapped her hands.

"Your mom hasn't said *yes*," Julian cautioned the little girl.

"P'ease, Mommy!" The little girl wrapped herself around Ruby's legs and looked up, a pleading expression on her face.

"Let me think about this a minute," she said, tapping a finger against her chin as she pretended to contemplate. "If you're suggesting that I stay here with Jay, where it's warm and dry, while you go to the park to slide down snow-covered hills with Emery, then *yes*, I can agree to that plan."

"Yay!" Emery said again, racing to the hall closet to retrieve her coat and snow pants and boots.

"Do you have any idea what you're in for?" she asked Julian, when her daughter was out of earshot.

"I've been tobogganing before," he assured her.

"With a four-year-old?"

"Probably not since Marisa was four."

"Then I wish you luck."

AFTER HIS THIRD trek up the hill, dragging the sled with Emery on it, Julian was thinking that Ruby should have wished him energy instead of luck. He worked on a ranch, for goodness' sake. He was accustomed to physical labor. But apparently hauling a four-year-old kid on a sled was a different kind of physical labor. Or maybe it was that he'd volunteered for this assignment after working six hours at Blue Sky Beef earlier that day.

Whatever the reason, he was ready to drop when he finally managed to convince Emery that the hill was "all tobogganed out for today" and it was time to head back home. It helped that several other parents were rounding up their kids to leave the park, which suggested to Julian that it was probably close to dinnertime.

Of course, Emery wasn't his kid, but when he was with her and Ruby, he couldn't help but wonder how his life might have turned out if he'd met Ruby first… For sure, he would have treated her a lot better than Owen McKinley did.

But that was all ancient history, and Julian was focused on the present.

"Look at you guys," Ruby said, when she met them at the front door. "All rosy cheeks and big smiles."

"Am I smiling?" Julian asked. "I can't feel my face."

"But you had a good time?"

"Yeah, it was pretty great," he said, and meant it.

"It was *the best*," Emery added.

"I'm a little surprised that you stayed out as long as you did," Ruby admitted. "Usually after four or five runs, she's worn out from the long walk back up to the top of the hill."

"Walk?" he echoed, his brows lifting.

Ruby looked at her daughter. "You didn't walk up the hill?"

Emery grinned. "Unca Julian pulled me on the sled."

Julian's gaze narrowed. "You told me that's what your mom does."

She responded with a cheeky grin.

"I did it *once*," Ruby acknowledged. "Then I decided that she could walk."

"I was conned," he realized. "Apparently by a master."

"It was fun," Emery said. "Thank you for taking me 'bogganin', Unca Julian."

"It was fun," he agreed, ruffling her hair. "And I would do it again."

She beamed at him.

"But next time, you're pulling *me* on the sled."

Emery giggled. "Uh-uh. You're too big."

"I guess we'll find out, won't we?" he said.

"It sounds like you burned off a lot of energy on the hill," Ruby remarked. "Are you hungry?"

*"Starving,"* Emery said.

"Go wash up for dinner then while I pop the garlic bread in the oven."

The little girl scurried off to do as she was told.

"I'll get out of your way and let you have dinner," Julian said.

"Oh, no, you don't," Ruby told him.

"No?" he asked, the question tinged with amusement.

"You fixed my dishwasher, and you pulled Emery up that hill countless times—I owe you dinner. It's not anything fancy," she said hurriedly, as he started to protest. "Just chili that I took out of the freezer this morning."

"And garlic bread," he noted.

"Which needs to go in the oven," she suddenly remembered.

After a moment's hesitation, he shed his coat and boots, then followed her into the kitchen. "Hot chili and garlic bread sounds like the perfect meal after several hours on the slopes."

"You were gone seventy-five minutes."

"Well, it felt like several hours."

She laughed softly. "I'm sure it did. So…you'll stay? Or did you have other plans for dinner?" she asked, realizing she didn't know what he did with his nights.

Julian held her gaze. "What kind of other plans do you think I might have?"

She shrugged. "A date, maybe."

"No," he said. "I don't have any other plans. And, Ruby?"

She'd turned to stir the chili in a pot on the stove, but looked back at him now.

"There's nowhere else I'd rather be."

# CHAPTER SEVEN

*Mustang Pass, Montana*

SHE COULDN'T SLEEP.

Winnie squinted at the glowing numbers of the clock on her bedside table.

2:17

She'd turned in hours earlier.

Long before midnight.

"I'm sorry," she'd said. "I don't think I can stay awake until the end of the movie."

The man in the La-Z-Boy recliner had shifted his attention from the television to her.

Not *the man*, she admonished herself. *Her husband*.

"Headache?" he'd asked.

She'd responded with a shake of her head. "Just tired."

"Okay," he'd said, as he paused the movie. "Get some rest. We'll save the ending for another time."

She'd kissed his cheek, grateful for his understanding, and made her way to her bedroom.

She *had* been tired, but sleep eluded her.

The same questions that ran on a seemingly endless loop through her mind all day continuing to plague her into the night.

So many questions.

Never any answers.

Beside the clock was a photo in a silver frame.

Though she couldn't see it in the dark, she knew it was there. Her wedding photo.

Wasn't a wedding supposed to be the happiest day of a woman's life?

Why did she have no memory of that day?

No memory of her husband even?

"Post-traumatic brain injury," the doctor called it.

She'd responded to his diagnosis with questions:

"How long will it last?"

"When will I remember?"

Questions he'd been unable to answer with any certainty.

"It could be a few weeks. It could be several months. It might be that your memories of the past never come back."

At the time of his initial visit, it had already been weeks.

Since then, months had passed.

Still, she refused to consider that her past might be gone forever. There had to be something she could do to unlock the door to her memories.

Or pry it open, if necessary.

The man—*her husband*—had tried to help.

He'd taken her to all their favorite places around town in the hope that one of them might spark a memory.

The bank on Queen Street where they'd first met when he was a teller and she was making a deposit for Knit & Pearl, where she worked part-time.

Except that the bank was a pizza place now and the knitting shop had become a tattoo parlor.

"Signs of change," he'd noted with obvious regret.

But Winnie had no memories of what they'd been and so couldn't mourn their transformation.

Their next stop had been Riverside Park, where they'd apparently crossed paths a few weeks later and he'd picked a flower for her from the public garden and nearly been arrested for his efforts. A peony, he said. Pink and lush and fragrant.

She'd smiled at the story, though she had no memory of the meeting. But Victor claimed that she'd pressed the bloom in a book to preserve it as a memento, so it must have been a good day.

After the park, they'd gone for a bite to eat at the Main Street Grill—the diner where they'd gone on their first date.

It hadn't been anything fancy back then, either, he'd confided. Because he hadn't been able to afford fancy, but he'd wanted to ensure she got a good meal and there was a reason the diner had been an institution in Mustang Pass for more than fifty years.

She was grateful for his efforts, and it pleased her to hear the affection in his voice when he recounted events of their shared past. But visiting the gazebo where they'd shared their first kiss and the church steps upon which he'd proposed—also the church in which they'd exchanged their vows—triggered no memories for her.

Her mind remained blank, like a brand-new canvas awaiting an artist's brush.

Or like a newborn child who had yet to experience any of what life had to offer.

Except that she wasn't a baby—she was an old woman.

She didn't need to know her actual birthdate to know that— she just needed to look in the mirror. Her hair was white (though gloriously thick for a woman her age, if she did say so herself) and her face was deeply lined, like a road map of crisscrossing routes, proof of the miles that she'd traveled.

But why couldn't she remember any of them?

The loss of so many years wasn't just a source of frustration but sadness.

And while her husband was happy to fill in the blanks of the time they'd spent together, what about all the years that had come before?

She had absolutely no insight into those years.

It was almost as if she hadn't existed before she met Victor.

Was her husband the only family she had? The only friend?

*Where was Beatrix?*

She frowned at the question that popped into her mind seemingly out of nowhere—followed logically by another: *Who* was Beatrix?

Winnie felt a frisson of excitement, a tentative spark of hope.

Because even if she didn't remember *who* Beatrix was, she remembered her name. And now that she had, she instinctively knew that Beatrix was someone important to her.

A longtime friend?

A sister?

A daughter?

Her breath caught.

*Beatrix is my daughter.*

The burst of happiness was immediately smothered by darkness.

*"Don't take her away. Please. I need to see my daughter. My Beatrix."*

*"I'm sorry."* But there was no remorse in the tone, no sympathy. *"Your baby's dead."*

*"No!"*

*Strong hands gripped her arms, held her down.*

*A needle slid into her skin.*

A tear slid down Winnie's cheek as she finally drifted into slumber.

# CHAPTER EIGHT

*Tenacity, Montana*

JULIAN WAS SURPRISED to get a text message from Hayes Parker early Friday morning, asking if he was available to meet. Intrigued by the request—and grateful for any kind of distraction that might keep his thoughts off Ruby for more than three minutes, Julian said that he was. Hayes replied with a time and a location.

But as he drove to the meeting location, his mind continued to drift back to Ruby—specifically the time he'd spent with her the night before. Conversation had flowed easily at the dinner table, and he'd been happy to stick around after the meal to occupy the baby while Ruby dealt with her daughter's usual bedtime routine. He'd been fighting his feelings for Ruby for a long time, but he had no weapon capable of combating his instinctive affection for her daughter. Maybe because he'd fallen for the little girl the first time he'd held her in his arms, when she was no more than a few weeks old. And he'd missed her, almost as much as he'd missed Ruby, when he'd ended his friendship with Owen.

The time he'd spent with them over the past couple of days had reminded him how much he'd enjoyed their company— and made him acknowledge that he was in danger of falling for the baby, too. But an even bigger problem was the feelings that had stirred inside him when he was alone with Ruby, after the kids were asleep.

If he thought that his feelings were one-sided, he might be able to ignore them, but the unexpected electricity that sparked whenever he and Ruby touched combined with some flirtatious banter and warm glances suggested otherwise. And if there was any chance that she might be attracted to him, he didn't want to ignore it.

Of course, figuring out what to do about it was a whole other issue. And one that would have to wait for further contemplation, because he'd arrived at the address Hayes had given him—which turned out to be directly next to the End of the Road Ranch, the property owned by Hayes's family.

Julian parked his truck on the road, behind the other man's vehicle.

"I'm guessing that you didn't have to travel too far for this meeting," he remarked, when he joined Hayes by the fence that ran parallel to the road.

"Not too far," Hayes agreed.

Julian tucked his chin into the collar of his coat and his hands into the pockets.

"I used to call it the End of My Rope Ranch," Hayes admitted. "When I left Tenacity, I never imagined coming back, never mind coming back to work as a rancher here."

"Ranching isn't for everyone," Julian noted.

"But for others, it's in the blood."

He nodded. "What is this place?"

"It's 800 acres that Henry Burkholder severed from his ranch and sold to Sam Gibson several years back. Sam planned to build a house on the land and start his own herd, but shortly after the papers were signed, his wife's grandfather invited them down to Texas to oversee his operation there."

"There are days that I'd choose Texas over Montana, too, if I had that choice."

"Winter days like this one, I'd guess," Hayes said.

"And you'd be right," Julian confirmed. "So why are we here?"

"Sam still owns the land. He wanted to make sure things

worked out in Texas before he sold it—and then he forgot about it, or so he said when he contacted me to see if I might be interested in buying it and adding it to End of the Road."

"I assume you didn't call me out here to tell me that you're buying it."

"No," Hayes confirmed. "I called you out here because I thought *you* might be interested in buying it."

Hayes would know, because Julian had approached him a few months earlier, when he'd learned that End of the Road Ranch had fallen on hard times when Hayes's father, Lionel, was sick. But Hayes had rejected his offer to buy part of the land, determined to save every last acre—and perhaps prove himself to his always disapproving father.

A smile spread across his face as Julian nodded, overjoyed that his longtime dream might finally be within his grasp.

RUBY AWOKE FRIDAY morning with mixed feelings.

Friday was usually the day that she looked forward to the weekend: two whole days to focus on Emery without giving a single thought to work. But this Friday came at the end of two weeks of holidays (aside from the New Year's Eve shift her boss had begged her to cover) and after the weekend, she and Emery would have to get back into their usual routines—and figure out how to fit Jay into them, too.

It hadn't taken any figuring—or even any effort—to find a place for the baby in her heart. From the first moment that Hazel Browning had thrust his car seat into her hands and he'd looked up at her with his big blue eyes, his expression far too solemn for someone so young, her mama bear instincts had kicked in. He was now one of her cubs, and she would do anything to protect him.

But how was she going to protect her own heart? Because she knew it would break into pieces when it was time to give him up.

And how was she going to protect her daughter's heart? Because Emery was growing more and more attached to the baby every minute of the day.

Thankfully, the little girl would be going back to preschool soon. Every day, she asked her mom how many more days before school started again. Ruby suspected she was more excited about seeing Mia, her best friend, than learning, but she figured the motivation wasn't as important as the desire to go to school.

Ruby had hoped to make arrangements for Emery and Mia to get together for a couple of playdates over the holidays, but the other girl's parents had taken her to Anaheim to visit her grandparents—and Disneyland.

Ruby's mom and dad had similarly tried to lure her to Florida with promises of visits to Disney World, but they didn't only want her to visit—they wanted her to move to the Sunshine State and had dropped more than a few hints about the abundance of job opportunities available to someone with her education and qualifications. And while Florida did boast over four thousand hotels compared to Montana's three hundred, Ruby couldn't imagine taking her daughter away from her paternal grandparents to placate the maternal ones.

Not to mention that Owen would likely have something to say about any decision to take their daughter out-of-state. And even if he didn't exercise his access on anything close to a consistent schedule, Ruby hadn't entirely given up hope that he might someday step up and be the kind of dad Emery deserved.

"Maybe Unca Julian will bring choc'ate doughnuts today," Emery said, drawing Ruby's attention back to the present.

"I don't know that we're going to see Uncle Julian at all today," she cautioned her daughter, reminded of the fact that he'd been a regular fixture in both of their lives before the divorce—and done a disappearing act afterward.

Thankfully, Emery had been too young to really remember him—or maybe, on some level, she did remember, and that's why she was already starting to get attached to him again.

"Why not?" Emy asked now.

"Because Uncle Julian has a job and other responsibilities. And it was nice of him to take time away from those things to hang out with us, but you shouldn't expect that he'll be a regular visitor."

Emery frowned at that, but before she could say anything else, Ruby's phone chimed with a text message.

She glanced at the screen and immediately chastised herself

for the quick spurt of disappointment she felt when she saw it wasn't Julian's name on the display but her friend Lynda Slater's.

Apparently Emery wasn't the only one who'd hoped to see Julian again today.

An unexpected trial delay = time on my hands. Are you up for a visit?

She immediately replied:

Would LOVE a visit.

While she waited for her friend, Ruby found herself reflecting on their first meeting, three-and-a-half years earlier.

Emery hadn't been even six months old when Ruby started to hear rumors about her husband's infidelity. Though Owen denied having an affair, she knew that she had to take control of her future. So she made an appointment to meet with Megan Grant, the owner and manager of the Tenacity Inn, prepared to beg to get her old job back.

Thankfully, no begging had been required, and Ruby had been behind the desk the following Monday when a group of local lawyers arrived for a workshop. The subject was "Mediation vs. Litigation—Choosing the Right Path for Your Divorce."

Though she hadn't yet set her mind on ending her marriage, Ruby was intrigued by the title. And when there was a lull at the desk, she'd snuck into the back of the conference room in the hope that she might pick up some insights.

Apparently she hadn't been as unobtrusive as she'd hoped, because when the group adjourned for lunch, Lynda Slater—the keynote speaker—came to the front desk and introduced herself to Ruby.

That impromptu conversation led to an unexpected friendship and they'd been besties ever since.

"Why doesn't anyone ever bring a veggie tray?" Ruby wondered aloud, as she took the dome-covered plate her friend offered.

"Because a veggie tray doesn't go nearly as well with coffee as cake does," Lynda replied, stepping into the foyer.

"Auntie Lynda!" Emy raced down the hall to throw herself at their visitor, wrapping her arms around her honorary aunt's legs.

Laughing, Lynda dropped her purse and the gift bag she still carried to lift the little girl into her arms.

"We got a baby," Emery told her. "A boy baby."

Lynda glanced at Ruby. "You finally got a call from Family Services?"

She nodded. "New Year's Eve. Or morning, I guess."

"Congratulations?" her friend said cautiously.

"It's a good thing," Ruby insisted.

Emy, bored with the conversation now, wriggled to be released. When Lynda set her down, she spotted the gift on the floor. "Is that a present?" she asked hopefully.

"It's a Christmas present," Lynda confirmed, in case the rosy-cheeked Santa on the bag wasn't an obvious giveaway. "Why don't you look at the tag and see who it's for?"

Emery peered at the tag tied to the handle, her eyes growing wide. "It has my name on it. It's a Christmas present for me?"

Lynda nodded. "Sorry I didn't get it to you before Christmas, but work was crazy busy right up until Christmas Eve and then, well, the holidays are always chaotic."

"Also, you don't have to bring something for her every time you come to visit," Ruby said to her friend.

"I don't bring something *every* time."

"Can I open it?" Emery asked.

"Of course you can open it," Lynda said, and Emery immediately started pulling tissue out of the bag.

"Take it into the living room," Ruby said. "I'll bring the cake and coffee in there."

By the time Ruby loaded up a tray with the coffee service, slices of cake and a juice box, Emery had the contents of the gift bag scattered on the living room carpet.

Jay, who had been fast asleep in the playpen when Ruby went into the kitchen, was now wide awake in her friend's arms.

"Look, Mommy. I got a coloring book and crayons and a new game and a Squishmallow and a LEGO set."

"Because Auntie Lynda doesn't spoil you at all," Ruby remarked dryly.

Her friend shrugged. "It's fun to shop for kids."

"Unless it's for formula and diapers."

"Good point."

"And you don't get your coffee until you give up the baby."

Lynda sighed but laid him down on the quilt Ruby had spread out on the floor.

Emery moved the box of LEGO closer to Jay and pointed to the 2+ age recommendation on the corner. "You can't play with this," she told him. "Cuz you're too little."

"I don't think you need to worry about him stealing your toys," Ruby assured her daughter. "He's not even crawling yet."

"I'm just telling him now so that he knows," Emery said.

"Well, he's probably going to need a reminder by the time he's mobile," Lynda told her.

The little girl wrinkled her nose. "What's mobile?"

"It means able to move around."

"When will he be mobile?"

Lynda looked at her friend, deferring to the expert on that question.

"Most babies start crawling when they're around eight months old and take their first steps around their first birthdays," Ruby said. "You took yours when you were eleven months old."

"Eleven?" Emery's brow furrowed. "Eleven's more than ten and I'm only four."

*Four going on fourteen*, Ruby thought.

"Eleven *months*, not eleven years," she clarified. "So it was about a month before your birthday that you started to walk."

"When's Jay's birthday?"

"November." Early November, according to the Family Services file, though the exact date of his birth was currently unknown.

"Is that a long way away?" Emery asked.

"It's January now," Ruby reminded her daughter. "Then

comes February and March and…" She continued to recite the subsequent months of the calendar for her daughter.

"November's a long way away," she concluded, with a heavy sigh.

"After Halloween," Lynda said, to offer some additional context.

Em considered this for a long moment while she sorted her blocks into piles according to their color. "Maybe we can take him back and get a different baby," she finally said. "One that walks and talks."

Lynda choked on a mouthful of coffee.

Ruby slid her friend a look as she bit down, hard, on her own lip so she didn't laugh.

"Don't you think you'd be sad if Jay didn't live with us anymore?" she asked her daughter.

Emery nodded, apparently not needing so long to think about that question. "So maybe we can keep Jay and get another baby?"

"Or maybe we can be happy that we have Jay and take the best care of him that we can for as long as he gets to stay with us."

"Okay," Em agreed, picking up her new coloring book and crayons and carrying them to her child-size table on the other side of the sofa.

"So how was your New Year's Eve?" Ruby asked her friend now.

"A lot less eventful than yours," Lynda said, looking pointedly at the baby on the quilt.

"Didn't you have a date with… Brandon?" she prompted, remembering how excited Lynda had been when she told her about their plans.

"Brendan," her friend said. "And yes, I did."

"I'm guessing it didn't go quite as you'd hoped."

"Not quite," Lynda agreed. "He hit the bar early and got so drunk, he was passed out before midnight."

"I'm sorry."

Her friend shrugged. "So I hooked up with Callan."

Now it was Ruby who choked on her coffee. "Who's Callan?"

"Brendan's brother."

"O-kay," she said cautiously.

"Don't judge me," Lynda pleaded.

"I'm not judging you," Ruby promised. "I'm just… I'm not sure what I am, though envious is probably part of it because I haven't had sex since… I can't even tell you how long it's been."

Her friend frowned. "Please tell me that your worthless ex-husband isn't the last guy you slept with."

Ruby lifted her mug to her lips and swallowed another mouthful of coffee.

"You're not saying anything," Lynda noted. "Does that mean Owen *is* the last guy you slept with?"

"I don't know how to answer that question without telling you what you told me not to tell you," Ruby admitted.

"You've been divorced more than a year—and separated almost two years before that."

"I'm aware," she assured her friend.

"Are you telling me that you haven't had sex in *more than three years*?" Lynda's tone was incredulous.

Ruby nodded.

It was another fact of which she was well aware.

But truthfully, she hadn't given much thought to sex until very recently. In fact, not until she'd met up with Julian again.

"Well, I know what my resolution is for this new year," Lynda said. "To get you laid."

Ruby felt her cheeks grow hot. "I appreciate your interest in my personal life," she said dryly, "but getting naked with a man isn't on my 'to-do' list at the moment."

"Apparently it's been so long, you've forgotten how enjoyable sex can be," her friend noted. "Otherwise it would be at the top of your 'to-do' list."

"Maybe I have forgotten," she allowed. "But it's definitely not a priority right now."

"Sex—with the right man—should always be a priority."

"Well, having to be tested for STDs because my husband was cheating on me with multiple women should be proof enough that I don't have a lot of experience with the right kind of man."

"You won't hear any disagreement from me on that score,"

Lynda assured her. "But Owen was your past. It's time to move on from the past and enjoy your present."

Not wanting to discuss her current infatuation, Ruby retrieved the carafe from the kitchen to refill their mugs of coffee.

"Or maybe you already have moved on," her friend said in a considering tone.

"Of course, I've moved on," she confirmed. "My relationship with Owen McKinley is very much in the rearview mirror."

Lynda spooned more sugar into her mug. "Speaking of rearview mirrors—was that Julian Sanchez's truck parked in your driveway Wednesday afternoon?"

Ruby had to laugh. "That was a creative segue."

"Well, was it or wasn't it?" her friend prompted impatiently.

"It was," she confirmed.

"I didn't know you were…friends?"

"I'm not sure we are," Ruby admitted. "I always knew him as Owen's friend. But I guess we became friends, too, though we lost touch when Owen and I separated."

"So what was he doing here?" Lynda asked now.

"He brought juice boxes."

"Juice boxes?" her friend echoed dubiously.

"Apple and grape," Ruby said.

"I need more information than that," her friend insisted.

She sipped her coffee. "Julian was at the inn for the party on New Year's Eve when I got the call from Family Services, and he offered to come home with me to put the crib together so it would be ready for the baby when he arrived. Then he called the next day, to see how we were doing, and he heard Emery in the background, whining that we didn't have juice boxes, so he picked some up and brought them over."

"Well, isn't he a clever man?" her friend noted with a sly smile. "Currying favor with the child to score points with the mom."

"I think he was just being nice," Ruby said.

Lynda lifted a brow. "He just dropped off the juice boxes and then continued on his way?"

"Not exactly," she admitted.

"So why don't you tell me—*exactly*—what happened?" her friend suggested.

"He brought doughnuts as well as juice boxes, so I invited him to come in for a cup of coffee and a doughnut."

"And of course he said *yes*."

"He said *yes*," she confirmed. "And we had coffee and doughnuts."

"And then?" Lynda prompted.

"How do you know there's an 'and then'?" Ruby challenged. "Maybe that's the end of the story."

"It's not," her friend said confidently. "I know you—and the flush of color in your cheeks is a sure sign that you're flustered."

"Maybe because I feel like I'm being interrogated."

"Or maybe because a handsome, charming man is interested in you."

"Julian hasn't given any indication that he is interested in anything more than being friends." She sipped her coffee, then added, "Although he did stop by again on Thursday."

"With more juice boxes?"

"No. With a new drain hose for my dishwasher."

Lynda lifted her mug to her lips. "I cannot tell you how much I'm struggling not to say something totally inappropriate right now," she confided.

"I can see it on your face," Ruby said. "And I appreciate your restraint."

"Instead I'll just say that I'm glad you finally got the dishwasher fixed."

"Julian fixed it."

"Handsome *and* handy," her friend mused.

"And then Emery finagled him into taking her to the park to go tobogganing."

Her friend smirked. "Just being nice, huh?"

"You've tried saying 'no' to Emery," Ruby reminded her, rising from her seat to pick up the baby, who was starting to fuss.

"Okay, I'll give you that one," Lynda said. "And after tobogganing?"

"By the time they got back, it was dinnertime, so I invited him to stay and eat with us."

"It sounds like he spent the better part of two days with you."

"I guess he did."

"And after dinner?" her friend prompted.

"He said *thanks* and he left."

Lynda frowned. "Did he at least kiss you goodbye?"

"It wasn't a date."

"But did he kiss you goodbye?"

"No."

Her friend was visibly disappointed.

"But…" Ruby hesitated. "There was a moment. Or maybe a couple of moments."

"Tell me," Lynda urged.

And because Lynda was her closest friend in Tenacity and she desperately wanted to talk to someone about the unexpected stirrings she'd experienced when she was around Julian, she told her.

About the moment when his fingertips brushed against her palm when they were putting the crib together, and when their eyes locked in the foyer when she walked him to the door, and what he said about her smile lighting up the room.

"So there's something there," Lynda noted approvingly.

"Maybe," Ruby acknowledged. "But he was Owen's friend."

"And you were his wife," her friend retorted. "We all make mistakes."

"Touché."

"So when are you going to see him again? Tonight?"

"I don't know. He didn't say anything about tonight."

"And you're disappointed about that, aren't you? Because you want to see him tonight."

"I don't know what I want," she admitted. "But I do know this isn't a good time for me to be thinking about starting a romance."

"It's past time for you to move on," her friend said firmly.

"But I don't just have Emy to think about now—I've got Jay, too. And he's been through so much in his short life already."

Lynda looked pointedly at the baby now snoozing in Ruby's arms. "I think Jay's doing just fine. And God knows Emy could benefit from a father figure in her life."

"Mark spends a fair amount of time with her," she reminded her friend.

"And that's great. But he's her grandfather, not her father."

"Well, Julian isn't her father, either. And I wouldn't want her to start thinking about him as such and then have him disappear from her life...like Owen did."

"I don't think you need to worry about her getting too attached after one outing to the park."

"You're right," Ruby decided. "I'm being ridiculous."

"Or maybe you're worried that *you* might get too attached, because you already have feelings for him."

"I'm definitely attracted to him."

"A very good sign," Lynda assured her. "The question now is—what are you going to do about it?"

It was a question that Ruby continued to ponder long after her friend had gone.

## CHAPTER NINE

As soon as Julian got home after his meeting with Hayes, he sat down at his computer and began crunching numbers, eager to put together an offer for the property.

"It's open," he called out, in response to the knock on his door.

"¡Hola!"

Recognizing his mother's voice, he closed the lid of his laptop and pushed away from the breakfast bar to greet her with a hug and kiss. "This is a pleasant surprise."

"I haven't seen you since the party at the inn on New Year's Eve," Nicole Sanchez said, the slightest note of accusation in her voice.

"I've been busy," he hedged.

"That's a surprise, as January tends to be a relatively slow month in ranching." Of course, she would know, as her husband worked in the same industry.

"And yet, there are always things to be done," Julian noted.

"Apparently," she agreed.

"Coffee?" he offered.

"A cup of decaf would be great."

He slid a pod into his single serve coffee maker and set a mug beneath the spout.

"*Gracias,*" she said, when he handed her the hot drink. "I

stopped by yesterday afternoon with some leftover pozole, but you weren't home."

He brewed a second cup for himself. "I hope you left the soup."

She nodded. "It's in your freezer."

"Thank you."

His mom sipped her coffee. "Are you going to tell me where you were?"

"Visiting a friend."

"A *friend*," she echoed.

He immediately realized his mistake.

He was being evasive, and he was never evasive.

Not with his mom.

"A woman," she concluded.

"Yes, a woman," he admitted.

"Are you interested in this woman…romantically?"

"I am," he admitted. "But I'm not sure if my interest is reciprocated."

"Well, why wouldn't it be?" Nicole demanded.

Her indignant tone made him smile.

"I can only think that it's because she doesn't know me very well yet," he said dryly.

"When are you going to bring her home for Sunday dinner?" she asked, clearly unwilling to let the subject drop.

"I'll let you know."

"It's Sunday the day after tomorrow," she pointed out.

"So it is," he acknowledged.

"You'll be home for Sunday dinner?"

"When have I ever missed it?"

"Only when you've had plans with a woman."

"No plans this Sunday," he assured her.

"Well, there's always room for one more at the table, if that changes."

"It's very early days, *Má*. Too early to bring her home to meet the family."

"You let me know when you're ready and I'll make something special."

"Shouldn't you be busy making plans with Marisa for her wedding?"

"She doesn't want a big wedding or a big fuss—she just wants to marry the man she loves."

"And that's why you came here to fuss over me?"

"I can—and do—worry about all my children at the same time," she assured him. "Diego, Luca, Nina and Marisa as much as you."

"Your children are all grown up now, *Má*. Don't you think it's time for you to stop worrying and let us live our own lives?"

"I'll stop worrying when you've got a wife to take care of you," she retorted.

"I can take care of myself."

"Well, of course you can," she said. "I didn't raise my kids to be *tontos indefensos*. But a man alone isn't happy. You need a partner—*una esposa*—to share the good times and the bad."

"Thank you for the pozole, *Má*."

"You're welcome." She kissed his cheek. "Remember what else I taught you—to be respectful and careful. I want to be a *suegra* before an *abuela*."

JULIAN HAD MANAGED to come up with an excuse to stop by Ruby's house every day since New Year's, but after assembling her crib, delivering juice boxes and fixing her dishwasher, he was running out of excuses.

So he was pleasantly surprised when, shortly after saying goodbye to his mother early Friday afternoon, his phone chimed with a text message from Ruby

Ran the dishwasher this morning... :)

His grumpy mood was immediately improved.

Because the brief—and admittedly impersonal—content of the message didn't matter as much as the fact that she'd initiated contact.

He pondered his reply for several minutes, because of course he was going to reply, and finally tapped out a message on his keypad.

The money-back guarantee is good for 60 days.

She answered quickly.

Since I didn't pay for the repair (and not even for the part!) I was hoping you'd let me make dinner as a 'thank you.'

Not such a brief or impersonal message this time, he mused.

And after a brief moment's hesitation, he tapped the telephone icon on the screen.

Ruby answered on the first ring.

"I'm not an efficient texter, so I thought I'd give you a quick call," he said.

"Apparently you have more to say than *yes* or *no*."

"I appreciate the offer…"

"But?"

"But you've got two kids to take care of—the last thing you need is to be cooking dinner for someone else."

"We all need to eat," she pointed out reasonably.

"Do you like pizza?"

"Doesn't everyone like pizza?"

"I assume that includes Emery?"

"It's only her second favorite meal in the whole wide world," she told him.

"So then is six o'clock okay for dinner?"

"Six is great, but I invited you," she reminded him. "So I should be the one to get the pizza."

"Next time," he said.

"PIZZA!" EMERY SAID, immediately identifying the flat box in Julian's hands. "Mommy, Unca Julian bringed pizza!"

"Well, I now know where I rank on her list of importance," he noted. "Below juice boxes, chocolate doughnuts and pizza."

"The way to a four-year-old's heart is through her stomach," Ruby told him.

"And the way to her mom's?" he asked, offering her a bottle of wine.

"I do like a nice chianti," she said, examining the label.

"Good, because the selection in the grocery store was limited, but a quick Google search promised that the simple flavors of a chianti would pair nicely with pizza."

"Well, I made a salad to pair with the pizza, too," she said.

"Because it's not okay to just have pizza?"

"The vegetables with dinner rule," she reminded him.

"Is that your way of guilting me into having salad, too, so that I'm not a bad example for your daughter?"

"You can eat whatever you want," she said, as she scooped some salad into Emery's bowl. "Your choices are between you and your mother."

She used salad dressing to make a smiley face on top of her daughter's salad and nudged the bowl closer to the little girl.

After Emy finished her salad, she ate two slices of cheese pizza. When she was done, Ruby excused her to go wash up and play.

Julian helped himself to another slice of pizza. "I seem to recall hearing that your family lives in Florida, which leads me to wonder how you ended up here."

"My parents are in Florida," she told him. "They moved down there about nine years ago. I actually grew up in Cody, Wyoming, where my dad worked on a cattle ranch until he was injured on the job and couldn't work anymore. After that, they took the insurance settlement he got and bought a little place in Madeira Beach.

"My brother, Garnet, is still in Wyoming. He works as a foreman on a different ranch there. And my sister, Scarlett, is a magazine editor in San Francisco."

"None of which tells me how you found your way to Tenacity," Julian pointed out.

"I went to Sheridan College in Wyoming to study hospitality and tourism management. After graduation, I stayed in Sheridan for a few years, working as a desk clerk at a local boutique hotel. It was a decent job for a new graduate, though working the night shift was a bit of a challenge.

"I'd been there almost a year when I was contacted by one of those head-hunting agencies. They were looking for a suitable candidate to fill a vacancy at the Tenacity Inn. It was essentially the same job that I'd been doing in Sheridan, but days rather than nights and with the possibility of working my way up to a management position."

She shrugged. "And then I met Owen and got swept up into his vortex, which led to my career goals taking a back seat to his. And after Emery was born, I was happy to be a stay-at-home mom, to spend every minute with my baby. Owen approved of the arrangement, because it showed his colleagues that he was the breadwinner taking care of his family. But when he was at home with us, it was evident that he resented the time I spent caring for our daughter.

"He started spending more hours at the office and fewer at home. At least, he said he was at the office. And while I wanted to believe him, I'd heard rumors that he was hanging out at the Grizzly Bar a lot—especially when Debby was working."

Julian saw the emotion on her face and felt compelled to remind her, "Which only proves that he wasn't smart enough to appreciate what he had at home."

"You said something similar the other night," she noted cautiously. "But I thought you and he were good friends."

"We were back then," he agreed.

"Did he cheat on you, too?" she asked lightly.

"No, but he cheated on you, and I refused to pretend that his infidelity didn't bother me."

"So why didn't you tell me what he was doing?"

"There was a part of me that wanted to," he confided. "But a bigger part knew that the truth would hurt you, and that was something I never wanted to do."

She nodded. "When we exchanged our vows, I really did believe it was 'till death do us part.' And, I'll admit, I considered staying with him for Emery's sake, because I thought it would be best for her to grow up in a home with a mom and a dad."

"What changed your mind?" he asked, as she settled back in her seat to give the baby his bottle.

"The realization that he wouldn't change—and that it was more important for me to be a good example to my daughter than stay in a marriage in which no one was happy."

"For what it's worth, I'd say you did the right thing. Emery is obviously thriving in the home you've created for her here."

"Thriving and impatient," Ruby noted, when her daughter interrupted them to announce that the numbers on the clock were an eight and a zero and a two.

"I know it's after eight o'clock, but I'm feeding the baby, so you'll have to give me a few minutes."

"But it's story time *now*." Instead of waiting, as her mom had suggested, she turned to Julian. "Will you read me a story, Unca Julian?"

He looked at Ruby for guidance.

She shrugged.

"Sure," he said.

The little girl beamed at him, and his heart swelled inside his chest. Oh, yeah, he was head over heels for this kid as much as her mother.

"You have to come up to my room," Emery said.

He rose from the chair. "What kind of books do you like? The *Twilight* series? *Harry Potter*? *War and Peace*?"

Her little brow furrowed. "I like *Max & Ruby*."

"Well then, I guess I'm going to have to learn about Max and Ruby."

"One story," Ruby said, calling out the reminder as Julian and Emery made their way upstairs.

"This is my room," Emery told him. "That's my bed and that's my dresser and that's my toy box and that's my book-case and that's the chair where Mommy sits when she reads me stories." As she inventoried her furniture, she pointed to each item in turn.

Her room was decorated like a little girl's paradise, the walls painted a soft purple with ruffled white curtains on the windows and a chandelier dripping with sparkly glass crystals hanging over a bed that boasted a padded headboard in the shape of a crown and a hooked rug of Cinderella's carriage on the floor beside her bed.

No wonder the little girl ruled everyone in her world like a princess—she was born to the role.

"Is that where I'm supposed to sit?" he asked, gesturing to the glider rocker.

She nodded.

He took a seat while Emery perused the bookshelf. She picked one book, then a second and a third, then carefully carried them over to him. She set them on the small table beside the chair, then nimbly climbed into his lap.

"This one first," she said, reaching for the top book and offering it to him.

"Your mom said *one*," he reminded her.

She nodded. "*This* one."

He opened the cover and began reading *Max & Ruby's Snowy Day*, a story about a young bunny who wanted to play outside and his older sister's efforts to keep him occupied inside.

The story wasn't very long, and as soon as Julian had turned the last page, Emery reached for the next book on the pile.

"Now this one," she said.

Before he could protest, she tipped her head back to look at him with big blue eyes and said, "P'ease."

And there was no way he could refuse her.

And when he finished *Bunny Cakes*, he automatically reached for the last book.

He was nearly finished *Max's Bedtime* when he sensed Ruby standing in the doorway, her arms folded across her chest.

He flipped back several pages in the book to point to a photo where Ruby—the big sister bunny—was standing in an almost identical pose.

Emery looked from her mom to the picture and giggled, and Julian was certain it was the sweetest sound in the world.

"I said one story," Ruby reminded her daughter. "And now it's way past your bedtime, Emery Rose McKinley."

"Whoops!" Emery gave her mom a cheeky smile.

"Into bed with you," Ruby told her. "Now."

"Okay," the little girl said agreeably. But she gave Julian's cheek a smacking kiss before she slid off his lap, and his heart completely melted. "Thank you for reading to me."

"Anytime," he said, and meant it.

She smiled at him again, then hurried over to the bed, sliding beneath the covers her mom had pulled back.

"Night night, Em." Ruby bent down to give her daughter a hug and kiss. "Sweet dreams. I love you."

"Love you, too," the little girl said, her eyes already drifting shut.

"Am I in trouble?" Julian asked Ruby, as he followed her out of the room.

"I know it wasn't your fault," she said. "It's a little scary to see how easily she manipulates all the adults in her life."

"I did try to stick to the one-book rule," he said.

"Let me guess—she looked at you with her big blue eyes pleading as she handed you the second book."

"Apparently she does the same thing to you."

"She *tries* to do the same thing to me," Ruby said. "But mothers are made of tougher stuff than other mere mortals so that we can resist such obvious ploys. Most of the time, anyway."

He chuckled.

"But thank you for reading to her. I've been trying to keep her on her usual schedule as much as possible, but having a baby in the house has required us to make some adjustments."

"She's a great kid," he said. "I enjoy spending time with her."

"Is that why you've been here every day since New Year's Eve?"

"Well, I kind of like spending time with her mom, too. And I'm hoping, if she has a chance to get to know me better, she'll find that she likes me, too."

"Of course, I like you," Ruby said. "You're thoughtful and kind and patient and obviously great with kids."

"Maybe the word *like* doesn't paint an accurate picture," he allowed. "So I'll add the fact that I'm incredibly attracted to you."

She blinked. "You are?"

"I am," he confirmed.

"But…"

"But what?" he prompted, when she failed to complete her thought.

"But…you haven't even kissed me."

"No, I haven't," he agreed. "Because I've been waiting for some kind of hint that you might want me to kiss you."

Maybe it was the almost two glasses of chianti that she'd drunk, or maybe it was that being close to Julian made her feel a little wanton and reckless. Or maybe it was a combination of the wine and the man.

Whatever the reason, she stepped forward, breaching the distance between them, and said, "How's this for a hint?"

Then she touched her mouth to his.

It was supposed to be a casual, friendly kiss. A test of the chemistry that had been sizzling between them.

Instead, it turned out to be a spark that set off a firestorm of want inside her.

And maybe it had the same effect on Julian, because his arms came around her and he pulled her close, his tongue sliding between her lips, not just deepening the kiss, but fanning the flames already in danger of burning out of control.

She knew that playing with fire was a good way to get burned, but it felt so good to be in his arms.

To touch and be touched.

To want and be wanted.

But as much as she wished this moment would never end, she was achingly aware of the fact that she had a little girl not yet asleep upstairs who could wander down at any minute.

And so, with extreme reluctance, she finally eased her mouth away from his. But she stayed in the circle of his arms, her forehead tipped against his chest as she struggled to draw air into her lungs.

"That was...a pretty good hint," he said.

"A little more potent than I was anticipating," she admitted.

"And now I'm wishing we'd had this conversation on day one, then we might have enjoyed sharing kisses like that every day since then."

She laughed softly and looked at him, her expression serious. "I'm incredibly attracted to you, too, Julian."

"I'm glad to hear it," he said.

She should have taken a moment to think before she responded, but as if of its own volition, her mouth opened again and she heard herself say, "I might be lousy in bed."

The hint of a smile played at the corners of his mouth. "I don't think so," he said.

"But you don't know," she said. "After all, there must have been a reason that Owen preferred sleeping with other women to his own wife."

"Owen sleeping with other women was more about him than you. For as long as I've known him, he's always had to be the center of attention. When you had Emery, he had to compete for your attention—or seek it elsewhere."

"That's an insightful observation."

He cupped her cheek with his hand, his thumb rubbing gently. "I'm sorry he hurt you."

She put her hand over his, savoring his touch. "I think I might finally be ready to move on."

"I'm glad to hear that."

They'd barely reestablished a friendship and their relationship was already changing again. And maybe it was too fast, but she was twenty-nine years old and she'd been alone for more than three years.

And Ruby didn't want to be alone anymore.

"Emery is going to her grandparents' house for a sleepover in a couple weeks," she told him.

"I'm sure that will be fun for her."

"It could be fun for us, too." She knew she was taking a step toward the point of no return and felt her cheeks flush as her body filled with tension.

Excitement.

Desire.

For Julian.

"If you wanted to have a sleepover here," she concluded.

His dark eyes immediately heated.

"It's a date," he promised. "Is there anything you want me to bring?"

She smiled. "A toothbrush."

# CHAPTER TEN

*Mustang Pass, Montana*

"WHAT ARE YOU doing up, Winnie?"

She finished pouring the water into the pot before turning to face her husband. "I'm making tea."

"It's the middle of the night," Victor pointed out.

"I know, but I couldn't sleep." She reached into the cupboard for a mug, frowned at the row of cream-colored cups. Where was her favorite mug? The purple one decorated with the Mexican cherry flowers.

She gripped the counter as a sharp pain sliced through her head.

Victor was immediately at her side. "Are you okay?" He took her gently by the shoulders and steered her toward the table. "Sit down. I'll bring the tea to you when it's ready."

She sat and closed her eyes, and the pain in her skull receded a little further.

"Actually, it's not true that I couldn't sleep," she told him now. "I didn't have any problem falling asleep, but then I woke up."

"Bad dream?" he asked gently.

She shook her head, still mesmerized by the image of the brightly colored mug in her mind... "Strange dream."

"Do you want to tell me about it?"

"I dreamed about a man."

"Should I be jealous?" Victor was obviously teasing, and yet, Winnie had an uneasy feeling that the man in her dream was someone important to her.

"He was looking for something," she said, ignoring his question. "And he seemed...frantic. Or maybe desperate. Whatever it was that he'd lost was obviously important to him, and I wanted to help, but I couldn't get close enough to communicate with him. Every time I thought I was catching up to him, he'd go through a door, and when I went through the same door, I found myself in a big room, empty except for an old-fashioned writing desk."

"That is a weird dream," Victor agreed. "But you've always wanted to help other people."

"Have I?"

It was so frustrating that he seemed to know so much more about her than she knew about herself.

Nothing about this house or this town—or even her husband—was familiar to her.

"You have," he confirmed. "You are a warm, caring, loving woman, Winnie Thompson."

She could only take his word for it.

After she'd fallen and hit her head, she'd tried to do some research on traumatic brain injuries and amnesia, but it was hard to sort through all the information that was available online. And, truthfully, spending too much time looking at the screen made her head hurt.

So many things made her head hurt.

But her heart ached, too. Like there was a piece of it missing.

Victor carried her tea to the table and set it in front of her. "Have you had this dream before?"

"I don't think so." But even as she responded to his question, images flickered through her mind—like one of those old books with the pictures that seemed animated when you flipped through them quickly. The same room, the same desk, but different words written on the page.

*Don't believe them.*

*Help me.*

*Find me.*

*I want to go home.*

She lifted her mug to her lips and carefully sipped the hot tea.

"I just wish I knew what was real and what was fantasy," she said to Victor.

"You know I'm happy to answer any questions you have."

He was right—she did know. So why was she reluctant to ask the question that was at the forefront of her mind?

Finally she said, "Do we have a child?"

His face seemed to drain of color. He swallowed.

*Your baby's dead.*

The words echoed in her head again.

Had she and Victor lost a child? Was that why he seemed so shaken?

She reached out to touch his hand, feeling guilty for asking a question that obviously caused him pain.

He turned his hand over, to link his fingers with hers. "Don't you think, if you'd had a child, you'd remember her?"

"I don't remember you," she pointed out.

A flash of pain was reflected in his eyes, adding to the guilt already weighing heavily on her shoulders.

"I'm sorry."

"It's okay," he said, slowly withdrawing his hand from hers. "I understand that you're frustrated. I would be, too, if our situations were reversed."

She swallowed another mouthful of tea.

"Maybe we should talk to the doctor about giving you something to help you sleep," Victor suggested.

"I don't think a pill is the answer."

Maybe there weren't any answers.

Maybe it was time for her to accept that.

It was only when she was back in bed and staring at the ceiling in the dark that Victor's words echoed in her mind.

*Don't you think, if you'd had a child, you'd remember her?*

She'd asked about a child; he'd specified *her*.

Did he know more than he was telling her?

And if he was keeping secrets, were they to protect her? Or himself?

# CHAPTER ELEVEN

*Tenacity, Montana*

THERE WAS A TIME, Ruby mused, when visitors called or texted before stopping by.

Of course, it was possible that the woman standing at her front door Saturday afternoon was selling something or at the wrong address, because Ruby was certain she'd never seen her before.

"Can I help you?" she asked politely.

"Ruby McKinley?"

"Yes," she said cautiously.

"Danica Townsend." The woman held up the ID badge hanging on the lanyard around her neck. "Family Services."

"Oh," she said, admittedly taken aback. "Did I know that you were going to be stopping by?"

"No. This is what's called an unscheduled visit. I'm sure when the baby was left in your care, you were informed that a worker would follow up with both scheduled and unscheduled visits."

Ruby nodded. "Yes. Of course, I just didn't expect a visit so soon."

"I'd say that I had a break in my schedule," Danica said, "but the truth is, there are no breaks in my schedule so I squeeze in these visits whenever I can."

"Understandable."

"Can I come in?"

"Of course," Ruby said again, because she knew it was the only acceptable response.

The social worker unbuttoned her coat, which Ruby took from her. As Danica removed her boots, Ruby suspected that this unscheduled visit was not going to be a quick one.

"Mind if I take a look around?"

"Please," Ruby said, gesturing with her arms wide.

*My life is an open book.*

*Please let me keep the baby.*

*Maybe even forever.*

The last thought popped into her head without warning, making Ruby's heart jolt inside her chest.

She'd applied to be a foster parent to give a home to a child who needed one on an interim basis—she hadn't ever considered fostering as a stepping-stone to adoption. But now that Jay was here, she didn't want to imagine ever saying goodbye to the little guy.

Of course, she had to be prepared for exactly that eventuality. Without knowing the reasons that he'd been abandoned at the church in Bronco, she couldn't know that whoever had left him wouldn't come back for him at some point in the future—or that another family member wouldn't learn of his existence and want to give him a home.

Hers was only intended to be a temporary home for him, until his relatives—or a more permanent placement—was found.

Pushing that uneasy thought to the back of her mind, she refocused her attention on the social worker who'd started her self-guided tour in the living room. As Danica's gaze moved slowly around the space, Ruby tried to see it through her eyes—the blue faux-suede sofa and chairs with purple and turquoise throw cushions. The sharp edges of the coffee and end tables covered with clear silicone bumpers. The TV stand and bookcases anchored to the wall. Framed pictures of Emery—some posed and some candid shots—from birth to present, in silver frames on the wall.

The little girl's dedicated play corner was admittedly a bit untidy, but the colorful bins were filled with age-appropriate toys, puzzles and games. A playpen for Jay, empty except for a couple of soft fabric books and squishy blocks. Spread out on the floor in front of the playpen was the quilt made with different colors and patterns and textures that she used for tummy time with the baby.

The social worker checked some boxes on a page on her clipboard and scribbled some notes. Then she moved on to the kitchen.

"I've caught you in the midst of dinner preparations," she noted.

"Actually, dinner's ready to go in the oven," she said, sliding the pan of lasagna into the now preheated appliance. "You caught me before I had a chance to clean up."

Danica waved a hand, dismissing the smear of pasta sauce on the counter and the dishes in the sink. "You make your lasagna from scratch?"

"When I've got the time."

"I'm impressed."

She opened the refrigerator, surveyed the contents, added a couple more check marks to her page.

"Can I offer you anything to drink?" Ruby asked.

"I'm good, thanks." She eyed the high chair—empty. "Where is the baby?"

"He's sleeping. Upstairs." She gestured to the iPad on the counter, showing the video feed of the baby's crib.

"Is this his usual naptime?"

"One of," Ruby said. "He usually wakes around 7:00 a.m., then has a nap from ten thirty until noon and another between three and four thirty."

"Bedtime?"

"Between seven thirty and eight."

"Does he sleep through the night?"

"Not yet. He's usually up once around eleven thirty and then again at 3:00 a.m."

"Tough schedule for you," Danica noted.

"I can handle it," Ruby assured her. "It probably helps that I've been through it before, so I know this stage doesn't last forever."

"That's right, you've got a—" another glance at her file "—four-year-old daughter? Emery?"

She nodded.

"Is she in school?"

"Preschool. Half days, three days a week."

"Where is she now?"

"Building a snowman in the backyard."

"By herself?" Danica frowned as she made her way to the window.

"No." *As if.* "She's with a…friend of mine."

The social worker watched Emery and Julian for a few seconds before turning back to face her. "Boyfriend?"

"Male friend," she clarified.

"So you're not romantically involved with this friend?"

"No. I don't think so."

Danica's brows lifted. "You don't think so?"

Ruby felt her cheeks grow warm. "I'm trying to be honest with you," she said. "The truth is, I haven't dated since my divorce. Julian is a friend and we hang out together sometimes, but he did kiss me the other night."

"I didn't mean to put you on the spot or embarrass you."

"It's okay," Ruby said. "I know you need to have a complete picture of Jay's home environment and everyone in his life."

The social worker nodded. "So what is Julian's surname?"

"Sanchez."

"Any relation to Nina?"

"He's her brother."

"I went to high school with Nina."

"Small world," Ruby noted.

"Small town, anyway," Danica said with a smile.

Another glance at the iPad indicated that Jay was starting to awaken from his nap, so Ruby led the way upstairs.

The baby smiled when he saw Ruby—she hoped that earned

her another check mark in the social worker's file—and snuggled into her when she lifted him out of his crib.

"He shares a room with you?"

"I thought it made sense to have him close—at least until he's sleeping through the night—so that he doesn't disturb Emery every time he wakes up." She set him on the makeshift change table to swap his wet diaper for a clean one, going through all the usual motions in the hope that the social worker wouldn't realize how unnerved she was by her presence. "When he's sleeping through the night, I'll move him into his own room across the hall."

Danica made some notes.

"Is it a problem that his crib is in my room?" Ruby asked, feeling a little anxious. "Ms. Browning didn't seem to think it was a problem."

"It's not a problem."

"He seems happy," Ruby said, refastening the snaps on his sleeper. Jay smiled at her again, doing his part to convince the social worker that he was content with the status quo. "I know he's only been here a few days, but he seems to have settled in."

"He does seem happy," the social worker agreed. "And, judging by the way he tracks the sound of your voice and responds to your touch, has already bonded with you."

"Well, that's good, isn't it?"

"It's good. And a little surprising, considering that he was with his previous foster mom for several weeks and has only been with you a few days."

She exhaled a cautious sigh of relief.

"I don't know if you want to look around up here some more," she said, "but this little guy is going to start fussing for his bottle."

"I think I've seen everything that I need to," Danica said, following Ruby down the stairs.

"Sounds like my snowman builders have come in from outside," Ruby noted, hearing voices in the laundry room, through which the backyard was accessed.

"Mommy! Mommy!" Emery charged through the door, her eyes sparkling with joy, her nose and cheeks rosy from the cold.

"We made a whole snowman family. A mommy and a daddy and a little girl snowman and a baby snowman."

She skidded to a halt when her gaze landed on the strange woman standing beside her mom.

"Who are you?" she immediately wanted to know.

"Manners, Emery," Ruby admonished.

"I'm Danica Townsend," the social worker told her.

"Can you say 'hello' to Ms. Townsend?" Ruby asked.

"Hello, Ms. Townsend," Emery said politely, albeit warily, understanding that her mom's words had been more a directive than a request.

"Ms. Townsend is a social worker with Family Services," Ruby explained, not just to her daughter but also for the benefit of Julian, who stood in the background looking every bit as wary as Emy. "She's here to make sure that we're taking good care of Jay."

"We are," the little girl was quick to chime in. "We feed him and burp him and change him. But only Mommy does the stinky ones."

The hint of a smile tugged at the corners of the social worker's mouth. "Are you happy that Jay lives with you?"

Emy nodded again. "It's like I have a brother now."

"What kind of things do you do with him?"

"*He* doesn't do *any*thing," the little girl confided. "But I read him stories and tell him about numbers and colors and hide behind my hands and then say peek-a-boo."

"Well, it sounds to me like Jay is a lucky little boy to have you."

Emy beamed proudly.

"And now I'll let you get back to your day," Danica said to Ruby.

She retrieved the woman's coat from the closet in the foyer. "It was nice to meet you."

"And all of you," the social worker said, accepting the proffered garment. Then she nodded to Julian. "Say 'hello' to Nina for me, Mr. Sanchez."

"Will do," he promised.

Ruby exhaled an audible sigh of relief when she closed the door at the visitor's back.

"Was it that bad?" he asked her.

"Actually, it wasn't bad at all," she realized, making her way to the kitchen to prepare Jay's bottle. "But I wasn't expecting a visit today, and then she was here, and I had a flashback to high school—to Mr. Zold announcing a pop quiz the one time that I didn't do my math homework."

"I would have bet you always did your homework," he said.

*"One time,"* she said again.

"Did you pass the quiz?"

"Barely. But Mr. Zold was concerned enough by my 'uncharacteristically low grade' that he made me take the paper home to get it signed by my parents."

"Ouch."

She nodded as she moved the bottle toward the baby's mouth. He immediately latched on to the nipple and started suckling. "The worst part is that my mother was 'disappointed.' As the big sister, I was supposed to be a good example to my siblings."

"I've heard that one, too," he assured her. "And I have two of each."

"Family dinners at your parents' house must be interesting with you, Diego, Luca, Nina and Marisa around the table. And Dawson now, too," she mused, adding his youngest sister's fiancé to the mix.

"You could come for Sunday dinner and experience it firsthand," he said.

She gauged that Jay had finished half his bottle and gently eased the nipple from his mouth so that she could burp him. "I don't think so."

"Why not?"

"Because…"

*"Because* isn't a reason," he chided.

"Because meeting the family is a big deal," she said, shifting the baby again to resume his feeding.

"You've already met my parents," he reminded her. "And you know Marisa."

"I met your parents the day I married another man."

"They won't hold that against you," he promised. "But since the idea of Sunday dinner with my family obviously makes you uneasy, we'll put it on the back burner for now."

"Thank you," she said. "And speaking of dinner, lasagna will be out of the oven in about twenty minutes, if you're interested."

"I think you know by now that I'm interested," he said, dipping his head to brush a light kiss over her lips.

"I was referring to dinner," she clarified.

He winked. "That, too."

RUBY WORKED 9:00 A.M. to 3:00 p.m. Monday through Friday, and occasionally picked up weekend shifts to pad her paycheck a little. Emery went to school on Tuesdays, Wednesdays and Thursdays, but only until 12:30, at which time her grandmother picked her up from school and then Ruby collected her from her grandparents' house when she finished work. On Mondays and Fridays, Emery went to daycare.

Except the Friday of her first week back at school following the holidays, when Caroline asked if she could take Emery to the new aquarium in Wonderstone Ridge. Apparently the facility was offering a special presentation for preschoolers, to introduce them to the various inhabitants of the oceans.

Ruby was grateful that Emery's paternal grandparents didn't only enjoy spending time with her but also made an effort to find activities that engaged her. As a result, Emery was always keen to go on "adventures"—as Caroline and Mark referred to their outings—with Mimi and Papa.

It was almost four o'clock Friday afternoon before they returned from Wonderstone Ridge.

"Did you want to come in for a cup of tea?" Ruby asked her former mother-in-law.

"That would be nice," Caroline agreed, ushering her granddaughter into the house.

"Did you have fun at the aquarium?" Ruby asked, as she helped Emery remove her coat and boots.

"So. Much. Fun," the little girl enthused.

"We always have a good time together," Caroline said, smiling affectionately at her granddaughter.

"I know you do," Ruby agreed. "And I'm grateful for all the time you spend with her."

"It's my pleasure."

Ruby knew she meant it. And it made her a little sad to think about everything that her own parents missed out on because they were so far away. But the move to Florida had been their choice, though one that had been made long before Emery was born.

Of course, Ruby made sure they got to FaceTime with their granddaughter every week, but a five-minute online chat was a poor substitute for in-person cuddles.

"What's that?" Ruby asked, when Caroline offered Emery the bag she'd carried in.

"Oh, just a couple of souvenirs that she picked out."

"You don't have to buy her something every time you go somewhere."

"I know," Caroline agreed. "But she really loved the dolphins, and they had an adorable stuffed dolphin in the gift shop. But then she couldn't decide between the dolphin and the orca. Then she saw the beluga whale and the sea turtle and the octopus."

As she inventoried the collection of toys that she'd purchased, Emery took them out of the bag and lined them up on the table.

"I appreciate your generosity," Ruby said sincerely. "But she already has so many stuffed animals on her bed there's barely room for her."

"It's hard to resist spoiling her a little," Caroline admitted. "Because she's my only grandchild—and likely the only one I'm ever going to have."

"Perhaps Emery can pick one to keep here and the rest can go to your house for her to play with when she's there?"

"That sounds like a fair compromise," Caroline said.

Emery apparently thought so, too, because she immediately picked up the dolphin and hugged it to her chest.

"Now put the rest of them in the bag so Mimi can take them home," Ruby instructed her daughter.

Emy dropped the octopus in the bag, then the beluga whale. Then she picked up the turtle and, after a moment's hesitation, tucked it into the crook of her arm with the dolphin.

"Emy."

She quickly added the orca to the bag.

"And the turtle," Ruby told her.

"This one's for Jay," Emy said.

"You know he can't have toys in his crib," Ruby reminded her.

"I know," her daughter confirmed. "But he can have it on the dresser, where he can see it."

"He can have it on the dresser," she relented, because how could she object to her daughter wanting to share her toys?

Emery skipped out of the room to take the turtle up to the baby's room.

"She is certainly fascinated with that baby, isn't she?" Caroline mused. "She hardly stopped talking about him all day."

"She is," Ruby agreed. "If a little disappointed that he doesn't yet walk and talk."

"It will happen soon enough." Caroline selected a couple of grapes from the fruit plate that Ruby had set out on the table. "She had a lot to say about Julian Sanchez, too."

The comment caught Ruby off guard, and she realized it shouldn't have. Even if she hadn't been prepared for her four-year-old daughter to tell tales out of school, she should have been prepared for the fact that people might talk about his truck being parked in her driveway on several occasions over the past week.

"We happened to cross paths at the inn on New Year's Eve and rekindled our friendship."

"He and Owen used to be quite good friends."

"I'm aware."

"Of course you are," her former mother-in-law acknowledged. "He was the best man at your wedding."

"Would you disapprove of me having a relationship with Julian?" she asked cautiously. Because while she didn't think her personal life was any of the woman's business, she also didn't want to create any tension in their relationship.

"Would you stop seeing him if I said *yes*?"

She considered the question for a moment before shaking her head. "No."

Caroline nodded approvingly. "Good."

"Good?" she echoed, surprised.

"I hope that Mark and I will always be part of Emery's life—and yours—but you need to live your own life. To make plans for your own future and Emery's. And, because Owen and Julian were good friends for a long time, I can say, with some degree of authority, that he's a good man."

"He is a good man," Ruby agreed.

"You deserve a good man. You deserve to be happy. And it wouldn't hurt Emery to have another positive role model in her life.

"Don't get me wrong—Owen's my son and I love him with my whole heart," Caroline continued. "But I'm not completely blind to his faults. I know he wasn't a good husband. He didn't honor the vows you made and—even worse, in my opinion—he didn't respect you enough to end your marriage before breaking those vows. And he has a lot to learn about being a father.

"Which I really don't understand, because he had a wonderful example in his own father." She sighed now. "Mark and I wanted more children, but it wasn't meant to be. But when Owen married you, we got the daughter we'd always wanted, and the divorce didn't change that."

Ruby had to swallow the lump that rose in her throat before she could reply. "You and Mark have always been good to me and Emery."

"We'd be honored to be an interim Mimi and Papa to Jay, too."

"If he's still with us when he starts to talk, I have no doubt you will be."

"I don't think you need to worry about Family Services finding another placement for him," Caroline said. "Anyone can see that baby is exactly where he belongs."

Though obviously pleased by her former mother-in-law's observation, she was trying hard not to get her hopes up. Because Ruby knew that a reunion with his birth mother would probably be the best thing for the little guy, even if the possibility made her heart ache.

"The last I heard, they were still trying to track down his

family," she said. "And the availability of family is an important factor in placement decisions."

"As it should be," Caroline agreed. "But family doesn't only mean those who are related by blood."

# CHAPTER TWELVE

*Bronco, Montana*

STANLEY WAS LONELY.

More than five months after his planned wedding, he still hadn't heard a word from his missing bride.

His family had urged him to get over his heartache and move on, but he couldn't. And despite what everyone was telling him, he didn't believe for a minute that she'd run away.

If Winona had changed her mind about wanting to marry him, she would have told him so. She wouldn't have left him to wonder and worry.

And he was worried, because it was obvious that something untoward *had* happened. The blood on her porch proved it, even if his family had tried to keep that discovery from him, concerned that his broken heart would give up on him if he heard about it.

But his broken heart was somehow still beating, though his blood pressure went up every time he thought about how the police had bungled their investigation into Winona's disappearance. They'd been less than useless, insisting the blood wasn't proof of anything. And that was before Winona's daughter got a letter in the mail, purportedly from her mom. Because apparently a postmark from Portland, Oregon, trumped blood on a porch in Bronco, Montana.

Maybe he shouldn't blame the police, but he wished they'd shown a little more interest in the fact that his bride-to-be had told him, just a few days before their planned nuptials, that she'd seen a dark cloud in their future.

But even he'd brushed off her premonition as pre-wedding jitters, and she'd acknowledged that was a possibility. Despite being ninety-seven years of age, she'd confessed that she was as nervous as a virgin bride at the prospect of becoming a wife for the first time. Probably because she was afraid of change.

For Stanley, the wedding was an even bigger deal. Maybe because he'd done it before and appreciated the significance of promising "till death do us part" in front of family and friends.

Was it death that had taken Winona from him, as it had already taken his beloved Celia?

No, he didn't believe death—or God—could be so cruel.

Like him, Winona had been in love before. But only once, when she was very young. She'd told him the whole story about her relationship with Josiah—the forbidden teenage love affair resulting in an unplanned pregnancy that caused her to be placed in a home for unwed mothers.

For years—decades!—Winona had believed that the baby she'd birthed had died almost immediately after. And she'd been so distraught by the loss of her child that the doctors had locked her up "for her own protection." Of course, when the truth came out—that her healthy baby girl had secretly been placed for adoption—she realized it had been for *their* protection. Because they'd known that she would have kicked and screamed until she found out what happened to her baby.

She'd been through so much in her life, endured so many ups and downs, experienced so many joys and sorrows. But she'd never been a bride. And while she'd originally pushed back against his efforts to set a date for their wedding, the closer they got to the day of the big event, the more excited she'd confessed to being.

So no, there was no way anyone was going to convince him that she'd simply changed her mind and walked away.

And, of course, he blamed himself for discounting Winona's concerns. Obviously, she'd been right to be worried.

But who would abduct a ninety-seven-year-old woman? Why?

Stanley pondered that question as he measured coffee grounds into the filter and slid the basket into place.

He wasn't sure he even wanted coffee, but it was part of his routine, and going through the motions of his day-to-day routine was all he could do at this point.

But no matter what he did to occupy himself, he couldn't get Winona's disappearance out of his mind.

There had been no ransom demand.

Not that he had a lot, but he would gladly give everything that he had to get his fiancée back.

He was pouring coffee into a mug when someone knocked at the door. He started at the sound—and poured coffee all over the counter.

Cursing under his breath, he wiped it up and made his way to the door.

"Evan," he said, finding Winona's great-grandson standing there. "This is a surprise."

"Is it a bad time?" the other man asked.

"It's been nothing but bad times since my fiancée disappeared," he said. "But come on in."

Evan stepped over the threshold.

"How's your wife doing?" Stanley asked.

"Daphne's well. Eager to be done with being pregnant and get on with being a mom."

"And you?"

"Equal parts excited and terrified about being a dad."

"Kids are exciting and terrifying creatures," Stanley agreed.

Evan smiled at that.

"Can I pour you a cup of coffee? It's fresh."

"Coffee sounds great."

Stanley filled another mug and set it on the table. He gestured for Evan to sit, then took a seat opposite him.

"What's on your mind?" he prompted.

"I can't believe I'm going to tell you this," Evan said. "You know I don't believe in all that woo-woo stuff my great-grand-mother is into."

Stanley nodded, because he did know—and that Evan had made Bronco Ghost Tours into a successful business despite not believing any of the otherworldly stories that he recounted for his guests. At least not until he'd met Daphne Taylor—now his wife—and the ghosts that lived at her Happy Hearts Animal Sanctuary.

"I feel silly even saying this out loud," Evan continued. "But... I think Winona is trying to send you a message."

He felt a frisson of excitement skitter down his spine. "And how exactly is she doing that?"

"Through my dreams."

"You've dreamed about your great-grandmother?"

"No. Well...not exactly."

"Well, what *exactly*?" he asked impatiently.

"For several weeks now, I've been having the same dream. About a locked room. The only thing inside the room is an old-fashioned writing desk, a feather quill and ink pot, and a piece of parchment upon which is written 'Don't believe them.'"

"'Don't believe them'?" Stanley echoed.

Evan nodded.

"Don't believe *who*?"

Now the other man shrugged.

"And you've had this dream several times?"

Winona's great-grandson nodded again. "The room and the desk are always the same, but sometimes the message on the paper is different. I've also seen 'Help me,' 'Find me' and 'I want to go home.'"

"You'd think, if she was sending a message, she'd be a little more direct about it," he grumbled.

"Knowing my great-grandmother, do you really think so?"

Stanley had to chuckle. "No, you're right. Winona always got a kick out of tangling people up with her cryptic messages."

He was surprised by the sound of his laugh—when had he last heard the sound? When had he felt so light?

But he had no doubt that Evan was right, that his dreams were evidence Winona was trying to communicate with him.

And while he might wish that she could have bypassed the middleman and come directly to him in his dreams, he understood that Evan—because he shared blood with his great-grandmother—might be more susceptible to receiving that sort of transcendental communication.

"Anyway, I don't know what it means," Evan said now. "And maybe it doesn't mean anything. But I thought you should know."

"You mean your wife insisted that you tell me?"

The young man's smile was wry. "That, too."

"Have you shared this information with the police?"

"No. And I'm not going to."

Stanley couldn't really blame him. The police had been skeptical enough about the blood; he suspected they'd put even less stock in dreams.

Which meant that he was going to have to figure this out himself.

And when he finally did, he was going to bring his bride home.

# CHAPTER THIRTEEN

*Tenacity, Montana*

ON MONDAY, JULIAN took the pozole out of the freezer and heated it up for his dinner. As he savored the first mouthful, he decided that the hearty soup was good enough to forgive the intrusive questions his mother had asked on her previous visit.

He'd always been able to talk to her about anything, but he was admittedly a little bit worried that she might not approve of him dating his former friend's ex-wife. If what he and Ruby were doing could even be called dating, considering that all the time they'd spent together had been at her house.

Not that he was complaining.

He was just happy to be with her.

He enjoyed hanging out with Emery and Jay, too, but he couldn't deny that he was really looking forward to the night that Emery had a sleepover scheduled at her grandparents' house.

Of course, he knew Mark and Caroline McKinley well, having spent a fair amount of time at their house when he and Owen were in high school. They were good people and they'd always made him feel welcome in their home. He suspected they might look less fondly upon him now if they knew he was spending time with their former daughter-in-law.

He was just finishing up the dishes when a knock sounded

on the door. Without waiting for an invitation, his sister Nina walked in.

"I need to start locking my door," he remarked, as she opened his refrigerator and helped herself to a can of Coke.

"I have a key," she pointed out.

"Remind me again why I gave that to you?"

She popped the tab on the can. "For emergencies."

"And is this an emergency?"

"Nope." She lifted the can to her lips and sipped.

"So what are you doing here, Nina?"

"*Má* sent me on a reconnaissance mission."

"Did she?"

"Of course, I'm not supposed to tell you it's a reconnaissance mission. I'm supposed to come up with a credible reason for dropping by and then work my way around to asking subtly probing questions about your new girlfriend."

"You wouldn't recognize subtle if it slapped you in the face."

"Which is why I didn't even try to go that route," she admitted.

"Am I supposed to applaud your forthrightness?"

"No applause necessary," she said. "Just give me something to take back to her."

He handed her the now clean and dry soup container.

"Ha ha."

"Tell her that it was delicious, as always."

"I need more than that, *mano*."

He pursed his lips, as if giving serious consideration to her request. "You could also mention that I finished the last of the tamales."

His sister muttered, creatively and colorfully, in Spanish.

"And that she should wash your mouth out with soap."

"She knows there's a new woman in your life," Nina said. "Someone that you're being uncharacteristically tight-lipped about."

"She's not a new woman."

"So…an old woman?" she quipped.

He rolled his eyes.

She narrowed her gaze. "An old friend?"

"Not any of *Má*'s business—and definitely none of yours."

"Which means she's someone we know," Nina realized.

"Why would you immediately jump to that conclusion?"

"Because if she wasn't, you'd tell me her name."

"No, I wouldn't," he denied. "Because you'd go home and cyberstalk her."

"I don't stalk," she said indignantly. "I creep."

"That's creepy, *mana*."

"*Creeping* just means following someone without their knowledge."

"Which is creepy," he said again.

"You can call it whatever you want," she told him. "But you know that I always find what I'm looking for."

RUBY WASN'T EXPECTING company when she was home with Jay on Tuesday—having booked a day off to accommodate his well-baby checkup, but recently Julian had been in the habit of stopping by, and the possibility that it might be him ringing the bell made her heart happy.

She should have peeked through the sidelight to confirm her suspicion, because it wasn't Julian.

Her smile slid from her face when she opened the door.

"Owen. What are you doing here?"

"I saw your car in the driveway and thought I'd stop in to see how you're doing."

It was credible that he was in the neighborhood; his office was only a few blocks away. But he'd never before stopped by without first communicating his intent—and even that was a rare event.

"I'm fine," she said shortly.

"You look good." His gaze skimmed over her, from the hair she'd pulled back into a ponytail to keep it out of the baby's reach, to the soft red sweater she wore over slim-fitting dark jeans. "Really good."

Once upon a time, it had taken nothing more than the look he was giving her now to make her knees quiver.

She felt nothing—which was sad but also a relief.

"Aren't you going to invite me in?" he prompted, when she failed to do so.

Ruby hesitated.

This was *her* house.

Her sanctuary.

Not that he'd never been inside, but he'd only been there half a dozen times before—and always to see their daughter.

"Emery's at preschool."

"I know."

But the slight hesitation before his response made her think that he didn't—that he hadn't thought about their daughter at all before he'd knocked on the door.

"I wanted to talk to you," he said.

Though she was still reluctant to let him in, she was even more reluctant to let all the heat inside her house escape through the open door. She finally stepped back.

She'd had no regrets about leaving the house where she'd lived as a bride and new mother. Divorcing Owen hadn't been an easy decision to make but it had been a necessary one, and she was grateful to be able to move on and make a fresh start with her daughter.

This house wasn't anything like the one she'd left behind, and it was filled with nothing but good memories.

It was hers and Emery's.

And baby Jay's, too.

*If only I could keep him.*

But she pushed those thoughts out of her mind as her ex-husband stepped over the threshold.

As he turned to close the door at his back, a muffled sound emanated from the baby monitor she'd left on the bookshelf in the living room.

Owen looked at her quizzically.

"I'll be right back," she said, ignoring the unspoken question in the lift of his brows.

She made her way up the stairs and into her bedroom, smiling when she saw Jay was on his side and peering through the slats of the crib.

"Look at you," she crooned softly. "You're going to be rolling over in no time—you're already halfway there."

He fell onto his back again as she approached and offered her a gummy smile.

"That wasn't a very long nap you had today," she noted. "Are you wet? Hungry?"

He responded with a gurgle.

"All of the above," she concluded.

She made quick work of his diaper change, reluctant to leave Owen unattended any longer than necessary. Not that she expected him to poke around—and not that she had anything to hide—she just wanted him gone.

When she returned to the main level with the baby in her arms, she discovered that her ex-husband had made himself at home—removing his boots and coat and helping himself to a cup of coffee from the pot on the counter.

He looked at the baby in her arms as he sipped his coffee.

"I didn't think that much time had passed since I last saw you," he remarked.

"Time really does fly, doesn't it?" she said lightly.

He frowned, as if not entirely sure she was joking.

"This is Jay," she said, setting the baby in his chair to free her hands to mix up his formula. "And he's hungry, so whatever you want to talk about, you can get started while I get his lunch."

"You're babysitting?" he asked, still stuck on the fact that she was caring for an infant.

"Fostering."

"Really?" he said, obviously surprised.

"Yes, really."

"Why?"

He was hardly the first person to ask her that question. Though he was the first to do so without any pretension of curiosity rather than disapproval.

"You know I wanted to have more kids."

It had been only one of many bones of contention during their short marriage.

"So this is how you're going about it?"

"Obviously this is a temporary arrangement," she said, more

as a reminder to herself than an explanation to him. "But it's kind of fun to have a baby in the house again, and Emery is learning to be a big sister."

It was the perfect opportunity for him to follow up with a question about their daughter, to show an interest in Emy.

"I don't remember the early days being much fun," he said.

Dropping the ball, as usual.

*How would you know? You were never there.*

She managed to bite back the retort that sprang to her lips, because there was no point in rehashing old arguments.

Instead, she said, "Why are you here, Owen?"

"There's a rumor going around town that you've been spending time with Julian Sanchez," he finally said.

"Is there?"

His gaze narrowed. "Is it true?"

"My personal life isn't any of your business."

"I always suspected he had a crush on you."

"And I'm not interested in your speculations. But I am curious to know what makes you think you have any say about what I do in my personal life."

"You're my wife."

"*Ex*-wife."

"You're right," he acknowledged. "But the fact is, you were mine first—and that's the only reason he wants you now."

"My relationship with Julian has absolutely *nothing* to do with you."

"I can understand that you'd want to think so, but history would suggest otherwise."

"What are you talking about?"

"Ask your boyfriend about Laura Bell," he suggested.

Ruby shook her head. "No, I don't think I will," she said. "I'm not playing your games."

"Okay, I'll tell you," he said. "When we were in high school, Laura dumped Julian to go out with me, and ever since then, he's been looking for a way to get back at me."

"Julian doesn't strike me as the type of man to hold a grudge for—what?—seventeen years?"

"Maybe you don't know him as well as you think you do."

She eased the nipple from Jay's mouth and lifted him to her shoulder to burp him.

Owen watched her with the baby, an almost wistful expression on his face.

"I sometimes think I would have been a better dad if we'd had a son."

"Well, we had a daughter," she reminded him. "And you could be a better dad if you wanted to be."

"I just don't know what to do with her."

"What would you do with a son?"

He shrugged.

"Anything you think you might do with a son, you could do with your daughter," she pointed out. "Kick a soccer ball around, build Lego, go tobogganing."

"You think she'd like those things?"

"I *know* she likes those things."

He looked skeptical.

"The Winter Carnival is at the end of the month. You could start by taking her there."

"I've already got plans that weekend," he hedged.

"The whole weekend?"

"Yeah. I'm going to Big Sky to ski."

"She might like to learn to ski. I'm not suggesting that you take her to Big Sky," she hastened to assure him. "As I'm guessing your weekend plans include a woman."

He didn't try to hide his smile. "You know me well."

"But you could plan an afternoon outing someplace closer," she said, determined to get him back on track, to focus on what really mattered—before Emery was old enough to dismiss him as he'd dismissed her and the opportunity to know his child was lost to him forever.

"You don't think four is a little young to try skiing?" he said dubiously.

"She started skating lessons in October—you should see her on the ice now."

"My mom showed me a video," he admitted. "I was impressed."

She was lucky that Caroline and Mark took an interest in

their granddaughter's life. She only wished Emery's father would show a fraction of the same.

"Speaking of Emery—it's almost time for me to pick her up from preschool."

"Oh." He glanced at his watch, frowned. "Doesn't my mom pick her up on Tuesdays?"

"When I have to work," she confirmed. "I took the day off because Jay had an appointment."

"Can you afford to be giving up shifts for a kid that isn't even yours?"

"Lucky for me, I get generous spousal support from my ex-husband," she said, tongue firmly in cheek.

"You didn't ask for spousal support," he reminded her.

It was true. When she discovered that he'd broken their vows, she'd wanted only two things—out of their marriage and custody of their daughter.

It was guilt, she guessed—or maybe pressure from his parents—that induced him to sign over title of the home they'd shared. And she knew he'd been annoyed that, as soon as the divorce was final, she'd sold that house to buy this one.

"Do you want to come with me—to say hi to Emery?" she asked him now. "I'm sure she'd be happy to see you."

He glanced at his watch. "Actually, I have to get to the office. I've got an appointment in fifteen minutes. But you can tell her that I said hi."

"Yeah, I'll do that," she said.

But it was a lie. She had no intention of mentioning his visit to her daughter, who'd already been disappointed by her dad too many times in her short life.

BETWEEN HER JOB and caring for Emery and Jay, Ruby didn't have much time for anything else, but she was glad to spend that little bit of time with Julian, who stopped by almost every day. Sometimes his visits were brief; sometimes he stayed for a few hours. Ruby was always happy to see him and so focused on their blossoming relationship that, by the next night, she'd almost entirely forgotten about her ex-husband's impromptu visit.

Emery poked at the meat loaf on her plate.

"I don't like this."

"It's hamburger, Em."

Her daughter shook her head. "Hamburger has a bun."

"But it's the same kind of meat as a hamburger."

"I like hamburgers with ketchup."

Ruby got the ketchup and squirted a puddle of the condiment on her daughter's plate.

Though Emery still looked wary, she jabbed a piece of meat with her fork and dipped it in the ketchup. "Is Unca Julian coming tonight?"

"I don't know."

"He didn't come yesterday."

"He was probably busy."

Emery nibbled on the meat, made a face. "I don't like this hamburger."

"I'm sorry to hear that, because if you don't eat all your dinner, you can't have ice cream for dessert."

In short order, her daughter had cleaned her plate.

And maybe bribery wasn't recommended in any of the parenting books Ruby had read, but there were times when it was the only thing that worked.

As an added benefit, Emery's attention was so focused on her food that she dropped her questions about Julian.

But Ruby's worry lingered as she bathed Emy after dinner and dressed her in her pj's and helped her brush her teeth in preparation for bed. Because apparently her daughter had already developed an expectation of seeing him every day, and maybe she shouldn't have been surprised. Julian had been spending a lot of time with them and Emery was a little girl without a father figure, and obviously looking for a surrogate.

She'd always tried to do what was best for Emery, and she couldn't help thinking that the best thing might be for Ruby to stop seeing Julian before her daughter got too attached. The problem was she didn't want to stop seeing him.

Did that make her a bad mother? Or merely a selfish one?

But spending time with Julian had been good for Emery, too. Especially considering that, after Owen's most recent visit,

Ruby didn't think he was going to step up to be a role model for his daughter anytime soon.

Or maybe she was just making excuses to justify her own relationship with Julian, because he made her happier than she'd been in a long time.

"Speak of the devil," she mused, when she peered through the sidelight (because that was a mistake she wouldn't make a second time!) and saw him standing on her porch.

Emery, having also heard the knock, had climbed on the sofa to look through the curtains. "It's Unca Julian, Mommy! He's here!"

She unlocked the door so that he could enter.

Before he could greet Ruby, Emery was there, jumping up and down to get his attention. "Hi, Unca Julian!"

"Hi," he said, lifting her into his arms for a hug. Then he met Ruby's gaze over the little girl's head, and his lips curved. "And hello to you, too."

It was crazy how his smile was enough to make her toes curl and her insides tingle, and to make her eager to know what other responses he might be able to elicit from her body.

"We didn't know if you were coming tonight," Emery said.

"I didn't know, either," he said. "I had some errands to run with my brother and I wasn't sure how long I was going to be." This time the look he gave Ruby was one of apology. "I should have called."

"It's fine," she said.

"It's late," Emery admonished. "You almost missed my story time."

"But *almost* means I didn't miss it, right?"

She nodded. "Are you gonna read to me?"

"If it's okay with your mom—" he glanced at her and got a nod of confirmation "—then I would love to read to you."

"Did you eat?" Ruby asked. "I could reheat some meat loaf for you."

"Thanks, but I grabbed a burger and fries with Luca."

"I had meat loaf and potatoes and carrots," Em told him. "*And* ice cream."

"What kind of ice cream?"

"Pink!"

"Strawberry?" he guessed.

She nodded.

"Can I tell you a secret?" Julian asked.

She nodded again.

He lowered his voice to a conspiratorial whisper. "Strawberry's my favorite."

"If you're hoping I'll offer you some, you're out of luck," Ruby said. "Em finished it off."

He pouted, doing a fair imitation of the little girl.

"But there's mint chocolate," Emery told him.

"Is there?"

"Uh-huh."

"Do you want some mint chocolate ice cream?" Ruby asked.

He shook his head. "I'm good, thanks. Besides—" he winked at Emery "—I don't want to be late for story time."

"Teeth need to be brushed before story time. Did you remember to brush your teeth after your bath?" Ruby asked her daughter, well aware that she had not.

"Whoops!" She immediately wriggled to be let down.

"Go do it now," she said, when her daughter's feet were on the ground. "And Julian will be up for story time in two minutes."

"That's how long the timer on my toothbrush is," Emery told him. "Don't be late."

"I won't be late," he promised. As soon as she was out of sight, he drew Ruby into his arms. "So I guess I have about a minute forty-five to say a proper *hello* to you?"

"Less than that, if you keep talking," she warned.

"Shutting up," he promised, and lowered his mouth to hers.

JULIAN ENJOYED BEING part of Ruby's kids' bedtime routines. Even more, he enjoyed the long, lingering kisses he shared with her after Emery and Jay were settled down for the night. She was so passionate and responsive, and the soft sighs and quiet murmurs that emanated from her throat when he touched her drove him wild. But as much fun as it was to make out on her sofa as if they were teenagers, he was really looking forward to the opportunity—hopefully the following Friday night—to take their relationship to the next level.

First, though, tonight, there was something he needed to tell her. But it was hard to remember what that something was when she was on his lap, her knees straddling his hips, her lips cruising over his.

After several long minutes, she eased her mouth from his. "I'm really glad you decided to stop by tonight."

"Me, too," he said, sliding his hands beneath the hem of her sweater. "Because spending a little bit of time with you beats the hell out of no time at all."

She pouted. "Is that your way of saying you have to go?"

"Not just yet," he said. "There was something I wanted to talk to you about first."

"That sounds ominous."

"It's not," he promised, struggling to maintain his train of thought while she nibbled playfully on his lower lip. "I just thought you should know that Luca and I ran into Owen tonight."

She eased back now to look at him. "When you mentioned burgers and fries, I wondered if you'd gone to the Grizzly Bar," she admitted.

"That's it?" he said, surprised by her lack of reaction. "You're not interested in what he had to say?"

"Not the least bit," she promised.

"Because you heard it all when he stopped by to see you yesterday?" he guessed.

"And because he's my ex-husband," she reminded him. "Which means that I no longer have to care about his opinions on anything."

"So why didn't you tell me that he was here?"

She huffed out an exasperated breath. "Are we really going to waste the little bit of time we have talking about my ex-husband?"

It certainly wasn't his first choice, but now that he'd started down this path, he felt compelled to know where it ended. "I'm just curious to know why you didn't say anything to me about his visit."

"Because the only reason he stopped by was that he heard we've been spending time together and he wanted to stir up trouble, and I refused to give him the satisfaction."

Julian heard the annoyance in her tone, but he wasn't entirely sure if she was annoyed with him or with her ex.

Likely both, he acknowledged.

"What did he say to make you think he was stirring up trouble?" he asked her now.

"He told me to ask you about Laura Bell. And now my curiosity is piqued," she admitted.

"Are you asking me about Laura?"

"I guess I am."

"She and I dated through most of our junior year in high school—until she ditched me to go out with Owen."

"And now you're spending time with Owen's ex-wife," she noted.

"One thing doesn't have anything to do with the other," he assured her.

"Owen certainly thinks it does," Ruby countered.

"Well, he's wrong."

"So why are we even talking about this?" she wondered aloud.

"Because I know he isn't happy about the fact that we're together and I don't want him making trouble for you."

"He can't make trouble for me anymore," she assured him. "The only way he could hurt me would be to take Emery, and no judge is going to give custody to a man who sees his daughter—at most—three times in a calendar year."

"Okay," Julian said. "I just wanted to know that you were sure about us."

"I'm sure. And, anyway, whose happiness do you care about?" she challenged. "Owen's or mine?"

"Yours," he said, skimming his palms over the bare skin of her torso. "Only yours."

"Then maybe you could forget about my ex-husband and focus on me?" she suggested.

"I can do that," he promised.

And proceeded to prove it to her.

## CHAPTER FOURTEEN

As Will and Nicole Sanchez's kids grew up and got busy with their own lives, it became difficult to coordinate all their schedules and sit down for a meal together. The exception was Sunday night, when everyone gathered for a traditional family meal and the chance to catch up with what was going on in all of their lives.

On most nights, conversation flowed as freely as the sangria, but tonight, Julian was aware of pointed looks between his parents and awkward breaks in the conversation whenever a question was directed at him.

"Why do I feel as if this is some kind of intervention?" Julian asked warily.

"Is something going on in your life that makes you feel as if you need an intervention?" Luca asked.

"I could use some help with my interfering family," he said.

"Ha!"

"It's not an intervention," his mother said. "It's just Sunday night dinner." She passed him the roasted potatoes. "But I'd be lying if I said we weren't concerned about your relationship with Ruby McKinley."

He looked around the table. "Is that a collective *we*?"

"To be honest, I didn't even know you had a relationship with Ruby McKinley until right now," Diego said.

"Wait a minute," Nina chimed in. "This would be Owen's ex-wife?"

"Which is one of the reasons for our concern," Will remarked, turning his attention to his firstborn son. "You and Owen were friends for a long time."

"*Were* friends," he agreed, emphasizing the past tense. "We stopped hanging out when I learned he'd cheated on his wife and then walked out on his marriage and his daughter."

"And that's another reason," Nicole said.

"What's another reason?" he demanded, frustration seeping into his voice.

"Ruby has a little girl. And a foster child now, too."

"She has an adorable little girl," Julian noted. "And her foster child is pretty darn cute, too."

"Children are a complication, no matter how cute they are."

"And *Má* would know," Marisa chimed in. "Because she had five."

"I'm not saying it's not complicated," Julian allowed. "I'm just asking you to trust me to make my own choices."

"We do, *hijo*," his mother assured him.

"Apparently not."

"But we worry," she said.

"Don't you have enough to worry about with Marisa's wedding only a few weeks away?"

"As your brother pointed out, I have five children—I know how to multitask."

Julian didn't doubt it was true, but as adept as she might be, he knew there was no way she—or anyone else—would dissuade him from romancing Ruby.

"You seem a little distracted," Julian noted, as he helped his mom load the dishwasher after the interrogation masquerading as Sunday night dinner had ended.

"I'm worried about your great-uncle Stanley," she confided.

"Has something else happened?" Julian asked now.

"Denise called," she said, naming his dad's brother's wife who lived in Bronco and had daily contact with *Tío*. "Apparently Winona's great-grandson stopped by to see Stanley and got him all stirred up."

"Stirred up how?"

"He claimed to have some recurring dream that he believes is his great-grandmother's way of telling him that she's being held against her will."

"Do you believe it?" Julian asked her.

"It doesn't matter what I believe," she said. "What matters is that your great-uncle believes it. And now he's apparently made up his mind to go find her."

"It might be good for him to have a focus," Julian noted. "Since the wedding-that-never-happened, he's been…drifting."

"It would be good for him to forget about that woman and move on with his life," his mother said firmly.

"That woman was his fiancée," he reminded her.

"Who walked out on him the day of their wedding. And who does that to someone they claim to love?"

"I don't know," he said. "But I'm sure there's more to the story."

"Unfortunately, I don't think it's a story that's going to have a happy ending."

RUBY DIDN'T REALIZE how much of her daily routine revolved around her daughter until Emery wasn't there. Only an hour after Caroline had picked up her granddaughter for the planned sleepover, Ruby was showered, with dinner prepped and the dining room table set—complete with wineglasses, linen napkins and candles.

Without Emy flitting around the house, asking questions about this or wanting help with that, she was able to complete the requisite tasks in about half the time they would ordinarily have taken her. Not that she ever objected to her daughter's assistance, and if she hadn't been preoccupied by the fact that she was preparing for a DATE, she would have already been missing her daughter like crazy, though she had no doubt Emy was having the best time with Mimi and Papa and not missing her mom at all.

But she was preoccupied by the fact that she had a DATE and

so she was relieved when Jay woke up from his nap and started fussing, because it gave her something else to focus on for a while. But after she'd changed him and supervised tummy time and read him some stories, he was content to sit in his bouncy chair and reach for the toys dangling above him while Ruby finished getting ready.

And now that was done, she had nothing to do but think about the fact that the evening was most likely going to end with her and Julian naked in bed.

Ruby hadn't been this nervous about a date since…

Since her first date with Owen, she realized with chagrin.

He'd been so handsome and charming in the beginning.

And the way he'd looked at her made her feel beautiful.

When had all that changed?

She couldn't say for certain, and really, the *when* didn't matter as much as the fact that it had changed. And the man who'd promised to love, honor and cherish her had broken every one of those promises.

Julian had made no such promises, and that was okay.

She knew that he was attracted to her, that he wanted to be with her, and for now, that was more than enough.

She fed Jay, then checked the potatoes roasting in the oven and stirred the chicken and vegetables in the pan on the stove. She sliced the crusty bread and set it in a basket on the table, then opened the wine—another bottle of chianti—so it would have time to breathe before dinner was served.

"What are the chances that you'll sleep until we're finished our dinner?" she asked the baby, as she carried him up to his crib.

He replied with a yawn.

"I'll take that as a good sign," she said, then gently touched her lips to his cheek. "Sweet dreams, baby."

HE BROUGHT HER FLOWERS. A gorgeous arrangement of white roses, soft blue hydrangeas and deep blue delphiniums in a cobalt blue vase.

"I don't know much about flowers, but I thought they'd go well in your kitchen," he said.

"They will," she agreed, taking them there. "And they're beautiful. Thank you."

"Something smells amazing."

"Chicken cacciatore," she said. "And it's ready whenever you are."

"I could eat," he said. "But first…" He drew her into his arms and kissed her, long and slow and deep.

"I think I should cook for you more often," she mused, when he finally lifted his mouth from hers.

"That wasn't because you cooked for me. It's because I really like kissing you. And because I've been thinking about you—and about tonight—all day."

"Did you bring a toothbrush?"

"A toothbrush…and a box of condoms."

She was grateful he'd thought to come prepared, because that little but essential detail had slipped her mind.

Still, she couldn't resist teasing, "A whole box?"

"I don't expect we'll use them *all* tonight."

"But it's good to have goals," she told him.

He chuckled and kissed her again. "We could get started right now."

"Or we could have dinner first," she said.

"Whatever you want."

"Why don't you pour the wine while I dish up the food?"

They chatted easily over the meal, and by the time she was clearing their plates from the table, Ruby was feeling a lot more relaxed than she'd been a few hours earlier.

She was just about to take the lemon panna cotta out of the fridge when the baby started to cry.

"Looks like we're going to have to hold off on dessert until after I change and feed the baby."

"I don't mind at all," he assured her, rubbing his flat belly. "Because I didn't know there was dessert when I agreed to that second helping of chicken."

"I shouldn't be too long," she said. "Why don't you see if there's a baseball game or something to watch on TV?"

His lips twitched as if he was fighting a smile.

"What's so funny?"

"You're not much of a sports fan, are you?"

"What gave me away?"

"It's January," he pointed out. "Not even the Grapefruit League plays in January."

"Hockey then?" she suggested as an alternative. "I know you need ice to play hockey, so I'm guessing it must be a winter sport."

"It is," he confirmed.

But he didn't turn on the TV.

As Ruby discovered when she returned to her now spotless kitchen and found him folding a tea towel over the oven door.

"Not a hockey fan?" she guessed.

"You did the cooking, so I did the cleaning—your rule," he reminded her.

"Well, thank you."

"You might not be so grateful tomorrow when you discover that I've put everything away in the wrong places, but you're welcome."

"Are you hungry for dessert now?" she asked.

"Yeah," he agreed, drawing her into his arms.

"I was referring to the panna cotta."

"I wasn't," he said, and lowered his head to kiss her again.

And her nerves were immediately dissolved by the heat that raced through her veins. Or maybe they hadn't completely dissolved, because he eased his lips from hers and tipped her chin up, forcing her to meet his gaze.

"Are you having second thoughts?" he asked gently.

"No," she said. "I'm a little nervous, but no second thoughts. Are *you* having second thoughts?"

"The only thought in my head right now is—how fast can I get her naked?" he admitted.

Ruby couldn't help but smile at that. "I just hope your…expectations…aren't too high."

"Is that your way of telling me that you don't have a stripper pole and a sex swing in your bedroom?" he asked teasingly.

"You've been in my bedroom," she reminded him. "Did you see either of those things there?"

"Maybe you put them in the closet when they're not in use," he suggested.

"You definitely need to lower your expectations," she warned.

"I don't think I do," he said. "Because all I really want is to be with you."

"It's been a long time for me," she cautioned.

"They say it's like riding a bike—as soon as you climb on, it will all come back to you."

She had to laugh at that. "Like riding a bike, huh?"

But as she took him by the hand and led him upstairs to her bedroom, she found the idea of climbing on wasn't a laughing matter but an arousing one.

Julian halted abruptly inside the doorway.

"What's wrong?" she asked.

"I forgot that there was a baby sleeping in your room," he admitted.

"The key word is *sleeping*."

He continued to hover by the door. "What if he wakes up?"

"I don't think he's going to have any idea what we're doing."

"Still... I'm not sure I'm comfortable getting naked with you in front of the baby."

Surprisingly, his apprehension made her less so.

She took a decorative throw off the arm of the chair in the corner and draped it over the slatted side of the crib facing her bed, so that even if Jay woke up, he wouldn't be able to see them.

"Is that better?" she asked.

"You're laughing at me, aren't you?"

"A little," she said. "But I also think it's sweet that you'd worry our...carnal activities might scar the baby."

"Carnal activities?" he echoed.

"Now you're laughing at me," she noted.

"A little," he said, drawing her into his arms.

He kissed her again then, long and slow and deep, until every last thought in her brain slipped away so that there was nothing but Julian. And still he continued to kiss her, making her feel not just wanted but cherished, and as he kissed her, his hands skimmed over her, touching her in a way that made her feel not just desired but adored.

She didn't realize he was unfastening the buttons that ran down the front of her blouse until she felt the air on her skin when the fabric parted.

He pushed the garment over her shoulders, let it fall to the floor. Then he unfastened her jeans and hooked his fingers in the belt loops to drag the denim over her hips and down her legs to pool at her feet.

He took a step back then, and his gaze was hot and intense as it skimmed over her.

"I really like your underwear."

"It's new," she told him.

His brows lifted. "For me?"

"For you," she confirmed.

"I appreciate the effort," he assured her. "But I think I'm going to like what's beneath the silk and lace even more."

He hooked his fingers in the straps of her bra and started to draw them down her arms, but she took a step back, shaking her head.

"No way am I getting all the way naked when you're still mostly dressed."

"I can catch up," he promised, already lifting his sweater over his head.

"Let me help."

She tugged his T-shirt out of his jeans and slid her hands beneath the hem. She explored the warm, taut skin of his stomach, tracing every ridge of his abdomen, the muscles quivering in response to her touch.

She hadn't thought about the fact that his work as a rancher would keep him in optimal physical shape, but she was thinking about—and appreciating—it now.

She touched her mouth to his chest, where his heart was beating as rapidly as her own. Then she tugged to release the button fastening his jeans and slid the zipper down. She dipped a hand inside, and he moaned as her fingers wrapped around him. He was hard—and huge—and that realization caused some of her hesitation to resurface.

It had been a long time, and she'd never been with a man as... built...as Julian. As she continued to stroke his velvety length, it occurred to her that inserting Tab A into Slot B might not always be as simple as it sounded.

He linked his fingers around her wrist, forcing her to halt her ministrations. "If you keep that up, *corazón*, I'm not going to be of any use to you."

Before she could respond, he lifted her into his arms, making the breath whoosh out of her lungs. It was such an unexpected and romantic gesture that she actually felt her heart flutter. Then he laid her gently on top of the mattress and lowered himself over her, straddling her hips with his knees.

"You are so beautiful."

It was hardly a unique line, but spoken in the husky timbre of Julian's voice and accompanied by the heat in his gaze, it didn't sound like a line at all.

"The way you look at me makes me feel beautiful," she confessed.

He brushed his thumbs over the tight buds of her nipples, through the silky lace of her bra. The brief contact made her gasp as arrows of pleasure streaked from the tips to her core. Julian hummed with satisfaction as his thumbs stroked the rigid peaks again, making her sigh. Then he lowered his head and suckled her through the fabric, first one breast, then the other.

Finally he located the clasp and released it, peeling back the lacy cups to reveal her bare flesh. Then his mouth was on her again, hot and wet, and his suckling was making her the same.

She was so distracted by what he was doing with his mouth that she didn't realize his hands were exploring farther south until he hooked his thumbs in the sides of her panties and drew them down her legs and tossed them aside.

"Julian." His name was a plea on her lips.

"Tell me what you want, *corazón*," he urged.

"I want you."

"I'm yours." He kissed her softly. *"Soy tuyo para siempre."*

He slid a knee between her thighs, urging them apart.

She opened for him willingly, eager to feel his weight on top of her, his length inside her.

"Condom," she suddenly remembered.

He held up the square packet in his hand.

"Let me."

*"Un minuto,"* he said. "There's something I need to do first."
Then he lowered his head between her thighs.

"Julian," she said again.

He parted the soft folds at her center and put his mouth on
her and her mind went completely, blissfully blank.

He tasted and teased with his lips and his tongue until everything inside her tensed and tightened and…finally… shattered.

She had to bite hard on her lip to hold back the cries of ec-
stasy that she wanted to shout out. He held her while she continued to shudder with the after-effects of her orgasm, and only
when she stopped trembling did he speak.

"See?" he said. "Just like riding a bike."

The unexpected remark surprised a laugh out of her.

"I can assure you, if I'd ever experienced anything like *that*
riding a bike, I would have spent a lot more time on my bike."

"Well, we're not done yet," he promised.

She took the square packet from his hand now and teased
him with her touch as he'd teased her. When he was finally and
fully sheathed with the condom, he again parted her thighs with
his knees. But this time, when he settled between them, it was
to bury himself deep inside her.

She wasn't prepared for the waves of pleasure to start again,
but the sensation of him inside her was more than she could
bear. And then he began to move, thrusting deep—and then
deeper—and before she could catch her breath, she was free-
falling again.

JULIAN WAS DONE.

No matter what happened between them going forward, he
knew that there would never be another woman for him.

He'd been enamored with her from their very first meeting,
but he'd had no choice but to get over his infatuation—or at
least pretend that he'd done so. And while he'd dated plenty of
other women in the past five years, he'd never felt about any of
them the way he felt about Ruby.

He wanted to tell her that he loved her, because he knew

that he did. But he also knew it was too soon—at least from her perspective.

By her own admission, she hadn't even dated since her divorce, so he didn't think she was prepared to hear such a declaration from the first man she'd slept with the first time she invited him to share her bed.

So instead of telling her, he showed her. With every brush of his lips and every pass of his hands, he showed her that she was desired and cherished. And when their bodies joined together, again and again in the night, he whispered what he knew in his heart.

*"Eres la única, mi corazón para siempre."*
*You are the only one, my heart forever.*

WHEN RUBY AWOKE the next morning, in the warm comfort of Julian's arms, she was stunned to realize that it was almost seven o'clock.

"Good morning," he said, close to her ear.

"Good morning." She shifted so that she was facing him. "Did you sleep okay?"

"Very okay. How about you?"

"Better than I've slept in a long time. Apparently multiple orgasms are the key."

He smiled. "Happy to be of service."

She snuggled deeper into the warmth of his embrace. "It helped, too, that Jay slept through the night."

"Not quite," he said.

She tipped her head back to look at him. "What do you mean?"

"He was awake around four, fussing a little."

She frowned at that. "I didn't hear him."

"I'm glad."

"You changed him and fed him?"

"I've spent enough time here to know the routine."

"How is it that some lucky woman hasn't snapped you up long before now?" she wondered aloud.

"Maybe I was waiting for you."

She wanted to believe it could be true, that this amazing man really wanted to be with her, but she was wary.

Because she knew that she could easily fall in love with Julian, but she'd been in love before and look how that had turned out.

But even as the thought crossed her mind, she knew that she was being unfair to Julian. He wasn't anything like her ex-husband. And when it came to the day-to-day stuff, he'd already proven willing to show up and do the work that needed to be done.

Still, she was reluctant to rush into anything.

And she couldn't help but feel as if they were moving a little too fast.

Yes, she'd known him for years, but they'd shared their first kiss only two weeks earlier, and now she'd woken up with him in her bed.

And it wasn't that she regretted spending the night with him—how could she regret being with a man who had seriously rocked her world?—it was more that she had no idea where they were supposed to go from here.

Or even where she wanted to go.

"I forgot to ask if you had to be at the ranch early this morning, but I guess you don't."

"I texted the foreman last night and told him that I was going to be late today."

"How late can you be?" She slid her hands over his shoulders to link them behind his head. "I could fry up some bacon and scramble some eggs."

"As tempting as that sounds, there's something I'm even hungrier for right here."

So they made love again.

And a long while later, she sent him off with a lingering kiss and a travel mug filled with coffee.

"Can I see you tonight?" he asked at her door.

"Emery's going to be home."

"I'm not asking to spend the night," he said. "Just to spend some time with you—and Emery and Jay."

"We'll be here," she promised.

"Okay if I bring pizza?"

"You're angling to get my daughter to like you more than she likes me, aren't you?"

"If that was my goal, I'd bring pizza *and* strawberry ice cream."

And, of course, when he returned, it was with pizza and strawberry ice cream.

# CHAPTER FIFTEEN

*Mustang Pass, Montana*

"WHAT SHOULD WE do for dinner tonight?" Victor asked.

Winnie looked up from the book she was reading—or at least pretending to read, while her mind wandered far away from the words on the page.

"Dinner?" She glanced at the clock on the wall, surprised to realize that the day was more than half over already.

"Are you in the mood for anything in particular?" he prompted.

She slid her bookmark between the pages and closed the cover. "Since you asked, I've been craving tamales recently."

"Tamales?" he echoed. "Are those the Mexican things?"

"They're masa filled with meat and beans steamed in corn husks."

He made a face. "Doesn't sound appealing."

"What are you talking about? You love tamales. You must have eaten half a dozen last New Year's..." Her voice trailed off when she saw the worried look on his face. "Didn't you?"

"I don't think I've ever had tamales," he said. "Never mind eaten half a dozen of them."

"I could have sworn..." She frowned and rubbed at her

temples. "Denise makes them with spicy pulled pork or slow-cooked chicken."

"Denise?" he immediately latched on to that name. "From the Main Street Grill?"

That's right, she suddenly remembered. Denise was the name of one of the servers at the local diner. The young one with the nice smile who wore her auburn hair in two braids.

So why was she suddenly certain that she was thinking about someone else named Denise?

Why could she picture a homey kitchen crowded with people and overflowing with laughter and love?

The memory—if it was a memory—made her heart swell with joy, if only for a moment.

"We don't know anyone else named Denise?" she asked.

Victor took her hand and gave it a reassuring squeeze. "I think maybe you've had one of your dreams again."

"Maybe," she said. "So many things are muddled up in my head."

"I know."

But she didn't want to spend any more time talking about the empty void where her memories should be. Instead, she asked, "What were your thoughts on dinner?"

"I was thinking that fish and chips sound good. We could go to the diner—maybe Denise will be working tonight."

"That sounds good," she agreed.

He smiled, obviously pleased by her response.

But it was a lie.

She didn't want fish and chips.

She wanted tamales, with a side of beans and rice.

Why was she lying to her husband?

Victor had never been anything but good to her.

Or at least for as far back as she could remember—which was admittedly only a few months.

Apparently when she'd tripped and fallen, she'd banged her head on the way down.

"You're lucky you didn't break anything," Dr. Hammond had said, when he'd come to the house to examine her.

But she didn't feel lucky.

Maybe her old bones were intact, but obviously something had broken in her mind and now everything in her past was hidden behind a dark curtain.

Like the heavy velvet curtains that separated the waiting area from the consultation chamber in a fortune teller's shop.

If only she could pull back those curtains and let in the light, illuminating the memories that were currently in the dark.

She closed her eyes, as if visualizing it might make it happen.

But instead of velvet curtains, she saw a purple door on a turquoise building decorated with stars and crescent moons. She instinctively knew the building was real—that it existed somewhere outside of her mind. And when she drew in a breath, she could almost smell sandalwood and vanilla.

She'd asked Victor about the possibility of seeing another doctor, but he told her that he'd consulted with three different specialists and they'd all said the same thing—that head injuries took time to heal.

"And even if you never remember what came before, we've got plenty of time to make new memories together," he'd said.

She wasn't entirely convinced it was true.

She was an old woman—whatever time she had left in this world couldn't be but a fraction of the years that had come before.

With a sigh, she opened her eyes first and then the cover of the book she still held in her hand.

But her mind continued to wander and her heart continued to ache.

So much time lost.

So many people forgotten.

*I'm sorry, Stanley.*

# CHAPTER SIXTEEN

*Tenacity, Montana*

JULIAN HAD GROWN up hearing the stories about his family history. His paternal grandparents had emigrated from Mexico shortly after they married, believing they could make a better life for themselves and their children in America.

Miguel had a knack with horses and quickly found work on a cattle ranch in Tenacity, Montana, and Liliana was hired to cook for the ranch hands. They eventually had two sons—Aaron and Will—and when the boys were old enough, they, too, were put to work on the ranch, learning everything they needed to know about ranching from their father and the other men they worked with.

Miguel's dream had been to earn enough money working on other ranches to eventually buy his own spread, then Liliana got sick, and a big chunk of his savings had gone to pay the medical bills. When the boys were old enough to follow their own paths, Aaron chose one that led him to Bronco, Montana, where he got a job with the post office and married a woman who worked in a hair salon. But Will only ever aspired to work the land as his father had done, and he remained in Tenacity doing just that, eventually marrying Nicole, another second-generation Mexican-American who helped support the family by tending their vegetable garden and working as a seamstress.

Julian was the oldest of their five children, and if at times it had felt cramped in their modest three-bedroom home, he'd been taught to appreciate what he had—a roof over his head, food on the table and family all around. And while money was often tight, there was always an abundance of love in their family home.

And Sunday dinner was an occasion not to be missed. Especially now that the kids were grown and living their own lives, it was an opportunity for them to reconnect and catch up.

Tonight they were dining on tacos al pastor.

"I have some news," Julian said, as bowls of meat and rice and various toppings were passed around the table.

"What news?" Will asked.

"I put an offer in on a parcel of land between the Barnhart property and the Parker ranch."

"To buy it?" Luca asked.

"No, to build a bridge on it," he retorted dryly.

His youngest brother rolled his eyes.

"And?" Nicole prompted.

He couldn't hold back the smile that spread across his face. "I got a call from the real estate agent on my way over here. My offer was accepted."

His mom's eyes filled with tears. "You're going to have your own ranch."

"You're going to be your own boss," his dad noted, nodding with satisfaction.

"That's the dream, isn't it?" he said lightly.

"Absolutely," Will agreed.

"You could be my boss, too, if you're hiring," Diego said.

Julian laughed. "I'm sure I'll be able to put you to work, but the final papers won't be signed until Tuesday and it's going to be a while after that before I get things up and running."

"But less if you had help," his middle brother pointed out.

"This is wonderful news," Nicole said, her eyes still misty. "Is there a house on the property?"

"Not a house," he said. "But there's an old hunting cabin.

Just a couple of rooms in desperate need of repair—or perhaps demolition."

"Are you planning to live in that?" His mom sounded worried.

"No. As soon as the ground starts to thaw, I'll get started building a new house."

"Maybe by the time you do that, you will have met a nice girl to marry. Make sure you have lots of bedrooms for all the grandbabies you're going to give me."

He rolled his eyes, not yet ready to admit that he already had plans in that direction. "I'm not your only child," he reminded her. "Maybe one of your other kids can work on giving you grandbabies."

"I know, but you're the oldest."

"But Marisa will be the first to marry. In just a few weeks, in fact. So maybe you'll be an *abuela* in nine months...or less."

The bride-to-be, seated on the opposite side of the table, drew back her foot to kick his shin—but connected instead with Nina, seated beside him.

"Ow. What the hell, Marisa?"

Ordinarily her language would have drawn the ire of both parents, but Will was currently preoccupied looking daggers at his youngest daughter's fiancé.

"She's not pregnant," Dawson John hastened to assure his future father-in-law.

"I'm not pregnant," Marisa confirmed—this time finding her intended target with her kick.

"Of course, she's not pregnant," Nicole interjected, attempting to soothe her husband's wounded sensitivities.

"But I'm still hungry," Diego said.

Nina snorted. "There's a surprise."

And that quickly, the tension dissolved.

"Luca, pass the meat to your brother," Will said.

"Do we have more tortillas?" Marisa asked.

"Of course," her mom said, already pushing her chair away from the table to retrieve them from the oven.

As everyone refilled their plates and then their bellies, conversation ebbed and flowed around the table. Glasses were raised—and sometimes voices—as numerous and various topics were discussed.

To an outsider happening upon the scene, Julian imagined it might look like chaos.

To him, it was Sunday night dinner with *la familia*.

He loved each and every one of them, and he was looking forward to the day when Ruby, Emery and Jay had designated places around the table.

WHEN RUBY DECIDED to apply to be a foster parent, it hadn't crossed her mind that she might end up with an infant.

Of course, she'd been thrilled to get the call from Hazel Browning on New Year's Eve and would have happily opened her home to any child in need. But within the first twenty-four hours of Jay's arrival, she'd wondered how she'd ever managed to forget the work that was involved in caring for an infant.

Not that Emery was easy, but a preschooler was demanding in a different way. And when Emery was hungry or thirsty or tired, she told her.

Babies cried.

It didn't matter if they were hungry or wet or tired, they cried.

And it seemed as if Jay was *always* hungry or wet or tired.

But after only a few days, she started to distinguish his different cries.

It had taken a lot less time than that for her to fall head over heels in love with him.

And now, after almost three weeks together, they seemed to have settled into something of a routine.

When she was working, she put him in his playpen behind the counter, where he worked his charm on any and all of the guests who stopped by.

But nobody adored him as much as Emery.

Whenever Ruby picked her daughter up from Mimi and Papa's after work, the little girl greeted her mom with a big hug and immediately turned her attention to Jay.

Of course, most people couldn't resist a baby—especially one who had a smile for everyone he met. And that included Lynda, who came to the inn just before lunch on Tuesday with a paper bag bearing the logo of the local sandwich shop.

"This is a surprise," Ruby said.

"I brought meatball subs and pasta salad," her friend said, setting the bag on the counter so that her hands were free to steal Jay out of his playpen. "All I want in return are baby cuddles and details."

"What's the occasion?"

She stretched out her arms so that the baby was high in the air. His eyes went wide, then his mouth curved in a smile and he gurgled happily. "I kicked butt in court this morning and wanted to celebrate."

"You hate going to court," she said, well aware that her friend was a passionate advocate for mediation over litigation.

"But sometimes there are reasons the parties can't meet in the middle. In this case, the reason was my client's now ex-husband." She brought the baby close again, rubbed her nose against his, then lifted him high again.

"He just ate," Ruby cautioned.

"He wouldn't be the first one of your kids to throw up on me," Lynda noted, but she heeded her friend's warning and cuddled Jay close to her body. "Any update on the search for his parents?"

"Not that Family Services has shared with me."

"Want me to make some calls—see what I can find out?"

Ruby blinked. "You'd do that?"

"Anything for you, my friend."

It was an admittedly tempting offer, but she was afraid to push, afraid to risk changing the status quo. And absolutely terrified to think about what would happen if one of the baby's relatives came forward and offered to give him a home. "Thanks, but I think I'll pass for now."

"Okay," Lynda agreed. "Just let me know if you change your mind."

"I will," Ruby promised.

"Now I want to hear about the other man in your life," her friend said.

"Julian?"

Lynda arched a brow. "Do you have a romance going with someone else?"

"No."

"The last time we chatted, you were waiting for him to make a move," her friend reminded her. "Considering his truck was in your driveway after midnight Friday night, can I assume he finally did?"

"How do you know his truck was in my driveway Friday night?" Ruby wanted to know.

"Because I drove by on my way home from Callan's place."

"Callan? The New Year's Eve hookup that didn't mean anything?"

"A second hookup doesn't retroactively make the first any more meaningful," Lynda assured her. "And you are not going to distract me that easily."

"I wasn't trying to distract you. I was expressing an interest in your life."

"Back to Julian," her friend said, making it clear that the subject of her personal life was currently closed. "When did he finally make his move?"

"Actually, I made the move," Ruby confided.

"Well, well," Lynda said approvingly. "The girl's got game."

"I don't know if that's true," she protested. "But I did kiss him. And then I told him that Emery had a sleepover scheduled at her grandparents' house and asked if he might want to sleep over at mine."

"I want details of the sleepover. Everything but the sleeping part."

Ruby had to laugh. "All I'm going to say is that I can now happily assure you that the last person I had sex with was *not* my ex-husband."

"At least tell me that Julian's amazing in bed," her friend urged.

"He's amazing in bed," she dutifully intoned.

Lynda sighed. "I knew he would be."

"What do you mean—you knew he would be?"

"I guess this is where I have to confess that I had a crush on Julian in high school."

Ruby's jaw dropped. "And you're only telling me this *now*?"

Her friend shrugged. "I was afraid that if I said anything to you before, you'd be all weird about getting together with him."

"Well, of course, I would," she agreed. "There's a code."

"*I* had a crush," Lynda said again. "As in, my heart sighed every time he walked past me in the halls. He never knew I existed."

"I'm sure that's not true."

"Believe me, it's true," her friend insisted. "He was a junior and I was a freshman. And he was dating Laura Bell." She sighed wistfully. "Oh, how I envied Laura Bell. Until—"

"Until what?" Ruby prompted.

"Until they broke up," Lynda finished.

Ruby's gaze narrowed. "Until she dumped him to go out with Owen, you mean."

"I wasn't sure you knew about that," her friend admitted.

"Owen told me."

"Of course he did," Lynda said darkly. "Trying to make trouble for you and Julian, no doubt."

"It didn't work," Ruby assured her.

"Good. And I'm glad to know that my instincts about Julian were correct."

"Of course, I only have one night—and one morning—as the basis for my assessment, but he certainly exceeded all of my expectations."

"So why are you not doing it every chance you get?" her friend wanted to know.

"Because we're usually in the company—or at least the proximity—of two children who, even when they're sleeping, could wake up at any moment," Ruby explained.

"You need to make time alone with him a priority. Make *him* a priority."

"It's a little scary, how quickly he's come to mean so much to me," she confided.

"Julian's not Owen," Lynda said gently.

"I know."

"And you deserve to be happy, Ruby."

"I am happy," she insisted. "I've got a good job, great friends and Emery and Jay. I feel like wanting anything more than that would be asking for too much."

"Trust me, wanting more orgasms is not selfish."

Ruby felt her cheeks flush. "You know that's not what I meant."

"I know," her friend admitted, with an unrepentant grin. "So tell me—do you have anything going on tonight?"

"No."

"Neither do I," Lynda said. "So reach out to Julian and set up a booty call."

She immediately shook her head. "I don't think so."

"You don't have to tell him it's a booty call. Just tell him that you've arranged a babysitter so that the two of you can have some time alone together. If he's half as smart as I think he is, he'll figure it out."

"You're really offering to babysit?"

"Why do you sound surprised?"

"Because it's not just Emery now," Ruby said.

"My sisters have six kids between them," Lynda reminded her friend. "Trust me—I've mixed more formula than a high school science class, changed a mountain of diapers and only once had to run to the emergency room because a kid got a Lego block stuck in his nose."

Ruby winced. "Thankfully Emy doesn't have any of the little blocks."

"It would require a concerted effort to shove a Duplo block into one of her nostrils," Lynda agreed. "But instead of thinking about that, go ahead and give Julian a call."

"Can I send a text message instead?"

"There are no hard and fast rules. You can do whatever you want."

She pulled out her phone and opened the messaging app.

"Sometime before seven o'clock tonight would be good," her friend remarked dryly, when Ruby continued to stare at the blank screen.

"I don't know what to say."

"Keep it simple. Something like—'Hey, Stud Muffin. Any plans for tonight?'"

She went with Lynda's suggestion, minus the 'Stud Muffin' part.

Any plans for tonight?

JULIAN GLANCED AT the screen of his phone when it buzzed, surprised—and pleased—to see the text message from Ruby.

It seemed as if he was always the one reaching out, asking to get together. This was a welcome change.

He immediately replied:

Not yet. What did you have in mind?

He watched the three dots on his phone, waiting for her to finish composing her reply.

I have a babysitter. Maybe we could spend some time at your place?

His place? Was she suggesting a booty call?

Are you suggesting a booty call?

No!

The immediate—and undeniably indignant—reply made him grin, then the three dots appeared again.

Maybe...

And he laughed out loud.

Would you be interested if I was?

Do you really have to ask?

What time should I come over?

How long is your babysitter available?

Until ten(ish).

How about dinner first?

You don't always have to feed me.

I like feeding you. And I need to eat, too. Especially if I'm going to keep up my stamina for...after dinner.

He imagined her cheeks flushing with color as she read his response.

In that case, dinner sounds good.

Can I pick you up at 6?

I'll be ready.

## CHAPTER SEVENTEEN

"YOU'RE NOT READY," Julian said, when Ruby came to the door with her hair in a ponytail, wearing a flannel shirt and leggings and a tired expression on her face. Not that he didn't think she looked great—because she did—but she didn't look like she had any intention of leaving the house.

She shook her head regretfully. "I'm sorry."

"Change of plans?" he guessed.

Now she nodded. "I tried calling you."

"I turned off my phone when I went into my meeting at the bank," he suddenly remembered, pulling the device out of his pocket now and discovering that he had three missed calls and a text message from Ruby. "Emery's sick?"

She nodded again. "Caroline called me after she picked Emy up from school to let me know she was complaining of a sore throat. So we stopped in to see the doctor on the way home and he did a rapid strep test, which was positive."

"Poor thing," he said, his personal disappointment immediately taking a back seat to concern for the little girl.

"She feels pretty miserable," Ruby agreed. "And is very unhappy that I'm making her keep her distance from Jay."

"Did the doctor prescribe antibiotics?"

She nodded. "I've got one dose into her so far. Anyway, I'm sorry about tonight."

"There's no reason to be sorry," he told her. "The only thing that matters is taking care of Em."

She blinked, as if surprised by his response. "Well, she's sleeping right now, so there's not much to do. But obviously I couldn't go out and leave her with a babysitter—not even her favorite honorary aunt."

"Obviously," he agreed. "And since we're not going to make our reservation at the restaurant, I'm going to call and cancel and then pop out to get us some food. Are you in the mood for anything in particular?"

She shook her head. "I'm not really hungry."

"Hungry or not, you need to eat—to keep up your strength so you can take care of your daughter."

"You're right," she acknowledged.

"How about a burger?" he suggested.

She considered for a few seconds, then nodded. "Actually, that sounds great."

"Do you need anything else?" he prompted. "Chicken soup for Em? Popsicles?"

"I've got soup. She might appreciate popsicles."

"What's her favorite flavor?"

"Banana."

He dipped his head to brush his lips over hers. "I'll be back in thirty minutes."

"I'll be here."

It took him a little longer than that, and the whole time that he was gone, he was anxious to get back to her, so that she wasn't alone.

It frustrated him to think how much she had to deal with on her own, as a single parent, because her ex-husband was less than useless. And though their relationship was still very new, he was eager to show her that she could count on him to be there for her and Emery and Jay, because he was as crazy about her kids as he was about Ruby.

When he returned, she was mixing formula and Jay was screaming in his high chair.

Julian put the popsicles in the freezer, set the bag of food on the table and unfastened the belt around the baby's middle to lift him into his arms.

The screaming immediately stopped.

"Thank God," Ruby said tiredly.

"I'm happy to help, but I don't think my assistance warrants deity status."

She managed a weary smile as she filled the baby's bottle.

"I'm sorry I was gone so long," he said. "It took me a while to track down Emery's banana popsicles."

"There's no need to apologize," she assured him.

When she reached for Jay, he instead took the bottle from her and nudged her toward the table. "Sit. Eat."

"I'll eat after I feed the baby."

"Do I have to call Chrissy to remind you that the correct response is, 'that would be helpful—thank you, Julian'?"

She lowered herself into a chair. "I don't mean to seem ungrateful."

"You don't seem ungrateful," he assured her, taking a seat across from her. "But you don't seem to know how to accept help when it's offered."

She didn't deny that it was true, choosing instead to focus on the contents of the bag. "Which one of these burgers is mine?"

"They're both the same." He settled the baby in the crook of his arm and offered him the bottle. Jay immediately latched on the nipple and began suckling.

"You got two orders of fries and onion rings," Ruby noted.

"I wasn't sure what you wanted—and I wanted both."

This time her smile came a little more easily.

"You mentioned earlier that you had an appointment today," Ruby remarked, as she unwrapped one of the burgers.

He nodded. "I planned to tell you about it over dinner, so that we could celebrate."

"What are we celebrating?"

He eased the empty bottle from Jay's mouth and lifted him to his shoulder to burp him. "I bought a ranch."

Ruby's eyes went wide. "What? You bought a ranch?"

"Well, I bought a parcel of land that's going to be a ranch," he clarified, returning the now satiated and sleeping baby to his high chair.

Her smile curved her lips and sparkled in her eyes. "That's exciting news."

"And a little bit scary," he admitted, unwrapping his burger. "Especially now that the papers have been signed."

"But this is your dream," she reminded him.

He nodded. "The first part of it, anyway."

She raised her paper cup. "Then I'm happy for you. And I have no doubt you will work hard to make it a success."

"It's definitely going to require a lot of hard work," he said. "I wish we had something other than watered down soda to celebrate with."

"I'm just happy to be able to celebrate with you," he assured her.

"I really am sorry," she said again. "I know this isn't what you had planned for tonight."

"Please stop apologizing. And really, it *is* what I had planned for tonight—because I got to spend the night with you."

"Well, it wasn't what *I* had planned for tonight," she promised.

He reached across the table to link their hands together.

Inexplicably, her eyes filled with tears.

Julian immediately pushed away from the table to kneel in front of her. "What's wrong?"

She shook her head, but the tears spilled over. "I just didn't expect you to be so understanding."

"What did you expect?" he asked, baffled. "Did you think I'd be upset? Angry?"

She didn't say anything.

"Let me guess—Owen would have been mad?"

"He didn't like having his plans changed at the last minute," she admitted.

"Why are you still making excuses for him?" He wanted to know.

"I'm not." Her immediate denial was followed by a frown. "I am."

"Why?" he asked again.

She seemed to consider his question as she swallowed another mouthful of soda. "I think I do it for Emery," she finally said. "I always try to put the best possible spin on his actions so that she doesn't have to know that her dad's an asshole."

"I can understand that, though she's going to figure it out for herself soon enough."

"I know," she agreed. "And I hope you know how much tonight meant to me. Not just that you were so great about having our plans upended, but because you were here for me."

"You don't have to do everything for yourself, anymore," he told her. "You know that, right? You can call me if you need anything."

"I'm starting to believe that might be true."

"It *is* true," he assured her. "I'm here for you. Anytime."

"Thank you."

"I don't want your thanks. I want you to promise that you'll call."

"I'll call."

"Promise?"

She nodded. "I promise."

BUT SHE DIDN'T need to call Julian, because he called her.

He texted the morning after their aborted date to check in on the little girl, then again later that day, and the following morning. Now it was Thursday afternoon, and he was on the phone again.

"How's Emery doing?"

"I'd say she's almost back to one hundred percent," Ruby told him. "In fact, she asked if she could go to preschool this morning."

"Did you let her?"

"No, I decided to keep her home another day to ensure she's fully recovered, though the way she's been bouncing off the walls should have convinced me." She was relieved that the antibiotics were working and her daughter was feeling so much better, grateful that her efforts to keep Emery and Jay apart had prevented him from getting sick, and wondering how she'd been lucky enough to have found a guy like Julian who seemed almost too good to be true. Someone who wasn't just a good man and a spectacular lover, but who made butterflies take wing in her stomach every time she saw his name on the display on her phone. Someone who made her want to trust and believe and take a chance on falling in love again.

"Good," Julian said, drawing her attention back to the present. "Because the Tenacity Winter Carnival is this weekend."

"We've never actually been to the carnival," Ruby admitted. "I considered taking her last year, but I wasn't sure if there would be much for a kid her age."

"There's something for kids of all ages. Snow sculpture contests, snowshoe races, sleigh rides, cocoa and cookies, and story time by the bonfire."

"It does sound like Emery might have fun," Ruby acknowledged. "But I'm not sure Jay would get much out of it."

"Nice try," he said.

"What do you mean?"

"You think I don't know that you're waiting for me to offer to take Emery so that you can stay home, cozy and warm, with the baby?"

She sighed wistfully. "Actually, that does sound like a better plan."

"Well, it's not going to happen," he assured her. "You're going to put on your thermal underwear and bundle up the baby and join us at the carnival."

"What if I'd rather wear the black satin underwear that was delivered today from Victoria's Secret?" She'd bought it on a whim, no doubt because Julian seemed to bring out the sexy side of her that had been hidden for so long.

"You do *not* play fair," he protested in a husky voice.

"I'm just curious to know what kind of underwear you'd prefer me to wear on the weekend."

"Wear the black satin under the thermal," he suggested. "The layers will help keep you warm and thinking of you in the black satin will keep *me* warm."

JULIAN WAS RIGHT—the Winter Carnival was fun.

And busy.

It was as if every single resident of Tenacity had come out for the event.

Emery loved every bit of it.

Ruby would have been happy to stay in the background, keeping Jay entertained—and warm!—while Emery dragged Julian from one activity to the next, but her daughter wasn't having it. Oh, she was happy to make snow sculptures with Julian, but she wanted her mom to be her partner for the snowshoe race. Then she dragged Julian around for the scavenger hunt and conscripted Ruby for the snowball relay. But the best, according to Emery, was the sleigh ride, because they all got to do that together—even Jay.

And though the air temperature was cold, it warmed Ruby's heart to see the joy on her daughter's face. When was the last time she'd seen Emery smile so widely? Or heard her laugh with such complete abandon? She honestly couldn't remember.

"Someone looks like she's having a good time."

Despite her earlier observation that all the locals seemed to have turned up at the event, it hadn't occurred to Ruby that her former in-laws might be there—or that, in the midst of the crowds, their paths would cross.

"I suspect this is going to become a yearly thing," Ruby said.

"It is for us," Mark said, smiling at his wife. "Every year since the carnival started."

"In the beginning, I don't know how they justified calling it a carnival," Caroline noted. "It didn't consist of much more than a snow-sculpting contest and a single booth selling hot cider back then."

"It's obviously a lot more than that now, because we've been here since noon and Emery has been going nonstop from one activity to the next."

"Kids do bounce back, don't they?" Caroline noted. "Looking at her now, you'd never know she was sick only a few days ago."

"They do," Ruby agreed.

"And how's this little guy holding up?" Mark asked, peering at the baby snuggled in the carrier attached to her chest.

"Surprisingly well," Ruby said. "I'm the one with frozen fingers and frostbit toes."

"You could head over to the bonfire to warm up."

"I'm hoping to head home to warm up, as soon as Emery gets her prize for completing the scavenger hunt."

"Mimi! Papa!" Emery, having spotted her grandparents, came racing over, waving her activity pack "prize."

Mark caught his granddaughter up in his arms. "How's Papa's princess?"

"I want snow taffy," she said.

"Well, who wouldn't?" he agreed.

"But wanting and getting are two different things," Ruby felt compelled to interject. "Because she's already had cotton candy, cookies and hot cocoa."

"That's a lot of treats in one day," Caroline remarked.

Emery tipped her head back against her grandfather's shoulder. "P'ease, Papa."

"I don't think your mom wants you to have snow taffy," he hedged.

"But do *you* want me to have snow taffy?"

Caroline pressed her lips together, obviously trying to hold back a smile.

"That child is going to rule the world someday," Julian remarked.

Mark lifted a brow. "Someday?"

"You didn't answer my question, Papa," Emery said.

"I want your mom to not be mad at me," he finally said. "So that means no snow taffy today."

"Tomorrow?"

He had to chuckle. "Let's wait and see what tomorrow brings."

"And right now, we need to be heading home," Ruby said. "So give Mimi and Papa hugs and kisses."

The little girl dutifully spread the love, and when Mark set her on her feet again, she returned to Julian's side to put her mittened hand in his.

"It was good to see you again, Julian," Mark said.

"And both of you," he replied.

As the McKinleys wandered off—in the direction of the

snow taffy booth—Ruby and Julian turned toward home with the kids.

"Was that awkward?" Ruby asked cautiously.

"A lot less than I expected," he said.

"Me, too," she agreed. "But they're important to Emy—and me—so I'm glad that they seem to be okay with you and me dating."

For several seconds, the only sound was the crunch of their boots in the snow, then Julian asked, "Is that what we're doing—dating?"

Ruby wasn't entirely sure how to interpret his question—or his guarded tone. "Isn't it?"

Before he could respond, Emery abruptly halted in the middle of the sidewalk and tipped her head back to look up at Julian. "My legs are s'eepy."

"Do you want me to carry you?" he offered.

The little girl nodded, making the red pompom on her hat bounce. "Yes, p'ease."

Julian lifted her into his arms and carried her the rest of the way home, and Ruby breathed a quiet sigh of relief that the discussion of their relationship was effectively shelved—at least for the moment.

But later that night, after the kids had been fed and bathed and were tucked into their respective beds, and she and Julian were settled on the sofa with glasses of wine, he picked up the conversation right where they'd left off.

"So, dating, huh?"

"You don't want to date me?" she asked, attempting to keep her tone—and the conversation—light.

"I was actually hoping that our relationship might have a slightly higher status," he said, unwilling to follow her cue.

Ruby sipped her wine. "Our relationship is important to me," she said carefully. "I just don't know that we need to put a label on it."

He was quiet for a minute, considering her response. "Maybe we don't," he allowed. "But several different people remarked to me today that I had a beautiful family, and it made me realize how much I want you and Emery and Jay to be my family."

She bobbled the glass in her hand, nearly sloshing wine over the rim.

"Now I've freaked you out," he realized.

"Maybe. A little." But she wasn't nearly as freaked out as she should have been, because the truth was, the idea of sharing a family with Julian was far more tempting than she wanted it to be—and *that* freaked her out much more than his declaration. She set the glass down and tucked her feet up under her on the sofa. "It's just that we really haven't been…together…very long."

He held her gaze for a long minute. "Does that mean it's too soon for me to tell you that I love you?"

"*Way* too soon." She realized, as soon as the words were out of her mouth, that her response might have been a tad too vehement. The stricken expression on his face only confirmed it.

"Apparently I don't need to ask if you feel the same way," he remarked dryly.

"Julian…" she said, aching for both of them.

"It's okay." He set his glass of wine aside with hers. "I don't need to be placated."

"I'm not trying to placate you," she denied. "But I'm also not trying to hurt you. You have to know I care about you. A lot."

"Yeah," he said. "I guess I do."

"But you're moving too fast and pushing for something I'm not ready to give," she told him, desperate to explain.

He nodded abruptly. "Point taken."

"I don't know what else to say to you," she admitted. "I wasn't prepared to have this conversation tonight."

"I didn't realize you needed designated prep time before talking to me about our relationship." There was an uncharacteristic edge to his voice, and it sliced through her heart.

"Please understand, Julian. You're the first person—the first man—I've let myself get close to since my divorce. And I'm worried that we might be rushing things a little."

He was silent for a minute, considering, before he asked, "Do you want to take a step back?"

The question surprised her—and maybe even unnerved her a little. Because she was still marveling over the fact that she'd found a man as wonderful as Julian and she definitely didn't want to lose him.

"That isn't what I said," she protested.

"Which isn't an answer to my question," he pointed out.

She shook her head. "No, I don't want to take a step back."

He exhaled audibly, assuring Ruby that wasn't what he wanted, either.

"But…"

There were other factors to consider, other hearts at risk in addition to their own. Most notably, Emery's and Jay's. Both kids were already growing attached to him, and both kids would be hurt if Ruby and Julian's fledgling relationship didn't work out. And the longer she let things go on, the greater the potential damage if it fell apart.

"…maybe we should," she concluded.

# CHAPTER EIGHTEEN

*Bronco, Montana*

STANLEY WAS ON a mission. He knew that if he was going to find his missing bride—and he was—then he needed something more concrete than cryptic messages in a dream. So he drove to Bronco Heights, to the house where Winona's daughter, Dorothea, lived with her daughter, Wanda.

"Stanley." His almost-daughter-in-law greeted him with a hug before ushering him into the warmth of her home.

He removed his boots and coat before following her to the kitchen for the coffee she offered.

"I'm guessing you're here because you talked to Evan," she said as she brought two mugs to the table and took a seat opposite him.

Stanley nodded.

"He told me about the dream a few weeks ago," she confided.

"The first time he had it?" he guessed.

"No, I'd imagine it was at least the second or third time," she mused. "He would have discounted it as meaningless nonsense the first time. Probably even the second."

"Do you believe he has some of Winona's gift?"

She smiled. "He certainly wouldn't consider it a gift, but yes, I do."

"Not as strong as yours, though?"

"Different than mine," she clarified.

He sipped his coffee. "Do you believe your mother pulled a runaway bride?"

She answered without hesitation. "Not for a minute."

"And yet, when you called to tell me about the letter, you told me that her note made it clear that she'd changed her mind."

"Okay, maybe for a minute," she allowed. "When I first read her letter. Because it was the first I'd heard from her in weeks—since our brief conversation the morning of the wedding—and I'd started to fear that she was lost to all of us forever. And suddenly I had proof in my hand—in her own handwriting—that she was alive, and I was so desperately relieved that I let myself believe the words on the page."

"What happened to change your mind?"

"Let me get the letter for you," she said.

He nodded. It was, after all, the reason he'd come—to read Winona's words with his own eyes.

When she returned with the letter, he pulled the single page out of the envelope and unfolded it to skim the brief words.

"It does look like her handwriting," he admitted.

Dorothea nodded. "You can tell by the loops of the *l*'s and the tails on the *y*'s."

"So you believe she *did* write this?"

"I read that letter over and over again, trying to reconcile the words on the page with what I knew about my mother. I traced my fingers over every letter of every word, and that's when I knew she *didn't* write it. Because the pressure on every letter is the same—as if the pen was never lifted from the page."

Stanley tried to follow her reasoning. "You're suggesting that it wasn't written but traced?"

She nodded again.

"Why didn't you come to me with this? Why would you let me wander, lost, worrying about her?"

"If we're not lost, we cannot be found."

"That sounds like something your mother would say."

"But now that you're here," she said. "I've got something else for you, too."

She retrieved a sketchbook from the counter and slid it across the table to him.

Dorothea was an incredibly talented artist who'd made a name for herself illustrating a series of popular children's books. What Winona was most proud of, though, was her daughter's ability to put on the page detailed images of real people she'd never met and places that she'd never been—proof of her gift.

He opened the cover, studied the sketch for a minute. A house with an old truck parked in the driveway.

"Am I supposed to know what this is?"

"I was hoping you might," she admitted. "Because I don't have a clue."

"You've never been to this house?"

She shook her head.

He flipped a few more pages, stopping at a drawing of a horse. "Are you thinking of buying a horse?"

She laughed. "Definitely not anywhere on my radar."

"A truck?"

She shook her head. "I don't know what the pictures mean, but I think they're connected somehow. I think, if you find the house and the horse and the truck, you'll find my mother."

"It might be easier if you'd put a number on the house or a license plate on the truck."

"Nothing worth having comes easy. But I can tell you not to go to Oregon. She's not there."

He didn't ask how she could be so certain, because it was apparent that she was, and that was enough for him.

He closed the sketchbook. "Can I take this?"

"Of course. I only wish I had something more to give you."

"You and Evan have given me hope," he said. "And I can't tell you how much I needed that after all these months."

She walked him to the door, hugged him again. "Promise to save me a dance at your wedding?"

"I promise."

# CHAPTER NINETEEN

*Tenacity, Montana*

JULIAN WASN'T PROUD of the fact that he'd walked out on Ruby after she'd decided to put on the brakes, but he'd been afraid that if he stuck around, the trajectory of their conversation would have gone from bad to worse. And as much as it hurt to hear her say that they should take a step back, he knew it would be infinitely more painful if she suddenly decided a single step wasn't far enough and wanted to end their relationship.

In the twenty hours that had passed since then, he hadn't reached out, because he hadn't known what to say or where they were supposed to go from here. There had been radio silence on her end, too, though he suspected that was more likely because she was busy with Emery and Jay than that she was tying herself up in knots over what had been said and not said the night before.

In any event, the last thing he was in the mood for was Sunday dinner with his family, but he knew that skipping the meal would only lead to questions he wasn't prepared to answer.

As it turned out, his parents and his siblings were all so busy fussing over his great-uncle that they barely gave Julian a second glance when he arrived.

"*Tío* Stanley." He greeted the old man with a hug. "It's good to know that *Má's* enchiladas inspired you to make the trip from Bronco."

"I'll definitely enjoy those," Stanley said. "But I'm here because I need your help finding my bride."

Julian was taken aback by this announcement—and leery of his uncle's request for his assistance. "Wouldn't you be better off hiring a private investigator?"

Stanley shook his head. "It needs to be me. I need to be the one to find her."

"What makes you think I can help?"

"I'm not sure I can explain it in a way that's going to make any sense to you," his uncle admitted.

"Try," Julian suggested.

"She told me to come to you."

He was taken aback. "You've talked to her?"

"Not directly," Stanley admitted. "Look, I get that you're probably already thinking I'm a crazy old man, but I need you to listen with an open mind. Okay?"

"Okay," Julian agreed cautiously.

"You know that Winona has a gift."

"That seems to be the consensus."

"Well, apparently her psychic abilities run in the family. Her great-grandson, Evan, is a skeptic, though, who hasn't embraced his talent. Nevertheless, he came to me a few weeks back because he had a dream…"

Julian listened patiently as his great-uncle recounted what Evan had told him, and then about his visit with Dorothea and the pictures she'd sketched.

Though he wasn't entirely convinced that Stanley was on the right path, he couldn't fault him for wanting to chase down any and every lead. If it was Ruby who'd disappeared, he wouldn't leave any stone unturned in his efforts to find her.

But he knew exactly where Ruby was—and she'd made it clear that she needed some time and distance to figure out her feelings for him. So maybe the best thing Julian could do right now was give it to her.

And even if *Tío* Stanley was on a wild goose chase, Julian

figured there wasn't any harm in spending a few days with the man. At the very least, it'd help keep his mind off Ruby.

"I CAN'T BELIEVE I let you talk me into this," Julian said, sliding behind the wheel of his truck the next morning.

"I don't think I talked you into anything," Stanley said. "I think you were looking for an excuse to get out of town."

Julian scowled at that, though he couldn't deny that there might be some truth in the old man's statement. Instead he said, "Where are we going?"

"Gray Horse."

"That's rather imprecise."

Stanley shrugged. "I don't have an exact address."

"Do you have anything other than a vague idea based on sketches and dreams?" he asked, punching the name of the town into his navigation app.

Instead of answering his question, Stanley asked one of his own. "Have you ever been in love, Julian?"

Immediately his mind went to Ruby. Because whether or not she was ready to accept his feelings, there was no denying that he was head over heels for the single mom and her kids.

"Yeah," he admitted.

Stanley nodded. "If someone took the woman you loved away from you, what would you do to get her back?"

*Anything.*

Which, he suspected, was his uncle's point.

"So… Gray Horse," he said, turning his truck in the requisite direction.

"Thank you."

"I just want you to be prepared for the possibility that this might not turn out the way you hope."

"I'm going to find Winona," Stanley said confidently. "Not finding her isn't an option."

IT WAS ALMOST lunchtime on Monday before Ruby realized that she'd left her cell phone in her car when she'd gone into work. Of course, her hands had been full, with Jay and all his requisite baby paraphernalia, so it wasn't surprising.

Or maybe she'd forgotten the phone on purpose—a subconscious attempt to prevent herself from checking the screen every five minutes to see if there was a message from Julian. And eliminate the temptation to reach out to him.

But she wasn't happy about the way they'd left things Saturday night and, as a result, she hadn't slept well since then.

He'd told her he loved her and she'd responded by telling him that she wanted to take a step back.

But was she supposed to say the words back to him when she really didn't know how she felt?

How would that be fair to either of them?

The fact was, no matter how many times she went over their conversation in her head, she couldn't make it play out any other way.

But she knew she'd hurt him, and she was sorry for that.

So when Chrissy stopped by the desk for a minute, Ruby left her to keep an eye on the baby while she hurried out to her SUV to retrieve her phone.

When Chrissy moved on, Ruby finally let herself steal a peek at her screen, her heart skipping a beat when she saw that she'd missed a call from Julian.

Actually three calls.

And he'd left one message.

She tapped the screen to access her voicemail.

*Hey, Ruby...*

Just hearing those two words in the warm, familiar timbre of his voice made her knees weak.

Was it any wonder that hearing him say "I love you" had completely unnerved her?

But why had she reacted so strongly to his declaration?

Why was she so reluctant to believe that his feelings could be real?

Or maybe the problem wasn't his feelings but her own.

Because if she let herself believe that he loved her, then she'd have to admit that she was more than halfway toward falling in love with him, too.

And loving Julian would require opening up her heart—a heart that was still a little battered and bruised as a result of being knocked around by her ex-husband during their short-term marriage.

*...Talk soon.*

When the message ended, she realized that her mental meandering had prevented her from actually hearing any of it.

She tapped the replay prompt.

*Hey, Ruby. I was hoping to talk to you before I left, but obviously you're not available right now. Anyway, my great-uncle from Bronco showed up unexpectedly and asked for my help with something, so it looks like I'm going to be heading out of town for a few days. I don't expect I'll be gone any longer than that, but I'll be in touch as soon as I get back. In the meantime, give Emery and Jay big hugs from me. Talk soon.*

She frowned at her phone, as if it was somehow responsible for the frustratingly vague message.

An unnamed relative showed up to ask for help with an unspecified *something* that required him to leave town for *a few days*.

If she didn't know better, she'd think that Julian was trying to put some distance between them.

And maybe she didn't know better.

They'd been together only a few weeks, and while they'd spent a lot of hours together in those weeks, it still wasn't a lot of time in the overall scheme of things.

Maybe there wasn't any mysterious errand and he had plans to hook up with another woman.

She immediately felt guilty for letting such a thought cross her mind, because Julian had proven to her, over and over again, that he was nothing like her ex-husband.

Still, it was possible that he'd changed his mind about what he wanted. That when he'd taken some time to think about their relationship, he'd realized it had gotten too real too fast.

After all, he was a single man who'd just bought his own ranch and she was a divorced mom of a four-year-old and a three-month-old foster child. There were days that, if she didn't love Emery and Jay to bits, she might think about running away, too.

Except that theory didn't jibe with what she knew about Julian, either. Since New Year's Eve, he'd been there for her and her kids. And not just for the fun stuff, either. In the short period of time that they'd been together, he'd seen that her life wasn't all Candy Land and story time snuggles. He'd borne witness to broken appliances and sick kids and stinky diapers. And he hadn't flinched at any of it.

Was it any wonder that she'd fallen in love with him?

She sank into her chair behind the counter, the realization hitting like a sucker punch to her gut.

*She loved Julian.*

Because apparently not wanting to fall in love didn't stop it from happening.

THEY SPENT THE night at the only roadside motel in the tiny dot on the map known as Gray Horse, sleeping in matching twin beds that were quite possibly as old as the ancient motel.

Julian did not have a good night's sleep.

But maybe it wasn't entirely the fault of the bed.

Maybe it was thoughts of Ruby that had kept him awake.

His mom had always said he led with his heart, as if that was a good thing. But he suspected that leading with his heart in his relationship with Ruby had scared her off.

He glanced at his phone, hoping for another message and experiencing a quick pang of disappointment that there was nothing new. The last communication from her was the text she'd sent the day before.

Enjoy your time with your uncle.

Well, he hadn't expected a string of heart emojis or a row of hugs and kisses, but something a little more personal would have been nice.

Was she annoyed that he'd gone?

But why would she be?

She was the one who said she needed time and space, and he was giving it to her.

"This isn't the right place."

Stanley's abrupt announcement interrupted Julian's musings.

"What is the right place?" he asked.

"I don't know," his uncle admitted.

It had occurred to Julian that *Tío* might not be in control of all his faculties, but notwithstanding his advanced age, he seemed lucid enough. Disregarding the fact that he was relying on dreams and sketches as some sort of mystical compass that he believed would lead him to his AWOL bride, of course.

They decided to stop at the little café beside the motel for breakfast before continuing their journey.

"Where to next?" Julian asked, as his uncle studied a map of Montana.

"Pony Crossing."

"You're just picking random towns with horse names, aren't you?"

"Dorothea's sketch of that horse means something."

"Maybe it means that Winona is somewhere near horses— which narrows our search down to…most of the Western states," Julian noted.

"Well, I know she's not in Oregon," Stanley said.

"And how can you be certain that she's not in the one place that you have actual evidence suggesting otherwise?"

"The postmark's a red heron."

"You mean a red herring?"

His uncle waved a hand dismissively. "Whatever."

Julian swallowed another mouthful of coffee, desperate for the caffeine to kick-start his sluggish brain.

In the light of a new day, he found himself questioning his willingness to accompany Stanley on this search. But *Tío*'s enthusiasm had been infectious, his determination inspiring, and maybe Julian had been feeling a little bit hurt by the realization that while he was preparing to go all in with his relationship with Ruby, she was pulling back.

"You're eager to get home," *Tío* guessed now.

He was, and yet—

"There's nothing I need to rush back for," he said, wishing it wasn't true.

"Not even the special lady in your life?"

"She can manage just fine without me."

"Is that what's bothering you?"

"I'm not bothered."

"You're definitely bothered."

Julian suspected his clenched jaw only supported his uncle's conclusion.

"Sometimes it helps to talk things through," Stanley said.

"If I wanted to talk, I would," Julian assured him.

"Just one more reason I wish Winona was here. You wouldn't have to tell her what was wrong, she'd know."

"Okay, fine. I'm bothered," Julian said. "I wish she needed me, but she doesn't. She's made that perfectly clear."

"But does she want you?" *Tío* asked.

"What?"

"It seems to me that it's more important to be wanted. To be chosen."

Something to think about, Julian mused, before shifting his attention back to his uncle. It was obvious that the old man was hurting, and he feared that Stanley would experience more heartache before this journey was over.

"Maybe we should go home, *Tío*," he suggested gently.

The old man's jaw set. "Not without Winona."

So Julian bit his tongue to hold back any further arguments.

Because he knew as well as anyone that love was sometimes stronger than reason.

## CHAPTER TWENTY

"Is Unca Julian coming tonight?" Emery asked, gliding the soapy sponge over Jay's round belly.

"Not tonight," Ruby said. "He had to go out of town."

"Will he come tomorrow?"

"I don't know. He said he was going to be busy for a few days."

Emery pouted.

"Don't get soap in his eyes," Ruby cautioned, attempting to refocus her daughter's attention on the task at hand while her own mind wandered.

She should have anticipated this.

She should have been careful.

Emery hadn't seen much of her dad since the divorce, and it was a source of continued frustration for Ruby that he rarely chose to exercise his visitation rights.

She helped rinse the soap off the baby, then lifted him out of the infant bath and into a soft hooded towel. Emy helped pat him dry, and it pleased Ruby to see how gentle her daughter was with Jay.

As she guided Emery through diapering and dressing the baby, her thoughts drifted again.

The last time Emery had seen her dad was her birthday in September. Ruby wanted to give Owen credit for remembering the day his daughter was born, but she suspected his mother had reminded him of the date. Caroline had probably bought and wrapped the gift that he brought for the birthday girl, too.

But he'd stayed only long enough to watch her open her present and accept the hug and thanks she gave him, then he was gone.

Sadly, his daughter was unfazed by his departure.

Or maybe she'd just been excited about the cake.

And then Owen hadn't even made an appearance over the Christmas holidays, because he'd been on a beach somewhere with his latest companion. He'd sent a bag of gifts, though. Or maybe it was more accurate to say that a bag of gifts had shown up for Emery with his name on the tags.

In any event, there wasn't much Ruby could do to make her ex-husband want to be a better dad. All she could do was temper Emery's expectations in an effort to lessen her disappointments.

But she hadn't done the same thing regarding Julian. And over the past three-and-a-half weeks, he'd been an almost daily presence in all of their lives.

He'd shared cooking and cleanup duties with Ruby. He'd played games with and read bedtime stories to Emy. He'd prepared bottles for Jay and even changed a few diapers. In short, he'd been a part of their family.

It was hardly surprising that Emery was disappointed to learn that she wasn't going to see him tonight.

And it was Ruby's fault.

She shouldn't have let her daughter get attached to someone else who might disappear from her life—as Julian had apparently done.

And as Jay would eventually do, too.

As much as Ruby hated to admit it, she might have made a mistake when she agreed to take the baby. Not because she didn't love him, but because she *did*—and she knew that Emery did, too. She also knew that their world was going to be left with a very big hole in it if his birth mother was found or another relative came forward or even if Family Services decided to find another—more permanent—placement for him.

Would they consider her application for adoption if she submitted one? Or would she face all the same barriers that she'd had to overcome to be approved as a foster parent?

Ms. Townsend had noted that the baby had bonded with Ruby—surely that had to count for something. Surely a judge would see that he was part of their family and let them stay together.

When her daughter had started preschool, her family consisted of two people—Mommy and Emery. Since returning to school after the holidays, her drawings reflected an expanded family that included baby Jay. And a dog, because Emy was adamant that she wanted a dog. (Though sometimes the dog had a horn in the middle of its head, making Ruby suspect that her daughter really wanted a unicorn.)

And though Ruby sometimes had a hard time saying no to her daughter, there was no way they could take on the responsibility of a dog right now.

Maybe if Julian—

No, she severed the thought before it had a chance to completely form.

She might not have been able to hold herself back from falling in love with him, but that didn't mean she had to depend on him for anything.

And after Emery and Jay were settled for the night (Emy seeking comfort from her thumb again), Ruby crawled under the covers of her own bed and deliberately stretched out in the middle of the mattress, as if that might somehow prove that she didn't need or want the complication of a man in her life.

But she couldn't deny that she missed him.

JULIAN HAD TOLD his boss that he needed a few days to deal with a family situation. Possibly a week, at the most. But he really didn't expect that they'd be gone that long, certain Stanley would recognize the futility of his search before then.

But when he woke up on day three in another crappy motel room in another obscure town—this one called Pinto Trail—his uncle was just as determined as ever to forge ahead.

"We're getting closer," Stanley said. "I can feel it."

So they forged ahead to… Mustang Pass.

And Julian resisted the urge to point out that, after three days of driving, they were now within fifteen miles of the starting point of their journey.

Beside the wooden sign that welcomed them to Mustang Pass was a life-size sculpture of the town's namesake standing on its hind legs, its forelegs pawing in the air.

*Tío* straightened up in his seat when they passed the sign, practically vibrating with excitement.

"Is that a restaurant up ahead?" Stanley asked, as Julian turned onto Main Street.

"Looks like," he agreed. "Do you want to stop for lunch?"

It was barely 11:00 a.m., but they'd been on the road for several hours already and Julian wouldn't mind at least stretching his legs.

"I could eat," Stanley said.

He hoped it was true. Over the past few days, he'd noticed that his uncle's appetite was severely diminished. Perhaps unsurprising, considering everything the old man was going through, but still worrisome.

He pulled into a vacant parking spot on the street, in front of the diner with a neon sign identifying it as the Main Street Grill.

"I need to show you something," *Tío* said to Julian, when the server whose name tag identified her as Denise had taken their orders.

Stanley opened the sketchbook he'd dug out of his duffel bag and thumbed through the pages until he found a drawing of a horse. "Look. It's a picture of the horse sculpture that we just passed. Dorothea drew this picture." His uncle stabbed at the page with his finger. "This proves we're in the right place."

Julian didn't think the sketch was proof of anything, though he thought it was possible that Winona's daughter had driven through Mustang Pass at some time in her life and noticed the statue.

It was equally possible that she'd been sketching the Ferrari logo, though he knew better than to point out that possibility to his uncle.

He smiled his thanks at Denise when she delivered his hot

roast beef sandwich with fries and extra gravy. Stanley had opted for a double bacon cheeseburger with onion rings.

"And this house," *Tío* said, flipping to another page in the sketchbook, "is in Mustang Pass. I'm sure of it."

Julian sipped his Coke.

"That house could be anywhere," he felt compelled to point out.

*Or nowhere*, he thought.

"The house is here," Stanley insisted. "Winona's here."

Denise returned to the table with a pot of coffee to refill his uncle's mug. As she poured, her attention snagged on the sketchbook open on the table.

"Are you friends of Victor's?" she asked.

"Victor?"

She gestured toward the image on the page. "That looks just like his place on Bridle Drive."

"I told you it was here," Stanley crowed triumphantly.

"How well do you know... Victor?" Julian asked the server, trying not to let on that they didn't know the guy at all.

"Not very," she admitted. "But I've only lived in Mustang Pass a few years, and he was something of a hermit when I first moved to town. Rumor has it that his wife walked out on him and broke his heart, but he's been a changed man since they reconciled a few months back.

"They come in together sometimes for a meal. They really are an adorable couple. He's fond of the fish and chips, and she usually gets the daily special, whatever that might be."

"The woman who comes in with him—would you happen to know her name?" Stanley asked.

Denise pursed her lips, trying to remember. "Winifred, maybe. Or something like that. No—Winnie," she decided. "I've definitely heard him call her Winnie."

Stanley sent his nephew a pointed look.

"It could be a coincidence," Julian cautioned, when the server moved on.

*"Tonterías."*

"Maybe it is BS," he acknowledged. "But if this woman who

comes in here with Victor is Winona, she's obviously not being held against her will."

"Nothing is obvious and not everything is as it seems," his uncle said stubbornly.

"Have you ever heard her mention someone named Victor?" Julian asked, trying a different tack.

"Never. And there's no way she met some other guy the morning of our wedding and ran off to marry him instead."

"I'm just asking you to consider the possibility that the situation isn't going to lead to the happy ending you're hoping for."

"Beginning," Stanley said.

"Huh?"

"Winona and me agreed that when we got married, it wasn't a happy ending but a happy beginning."

"I DON'T WANNA go to school today," Emery said, when Ruby set her breakfast on the table in front of her.

Ruby held back a sigh as she refilled her coffee. "Why are you doing this? You love school. And it's Wednesday, so you'll have story time and craft circles and Farmer Brown is visiting with Wilbur the Pig today."

The mention of the pig seemed like it might change Emy's mind, but then she shook her head stubbornly. "I wanna stay home today."

"Well, you can't, because I have to go to work."

"I can go to work with you."

"You would be bored to tears," Ruby said.

"Jay goes to work with you," Em pointed out.

"Jay eats and sleeps and poops," she reminded her daughter.

That got a giggle, then Emery's expression grew serious again. "Will you pick me up from school?"

"Mimi will pick you up from school and then I'll pick you up from Mimi's, like I always do."

"You won't go away?"

"Go away?" she echoed, baffled. "Where would I go?"

The little girl poked at her waffle with her fork. "Where did Unca Julian go?"

"Oh, honey." She set her mug on the counter and sat beside her daughter. "Is that what this is about? Are you missing Uncle Julian?"

Emery nodded. "Where did he go?" she asked again.

"I don't know," she admitted.

"Is he coming back?"

"Of course, he's coming back."

She felt confident in that assertion, because Julian's whole family was in Tenacity. Whether or not he came back to her and Emery and Jay was the unknown, and she wasn't going to make false promises to her daughter in that regard.

"But it might be that when he comes back, he doesn't hang around here as much as he did before."

"Why? Doesn't he like me anymore?"

"Honey, I promise that Uncle Julian likes you just as much as he always did. But sometimes, people get busy with their own lives and they don't have as much time to do the things they used to—or hang out with the people they used to hang out with."

"That's what you say about Daddy," Emery pointed out. "That he doesn't come see me cuz he's busy."

*Busted.*

"Because he *is* busy," she said.

He was also a selfish, self-centered jackass, but she kept that to herself. As Julian had noted, Emery would figure it out on her own soon enough.

"He has to work a lot of hours at the insurance company with Papa," Ruby reminded her daughter gently.

"Papa has time for me."

*Busted again.*

Apparently it was going to be one of those days.

"BRIDLE DRIVE," STANLEY reminded his nephew, as Julian fastened his belt. "She said the house was on Bridle Drive."

"I heard what she said," he assured his uncle.

"So why aren't you punching it into your map thingy?"

"Because we need to have a plan before we go racing off to confront a stranger."

"The plan is to get Winona back."

*"Tío,"* Julian said, in that patient tone that was starting to

drive Stanley crazy. "I think we should contact the local sheriff's department and ask them to check out Victor."

"I don't need to be patted on the head by any more useless deputies. I know Winona's here, in Mustang Pass."

So Julian punched the street name into his navigation app, and when the route directions loaded, he drove.

And in three minutes, he was turning onto Bridle Drive.

"Look!" Stanley pointed—shoving his hand right in front of Julian's face as he did so. "That's the house from the drawing."

Julian ducked his chin to peer around his uncle's arm and pulled his vehicle over to the curb on the opposite side of the road. The house on which his uncle was fixated did bear an uncanny likeness to Dorothea's sketch—right down to the boxwood hedges in the front yard and the ancient pickup truck in the driveway.

Stanley was already unbuckling his belt.

"*Tío, esperar.* Just hold on a second," Julian cautioned.

"I've been holding on for months," his uncle protested. "My fiancée is in that house, and I don't intend to wait another minute to see her."

"We can't just go barging in there without—"

But he was talking to air, because *Tío* Stanley was already halfway across the street.

Cursing under his breath, Julian pushed open his door and hurried after him.

## CHAPTER TWENTY-ONE

*Mustang Pass, Montana*

STANLEY POUNDED ON the door, his fist knocking on the wood in rapid concert with his heart against his ribs.

Dorothea hadn't sketched a picture of Victor, so he had no idea what to expect. When the door opened, he found himself face-to-face with a man of similar age, a couple of inches shorter with a slighter build. His salt-and-pepper hair was short, his bushy white eyebrows drawn together over pale blue eyes.

"Are you Victor?"

Those pale eyes narrowed suspiciously. "Yeah, but unless you've got Thin Mints, whatever you're selling, we're not buying," he said gruffly.

"I'm not selling anything," Stanley told him. "I'm here for Winona."

Something that might have been fear flickered in the other man's eyes before he squared his shoulders and lifted his chin. "Then you're obviously lost."

He attempted to push the door shut, but Stanley had shoved his foot in the opening.

"Winona!"

Victor threw his weight at the door.

It didn't budge.

"Winona!"

"If you don't get off my property right now, I'm going to call the sheriff's office," Victor warned.

"Goodness, Victor—what is all this yelling?"

When Stanley saw the house that matched Dorothea's sketch, he'd desperately wanted to believe that Winona was there. But apparently there had still been a smidgeon of doubt in his mind, because hearing her voice absolutely staggered him.

"Winona." He pushed past the other man to make his way to her, his gaze drinking her in like a parched man would a glass of water, as his nephew, having finally caught up with him, stepped over the threshold.

Stanley reached for Winona's hands and realized his own were shaking.

"Winona," he said again. "My Winona." He lifted her hands to his lips, kissing each one in turn. "I have missed you so much."

She looked at him warily as she withdrew her hands from his grasp, then turned to the man who'd taken up position beside her. "Who is this man, Victor? Do we know him?"

"Wait a minute," Julian said, stepping forward. "Are you saying that you don't recognize *Tío* Stanley?"

"Should I?"

Stanley exchanged a worried look with his nephew.

"I thought amnesia was something that only happened in books and movies," Julian remarked.

"The doctor said it was induced by traumatic brain injury, caused by my fall," Winona said.

"Do you remember the fall?" Stanley asked gently.

She shook her head. "Not the fall or anything that came before." Then her gaze narrowed. "Did he say your name's Stanley?"

"Yes. Stanley Sanchez."

*"I'm sorry, Stanley,"* she said, the words barely more than a whisper from her lips.

He frowned. "Why are you sorry?"

"I… I don't know," she admitted. "I've tried so hard to remember, but the most I've been able to come up with are occasional snippets of conversations and odd dreams. But I do remember thinking, *I'm sorry, Stanley.*"

"Maybe she's sorry that she left you to be with me," Victor said.

Stanley ignored the other man to take Winona's hands again. "Your name is Winona Cobbs and you're my fiancée."

"Fiancée?" she echoed uncertainly.

"We planned to get married in July, but then you went missing."

"I don't understand... Why would I plan to marry you when I'm already married to Victor?"

His blood ran cold. "You *married* this guy? When *in hell* did that happen?"

She turned to Victor again. "How long have we been married?"

"Well." The other man cleared his throat. "The truth is, we're not actually, officially, married."

Stanley was relieved, but Winona looked stunned.

"What do you mean—we're not married?" she demanded. "There's a picture from our wedding on my bedside table."

Stanley's gaze narrowed.

"Photoshop," Julian guessed.

Victor flushed guiltily.

"I don't understand," Winona said. "What's going on here, Victor?"

"What's going on is that these gentlemen are leaving." Victor opened the door again and gestured with a flourish. "And if they don't, I'm going to have them arrested for trespassing."

"Actually, I think calling the sheriff might be a good idea," Julian said, pulling his phone out of his pocket to do just that.

"The sheriff," Winona echoed, obviously flustered.

"Please, go," Victor said. "You're upsetting my wife."

"You mean your fake wife," Stanley said. "Who's actually my real fiancée."

"This is my fault." Winona rubbed her temples. "If only I could remember."

"It's not your fault," Stanley said gently. "And your memories aren't lost forever."

"How can you know?"

"Because your conscious mind might not remember me, but your heart does. And it reached out to your daughter and your great-grandson so that I would come find you."

"I have...a daughter?"

He nodded.

"Beatrix?"

"That was the name you gave her," he confirmed. "Her adoptive parents named her Dorothea. Some people call her Daisy."

"I have a daughter," she said again, not a question this time.

"You have a daughter, a granddaughter, a great-granddaughter, great-grandson and the next generation is well under way."

Her eyes filled with tears. "And I've forgotten every one of them."

"No," Stanley said. "You haven't forgotten. You just need some time to remember."

"I KNOW THIS isn't quite what you imagined for your reunion," Julian said to his uncle, while they waited for the sheriff's deputies to arrive. "And I'm sorry."

"I feel...gutted," *Tío* admitted. "I was sure she'd rush into my arms, as overjoyed to see me as I was to see her." He shook his head, his expression bleak. "She doesn't even remember me."

"She will. As you said, she just needs time."

"It's been more than five months."

"Five months during which she lived with a stranger in unfamiliar surroundings, listening to lies about her past and her present," Julian pointed out. "You can't really be surprised that none of that triggered her memories."

"No," he agreed. "But how much longer are we supposed to go on like this? How much longer am I supposed to wait?"

"Do you love her?"

"You know I do."

"So maybe the real question is—how long are you willing to wait for the woman you love?"

"Forever," Stanley admitted.

Julian nodded. If this trip to Mustang Pass with his uncle

had taught him nothing else, it had at least taught him to savor every minute with the ones you loved.

For him, that included his parents and brothers and sisters, his aunts, uncles and cousins—his whole family. And when he thought of his future, he knew without a shadow of a doubt that he wanted Ruby and Emery and Jay to be part of his family, too.

Now he just needed to convince Ruby that she wanted the same thing—but he suspected that might be a bigger challenge than finding his uncle's missing bride had been.

DEPUTY BURROWS AND Deputy Hernandez decided to separate Victor and Winona to get independent statements from each. To the surprise of Deputy Burrows, Victor indicated that he wanted to make his statement in front of the visitors to his home, certain he could make them understand his motives and his actions.

So now Victor and the deputy were seated on one side of the dining room table, with Stanley and Julian across from them.

"For the protection of everyone here, I'm going to record this interview," Deputy Burrows said, setting his phone in the center of the table. "For the record, we are at the home of Victor Thompson at 490 Bridle Drive in Mustang Pass, our attendance at the residence having been requested by Julian Sanchez, also present with his uncle, Stanley Sanchez. The senior Mr. Sanchez claims to be the fiancé of Winona Cobbs, a resident of Bronco, Montana, who was reported missing the day of her July wedding. He further alleges that the woman Mr. Thompson has been passing off as his wife is the same Winona Cobbs.

"Mr. Thompson's supposed wife does not appear to have any identification, but she has consented to a search of the premises to see if any might turn up. At this time, myself and Deputy Hernandez are proceeding on the assumption that the female resident of this address is, in fact, Winona Cobbs, based on her resemblance to photos of the missing woman provided to our office by the Bronco authorities, official confirmation pending fingerprint or DNA match.

"In the meantime, Mr. Thompson has indicated a willingness to make a statement. Though we are at the early stages of the investigation and don't know if any charges might be warranted, he has been advised of his Miranda rights and waived both his right to remain silent and his right to consult with an attorney."

Deputy Burrows then nodded to Victor. "Go ahead, Mr. Thompson."

"Okay, well, first I should probably confirm that my Winnie is Winona Cobbs. I was a loyal reader and big fan of her advice column, 'Wisdom by Winona.' I liked her spunky style and no-nonsense advice. So when my wife and I started having trouble in our marriage, I decided to write to Winona.

"She printed my letter, and I followed her advice. I complimented Marlene's hair and her clothes and her cooking—even when it was awful. But Marlene said six months of compliments didn't make up for thirty-six years of neglect, and she packed her bags and walked out."

"None of which explains how we've ended up here today," Julian noted.

"In the summer, I saw a notice in the paper about Winona's upcoming wedding," Victor explained. "And the closer it got to the date, the madder I got thinking that the woman who destroyed my marriage was planning her own happily ever after."

"A few lines of advice printed in a newspaper isn't to blame for the breakdown of your marriage," Stanley said.

"Anyway, it's not as if I planned to kidnap her. I just wanted to confront her—to let her know that she wasn't so wise after all.

"So the day of the wedding, I was waiting for Winona outside her house. I just wanted to talk to her, so I grabbed her arm, to make her listen. But she wrenched her arm free and lost her balance. As she fell, she hit her head on the porch railing... I didn't think she hit it too hard, but there was a lot of blood." He shuddered at the memory. "So much blood."

The deputy interrupted at that point to remind Victor of his rights, but he ignored the warning.

"She was just lying there," Victor continued. "Crumpled in a heap on the step, and I thought... I thought she was...dead."

"So why didn't you immediately call nine-one-one?" Stanley demanded.

"Because I was afraid I might have been arrested—"

"*Would* have been arrested," Stanley interjected. "Because you assaulted my fiancée."

"I only wanted to talk to her."

"What happened next?" Julian asked.

"Well, I picked her up and put her in my truck. I was sure no one would believe her death was an accident, so I decided to get rid of her body somewhere far away. But I hadn't been driving for very long when she started to moan. Scared me so badly I nearly ran my truck right off the road.

"I was relieved, obviously, to know she wasn't dead. But I was scared, too, because I knew I'd be in trouble for driving away with her."

"It's called kidnapping," Stanley snapped.

"I didn't mean to kidnap her," Victor insisted.

"What happened when you realized Winona wasn't dead?" Julian prompted.

"Well, I asked her how she was feeling, and she said her head hurt. I told her that she had a nasty fall—cuz that's the truth—and she told me that she didn't remember. I asked her what she did remember, and she didn't seem to know how to answer. I asked her simple questions—like her name and date of birth and where she lived—and she couldn't answer any of them. That's when I realized she had amnesia—just like you see in the movies."

"And that's when you decided to take advantage of her loss of memory to create your own history for her."

"I could hardly tell her the truth, not without causing a whole lot of trouble for myself," Victor said sheepishly.

"How about the worry and heartache that you caused her family? And me?" Stanley demanded.

"I didn't want anyone to worry. That's why I wrote the letter to Dorothea."

"So it was you who wrote the letter," Stanley said, with a pointed look at his nephew.

"I had her copy a passage out of a book—told her that the doctor suggested it would be a good exercise for her mind. Then I picked out the words that I needed and traced them onto a new page."

"In that letter, you said that she was fine. But she was knocked unconscious and lost her memory."

"I treated her good," Victor insisted.

"But why would you?" Julian wondered aloud.

His uncle scowled at him. "What kind of question is that?"

He shrugged. "I'm just wondering why a man who apparently blamed Winona for everything that went wrong in his life would want to set up house with her."

"When we first came back to Tenacity, I was still angry with her," Victor admitted. "But I figured that if she believed she was my wife, I could get her to cook and clean and do all the other things a wife is supposed to do."

"And you blame Winona for the fact that your wife left you?" Stanley muttered.

"But she was really weak at first," Victor continued. "So I had to take care of her before she could take care of me. And I realized that I liked taking care of her. That it felt good to be needed."

"He took good care of me," Winona said, as she reentered the room. "Aside from the fact that everything he told me about my life was a lie. He even took me shopping for new clothes, because someone broke in and stole the entire contents of my dressers and my closet." She frowned now. "But I suspect that was a lie, too."

Victor didn't deny it.

"I'm guessing he picked out your clothes, too," Stanley said. "Because neutral colors are not your style."

"They're not?"

"No," he confirmed. "And where is your jewelry?"

"Right here," Deputy Hernandez said, holding up an evidence bag.

"Is there an engagement ring in there?" Stanley asked. "A white gold band with a round amethyst surrounded by diamonds."

Hernandez nodded. "There is. But I can't give it back to you right now. It's evidence."

"Let him have it," Burrows decided. "This fool here just made a full confession—on tape—so I don't think we're going to need it to get a conviction at trial. And if we do, we'll just subpoena them to come back."

"What's going to happen to Victor?" Winona asked, sounding worried.

"We'll take him to the sheriff's office where he'll be held until formal charges are brought."

"Good," Stanley said.

"But fair warning," Burrows continued. "I suspect the local magistrate is going to order a fitness hearing to determine if he's competent to stand trial."

"What happens if he's not competent?" Stanley wanted to know.

"Then he'll be detained in an appropriate psychiatric facility."

"So long as he stays the hell away from Winona."

She looked at Stanley then, a pleat between her brows. "You really do love me, don't you?"

"With my whole heart," he told her.

"Do I love you?"

"I hope so, considering that you'd planned to marry me before you were kidnapped by Victor."

"Was it going to be a big wedding?"

"Big enough."

"Did I have a fancy dress?"

"I can't say for certain, because you refused to let me see it before the wedding, but I imagine it was fancy enough. You said you'd waited more than ninety years to finally be a bride and you were going to do it right."

"I think I've always wanted to get married, but I never thought I'd fall in love again."

"Again?" He jumped on that single word, as if it proved she had some memories of her past.

Winona frowned. "I think I fell in love when I was very young—hardly more than a girl."

"That's right," he said. "You were seventeen."

She closed her eyes for a minute. "Josiah," she finally said. "He was so handsome. So charming."

Stanley felt as if his heart was breaking all over again.

How was it that she could remember the man she'd loved almost eighty years earlier and not remember him?

Then she opened her eyes again and smiled. "But I think you're even more handsome."

"Do you?" he asked, her kind words a balm to his battered heart.

"Here's the ring," Hernandez said, holding it out to Stanley.

"Oh, that's so pretty," Winona said. "And unique."

"Just like you."

Her cheeks flushed. "You are a charmer, aren't you?"

"I know you don't remember me yet, but you let me put this ring on your finger once before and I'm hoping you'll accept it again—if only for safekeeping."

"I guess that would be okay," she agreed, holding out her left hand.

Stanley gently slid the ring onto her third finger.

But as he pushed the band over her knuckle, she made a soft sound, almost of distress, and looked at him with her blue eyes wide and shimmering with tears.

"Did I hurt you?" he asked, immediately concerned.

"No." Winona shook her head. "You didn't hurt me, Stanley." She lifted her hand then to touch his cheek. "I remember."

"You remember...*me*?"

"I remember *everything*," she said softly, her voice thick with emotion. "It's as if the little bits and pieces that were floating around in my mind finally came together to make my memories." She glanced at the ring again. "We got this at an antique sale. You found it inside an old teapot—a hidden treasure, you said."

"That's right," he confirmed, his heart swelling with joy.

"I remember our first date. We met at that little hole-in-the-wall bar in the valley called—" her brow furrowed as she searched for the name "—Doug's."

He gave her an encouraging nod.

"You were there with your nephew—Felix." She laughed softly. "And we stranded him at the bar when we left with the keys."

Her smile faded and her brow furrowed. "Okay, maybe I don't

remember everything," she acknowledged. "But it's starting to come back. And most important, I remember how much you love me—and how much I love you."

His throat was tight. His eyes misty.

He gently removed her hand from his cheek and brought it to his lips. *"Mi corazón."*

"*My* heart," she echoed, and smiled.

# *CHAPTER TWENTY-TWO*

*Tenacity, Montana*

RUBY WAS RELIEVED to note that Emery was in a much better
mood when she picked her up from Mimi's. And throughout
the ride home, her daughter chatted happily about the events
of her day—the highlight of which was the appearance of Wilbur the Pig.

"And one of the craft circles was finger painting and I made
a picture of my family," Emery said.

"Did you bring it home so I can put it on the fridge?"

"Uh-huh." She unzipped her backpack and pulled out the
picture.

Of course, at this early stage in her artistic development, the
people in Emery's drawings and paintings weren't much more
than round heads with arms and legs sticking out of them. This
time, she'd put four people in the picture.

"You and me and Unca Julian and Jay," Emery said, pointing to each one in turn.

"And a puppy?" Ruby guessed.

Em nodded.

When they got home, Ruby dutifully stuck the picture to the
refrigerator with a magnet advertising Pete's Pizza.

"How about stir-fry for dinner tonight?"

"Can we have pa'sghetti?" Emery asked hopefully.

She'd already taken the chicken out of the freezer but decided it would keep.

It had been a challenging day from the start, and though Emery seemed to have bounced back, Ruby decided that if her daughter wanted spaghetti, she was going to make spaghetti.

After dinner they played three games of Candy Land, then she let Emery have bubbles in her bath. During story time, she injected extra enthusiasm into the character voices, determined to make her daughter forget that she liked story time with Uncle Julian best.

"Sweet dreams, Emy." She kissed her forehead, inhaling the familiar scent of baby shampoo and little girl. "I love you."

Emery yawned. "I love you, too, Mommy."

And Ruby knew that she had everything she needed right here.

But she still missed Julian.

WHEN JULIAN FINALLY arrived back at his parents' house in Tenacity, where Stanley suggested he and Winona spend the night before making the longer journey home to Bronco, he discovered that news of the missing bride's rescue had preceded their arrival. Local TV vans, camera crews, reporters and media bloggers lined the path from the driveway all the way to the front door.

Stanley gallantly held them off and ushered his fiancée into a house overflowing with Sanchezes and all of Winona's family, too.

"Looks like somebody's having a party and didn't invite us," Winona remarked.

"Apologies for the oversight," Nicole said, giving *Tío*'s bride-to-be a warm hug. "Until a few hours ago, we didn't know where to send the invitation."

"Well, I'm glad I made it," Winona said. "Because I'm ready to celebrate. Today is the day I got my life back." She looked at the man by her side then and smiled. "My life and my love."

"But how did you all get here so fast?" Stanley wanted to know.

"Julian called his mom to tell her that you'd found Winona,

and she promptly called Denise in Bronco, and then the two of them burned up the phone lines spreading the news and, of course, everyone wanted to be here to welcome her home."

Technically, Tenacity wasn't her home—at least not where she lived. But she'd lived in a lot of different places in her ninety-seven years, and one of the things she'd learned was that home was more about the people than the place.

And all these people here were her family.

She was home.

But even in a house filled with love and laughter, she sensed that something—or maybe someone—was missing.

She made her way through the crowd until she found Julian in the kitchen, mixing up another pitcher of sangria.

"I thought you'd disappeared," she said. "I haven't seen you since we got back."

"It's easy to get lost in this crowd," he noted.

"Well, I've found you now, and I'm glad, because I wanted to thank you for helping Stanley find me."

"All I did was drive," Julian said. "*Tío* did the rest. With help from your daughter and great-grandson, as I understand it."

"He couldn't have done it without you," she insisted. "You were an important part of his journey."

He looked wary. "I was glad to help."

"And you called your family…"

"We weren't sure everyone would be able to make it on such short notice, but they did. Because they know how important you are to *Tío*, and that means you're important to all of us."

"I am humbled and overwhelmed by the love in this house," she said. "But not everyone is here."

He frowned as he scanned the crowd. "Who's missing?"

"The one who holds your heart."

"Ah, well." He looked at his great-uncle's fiancée with new respect—and perhaps a little bit of wariness. Because even if the old woman really was a psychic, that didn't mean he wanted her looking too deeply into his mind. Or his heart.

"Or perhaps I should say the *ones* who hold your heart," Winona mused thoughtfully. "She has a child? Children?"

He nodded, because it was true that Ruby and Emery and Jay all held his heart.

But did he hold any of theirs?

Or had the last few days that they'd been apart reminded Ruby that she could manage just fine without him?

Winona touched a hand to his arm. "They've missed you as much as you've missed them."

"I'm not sure that's possible."

"Trust your heart," she urged. "And hers."

He nodded, not certain how else to respond to her unnerving—but hopefully accurate—insights.

"You'll bring them to the wedding?" Winona prompted.

"Just say when."

"Soon," she promised. "Very soon."

Julian watched as she made her way back to her fiancé, who then escorted her to the buffet table and filled a plate with tamales for her.

"It was a good thing you did for *Tío* Stanley," Nicole said, when she found her son in the kitchen.

His smile was wry. "A few days ago, you said it was a wild goose chase."

She shrugged. "But you bagged the goose."

He chuckled. "Don't let Winona hear you call her a goose."

His mom peered past him to the living room, where the reunited lovebirds were seated side by side, their hands entwined.

"He really does love her," she murmured.

"Did you doubt it?"

"No," she said. "But when I believed she'd willingly left him at the altar, I wished it wasn't true."

"*Tío* Stanley said he knew, the first time he met Winona, that she was the woman he'd love for the rest of his life."

"Your dad said the exact same thing about me," she noted. "The Sanchezes are a romantic lot."

"So maybe it won't surprise you to hear that Ruby's the one for me. And that I've known it since the day I met her."

"You mean the day your friend introduced you to his girlfriend?"

"The very same," he confirmed. "I knew it in my heart—

and only a few weeks later, my heart ached, because I knew she was going to marry Owen."

"And so you waited."

"I couldn't do anything else," he said simply.

She took his face in her hands and drew it down to press her lips to his forehead. "Go get your girl. Be happy."

"That's my plan."

But there was one more thing that he needed to do first.

"DID YOU SEE the news?" Chrissy asked, when she stopped by the reception desk at Tenacity Inn on Thursday morning.

Ruby held up the newspaper that she'd been perusing while sipping her coffee. "I've got it right here."

"That's old news."

"Well, the *Tenacity Tribune* only publishes once a week."

"Which is why people who want to know what's going on get the details online. Or on TV."

"You know I don't watch the news when Emery's around—she doesn't need to know about all the bad stuff that goes on in the world."

"Well, if you'd watched it last night, you might have seen your boyfriend on TV."

"My... Do you mean Julian?"

Her friend's brows lifted. "How many boyfriends do you have?"

She didn't know how to answer that.

Definitely no more than one, but it was possible the number was now zero.

Because even if Julian had been her boyfriend prior to the Winter Carnival weekend, she didn't know that he was still, and she hadn't heard a word from him in three days.

"Tell me why Julian was on TV," she said to her friend.

"Do you remember hearing about that old woman from Bronco—the fortune teller—who went missing the day of her wedding last summer?"

Ruby nodded.

"Julian found her. Well, him and his uncle, who was the missing woman's fiancé."

"You're kidding."

"Nope."

"Where did they find her?"

"Mustang Pass," Chrissy said. "Can you believe she was so close all this time?"

"It doesn't take three days to get to Mustang Pass," she noted.

Her friend looked puzzled.

Ruby waved a hand. "Never mind."

"Anyway, it turns out the bride-to-be had *amnesia*. She completely forgot not only that she was planning to get married but even the identity of her groom."

"Sounds like the plot of a soap opera," Ruby mused.

"Complete with a hunky hero," Chrissy said with a wink, before she hurried off to check that the conference room was set up for lunch.

Although her friend had already given her the broad strokes of the story, when Chrissy was gone, Ruby opened a browser on the desktop computer to fill in the details.

So much for Julian's promise to be in touch as soon as he got back to town, Ruby mused, as she skimmed the online write-up. And she knew that he was back in town, because there were numerous photos and sound bites to prove it.

Obviously he'd been telling the truth when he said that he had something to do out of town, but not when he'd promised to be in touch as soon as he got back.

But that was okay, Ruby decided. Because she'd been the one to suggest that they take a step back. And if that step back and a few days apart had made him realize his feelings for her weren't as strong as he'd believed, well, that was something better discovered sooner rather than later.

It was even better that she hadn't told him that she loved him, too.

And maybe her heart ached to think that their relationship could be over already, but she would survive.

She'd gotten through the breakdown of her marriage; she had to believe she could get through this.

# CHAPTER TWENTY-THREE

"WHAT'S FOR SUPPER?" Emery asked.

"We literally just walked in the door," Ruby noted. "Are you really thinking about supper already?"

"I just wanna know what we're having."

"Chicken fingers."

Her daughter's expression brightened. "The kind like Julian makes?"

"No," Ruby said, as she buckled Jay into his high chair. "The kind that comes in the box from the grocery store."

"Oh." Em's disappointment was palpable.

"But I've got sweet potato fries to go with the chicken fingers. And ice cream for dessert."

"Pink ice cream?"

"Of course."

"With sprinkles?"

*Why not?* Ruby thought.

"Pink ice cream with lots and lots of sprinkles," she promised, putting some soft blocks on Jay's tray to keep him occupied while she prepared dinner. "And don't forget to take your lunchbox out of your backpack before you put it in the closet."

"Then can I watch TV?"

She glanced at her watch. "You can watch one episode of *Paw Patrol*."

"Yay!" Em clapped her hands together.

As she headed into the living room, a knock sounded at the front door.

"Someone's here," Emery announced.

"Let me get it," Ruby said, reminding her daughter of her cardinal safety rule.

"It's Unca Julian!" She bounced on the sofa cushion she was standing on to look out the front window. "He's back!"

Ruby took a deep breath to calm the butterflies suddenly winging around in her belly and smoothed a hand down the front of the dress she hadn't yet had a chance to change out of.

"Open the door, Mommy," Emery urged.

She opened the door, a carefully neutral expression on her face. "Hello, Julian."

He smiled, and her knees quivered. "Hello, Ruby."

He looked tired. She could see it in his eyes and the lines around his mouth, making her think the successful outcome of his trip hadn't been as effortless as the media reports implied.

"I saw you on TV at Mimi's!" Emery announced excitedly.

Which was news to Ruby. Her former mother-in-law was usually as careful as she when it came to protecting Emery from stuff like that, but obviously Caroline had figured the little girl would be interested, because it was about Julian.

"Did you?" he said.

"Apparently you're a local hero," Ruby remarked.

"My ten minutes of fame."

"I thought it was fifteen minutes of fame."

"That was pre–social media," he told her. "When people had attention spans longer than two hundred and eighty characters."

"Fair point," she acknowledged.

He waited a beat before asking, "Are you going to let me come in?"

She finally moved away from the door, carefully sidestepping her daughter, who was jumping up and down, practically dragging him over the threshold.

"I haven't seen you in days and days," Emery said to him. "Where'd you go, Unca Julian?"

"I had to go out of town with my uncle."

The little girl abruptly remembered that she'd been mad, because she fisted her hands on her hips. "You went away and didn't say goodbye."

"It was a last-minute trip," he explained. "And I knew I wasn't going to be gone for very long."

"It was *days* and *days*," she said again.

"It was longer than I expected," he acknowledged. "And I'm sorry for that."

"Mommy says I have to forgive someone when they say they're sorry, so I forgive you. But I'm still mad that you didn't say goodbye."

Julian set down the long cardboard tube in his hand to lift her up so they could continue the conversation eye-to-eye. "Would you stop being mad if I promise to never again leave without saying goodbye?"

"Maybe. If you pinky swear."

"Pinky swear," he said, linking his smallest digit with hers. "I also promise that, any time I go away, I will come back."

She seemed satisfied with this, because she nodded. "Okay."

Then she gave him a smacking kiss on the cheek and wriggled to be let down.

"Are you gonna stay for supper?" she asked, when her feet were on the ground again. "We're having chicken fingers and sweet potatoes and pink ice cream. With sprinkles."

"I'd like to stay," he said, with a questioning glance in Ruby's direction, "but I need to talk to your mom first, to make sure it's okay with her."

"It's okay, isn't it, Mommy?" Emery asked on his behalf.

Ruby narrowed her eyes on Julian as she spoke to her daughter. "Didn't you want to watch *Paw Patrol*, Em?"

"Oh, yeah," she suddenly remembered, skipping into the living room.

Julian held Ruby's gaze. "I'm getting the impression that you're not going to forgive me as easily as your daughter did."

"There's nothing to forgive," she said. "You don't need my permission to go out of town—or anywhere else."

"So why does it seem like you're mad?"

"Because I don't appreciate you making promises to my

daughter that you can't keep," she told him. "She's a little girl and she's counting on you to stick around—and maybe that's my fault. Maybe I should have limited the time she spent with you so that she didn't get too close, and I didn't, and that's on me.

"But you have no idea how hard the last few days have been. Every day, she asked about you, and every day, I struggled to answer her questions without giving her false hope."

"The last few days were hard on me, too," he said, taking a step toward her. "I missed you and Em and Jay like crazy."

She took a step back, preserving the distance between them. Because she knew that if she let him get too close, if she let him touch her, she'd forget that she was mad. In fact, she'd likely forget everything but how much she missed being held in his arms.

"But you're the one who left," she pointed out. "And your message said that you'd be in touch as soon as you got back."

"That's why I'm here."

"You got back yesterday."

His brows lifted. "Is that why you're giving me a hard time? Because I waited—" he glanced at his watch "—twenty-two hours before knocking on your door?"

She scowled. "It sounds ridiculous when you put it like that."

And maybe it *was* ridiculous, but she'd been hurt by his disappearing act, and she didn't know what to say or do—or even how to feel—now that he was standing in front of her, as if nothing had changed between them.

"I'm sorry I didn't come sooner, but there was something I needed to do before I could see you."

"You didn't even call."

"Because I missed you like crazy the whole time I was gone," he said again. "And I knew that if I heard your voice, there'd be no way that I could stay away."

The sincerity in his voice, in his gaze, chipped away at her lingering annoyance and knocked down the walls she'd tried to put up around her heart.

"No one said that you had to stay away."

And apparently he heard the softening in her tone, because his lips curved in a hopeful smile. "Did you miss me?"

*More than I ever could have imagined.*

Not that she had any intention of admitting it to Julian.

"You said there was something you needed to do before you could see me," she said instead.

"There was," he confirmed, reaching down to retrieve the cardboard tube he'd set aside earlier.

Her curiosity was immediately piqued. "What's that?"

"If you'll let me past the foyer, I'd be happy to show you."

He removed his boots and coat before making his way into the kitchen. When Jay spotted Julian, he dropped the block he'd been chewing on and gave him a gummy smile.

"Hey there, big guy," Julian said, returning the block to the baby, who immediately dropped it again.

He chuckled. "We'll play that game later," he promised, before popping the cap off the end of the tube he carried to withdraw the papers that were inside.

Blueprints, Ruby realized.

"Remember when I told you that I bought land to start my own ranch?" Julian asked her now.

"Of course." It was the night they'd had to cancel their date because Emery had strep throat. More important, it was the first time in all the years that her daughter had been alive that Ruby hadn't been alone in worrying about her little girl.

"Well, this is the plan for the house I was originally going to build," he told her, unrolling the papers. "Kyle Mitchell, an architect friend of mine, drew them up when he was in college several years back. The assignment was to interview a prospective client and draft a plan in accordance with the client's wishes. I was the prospective client, and he gave me the plans as a tangible reminder of my goals."

She looked at the simple ranch-style house with a wraparound front porch, main floor master bedroom and en suite bath plus an office and an open concept kitchen-living room combination.

"It's nice," she said, though she had no idea why he was showing her old plans for a house.

"But small," he acknowledged.

"Well, how much space do you really need?" she asked reasonably.

"Kyle tried to push me to add at least a second bedroom, but I was worried that if I had a spare room, one of my annoying siblings might want to stay with me."

Ruby couldn't help but smile at that.

"Anyway, Kyle has his own architectural firm in Bronco now, and though he specializes in commercial buildings, he agreed to tweak my old plans for me."

He slid the top page aside so that she could see the revised plan, with two additional bedrooms, a second bath, a bigger kitchen, separate dining room and expanded living space.

"That looks like more than a tweak," she noted.

"Well, once we got talking, I realized that I was going to need a lot more space to accommodate you and Emery and Jay."

Her breath caught in her throat, and she had to swallow before she could respond. "You want us to live with you?"

"Well, not today—or even tomorrow—because it's going to take a little while to build," he confided. "But at the risk of again being accused of moving too fast, yes, I want you and your kids to live at The Start of a New Day Ranch with me."

Joy—pure and unadulterated—filled her heart to overflowing.

"I also want you to marry me—that's just a heads-up, not a proposal," he hastened to assure her. "I'll save the whole down-on-one-knee thing until you can hear me tell you that I love you without freaking out."

"I didn't freak out," she protested, though without much conviction.

"You totally freaked out," he said, but the smile that accompanied his words assured her that she was forgiven. "But I should have anticipated that my declaration might come as a surprise to you, and I shouldn't have let myself be hurt by your apparent rejection of my feelings."

"I didn't reject your feelings," she denied. "I didn't know what to do with them. And before I had a chance to figure it out, you were gone."

"My uncle needed my help. And I thought you needed some time to figure out how you felt."

"I felt angry that you walked out on me," she told him, unwilling to let him off the hook completely.

He reached for her hands and drew her closer. "I left town," he said gently. "I didn't leave *you*."

"It felt like you'd left me—and Emery and Jay."

"I tried to call you," he reminded her. "And I know you got my message, because you replied by text."

"You're referring to the message in which you said that an unnamed uncle needed your help with an unspecified something which required you to be gone for an indeterminate amount of time?"

"Yeah," he admitted, drawing her closer still. "And now I understand how that might have seemed…inadequate."

She nodded.

"But what you need to understand, *corazón*, is that when I said I loved you, my feelings weren't contingent upon you saying the words back—or on anything else at all." He released her hands now to slide his arms around her. "I said I loved you because it's how I feel. And I will love you forever."

She linked her hands behind his neck. *"También te amo."*

He grinned. "Someone's been brushing up on her Spanish."

"I had some time on my hands while you were away," she said. "And some time to think about how I felt—and why I reacted so strongly when you told me you loved me."

"You mean why you freaked out?" he teased.

"I accused you of moving too fast and pushing for more than I was ready to give, but the truth is, I was scared. Not of your feelings so much as my own. Because I'd only just realized that I'd fallen hard and fast, and I wasn't close to being ready to admit those feelings out loud.

"And then you were gone, and I realized there was something even scarier than the way I felt—the possibility that I might have lost the best man I've ever known."

"Never," he promised, and finally lowered his mouth to hers.

It was a kiss of apology and forgiveness; a kiss of passion and promise; but mostly, it was a kiss of love.

"I really do love you," she told him.

"You want to prove it by being my date for Stanley and Winona's wedding on Saturday?" he asked.

"*This* Saturday?"

He nodded.

"I guess she wasn't kidding when she said she didn't want to wait," Ruby mused.

"So what do you say about being my *plus-three*?" Julian prompted.

Her brows lifted. *"Plus-three?"*

"I know you and Emery and Jay are a package deal, and I wouldn't have it any other way."

"In that case, you've got yourself a *plus-three* for the wedding."

WINONA'S ORIGINAL WEDDING dress had been destroyed by Victor, and she was glad, because she wouldn't have wanted to wear it again. Instead, she went to Cimarron Rose, a boho clothing boutique in Bronco, where proprietor Everlee Roberts Abernathy came through for her in a big way. And when Winona walked down the aisle in a stunning gown of crimson lace carrying a bouquet of lavender roses, purple carnations and red gerbera daisies, it was the consensus of the guests that she was a stunning and unique bride. (And that was before she lifted the hem of her skirt to show off the purple cowboy boots on her feet.)

Ruby didn't know that she'd ever seen a more radiant bride—or a groom more obviously in love. And when the elderly couple exchanged their heartfelt vows, she didn't think there was a dry eye left in the church.

"It was a beautiful ceremony," Ruby said to Winona, as she and Julian made their way through the reception line at The Library, the restaurant owned by one of the Bronco Sanchezes. All Winona's family was on the receiving line, including her great-grandchildren Evan and Vanessa.

"Short and sweet." The bride winked at her. "When you've waited more than nine decades to be a bride, you don't want to waste too much time on the vows or you might not live long enough to enjoy your honeymoon."

Ruby had to laugh, even as she felt her cheeks grow warm.

"But don't worry, honey," Winona continued. "Your turn will come before too long." Then the old woman laid a hand on her arm. "He wasn't the first, but he will be the last. And then your family will be complete."

Ruby had heard rumors about the old woman's psychic abilities, of course, but she wasn't entirely sure she'd believed them. Not even after Julian told her about Dorothea's sketches and Evan's dreams. Not until the warmth of Winona's touch seemed to penetrate all the way to her wary heart.

The bringing together of families and friends made a wedding ripe with opportunities for awkward encounters and embarrassing moments. Having already survived one, in her first introduction to the bride and the groom, Ruby tried to brace herself for the next: meeting up with Julian's parents.

Thankfully, that turned out to be neither awkward nor embarrassing. In fact, his parents were warm and welcoming in their greetings, and in no time at all, Nicole was cooing over the baby she'd stolen from her eldest son's arms while Will was being charmed by Emery, leaving Ruby and Julian to simply enjoy the moment and being together.

Bethany McCreery, the wedding singer Stanley and Winona had booked for their July wedding date, was unavailable for their rescheduled nuptials, but she'd previously made a recording of "their song" that she allowed them to play for their first dance. As they swayed together to the music, Winona's eyes sparkled with happiness and Stanley's smile stretched from ear to ear.

After the dancing there was cake. And after the cake had been served, Stanley and Winona mingled with their guests some more, preparing to make their exit from the reception to head off on their honeymoon.

"I need to ask another favor," Stanley said to Julian, when the newlyweds came to say goodbye.

"I don't think so," he said. "I'm still recuperating from the last favor I did for you."

"This one won't require sleeping in uncomfortable motel rooms," *Tío* promised.

"What is it?" he asked warily.

"Check out the real estate listings in Tenacity while we're on our honeymoon." The old man slid an arm across his new wife's shoulders. "Me and Winona have decided to split our time between Bronco and Tenacity when we get back from our honeymoon."

"Why would you do that? Don't you want to slow down and take some time to just enjoy being together?"

"Slow is for old people," Winona said with a wink.

"And we definitely plan to enjoy being together," Stanley said.

"But there are people in Tenacity who could use my guidance," the bride said.

"And maybe my help, too," her groom added.

"What is it you plan to do, *Tío*?" Nicole asked.

"I'm going to help find missing persons. After all, I found Winona when no one else could."

Julian considered reminding him that he'd found his bride because her daughter and grandson had given him all the clues, but he figured the old man's plans were harmless and that everyone should have a hobby.

"Are you really interested in detective work?" Nina asked her great-uncle.

"I really am," Stanley said. "And I've always had a knack for solving puzzles."

"In that case, I might have your first case for you."

"Tell me about it," he urged.

She shook her head. "It can wait until you get back from your honeymoon."

"Can't you at least give me a clue?"

"Alright," she relented. "It involves history and a mystery… and a long-lost love."

Stanley rubbed his hands together. "Sounds like just the kind of juicy case a hungry investigator could sink his teeth into."

"*After* his honeymoon," Winona said firmly.

"*Si, querida,*" he dutifully intoned, making everyone laugh.

"And here comes your ride," Luca chimed in, as an antique car with a "Just Married" sign on the back and streamers of cans hanging off the rear bumper pulled up in front of the restaurant.

"Thank you all for being here to celebrate with us today," Winona said, waving to the crowd of guests.

"Haven't you forgotten something?" Marisa asked, with a pointed glance at the bouquet in the bride's hand.

"I guess I have," Winona said with a laugh. "Come on, all you single women. Gather around for the ceremonial bouquet toss."

"You're not going to vie for the prize?" Julian asked Ruby, when she held herself back from the group of women pressing forward. A group that included Winona's almost eighty-year-old daughter, Dorothea.

"If my mother can find love again at her age, perhaps there's hope for me to do the same," she said, as she playfully elbowed her way to the front of the crowd.

But Ruby only shook her head as she put one arm around her daughter and tucked the other into the crook of Julian's arm, where the baby was sleeping. "I've already got everything I want right here."

Winona turned her back to the group and tossed the flowers over her shoulder.

The bride proved to have an impressive arm, because the bouquet sailed over the heads—and outstretched hands—of the group of single women to smack Ruby in the chest.

"You caught the flowers, Mommy," Emery exclaimed.

Apparently she had, though it had been a reflex more than anything that caused her fingers to clutch the flowers before they could fall to the ground.

"I guess that means you're next," Nina Sanchez said.

"Next after me, maybe," her sister, Marisa, chimed in, reminding everyone that she and Dawson would be exchanging their vows the very next Friday, having snagged the Tenacity Social Club for their after-party when another event was canceled.

"I'm not in any hurry," Ruby assured them. But she tipped her head back against Julian's shoulder then and smiled at him. "But I'm no longer opposed to the idea of another walk down the aisle, either."

"Meeting the right man makes all the difference," Daphne Cruise said, with a loving glance at her husband, Evan.

"It really does," his sister, Vanessa, agreed.

"Lucky for me," Ruby said, pitching her voice for Julian's ears only. "I met the best man of all."

# EPILOGUE

*Valentine's Day*

HE OPTED FOR red flowers this time, because they seemed more appropriate for the occasion. Red roses, white lilies, miniature red carnations and white chrysanthemums. He wanted to do something special for their first Valentine's Day together, but though there was a ring burning a hole in his pocket, Julian hadn't yet decided whether he would pull it out tonight. As eager as he was to move forward with plans for their future, he was conscious of Ruby's desire to take things slow.

As he approached her house, another vehicle was pulling out of her driveway. The driver smiled and waved as she passed going in the opposite direction.

Julian picked up the bouquet of flowers and made his way to the front door, sliding the key Ruby had given him only a few days earlier into the lock. She'd acted like the key was no big deal, but he knew it was, because it was tangible proof that she wasn't going to shut him out again.

"Mommy, Unca Julian's home!"

He managed to save the flowers as Emery leaped into his arms. He was sure he wouldn't always get such an exuberant welcome from the little girl, but he knew he'd never grow tired of it.

"Was that Ms. Townsend from Family Services I saw leaving just now?" he asked, as Ruby made her way into the foyer.

"It was," she confirmed.

Julian was having a little trouble deciphering her nonverbal clues, because her lips were curved but her eyes were shiny with unshed tears. He cautiously offered her the flowers. "Happy Valentine's Day?"

She laughed as she accepted the bouquet. "Thank you." She rose on her toes to brush her lips against his. "These are undeniably the second-best gift I got today."

"What else did you get?"

"Very good news. Family Services has approved my application to adopt Jay."

"That means he gets to stay with us forever," Emery chimed in.

"Definitely the best Valentine's Day gift," Julian agreed.

She nodded. "There's nothing I want more than for Jay to be my son—officially and legally—except maybe to make him *our* son."

His heart gave a cautious leap of joy inside his chest. "And how would we go about that?"

"The easiest way would be to get married," she said, her tone deliberately casual.

"You think marriage would be easy?" he asked, only half-teasing.

"Well, loving you is the easiest thing I've ever done, so I figure being married to you should be a piece of cake."

He grinned. "A piece of wedding cake?"

"Can we have choc'ate cake?" Emy piped up to ask.

Ruby had to laugh. "We can have whatever kind of cake you want, if Julian says *yes.*"

"Say *yes,*" the little girl urged.

"Why don't you take these flowers into the kitchen for your mom?" Julian said, handing her the paper-wrapped bouquet.

"Okay."

The happy light in Ruby's eyes dimmed a little as her daughter disappeared from sight.

"You're not going to say *yes*," she realized. "You wouldn't have wanted Emery out of the room if you were going to say *yes*."

He took her hands and drew her toward him. "I don't think I could ever say *no* to you. But I also couldn't let you hijack the proposal I'd been planning."

"There's no way you were planning to propose."

"No way, huh?" He pulled the ring out of his pocket and dropped to one knee.

Ruby's eyes grew wide at the sight of the sparkling diamond set in a simple gold band. The stone was on the smallish side, not intended to make a statement about anything other than the sincere love in his heart.

*"Ohmygod."* She pressed a hand to her heart.

"I hope you know by now that I love you, Ruby."

She nodded, her eyes glittering with emotion. "And I love you."

"So what do you say—will you marry me?"

"Yes." She responded to his question without hesitation. "Yes, Julian, I will marry you."

Emery came back as he was sliding the ring on Ruby's finger. "What happened, Unca Julian? Did you fall down?"

Her mom choked on a laugh.

"Actually, I did," he said. "I fell head over heels for your mom and you and your brother."

The little girl's brow furrowed. "Did you hurt your head? Do you want me to kiss it better?"

"I think a kiss right here—" he tapped a finger to his cheek "—would make me feel much better."

She dutifully kissed his cheek, and gave him a hug, too, for good measure.

Julian rose to his feet then. "Now that we're officially engaged," he said, snaking an arm around Ruby's waist to pull her close. "How about setting a date for our wedding?"

"What's your hurry?" she wondered.

"Only that I don't want to spend a single day of the rest of my life without you."

"Married or not, you're stuck with me now, cowboy." She lifted her arms to loop them over his shoulders and draw his mouth to hers. *"Soy tuyo para siempre."*

\* \* \* \* \*

# A Match For The Sheriff

Lisa Childs

MILLS & BOON

*New York Times* and *USA TODAY* bestselling, award-winning author **Lisa Childs** has written more than eighty-five novels. Published in twenty countries, she's also appeared on the *Publishers Weekly*, Barnes & Noble and Nielsen op 100 bestseller lists. Lisa writes contemporary romance, romantic suspense, and paranormal and women's fiction. She's a wife, mom, bonus mom, avid reader and less avid runner. Readers can reach her through Facebook or her website, lisachilds.com.

## Books by Lisa Childs

### Harlequin Heartwarming

#### *Bachelor Cowboys*

*A Rancher's Promise*
*The Cowboy's Unlikely Match*
*The Bronc Rider's Twin Surprise*
*The Cowboy's Ranch Rescue*
*The Firefighter's Family Secret*
*The Doc's Instant Family*
*The Rancher's Reunion*

Visit the Author Profile page
at millsanmdboon.com.au for more titles.

Dear Reader,

Welcome back to Willow Creek, Wyoming. Sadie March Haven-Lemmon isn't done matchmaking yet. Sheriff Marsh Cassidy, her grandson, is the last bachelor cowboy left, but he won't be for long if Sadie has her way. The sheriff has bigger things on his mind than romance, but somehow he can't stop thinking about his father's home nurse, single mom Sarah Reynolds. Sarah knows her patient no longer needs her, and she needs to start making plans to leave. But she's fallen in love with Willow Creek and with the Haven/Cassidy family.

She's not the only one. I've fallen in love with this series, too, and with this family. While Marsh is the last bachelor cowboy of the Haven/Cassidy family, there are some single Lemmons who are now Sadie's stepgrandsons. Their new cousins have already warned them to watch out for Grandma, so telling their stories is going to be a lot of fun!

I love writing about big families. I come from one myself, so I'm familiar with the dynamics and with strong women like Sadie who will do anything for the people they love. Sadie is one of my favorite characters of all of them I've written. While her meddling might bother her family, it's just proof of how much she loves them and wants them to be happy. I hope these books have brought you some happiness like they have me.

Happy reading!

*Lisa*

For Sharon Ahearne, my mother-in-law and
mother in my heart and my inspiration for
strength and resilience.

Love you!

## CHAPTER ONE

THE OLD DESK chair creaked as Sheriff Cassidy leaned back and stared down at the lighter that lay cupped in the palm of his hand. Two horseshoes, turned on their sides to represent the initials CC, were engraved in the pewter, which was old and soot stained. Irony struck him that the lighter was in his possession now, since he was the only one of his brothers not to have those initials. Unlike his older brother, Cash, and his younger brothers, twins Colton and Collin, Marsh had been named after an uncle he hadn't even known existed until recently. Michael March Cassidy was his full name, but Cash's pronunciation of it, as a toddler, had stuck: Marsh. So that was what everyone called him now.

"Marsh?"

He glanced up to find his brother Cash standing in the doorway to his office. Whereas Marsh and the twins were dark haired and dark eyed, Cash was blond and blue-eyed. Now they all knew why: they didn't have the same biological father. But they did have the same *real* father, the man who'd lovingly raised them all. JJ Cassidy. Despite how much he loved them, or maybe because of how much he loved them, he'd also kept some secrets from them. Like his real name. He wasn't really JJ Cassidy; he was Jessup Haven.

If only Marsh could be certain that there were no more secrets that his dad or anyone else was keeping from him...

But since he'd gone into law enforcement, people often lied to him to protect themselves or people they cared about. He knew that, and he usually could tell when people were lying and figure out the truth. But this time...

"Hey, you're giving me that interrogation-room stare again." Cash held up his hands as if Marsh had drawn his weapon on him. "I swear I don't know anything about how my lighter got into the house. I absolutely did not burn down our childhood home."

Marsh believed him, but he wasn't certain that he should. Cash had spent nearly two decades estranged from the family. When he'd learned, as a hotheaded teenager, that his parents hadn't told the truth about his paternity, Cash had taken off. But now that they'd all reconciled, it felt as if they'd spent no time apart. Like they were as close as they'd always been.

Or maybe that was just the way that Marsh wanted it to feel. He wanted his family to be together and happy. And they were now.

But for this.

For wondering how their old childhood home had burned down six weeks ago and who was responsible for starting the fire. Colton, the firefighter, had found the lighter in the cellar of the burned house and, knowing it was Cash's, had been hanging onto it before he'd recently turned it over to Marsh.

"No, I don't think you did it," Marsh said.

"Thanks for the vote of confidence, I think," Cash said. "But I wish that you *knew* for certain that I didn't."

Marsh sighed. "I'm not even sure something really happened. The Moss Valley Fire Department initially determined that it was because of poor maintenance of the property." He flinched with guilt at the thought of how the ranch had become run down while he and his brothers had all been so busy. He'd gone to college for criminal justice and started his career in law enforcement. Collin had gone for medicine and had become a cardiologist. Colton had been fighting fires and working as a paramedic for years, while Cash had just been gone.

Cash flinched, too, as if the thought and the guilt had crossed his mind as well. "I'm sorry…"

"Even those of us who were there couldn't keep up with school, then our jobs, as well as helping with Dad's doctor and hospital bills, not to mention all of his appointments and in-patient stays. Darlene did her best to take care of him and the ranch." He didn't know what they would have done without the woman they'd thought was their late mother's friend but was actually their aunt, the widow of the uncle they hadn't known they had.

"So, the fire could have been an accident," Cash suggested, his upbeat tone hopeful.

Marsh shrugged. He didn't know, but even though he'd left his job as a deputy in Moss Valley, and therefore the jurisdiction, to accept the interim sheriff position in nearby Willow Creek, Wyoming, he was determined to find out the truth. No more secrets.

"And if it was an accident, then the lighter had nothing to do with starting the fire," Marsh continued. That was what he wanted to believe—that it was just an accident. But he wouldn't be able to put his doubts to rest until he had proof.

"I hope it didn't start the fire," Cash said. "Because then it is my fault for losing it."

"But you weren't the one who used it," Marsh said. Someone else would have, if it had actually started the fire. But who? And why? "And even if they hadn't found your lighter, they probably would have found something else to start the fire, assuming it wasn't just an accident. But until I know for certain what happened, I can't give the lighter back to you."

"I'm not here for the lighter," Cash said. "And if it is what someone used to start the fire, I don't ever want it back."

It was a family heirloom. Their maternal grandfather's lighter. But they'd never met him or their maternal grandmother. They'd thought their paternal grandparents had died before they were born, too, but then they'd learned the truth.

Their paternal grandfather was gone, and that uncle, their father's brother, for whom Marsh had been named had passed away years ago, too. Just before Marsh and his brothers had learned they were really Havens, they'd also lost a cousin, when he and his wife had died in a tragic auto accident.

But they all suspected that cousin was still with them, in the heart transplanted into their father after years of a debilitating illness had destroyed his. Thanks to that heart, their father was the healthiest he'd ever been, and since Cash was back, he was happy again, too. He hadn't been happy in so long.

"Why are you here?" Marsh asked, and he tensed a bit with concern. "Any reason you need to be at the sheriff's office?" Had something happened?

Cash chuckled. "Like I said, I'm not turning myself in for something I didn't do. I'm here to ask the sheriff for help with something, though."

Marsh narrowed his eyes. "Help with what?"

He had never met anyone as independent as his older brother. But then Cash had always had Becca, so maybe he wasn't as independent as Marsh had always thought he was. Cash was finally taking his friendship with Becca to the next level; just a couple of days ago, he had proposed to her.

"Help getting married," Cash said. "I'm here to ask you to be my best man."

Marsh had to blink hard for a second before he could focus on his brother's face. Squashing down the emotions threatening him, as he usually did, Marsh grinned and said, "Of course I'm your second choice."

"What do you mean?"

"You can't ask your real best friend since she's the one you're marrying," Marsh pointed out.

"Becca is my best *friend*," Cash agreed. "I'm asking you to be my best *man*."

"Dad is the best man I know," Marsh said.

Cash blinked hard now and nodded. "He is the best man I know, too. But you're a pretty close second, Marsh."

"I've always been second," Marsh said. "But that was to you." He was just teasing him; that was something that he had never minded. He'd idolized his big brother.

Cash shook his head. "You were never second to *me*."

"I'm two years younger than you," Marsh reminded him.

"And yet, we sometimes felt closer than the twins were to each other."

"Until you left," Marsh murmured with a pang as he remembered how hurt he'd been when Cash had left, how alone he'd felt. The twins had had each other, and Darlene had been there to help their dad. But Marsh...

He'd been alone then. Like he was alone now. All his brothers had found the loves of their lives, or in Cash's case, finally realized his best friend was his soul mate. But Marsh was still alone.

That was the way he wanted it, though. He was used to being alone; he preferred it. That way, he couldn't lose anyone else close to him like he'd lost his mom to cancer, and like he'd nearly lost his dad so many times, and then he'd lost Cash, too, for nearly twenty years. But Cash had attended the college that he'd had a scholarship for, and he had become a veterinarian just as he'd planned. Then, after traveling for a while as a rodeo vet, he'd settled close to home in nearby Willow Creek, near family that they hadn't even known they had—all the Havens.

"I'm sorry," Cash said, his voice gruff with regret over leaving.

Marsh sighed and shook his head. "No, I'm sorry. And I won't bring it up again. I know we can't change the past."

"I wish I could," Cash said, his blue eyes glistening with unshed tears. "I wish I'd been there for you and Dad and the twins, and most of all, that I'd realized how I felt about Becca. I wasted so much time."

Despite being uneasy with emotion, Marsh stood up and hugged his brother. Then he pulled back and asked, "You know how to make up for that?"

Cash shook his head.

"Make the most of the time we have now."

"So, you'll be my best man?"

Marsh grinned and lightly slapped his brother's back. "Yes, I will."

"And then when it's your turn to get married, I'll be yours if you want me," Cash said.

Marsh snorted. "It's never going to be *my* turn."

"Yeah, that's what a lot of our cousins and even our own

brothers said, and then Grandma Sadie got a hold of them," Cash noted with obvious affection.

She wasn't his biological grandparent, but she had claimed Cash as her grandson. Maybe because they were so much alike: both stubborn.

Marsh shook his head. "Not going to happen."

"She's got a great track record as a matchmaker," Cash said.

"And if she wants to keep her streak alive, she's going to have to focus on someone else," Marsh said. "I'm never getting married."

"Ah…famous last words…" Cash teased.

At least, Marsh hoped he was teasing. But before he could make sure his brother understood that this best man thing was definitely going to be one-sided, his phone rang. Once his caller identified himself, Marsh waved his brother off. Cash left with a grin and a mouthed *thank you*.

"Sheriff Poelman," Marsh greeted his old boss from Moss Valley. "It's great to hear from you."

"No, you're not hearing from me," Poelman replied. "I never made this call. You know nothing about this."

Marsh let out a chuckle. Poelman wasn't as old as Marsh's grandmother and her new husband, but he was a lot like them in that he was quite the character. "Well, that's certainly true," Marsh agreed. "I have no idea what this is about."

"The fire."

Marsh's amusement turned to apprehension. "What about the fire?"

"The insurance company isn't accepting the fire investigator's determination on cause," Poelman said. "They want us to investigate."

"What? Why?" Marsh asked, and he closed his hand over the lighter, hiding it from sight as if Poelman could see through the phone line.

"For some reason, the adjuster has it in his head that it's arson," Poelman said. "I just wanted to give you a heads up. Your family has already been through so much."

"So, are you going to…?" Marsh couldn't bring himself to finish the question.

"Investigate?" Poelman's sigh rattled the phone. "We'll go over it all with the fire department, make sure there's nothing they missed."

Marsh tightened his hand around that lighter. "Well, uh, thank you for—"

"For nothing," Poelman interrupted. "This case isn't in your jurisdiction, and your family could be involved, so this call never happened." He chuckled then hung up.

With the way Poelman was joking around, he didn't seem to be taking the insurance company's request too seriously, but he was still a good lawman. He would investigate. And what would he find?

Marsh curled his fingers and stared down at the lighter in his palm. He couldn't hide it forever. He was going to have to turn over the lighter, but with the initial determination being that poor maintenance caused the fire, the lighter had nothing to do with anything. It was just like any other possession in the house. So hanging onto it wasn't breaking any laws. But, like Poelman had just pointed out, Marsh couldn't be part of the investigation because it was family and out of his jurisdiction, too.

But neither of those reasons was going to stop him from investigating. He had to learn the truth no matter what it was, just as he hoped his brother understood he'd spoken the truth. While he would be Cash's best man, his brother would never be his...because he was never getting married.

SARAH REYNOLDS NEVER should have gotten married. She'd been too young and naive to realize that what she'd felt for her high school boyfriend had been puppy love and friendship and not the real thing. Despite her parents' objections, she'd married him anyway and had realized too late the mistake she'd made. But she knew now, because of her child, what real love was.

She loved her son so much. And if she hadn't married his father, she wouldn't have six-year-old Mikey now. So, as humiliating and painful as the end of her marriage had been, it'd also been worth it.

Mikey was worth every moment of pain she'd suffered and every sacrifice she'd had to make. But ever since the fire at the

Cassidy ranch, he hadn't been himself. She'd tried to find out why—if the fire had scared him, or he was upset about leaving the ranch. But he kept shutting her down every time she asked.

She was so worried about him and about their future, but she couldn't let him, or anyone else, see that concern. So she stayed up after everyone else had gone to bed in the house that her patient, JJ Cassidy, had rented in the town of Willow Creek after his ranch in Moss Valley had burned down. She sat alone on the back deck and let the tears of exhaustion and worry roll down her face.

During the day, for Mikey's sake and everyone else's, she hid her fears behind a bright smile. But at night…she felt so alone. And so scared…

She'd been working as a home health nurse for JJ for nearly seven months now, two months prior to his heart transplant and now five months after it. He didn't need her help any longer. He'd had no issues with rejection; his body had readily accepted the new heart as if it had always been his. Or maybe a part of him…if it had once truly belonged to his nephew.

JJ was healthier and happier than he'd been since she'd met him. From what she'd heard about his family tragedies, he probably hadn't been happy for a very long time. He was such a kind man—his entire family was—that she wanted to stay, but she felt like she was already taking advantage of his new heart, which was as compassionate as his old one. Maybe that was how he'd worn it out. Maybe loving too much and too generously had worn it out and not the lupus that had ravaged his body.

She uttered a shaky sigh. That romanticism had gotten her in trouble her entire life just as her no-nonsense father had warned her it would. He'd been right, but she wasn't about to admit that to him. Even after her marriage had ended, she'd refused to go back home and had worked hard to support herself and her son.

She'd figured it out then, and she would figure it out now. There was just one thing that she was afraid to figure out: how the fire, which had burned down the ranch, had really started. She'd thought it was an accident, but JJ was still waiting for his insurance company to settle the claim. For some reason, they were hesitating or still investigating. Why?

Because they suspected there was more to it? She wondered...

"I didn't realize anyone was out here," a deep voice rumbled.

Sarah jumped and nearly let out a scream despite recognizing that voice. Or maybe because she recognized it. She turned her head to find Sheriff Cassidy standing behind her, wearing the white hat he'd worn even before he'd gone into law enforcement. Not that she'd known him then. She'd just seen the pictures of him when he was a kid. Those pictures, those memories, were all gone now, just like the house where he'd grown up.

She was afraid that she might be at least partially responsible for that loss. Was it something she'd done—or hadn't done—that had caused the fire? If it was, she wouldn't be able to forgive herself, let alone expect him to forgive her.

IF ANYONE HAD told Sadie March Haven, now Lemmen, that she would be this happy again, she would have called them a fool. Would've said it wasn't possible, not after all the losses she'd suffered in the eighty years she'd been alive.

Lem, her new husband, had suffered some losses, too, so he understood. He understood her better than even her first husband had, and it wasn't just because they'd known each other since they were kids. While they shared so many of the same memories and experiences from life, they also shared something deeper, a connection that she'd never had with anyone else, as if they shared a soul, or at least a heart.

So she could feel the turmoil inside him that she felt herself. But her happiness wasn't dimmed at all. This was just a part of life—at least, a part of theirs. They loved so many people, and when those people were upset, they were, too.

She smiled as Lem poured some milk that he'd warmed in the microwave into her mug. She sat at the long stainless-steel-topped island in the enormous kitchen of the ranch house. Usually Taye, Sadie's youngest grandson's fiancée and also the cook Sadie had hired to help out after the tragic accident, was behind that counter, taking care of everyone.

But Lem was taking care of Sadie now, just as she took care of him. Even though she was sitting on one of the stools and he was standing, she was still a bit taller than him. She was six feet, or she used to be, and he was probably closer to five. With his pure white hair and beard and sparkling blue eyes, he looked a lot like Santa Claus, which was why he'd been playing him every holiday season in the town square of Willow Creek.

Since marrying him a couple of weeks ago, Sadie felt as if every day was Christmas. She reached across the island and covered his left hand with hers. Her hand was bigger, her knuckles swollen with arthritis. They'd chosen tattoos instead of rings, and the infinity symbol wrapped around their ring fingers.

Lem turned his hand over and entwined their fingers. "If we want to sleep, we should probably skip the sugar."

But he'd set out a plate of cookies anyway. Snickerdoodles. Her favorite. Taye baked them perfectly every time, so they were kind of crunchy on the outside and perfectly soft inside. With her right hand, Sadie picked up a big one and took a bite. Cinnamon and nutmeg exploded on her taste buds, and she couldn't help but murmur, "Mmmmm."

Lem grinned. "Is Caleb right? Do cookies make everything better?"

She grinned, too. Five-year-old Caleb was one of the great-grandchildren new to their family, but it felt as if the young boy had been forever a part of it, and of her. Just as Lem had been. "You tell me," she said.

Lem hadn't touched the cookies or the warm milk he'd poured into his mug after pouring hers. A call from his oldest grandson had awakened them and their little long-haired Chihuahua earlier. While Feisty had fallen back asleep, they hadn't been able to.

"Are you okay?" she asked.

He nodded. "Yes, I'm just not sure if giving Brett what he asked for was enough or if I should do more…"

"And if you do more, you'll be accused of meddling," she finished for him. They often finished each other's sentences and thoughts. She sighed again but with regret, not bliss. "I'm sorry. That's my fault. I'm pretty sure that my grandsons warned yours at our wedding about my…"

"Penchant for matchmaking," he said. "It was my grandsons' father who warned them about my penchant for being overly involved, as Bob says, in the lives of my family."

It was one of the many things they had in common, loving their families so much that they wanted the best for them. They wanted them to be happy and healthy. But wanting that too much had driven away Sadie's oldest son, so she'd learned to step back when it was necessary. Or so she hoped.

"You gave Brett the phone numbers he asked for, for Ben and for Genevieve." Ben was the mayor of Willow Creek, but he was also a lawyer, like Genevieve, who had recently married one of Sadie's other grandsons, Dr. Collin Cassidy. Brett, Lem's grandson, needed legal advice. After the wedding, he and his two brothers had returned to the ranch they ran in nearby Hidden Hollow to turmoil and tragedy; their boss and friend had passed away while they were gone. "But we can go to Hidden Hollow, if you want to personally check on them," she said.

Lem sighed then took a long sip of the now cooled milk. "I think we should wait, at least until I find out what Ben has to say." As well as now being his grandson, Ben was Lem's friend and his boss. Ben was the mayor, and Lem was the deputy mayor. Roles they'd served in reverse before.

Just as Ben had turned Sadie's matchmaking back on her when he'd started bringing Lem around the ranch. That stinker…

She smiled with affection.

"What about your text?" Lem asked.

And her smile slid away. When Brett's call had awakened them, Sadie had automatically reached for her cell as well, and she'd seen the text Marsh had sent her: We need to talk.

That message filled her with dread because it usually did not mean they needed to talk about good things. But there had been more to it, something that brought her smile back now: Love you, Grandma.

Marsh was such a good man. With his sense of honor and his calm demeanor, he was so much like the man after whom he'd been named, his uncle, her younger son Michael. The two of them never having the chance to meet was yet another tragedy.

Marsh's text hadn't been the only one she'd found on her cell. Jessup had sent her one as well, with nearly the same message about needing to talk.

"If you're worried, you should just call them now," Lem advised her. "Then maybe you'll be able to sleep."

She was more worried about Lem and her new step-grandsons than she was about her son and Marsh. She sighed again. "I'm sure they both just want to warn me not to subject Marsh to any of my matchmaking." She shrugged, just like she would shrug off their warnings.

They had to see how happy the rest of their family was now. Marsh's brothers, Jessup's sons, had found the loves of their lives, or in Cash's case, realized his best friend was his soul mate. Marsh's cousins, Jessup's nephews, were all happy now, too, despite their recent loss.

So were she and Lem.

They'd all found love and happiness. That was all she wanted for Marsh and for Jessup. Now she just had to figure out how to make them want that for themselves.

## CHAPTER TWO

MARSH COULD HAVE stepped back from the open patio door when he'd noticed Sarah Reynolds, the home health nurse, sitting outside on the deck, her curly dark blond hair blowing softly in the night breeze. Then she'd turned her face slightly, and he'd noticed the tears sliding down her cheeks.

He really should have backed away then and left her alone. That was what he would have preferred if someone had caught him in a vulnerable moment—that they would pretend they hadn't noticed and just walk away.

But because she was taking care of his father, he needed to know why she was crying, in case it had anything to do with the man he loved most in the world. So he stepped through the open door and joined her. Not that he expected her to stay. Since he'd moved into the house his father was renting in Willow Creek, she'd been as skittish around him as that bronco they'd had out at Ranch Haven. The one that rodeo champ, and his cousin, Dusty Chaps, had won in a bet. The horse's owner had bet Dusty that he couldn't stay on the bronco for the required eight seconds. That day, Dusty had. But nobody else had before or since that day, not even Dusty. The owner had been so sure of himself that he'd wagered the horse, and he'd honored his bet, giving Dusty the bronco. Midnight. He was a beautiful animal. But he was a beast to those who didn't know him, pawing at the ground and making threatening noises.

Sarah, with her delicate features, big dark eyes and curly hair, was a beauty, not a beast, but she seemed jumpy around him. Like how she jumped when he spoke to her seconds ago, saying that he hadn't known anyone was outside.

He was lying, but only a little bit. When he'd headed toward the deck, he'd figured everyone else in the house was already asleep. He'd stayed late at the office, going over everything he knew about the fire, which wasn't much.

The day his family home burned down, he had arrived at the ranch after the fire had already started, after Dad had gone back inside to try to find Sarah's kid. The little boy hadn't been in the house, though; he'd been in the barn. Mikey was even more skittish than his mother. Marsh was pretty sure the kid had never uttered a word around him. Sarah hadn't uttered many herself.

But maybe their reticence was more about him than them—or more about his badge. A lot of people tended to be quiet around officers of the law, probably because the only time he saw them was when he was investigating a crime or assisting at the scene of a traffic accident. But even before he'd pinned on his badge, he hadn't been great with kids. Of course, he hadn't really been around them before, and after, he'd only seen them in the line of duty except for dropping in at the ranch after Sarah and Mikey had moved in with his dad. Now he'd moved in with them in the house his dad rented in Willow Creek.

"Are you all right?" he asked. And he wasn't wondering just about this night.

She rubbed her hand over her face, wiping away the tears he'd already seen, and nodded. "Yes."

"Is my *dad* all right?" he asked, his voice gruff with a rush of his own emotions. His father's health had been up and down for so many years. But he'd thought that had all changed now, with the new heart, which had put his lupus into remission. He'd thought that he could finally quit worrying about him.

Sarah jumped up then and touched his arm, as if she was the one comforting him now. "Yes, he's doing great. Better, I think, than anyone expected."

Marsh released a shaky breath of relief. "Good."

"Yes," she said. "He's doing so well that he really doesn't need me anymore."

"Is that the reason for the tears?" Marsh asked, and he reached out but pulled his hand back before he touched her face. He didn't want to make her any more skittish than she already was, and the thought of touching her made him a little skittish, too. Uneasy. Too aware.

Ever since she'd started working for his dad, he'd been interested in her. He'd wondered about her past, why she was raising her son alone. Why she'd chosen to be a home health nurse and not work at a hospital.

But he'd never asked her those questions, feeling that they were too intrusive. All that mattered was how well she took care of his father; she was a good nurse and clearly a compassionate person. And beautiful.

He'd dealt with his interest in and awareness of her the way he dealt with all his uncomfortable emotions: he just ignored them. But ignoring her wasn't as easy now that they were living in the same house.

Ignoring her was also counterproductive. To learn more about the fire, he should have talked to her about it sooner. She'd been there when it had started and had been living at the ranch in the months before it happened.

She swiped at her face again, as if worried that she'd missed a tear. "No tears. I'm just tired," she said.

Marsh had an innate ability to determine when people were lying to him, but he didn't need it with her. She was easy for anyone to read. In addition to lying to him, she seemed anxious to get away from him; her gaze kept darting away from his to the house behind him. But he remained where he was standing between her and the open sliding door.

"I need to get some sleep," she said.

He did, too, especially since he'd asked for a meeting with Sadie tomorrow. He had to be sharp to keep up with his grandmother's quick mind, or he might find himself getting talked into something he didn't want. Not that he would let even Sadie talk him into risking a relationship.

He had his family to worry about, like always, and now he had an upcoming election to worry about since he definitely wanted his interim sheriff position to become permanent. It wouldn't be fair to a romantic partner to come so low on his list of priorities.

"I don't want to keep you up," Marsh said. "But I don't often have the chance to talk to you alone. And I'd really like to talk to you, Sarah."

A pang of guilt struck him because he hadn't made more of an effort to have a conversation with her before, and now he just intended to question her about the fire. He had the excuse that he'd been too busy, but she was the one caring for his dad, so he should have talked to her. Instead he'd just talked to his dad and to Darlene, who'd hired her. And he wasn't sure why he'd avoided her except that he tended to avoid things that unsettled him.

And Sarah Reynolds, with her big soulful eyes, unsettled him, especially as she was staring up at him with those eyes now. And in that moment, he couldn't tell if she was scared or if *he* was.

SARAH WAS SCARED for so many reasons. It wasn't that she didn't trust Marsh Cassidy; he was the sheriff after all. If he hadn't scared her even before he became the sheriff, she might have thought that he frightened her *because* of his position. But there was more that intimidated her than the badge and the gun. He was so big, well over six feet tall, with broad shoulders. Yet his brothers were tall and broad as well, and she was comfortable around them.

JJ, their dad and her patient, was a big man, too. And she loved him like he was *her* father and really wished that he was. JJ was so kind and upbeat despite all the years of illness he'd suffered. Other patients with similar health challenges had been bitter and resentful and had lashed out at her. But he never had. After recently meeting his mother, Sarah knew where he got that strength and resilience. But unlike her son, Sadie Haven was an intimidating woman; maybe she'd passed that trait onto her grandson Marsh.

All edgy with nerves, she wasn't the least bit sleepy, but she feigned a yawn. "It's really late. Can we do this another time?"

"It won't take long," he said. "I just have a couple of questions for you."

"Questions?" She'd been working for his father for months, and he had never acknowledged or addressed her with anything other than a nod. "I've probably said more than I should have about your father's health."

She wouldn't have done that if JJ hadn't already assured her that it was fine to answer whatever questions his sons asked about him. He'd confessed that he'd already kept too many secrets from them, and he wanted them to be certain he wasn't holding back any longer, especially about his health. He'd told her how scared they'd all been, pretty much their entire lives, that they were going to lose him.

But then they'd lost their mom to cancer instead. Sarah couldn't imagine growing up like the Cassidy brothers had, and a pang of sympathy for them, and maybe especially for Marsh, struck her heart. Obviously they had inherited their grandmother's strength, just like their father had.

She released a shaky breath and asked, "What do you want to know?"

"About the fire," he said.

Another pang struck her heart, this one of pure fear. "I... I doubt I know any more than you do." And she didn't know anything for certain, but she'd recently started having suspicions, horrible suspicions that she felt guilty for even considering.

"You were there when it started," he said. "I didn't get there until after the house was already ablaze."

Ablaze. She and JJ and Darlene had been out in the barn, admiring Darlene's mare, when they'd smelled the smoke. When they'd stepped outside to see what was burning, they'd seen that the house was on fire. She and Darlene had rushed inside to get JJ's oxygen tanks out before they could explode. She shuddered as she remembered the heat of the flames devouring the worn wood of the old farmhouse. Once they were out with the tanks, she'd realized that Mikey was missing. And she'd been scared, so very scared, that her son was inside.

She'd tried to go back in to rescue him, but Darlene had held her back while JJ rushed inside to find him. Her patient could have died. He was more than a patient, though. And she'd been so scared for him, too. Then his sons Marsh and Collin had arrived, and they, too, had run into the fire to find Mikey and their father. They'd all come out except for her son. And in those moments, when she'd thought she'd lost Mikey, she'd nearly lost her mind. Just remembering it now made her tremble, tears rushing to her eyes again.

Marsh's big hands cupped her shoulders. "I'm sorry, Sarah. I didn't mean to upset you."

"It's just… I thought my son was in the house, in the…" Tears choked her now, making it impossible for her to voice her greatest fear aloud.

Marsh closed his arms around her, holding her gently as the tears rolled down her face. She could have pulled away from him. She should have pulled away from him. But it had been so long since anyone had held her like this…since she'd had anyone she could lean on like she was tempted to lean against him now, to slide her arms around him and hold on and…

Then he asked, "Why did you think he was inside?"

She tensed with fear, again, that he suspected the same thing she was beginning to, that her son might have…

No. She couldn't let herself go there, and she definitely couldn't let the sheriff go there, either.

She stepped back, pulling away from him, and his arms dropped back to his sides. "I guess I just panicked," she said. That had to have been why Mikey was so apologetic and tearful when she'd found him. He'd just been sorry that he'd upset her. "I should have known he was in the barn." That was where she and Darlene had found him, in the loft, with that stray cat who'd started coming around the ranch. "Mikey was *always* in the barn."

*So he couldn't have had anything to do with the fire starting.* But she didn't say that last thought out loud. If Marsh hadn't considered that someone might have started the fire, she didn't want him to consider it. And she certainly didn't want him to suspect her son; she didn't want to suspect him either. But he'd been even more upset than she'd been when she'd found him, and as he'd clung to her, he'd kept whispering, "I'm sooo sorry. I'm sooo sorry."

And every time she'd tried to talk to him about the fire since, he'd completely shut down and not spoken at all until she dropped the subject.

"It was good that he was in the barn," Marsh agreed, and a slight grimace crossed his handsome face.

She flinched as she remembered that Marsh had been hurt, along with his dad and brothers, while trying to find her son that horrifying day. "I'm not even sure I thanked you for going back into the house that day. I owe you my gratitude and an apology as…" Her voice cracked as she remembered the burns and smoke inhalation they'd suffered. It hadn't been too bad, but it could have been so much worse.

"It wasn't your fault," Marsh said, but he seemed to stare at her for a while, as if he was now considering that *she* could be a suspect.

"It was just an accident," she reminded him. "That was what Colton said the fire investigator had determined. That it was bad wiring or poor maintenance or something…" And the arson investigator would know better than she would what had caused it. Maybe the fire, and her reaction to not knowing where Mikey was, had scared her son so much that he'd apologized for upsetting her and didn't want to talk about it now.

He'd enjoyed living at the ranch, playing in the barn, but he hadn't wanted to go back the other day when the Havens had planned an impromptu excursion to the Cassidy ranch in order to find that stray cat and make sure it was all right. Mikey had loved that cat and the mare Darlene had in the barn, but he'd refused to go back with the others. No. He had more than refused; he'd seemed to panic at the thought. And that was when she'd started thinking that horrible thought she'd been thinking…

But maybe he'd just been traumatized from witnessing the fire and the destruction and the fear and also from the ambulance taking away the Cassidy men.

"I'm sorry that you and your father and your brother got hurt looking for my son," she said, clarifying her earlier apology. "I should have known where he was." And that was why this was more her fault than anyone else's. Mikey was her responsibility—hers and hers alone.

"I don't think my parents ever really knew where my brothers and I were," Marsh said. "We pretty much ran wild around the ranch."

"They didn't worry about any of you getting hurt?" she asked.

"We got hurt wrestling in our bedrooms," he said with a slight smile. "We were safer running around with the animals. And on the ranch, the animals were really just animals, not like some of the people I've arrested over the years."

She sucked in a breath. Did he know...

Heat rushed to her face with embarrassment and dread that he might know about her past.

"Not that there's a lot of crime in Willow Creek or that there was in Moss Valley," he added, as if he'd sensed that he'd scared her. "They're both safe places to live."

"Because you've been the law in both places?" she asked with a slight smile.

He chuckled. "I'm hardly *the* law. I just do my best to uphold it."

Maybe that was why he intimidated her, because he was so good. He was the kind of man who ran into burning buildings to rescue people and who wasn't afraid to take on dangerous criminals. He was the kind of man who probably saw everything in black and white. So there was no way he would understand her past.

She'd been there, and even she didn't understand it. But she forced another smile and held up her hand as if she was being sworn in to testify. "I promise that I haven't broken any..." But before she could finish, she got distracted...with the errant thought that maybe keeping her suspicions to herself was a crime of some kind. Or maybe the distraction was that he was smiling, too, his dark eyes as bright as the little twinkling lights dangling from the arbor over the deck.

"Any what?" he asked when she trailed off.

She blinked, trying to break that connection she felt to him through their gazes. "Laws, of course," she said. But then she couldn't help but ask, "What did you think I was talking about?"

"Hearts, Sarah," he replied, and his grin slipped away.

Her heart started pounding then, fast and hard. She had no idea how to respond. Was he flirting with her? Sarah wasn't even sure she knew how to flirt back if she was inclined. But she was not at all inclined to flirt with Marsh Cassidy, or with anyone else. She had to focus on her son, and she couldn't risk making another mistake that affected him.

Marsh said, "I have a feeling that you might have broken a few of those."

She wanted to laugh off his comment. But there was some truth to it. Hearts had been broken just as promises had been broken. But she hadn't been the one who'd caused the damage, who'd broken the promises.

She had learned from that damage, though. She'd learned never to risk that pain again, for herself—or for her son.

MIKEY REYNOLDS STOOD behind the frilly curtains at the window of the bedroom on the second story, where he'd been sleeping since the fire at the ranch. Except he really wasn't sleeping much, not since that fire.

So through that filmy lace, he tried to study the people standing on the deck below. He couldn't see much through the boards of the peek-a-boo roof thingy over the patio, but the twinkling lights dangling from the boards made his mom's golden hair even shinier, and made the sheriff's white hat glow in the dark.

His stomach ached, and it wasn't because he'd eaten too much. Like sleeping, he hadn't been eating that much since the fire, either. Not even when they'd gone to Ranch Haven for that end-of-summer party a few days ago. And there'd been a lot of food there, cookies that the other kids swore were so good.

But, like then, he felt sick over the thought of trying to eat. Of trying to sleep...

Of trying to talk to anyone...

He wanted to listen right now instead. He needed to know what the sheriff was saying to his mom, so with a shaking hand, he turned the lock and pushed up the window. But as he did, it squeaked, and both people tipped back their heads and stared up at him.

He jumped away from the window. But it was too late. He was pretty sure they'd seen him. So he left the window open and rushed back to his bed and climbed into it and pulled the light blanket over his body. Then he pressed his head into the pillow and squeezed his eyes shut. And he held his breath.

The stairs creaked first and then his door as someone turned the knob and opened it. Was it the sheriff or his mom? He wasn't sure which one it was, but he resisted the urge to open his eyes and look.

He had to pretend to be asleep, especially if it was the sheriff. He didn't want to talk to the guy, and he'd made sure that he hadn't. Not that the sheriff had ever really tried. They usually just nodded at each other. That was it.

And that was enough to make Mikey's stomach hurt, just like it was hurting now, probably because it was full of the air he was holding in.

Maybe he should have pretended to snore instead, but if he let out the breath now, it was going to be loud. But if he didn't, he might pass out. So the air escaped him in a heavy gust that stirred his blanket.

A soft laugh tinkled out. His mom's laugh. He didn't hear it that often, but when he did, it made his heart warm, and he smiled.

She touched his hair, brushing it back from his forehead. "Why are you awake?" she asked. "Are you nervous about starting school?"

He didn't feel like smiling now. He groaned. "Can't you just keep teaching me?" he asked.

"You'll like school here in Willow Creek," she said. "And you already know so many kids."

"Who?"

"All the Haven boys and Bailey Ann and Hope."

He'd met them at that party a few days ago, but he hadn't really talked to them. They'd tried talking to him, though, and they hadn't said the things the kids at his old school had. These kids had been nice, and he wasn't used to that.

He didn't know what to say when someone was nice to him or even when they were mean to him. So he never talked much, even before the fire.

"You're going to make so many more friends," his mom assured him.

He didn't make friends, though. Not with people. He made friends with animals, like Miss Darlene's horse and that cat that had hung around the barn—just like he'd hung around the barn. He'd rather be with animals. So would Miss Darlene. She'd told him that she got a job working with them now.

"Can't I just go to work with Miss Darlene?" he asked. "At the vet's office?"

Another chuckle reached his ears, a deep one. And he jumped and turned toward the open door. A big shadow blocked it. A big shadow with that white hat. "You sound like my brother Cash," the sheriff said. "He's one of the veterinarians who Miss Darlene's going to work with, and all he ever wanted to do was be with animals. But he knew he had to go to school first and get his high school diploma and then his degree so that he could take really good care of the animals. When Cash was in school, he found his very best friend, and they're still friends all these years later."

A best friend. Something inside Mikey yearned for that, for a really close friend, someone he could tell everything to… like…the secret he'd been keeping.

He sucked in a breath.

"You need to go to sleep, honey," Mom said. "You have to get up early tomorrow for school."

He got up early every day, usually because it was so hard to sleep lately. Tonight it was going to be even harder. Because of school starting, and because of the sheriff.

"Good night, you two," the man said, his voice just a low, deep whisper. Then his boots lightly struck the wood floor of the hall as he walked away.

Mikey thought for a minute how it might be to have a guy around to tuck him into bed like his mom did now. He couldn't remember his dad. Had he ever done it?

Or had he just done bad things and nothing good?

"Are you going to be able to get to sleep, honey?" his mom asked. "Do you want me to stay with you until you do?"

"No, Mom," he said. "I'm tired now." Then he yawned and closed his eyes and pretended that he'd fallen asleep. And this time, he made sure he breathed normally so that he didn't blow out all that air again. And finally, Mom walked away like the sheriff had.

But, unlike with his mom, Mikey hoped that the sheriff didn't come back. He didn't want to see him again.

## CHAPTER THREE

IF MARSH HAD had the time, he might have pulled over a couple of vehicles along the road to Ranch Haven. One was a big van that was speeding just a bit, but when the driver, a tall woman with a thick blond braid, saw him, she slowed down and waved.

Taye Cooper, probably driving the Haven boys to school for their first day. He waved back. Then, moments later, a red Cadillac sped past him. It stayed in its lane, but it was going much too fast. He flicked on his lights for a second, just as a warning, and in his rear view, he noticed the brake lights as the Caddy slowed down for him. That vintage Cadillac was pretty distinctive and belonged to the deputy mayor and Marsh's new step-grandfather, Lem Lemmon.

Having seen both those vehicles leaving, he shouldn't have been surprised when he arrived at the house a few minutes later and was greeted with silence. He'd been told, several times, not to knock or ring the doorbell, that only strangers or sales-people did that.

Family walked right in. He wouldn't have believed, when he'd first learned that he was a Haven, that he would ever feel at home here. But it hadn't taken him long to feel that he fit in, maybe because he looked so much like his cousins. Or maybe because the ranch was also in his blood like it was for the people with whom he shared some DNA. Or maybe it was just because of Sadie...

It was through the sheer force of her iron will that he hadn't had a choice but to feel like family because that was what she'd wanted. He wanted that, too, which was why he was here, stepping through the patio doors from the courtyard that opened onto the kitchen.

For once, the kitchen was empty, almost eerily so. But he'd passed Taye on the road, so he understood why the cook wasn't at her usual spot behind the long kitchen island. And the kids were with her in that van instead of gathered around like they usually were.

Lem had left, too, in that red Cadillac Marsh had passed. But where were the others?

Toenails scratched across the brick floor, and then a little yap cut through the silence. And Feisty, his grandmother's long-haired Chihuahua, rushed up to him. Her little teeth snapped, and she growled despite the wagging of her fluffy black tail. She climbed over his boots and tugged on the bottoms of his jeans. By now, he knew what she wanted, so he leaned over and scooped her up in his hands, bringing her toward his face. She snuggled close, kissing his chin until he pulled her away and grimaced.

Then, from upstairs, came the cry of a baby. And another cry chimed in with the first, echoing and almost harmonizing with it. "Shh," he said to Feisty. "We woke up the twins." His cousin Dusty and his wife, Melanie, had just welcomed their babies into the world a few days ago.

He grimaced again, but this time, it was at the thought of having infants around, totally dependent on him. He wasn't good with older kids because he somehow unsettled or intimidated them. He couldn't imagine how bad he would be with babies.

"If the boys getting ready for school a little while ago didn't wake them up, you certainly didn't," Sadie said as she walked into the kitchen.

Feisty wriggled in his grasp, and he leaned down to put her back on the floor, which she rushed across to dance around Sadie's well-worn boots.

Despite being eighty years old, Sadie still worked the ranch a bit. And it showed in those worn boots and the arthritis that had swollen every knuckle of her big hands. Maybe that was why she and her new husband had chosen tattoos instead of rings as the declaration of their love and commitment.

Marsh admired their commitment, but it was something he was never going to risk himself. He knew nothing lasted forever. Even if the marriage didn't fail, people died. Like Lem's first wife and Sadie's first husband, the grandfather Marsh had never gotten the chance to meet.

"I suspect their empty stomachs are what woke them up," Sadie said. Instead of being bothered by the crying, she smiled with affection. Nothing seemed to faze the woman; she was so strong.

Marsh was counting on that strength, or he wouldn't risk sharing his burden with her. He was also hoping her strength would shore up his, so that he could figure out what was the right thing to do for his family and for himself.

"How's your stomach?" Sadie asked, and she reached out as if she was going to pat it. But then she hugged him instead.

Marsh closed his arms around her and hugged her back. She was nearly as tall as he was so he was able to rest his cheek against her head for a moment. Her long white hair was bound in a thick braid that reached almost to her waist. And she wore jeans and a Western shirt like he did.

"I'm not hungry," he said. Thinking about the fire investigation being reopened had killed his appetite. He held her one more moment, borrowing her strength, before pulling away from her.

She gave him a speculative look, as if trying to figure out what was going on with him. Not that he hadn't hugged her before, but he wasn't as comfortable expressing affection as his younger brothers were. Which was another reason that he'd determined it was better for himself and everyone else that he remain single.

"Taye saved some fresh cinnamon rolls and banana nut muffins for us," she said as if trying to tempt him. Then she opened the microwave and pulled out a covered dish. Despite the cover, the scent of cinnamon and banana wafted over to him.

And his stomach growled.

Sadie grinned. "There's fresh coffee, too."

"Sold," he said. "But just be aware that I'm not this easily manipulated when it comes to other things."

She blinked and widened her eyes, obviously feigning innocence. "What things are you talking about?"

He chuckled. "I think you know. But I didn't come here to talk about that." Then he released a heavy sigh with the tension that had been gripping him.

"You didn't?" Sadie asked with another speculative stare.

"No," he said. "That's the least of my concerns right now. I'm worried about something else."

"Your dad?" she asked with a slight gasp. "Is he doing all right? Is his heart—"

"He's fine," he assured her, just like Sarah had had to assure him the night before when he'd found her crying on the deck.

Why had she been crying?

She hadn't actually told him because she hadn't even admitted she'd been crying.

He suspected there was a lot she hadn't told him. And he wanted to know...*everything*...about her. He wasn't about to ask Sadie for help with that, though, knowing that she would get the wrong idea entirely.

He didn't want himself to get the wrong idea, either. He didn't want to be interested in Sarah for anything more than finding out what had caused the fire at the ranch. Despite how pretty and compassionate she was, he didn't want to get involved with her—for his sake and for hers. He wasn't family man material; his family had always been so much of a mess growing up, with the health and financial strains, his mother dying and Cash running away.

Family life was too hard for him to risk for himself or to inflict on anyone else, especially a young mother raising her son on her own.

Sadie waved a mug in front of his face, the scent of coffee wafting from it. "You seem very distracted, Marsh," she said as she handed him the mug and a plate with a cinnamon roll and a muffin on it. She pulled out a stool from the counter and settled on it, in front of another plate and mug.

Marsh put his on the counter and pulled out a stool to join her. "Distractions that I don't need right now," he murmured. He needed to concentrate on the upcoming election, not on the fire and certainly not on Sarah Reynolds.

"Can I help?" she asked.

"I don't know," he admitted. "I'm not sure what to do myself."

"About the election?"

"No, I want to run," he said. "I like being sheriff." And it wasn't a role he was going to give up without a fight. He just hoped it wouldn't be a fight.

"I can definitely help you with the election," she said. "I've helped Ben in the past."

"It's not about that," he said. "It's about the fire at the ranch."

"What about it?"

"It hasn't been settled yet," he said.

She narrowed her eyes and nodded. "So that's what this is about…"

He nodded, too. "Yes, the Moss Valley sheriff gave me a courtesy call to let me know the insurance company wants a more thorough investigation."

"They think it's arson?"

"I guess…"

"Do you think it's arson?" she asked.

"I don't know…" he murmured again. "But Colton shared something with me…"

"That same something that had him so anxious to find your brother Cash?" she asked.

"You know about the lighter then," he said. He should have known that she would know. Some of the tension drained from his shoulders as he expelled another sigh.

"Of course I know about it…" she murmured around a mouthful of cinnamon roll.

"Cash swears he doesn't know how it got into the house. He lost it somewhere else on the property. And I'm not even sure it started the fire, but where Colton found it…"

"He's worried that it did," she said when he trailed off.

But she didn't sound that certain, more like she was guessing. Or maybe she just couldn't bring herself to think someone had deliberately set the fire, either.

"I don't know what he thinks anymore, but with the insurance company wanting the fire investigator to take another look..." He shrugged. "I don't know what to think..."

"It still could have been an accident," she said. "Maybe that lighter had nothing to do with it."

"But maybe it did," he said. "So, should I turn it over to the fire investigator or the Moss Valley sheriff?"

"You don't know that it started the fire," she reminded him.

"But I don't know how it got in the house, either," he said. "Cash swears he hasn't set foot inside it since he ran away all those years ago, so how did the lighter get there? And did whoever brought it into the house start the fire?"

"Why don't you find out?" she asked.

"It's not my jurisdiction," he reminded her. "Someone got me hired here in Willow Creek after she got the former sheriff to retire early."

She snorted. "Early? It was way past time for him to retire. You're smarter and harder working than he ever was. And you'll figure this out faster than the fire investigator or sheriff in Moss Valley will."

He smiled at her praise. "But what do I do if I don't like what I learn?"

"You'll figure that out, too," she said.

Torn between law and order and loyalty to his family, he wasn't as confident as she was that he would. But maybe that was why he'd come to her for advice.

"How can you be so sure?" he asked. Especially when he wasn't. "It's not like you've known me very long."

She smiled, etching lines by her mouth and dark eyes. But her eyes sparkled and her face lit up with a glow of happiness. The lines didn't detract at all from her beauty; in fact, they somehow added to it, as proof that she'd earned the wisdom she had. "I know you like I know myself. You're a part of me Michael March Cassidy, and I'm a part of you."

That was what family was and why this was so difficult. He didn't want any of his family to get hurt. But for some reason, when he thought of family, he also thought of Sarah and her son. They weren't family. Nobody had even known them that long or that well.

But maybe it was because of what they'd gone through together—his dad's heart transplant and the fire—that they felt closer than simply a nurse hired for medical assistance and her child. While Sarah had taken excellent care of his father before and after his transplant, Mikey had been unobtrusive and sweet. He was a sensitive, empathetic little kid, totally unlike how Marsh and his brothers had been at his age.

Sadie chuckled. "Are you all right, Marsh? Is the thought of being like me too horrible to comprehend?"

He chuckled now. "No. It would be an honor to be like you, Grandma." It really would. The woman was incredibly strong to have survived all the losses that she had. She hadn't just survived; she'd thrived.

She blinked furiously at the tears that momentarily brimmed in her dark eyes. "And here I thought you wanted to meet up today to warn me to back off…"

He chuckled again. "From your matchmaking?"

She nodded.

"I don't need you to back off because I'm not worried about that," he said. "Whatever scheme you concoct isn't going to work on me."

"Why not?" she asked. "You must see how happy your brothers and cousins are now."

"Yes, and I'm happy for them," he said. "And for you. But as much as I may be like you and them, I wouldn't be happy in a relationship." He would be on edge, like he'd been growing up, worried that he might lose someone, or worse, put them through the stress that he'd endured growing up. With his job, it was even more likely that whoever loved him might lose him.

As SARAH FOUND a spot in the nearly full parking lot at Willow Creek Elementary School, she wasn't sure which of them was more nervous: her or Mikey. She gripped the steering wheel tightly to still the trembling in her hands. But she had to remove one to shift the vehicle into Park and then shut off the ignition. As she did, she drew in a breath that was as shaky as her hands.

So many other parents were also driving their children to school on their first day. Mothers and fathers together, as well as other single parents like her, except that they probably weren't all single parents like her. The other parent was probably just at work, not where her ex was. Because of where he was, the other parents at Mikey's old school in their hometown hadn't treated her very well. They'd judged her by the actions of her ex, making it difficult for her to even find work because people hadn't trusted her in their homes. And with the way some of the people had talked to her, their kids had probably overheard the comments and judged Mikey as harshly as she'd been judged. And he was just a child. A sweet, loving child.

She glanced into the rearview mirror and studied his tense face. With strawberry blond curls and big blue eyes, he was so cute. And he was a good kid. He really was.

She knew it, and she felt so guilty that she'd even considered that he might have had something to do with the fire. And even if he had, it would have been an accident. He wouldn't have purposely done that, which could have been why he'd been apologizing so tearfully the day it had happened.

The one question she hadn't already tried to ask him that day was if he'd started the fire, and she didn't know if she could actually ask him that. She knew he struggled with self-esteem from the bullying at his old school, so she didn't want him to feel even worse about himself if he had accidentally started it. As a nurse, she could care for any of his physical wounds, but she wasn't certain how to care for that kind of injury, for the emotional and mental ones.

She cleared her throat of the emotion affecting her and said, "We're here." Then she turned around and forced a big smile for her son.

From his booster seat in the back, Mikey glanced out the side window. But he didn't make a move to release his seat belt or reach for the door.

"It's going to be fun," she said encouragingly as she secretly hoped she wasn't lying. Mikey looked at her with suspicion, like he thought she was. "You already met a lot of kids at Ranch Haven last week, and you know how nice they all are."

"At Ranch Haven," he said.

"You don't think they'll be nice when they're at school?" she asked.

His bony shoulders lifted in a shrug. "I dunno…"

"There's one way to find out," she said. "Let's go inside…"

She wasn't sure that she would be able to walk in with him, though, or if she would have to leave him outside the doors to the lobby at the center of the T-shaped school. She'd been in the building when she'd signed him up and knew the layout and how seriously they took security. All of the doors were kept locked, and there was even a retired deputy who acted as a security officer.

Her son would be safe here. After the scare she'd had at the ranch, when she hadn't been able to find him, she was happy she would always know where he was and that he wouldn't be in any harm. But she wanted him to be happy as well.

Yet the mention of going inside had his mouth pulled down at the corners in a frown and his blue eyes widened with fear. "I don't feel—"

Someone tapped on the glass of the driver's side window, and they both whirled toward it. Becca Calder stood next to their vehicle. Becca was a real estate agent in Willow Creek and Moss Valley. She was tall and beautiful with black hair and dark eyes. And her daughter, Hope, who stood next to her mother, was a mini version of her, with longer dark hair. She tapped on Mikey's window.

"We gotta get going," she told him. "The bell is going to ring soon." Then she tugged on the door handle.

Sarah pressed the button to unlock the doors, so that Hope could get it open. And as the door swung out, Mikey unclicked his belt and scrambled out of his booster seat as if he was embarrassed that he still had to use one. It was a struggle to get him into it because he protested that he was too big. But, legally, he wasn't.

He was actually small for his age. So much so that Hope

was taller than him when he stepped out to stand next to her. "Do you have your backpack?" Hope asked him. The second he hooked his hand through it, she tugged on him, pulling him toward the school.

Another little girl called out to her from the sidewalk. "Hurry up!" The girl had a profusion of dark curls and held the hand of a blond woman who wore a suit jacket, skirt and heels like Becca and looked as put together and professional as the Realtor was.

Sarah, in her faded scrub pants and shirt, felt hopelessly out of place and out of class in the presence of the other women.

But then Becca opened her door and held it for her. "Come on," she said. "I know how hard this is." And she took Sarah's hand just like her daughter had taken Sarah's son's hand. She squeezed it. "We're just as scared on their first day of school as they are." She smiled. "Or maybe we're more scared than they are."

Sarah smiled. "You must be more scared than Hope." Because her daughter had tugged Mikey along toward that other little girl, who was jumping up and down on the sidewalk. "And certainly everybody is more afraid than she is."

"Bailey Ann," Becca said. "She's thrilled to finally go to school like other kids."

Sarah had briefly met the little girl and her parents at Ranch Haven. "She had a heart transplant?"

Becca nodded. "Yes, like JJ."

But she was just a child, probably just a year or two older than Mikey. "That's so sad."

"You can't be sad around Bailey Ann," Becca said.

Sarah fervently hoped that was true, that the little girl could cheer up her son.

Like her daughter, Becca nearly dragged Sarah along down the sidewalk toward the other parents standing outside those double steel doors to the lobby. Their children stood closer to the doors, waiting for them to be opened, so they could rush inside toward their classrooms.

Well, Bailey Ann and Hope looked ready to rush inside while Mikey turned back and stared at Sarah, as if silently begging her to let him go back home.

But JJ's house wasn't their home. They hadn't had one for a while. Maybe it was time to put down roots somewhere. To make a life for them that wasn't moving from place to place anymore.

That was what she wanted for him, for them.

But what if...

She couldn't fixate on the fire anymore. He couldn't have had anything to do with it. As she'd told Marsh the night before, Mikey had been in the barn. And that was the only reason her son had apologized to her, because he'd scared her when she hadn't been able to find him.

He looked scared now.

But he wasn't the only one. The blond woman looked deathly pale as she stared at Bailey Ann. Becca let go of Sarah's hand to grab the other woman's. "Are you all right, Genevieve?"

The woman released a shaky breath. "Yes, it's just that I'm worried about her medications and her overdoing it."

"Is she still on three daily doses of her anti-rejection medication?" Sarah asked.

Genevieve nodded. "Yes, she has to take one of them at lunch, with food. Collin went over it all with the nurse, but he has concerns. He actually asked to speak with her again this morning." She bit her lip.

Sarah would have offered to speak with the nurse, too, but Collin Cassidy wasn't just a concerned father. He was a cardiologist. He could explain his daughter's situation better than anyone else.

"Hurry up! We're late!" Little bodies rushed through the crowd of parents. One belonged to a blond-haired boy, and the other had darker blond, almost brown hair. An older kid, with sandy hair, limped after the younger boys.

"Please, excuse us," he said with a long-suffering sigh. Miller Haven, at seven, seemed much older than his younger brother and step-cousin. But then all of the kids went through so much when Miller, his brother Ian and their toddler brother, Jake, were in an accident with their parents earlier that year. They had survived, but their parents hadn't. And the other child, Caleb Morris-Haven, had lost his dad a year or so before.

Tears of sympathy pricked the back of Sarah's eyes. She hated to see anyone suffer, but especially children. They looked good now, though. Happy.

Taye Cooper, who had started out as the cook at the ranch and was soon to be the Haven boys' aunt and co-guardian, joined them on the sidewalk. She held a toddler on her hip, and his head was snuggled against her, his dark curls mussed and his dark eyes bleary with sleepiness. "I forgot how far the ranch is from town," she said.

"You're not late," Becca assured her.

"Tell them that," Taye said with a chuckle as she watched Ian and Caleb move through the crowd of children now. They stopped by Mikey and Hope and Bailey Ann, and they greeted him with big smiles just like Hope had. Miller's smile slid away when he met Bailey Ann's though.

Sarah released a shaky breath. Hopefully, Mikey's and her fears were unwarranted. It looked as though these kids would be as nice to him here at school as they'd been at the ranch.

Then the big steel doors opened, and the children poured into the school. All but Mikey.

He turned back and stared at her again. Even though there was some distance between them, Sarah could see the panic on his tense face and in his eyes. And she could feel his fear pounding frantically in her heart, too.

She was tempted to rush forward to rescue him, to pull him out of the crowd and into her arms. But then Hope tugged on him, and he turned around and disappeared inside the school with the little, dark-haired girl.

"They will be okay," Becca said.

Sarah wasn't sure who she was talking to—her or Genevieve or Taye. They all released shaky breaths like she had.

"I'm glad I pushed back my appointments this morning," Genevieve said, "because I need to go back home for a while and recover from this. Please don't make me go back alone." She reached out and touched Little Jake's back. "Please, Taye, you can commiserate with me." Then she turned toward Becca and Sarah. "And you two have done this before, so you both need to come and assure us that it will get easier."

Becca chuckled. "So you want us to lie to you?"

Sarah laughed, too, despite herself. "That would be a whopper."

"Yes, lie to us," Taye said.

Becca made a tsking noise with her tongue and teeth. "No, Genevieve says we always have to be open and honest."

"Would have saved you a lot of trouble," Genevieve pointed out.

Becca sighed. "You're right. It is the best policy."

Sarah didn't feel like laughing now; she felt like crying. Because she knew that if she was open and honest with these women, they wouldn't be as welcoming as they were now being to her or her son.

WHEN JESSUP PASSED the Willow Creek Sheriff's Department SUV on the road to Ranch Haven, he beeped his horn and waved even as tight knots formed in his stomach. What was Marsh doing out at the ranch?

He could probably guess. A short while later, when he walked into the sun-drenched kitchen where his mother was sipping coffee from a big mug, he asked, "Did you summon Marsh out here for more of your scheming? Even after I warned you not to push him?"

Her throat moved as she swallowed. Then she smiled at him, but only with her lips. "I did not summon him. He requested a meeting."

"A meeting about what?"

Her forehead furrowed. "I can't quite remember…"

He snorted. "Don't try that with me."

"I am getting older, you know," she said.

"The hearing is the first thing to go," he said. "And that seems to be your problem. That you can't hear people telling you not to meddle."

She smiled. "I heard Marsh."

"He told you not to meddle?" So that was his reason for coming out to Ranch Haven. How typical of Marsh to be proactive and upfront. Just like his uncle, Jessup's younger brother, had been.

Sadie nodded.

"Are you going to listen?"

She held her hand up to her ear and leaned toward him. "What? What did you say?"

"Exactly," he scoffed then laughed and wrapped his arm around her shoulders. "I love you so much." How had he stayed away as long as he had? Because he'd been so convinced he was going to die and hadn't wanted to put her through that...

For her to feel helpless like she'd felt every time he'd gotten sick growing up. He knew how frustrating that feeling was because he'd felt helpless so many times in his life.

"I love you, too, my darling oldest child," she said as she wrapped her arm around him. "But I suspect that you're here to tell me to back off."

"Like father like son...at least about that," he said. He wished he was as honest and aboveboard as his son the sheriff. But every secret he'd kept had been for what he'd considered a good reason, to save the people he loved from pain and stress, but in the end, he'd just caused them more.

"Who do you think I would try to match you up with?" she asked, as if it was just out of idle curiosity.

But he knew better.

"You know Darlene is my sister, in my heart as well as by marriage," he reminded her. He doubted his mother considered Darlene a possible match for him, and that she was probably thinking of the same woman he couldn't seem to stop thinking about, the one currently staying at Ranch Haven to help out her daughter during her pregnancy and with the twins she'd just recently had.

As if thinking about her had conjured her up, Juliet Shepherd descended the back stairwell to the kitchen. Her auburn hair bounced around her shoulders, and she wore no makeup, but her face glowed. In one arm, she cradled an infant, and she stared down at the baby with such a look of love and fascination.

He lost his breath for a moment as something happened to his brand-new heart, something that wouldn't have happened to the old one, which had been too broken and worn out.

"Hi, Juliet," he said, when he was finally able to breathe again.

She glanced up from the bundle in her arm and smiled at him with that smile that lit up her whole face. "Good morning, Jessup," she said. "I didn't know you were coming out to the ranch."

But she seemed happy to see him, as happy as he was to see her. Juliet was his nephew's mother-in-law and a new grandmother to those twins, though she didn't look old enough to be anyone's grandmother. She looked so young, and something about her made him feel so young again.

So young and hopeful. Feeling like he did, he wasn't certain that he would mind his mother meddling...just this once. For him...

And if he wanted that happiness for himself, shouldn't he want it for Marsh, too?

Maybe it wouldn't be so bad for him or his son if his mother refused to listen to their requests for her not to play matchmaker with them.

# CHAPTER FOUR

SARAH WASN'T ENTIRELY sure how she'd wound up at Genevieve and Collin Cassidy's home with Becca, Taye and Little Jake. But when Genevieve had invited her, she hadn't had a reason to say no.

JJ didn't need her; he'd left her a note that morning that he was going out to Ranch Haven to see his mom. Marsh, as usual, was already gone when she'd awakened. Last night was actually the first time they'd ever really had a conversation.

A conversation that she couldn't get out of her mind, just as she couldn't get the man out of her mind. But he had actually been stuck in her head from the first moment she'd met him at the Cassidy ranch. His big build, the white hat, the intensity of him that she found intimidating, but also his love for his father and his camaraderie with his brothers, which she'd witnessed during his visits to the ranch and while he'd been staying with them in Willow Creek. And she would never forget how fearlessly he'd gone into that burning house for the people he loved.

A lot of the people he loved were in the house she'd been invited to. Of his immediate family, only his dad and his brother Colton, the firefighter, were absent. His brother Cash had stopped in to join Becca. His brother Collin was there. He'd been at the school, too, touching base again with the school nurse.

Another nurse was also at their home, an older woman who

usually worked at Willow Creek Memorial Hospital. "I wish you were the school nurse, Sue," Collin said to her. "I wouldn't be so worried about Bailey Ann being there without me or Genevieve."

Sue's icy blue eyes widened as if horrified. "Not me. I'm not good with children."

Genevieve snorted. "Yes, you are. Bailey Ann loves you."

"Bailey Ann is different," Sue said with a slight smile. "I love spending time with her. But a whole school of kids…" She shuddered slightly and shook her head. "No." She turned toward Sarah. "You're a nurse. You should apply for the job."

"I thought someone was currently in that position," Sarah said. After struggling to get jobs herself, she didn't want to take anyone else's from them if they needed it.

"Mrs. Howard would have retired years ago if there was anyone else willing to take her place," Sue said.

"She mentioned to me today that she'll be putting in her notice soon," Collin said.

Cash chuckled. "Was that because of a certain overprotective father?"

"Overprotective?" Collin repeated and shook his head. Unlike his brothers, he didn't wear a hat, but maybe one wouldn't go with his white doctor's coat. Collin's twin, Colton, always wore a black hat unless he was in his firefighter gear. Cash, a veterinarian, wore a brown hat, while Marsh wore a white one, maybe because he was the sheriff.

Cash held up his hands. "I know, I know. You have every reason to be protective of Bailey Ann."

From what Sarah had heard, the little girl had come close to death many times in her young life. Just the thought of that made Sarah's heart ache. She couldn't imagine losing a child, though there were times lately when she felt like she was losing Mikey. He'd always been a quiet and shy kid, but since the fire, he'd shut down even more and was shutting out everyone.

Even her, despite all her efforts to get him to talk to her.

Then she remembered how sweetly Hope had taken his hand and led him into the school. Maybe he wouldn't be able to shut her out just as Sarah hadn't been able to refuse her mother's urging to join them here to commiserate over their kids' first day of school.

"Will you consider applying for the position?" Collin asked Sue.

She shook her head. "I can't. I'm near retirement myself at the hospital. Sarah would be better suited to the position. She has a child of her own there, too, so it would be a great job for her."

Sarah felt a tug of yearning to take the job to be able to spend more time with her son. She'd happily homeschooled him during her time at the Cassidy ranch, so she was already missing him. But after how withdrawn he'd become after the fire, she'd worried that maybe he'd been too isolated out there and that he needed to be around kids his own age for socialization.

"It really would be a great job for you, Sarah," Becca said.

Did they all know JJ didn't need her anymore? Maybe they were trying to find her a new position, so that she would move out of their father's house.

"But what about Dad?" Cash asked, his face going a little pale, probably with fear over JJ's health. "He just recently got his transplant, and if his lupus flares up again, he's going to need medical help."

"He's doing really well," Sarah assured him. "I am sure that he would be fine without me." She really needed to find another job and a place for her and Mikey to move to. But would the school hire her?

While her professional record was exemplary, her personal life wasn't. She'd made a mistake that had cost her so much, and she was afraid that it would wind up costing her son, too. It already had since he'd been bullied at his old school. If she applied for that position and someone found out about her ex-husband, Mikey's father, the little boy might start getting teased and bullied here.

And given how fragile he'd seemed since the fire, she wasn't sure how much more he could take.

A TEXT HE'D sent had brought him to Ranch Haven that morning, but a text he received brought him to Collin and Genevieve's house in Willow Creek. Swing by. Cash and Becca are here along with Taye and Little Jake. Baker and Colton might stop in, too.

Marsh should have headed right to the sheriff's office, but the chance to see his brothers together drew him to Collin and Genevieve's. Cash had been gone too long, so any chance to see him again felt like a gift, kind of like seeing Dad healthy and happy was.

But Dad wouldn't be at Collin's. Marsh had passed him on the road to Ranch Haven. He trusted that Sadie wouldn't share his concerns about the fire with her oldest son; she would protect him like JJ had been trying to protect her during all the years they had been estranged.

Marsh wanted to protect his family from any more estrangements. He had to find out the truth about that fire and make sure that, whatever the truth was, it didn't hurt anyone he loved.

His grandmother was right; he would figure out what to do. But first, he had to figure out what happened. Hopefully it was just an accident and there was no point in worrying his dad about the lighter.

When he pulled up to the large ranch house in town, he couldn't help but notice the small car parked in the driveway behind Becca's SUV. Was it a coincidence that Sarah was here, or had his grandmother already enlisted his brothers to help throw them together? Was this the match she was going to try to make next? Him and Sarah Reynolds?

The nurse was single and beautiful and sweet. She deserved to be with someone, but she and Mikey deserved someone who would have more time and attention to give them. He assumed Mikey's dad wasn't in the picture at all anymore. She didn't wear a wedding ring, and nobody had come to visit her and Mikey at the ranch or at the house in town. And Mikey hadn't gone anywhere for visitation with his dad either.

Was he dead?

Or had he just abandoned them?

Or was there some other reason, something that Sarah wasn't willing to share? Maybe that was why she was so skittish around him; she was keeping secrets of her own.

And why was Marsh so interested in her?

All that should concern him about her was what she and her son knew about the fire. While she claimed not to know very much, he still needed to talk to Mikey.

With no other places to park in the driveway or along the curb, Marsh pulled the sheriff department SUV behind her car. He didn't intend to stay, especially if his brothers were just trying to aid and abet Sadie's matchmaking scheme.

Once he stepped out of his SUV and approached the house, he could hear the deep rumbles of his brothers' chuckles drifting out through the open door and windows. His heart warmed from hearing them all together, laughing like they used to, when they weren't squabbling over something. The squabbling had happened when they were teenagers; they were adults now. Not that they hadn't squabbled a bit with Cash's return. But that had been over that stupid lighter.

He wished he could get rid of it and never see it again. But it was potentially evidence, and he couldn't bring himself to destroy it even though it might implicate someone he loved. He wasn't as convinced as his grandmother was that he would know what to do with the truth once he learned it. Yet he still had to find out what it was, whatever it was.

He drew in a deep breath and stepped through the open door. He wasn't sure if he was bracing himself for whatever teasing his brothers might do or if he was bracing himself for *her*. With the way his heart jumped a little the minute he saw her, he had his answer. Last night…her tears…

Touching her shoulders to comfort her, holding her close as she relived the terror she'd felt when she hadn't been able to find her son the day of the fire…

It all rushed over him again, making his fingertips tingle and his head a little light.

*What in the world is wrong with me?*

Maybe he just wasn't getting enough sleep with all his worries about the fire and his family and the upcoming election. Maybe that was the reason he felt lightheaded when their gazes met.

Her face flushed a little, and she looked away from him.

Maybe she was embarrassed over getting so emotional the night before.

He wanted to look away from her, too, but she was so pretty with her dark blond hair pulled up in a clip, a few curls escaping to frame her heart-shaped face. Her eyes were so big and dark with dark circles beneath them. She must not have gotten any more sleep than he had after she'd tucked her son back into his bed the night before.

"Hey, everyone, simmer down now," Cash said. "The sheriff might be here to write us up for disturbing the peace."

They weren't the ones disturbing his peace. Or, at least, he hoped none of them had started the fire. But it wasn't just the fire disturbing his peace. For some reason, he couldn't stop thinking about Sarah.

But he forced himself to grin at his older brother. "You're right. I got a call about some disorderly conduct at this address."

"Good thing we have a lawyer in the family to defend us," Collin said as he wrapped his arm around his wife's slender shoulders.

Marsh still couldn't get over his shock that his younger brother was married. He knew that Collin and Genevieve had initially wed so that they would be able to foster and adopt Bailey Ann, but they had fallen in love quickly and deeply. Very quickly and very deeply.

Which was something Marsh wouldn't have believed could happen if he hadn't witnessed it himself. They not only loved each other very much, but they loved their daughter, too. Despite Collin's teasing, he looked tense.

"So, what is this party about?" Marsh asked. He glanced around and noticed that Collin wasn't the only one who looked tense. Taye and Baker did, too, and they cuddled Little Jake between them as if unwilling to let him go.

And Sarah seemed unwilling to even look at him. Not that that was unusual. She usually didn't spare him any more attention than he did her, even though they'd been living in the same house for weeks.

Becca and Cash were the only ones who actually looked happy and relaxed. "We're supposed to be celebrating the kids going back to school," she said. "But it's hard not to be with them as much as we're used to."

"Cab," Little Jake murmured. "Cab…" The toddler was obviously missing his favorite cousin, Caleb.

Marsh felt bad for the little guy as he had a sudden memory flash through his head of watching Cash go off to school when they were little. And then again, when Cash had left home for good.

He'd missed him so much. He glanced at his older brother, still hardly believing that he was here with them again after so many years apart. Cash's return was almost harder to believe than Collin marrying as hastily and happily as he had. But Cash wasn't just back in their lives; he was engaged as well, just like Colton was engaged to Livvy Lemmon.

All their lives, Marsh and his brothers had sworn they would never get married, probably because of the heartache their parents had suffered over their health and financial issues. Mom had always worried so much about Dad that she hadn't taken care of herself, and so it should have been no surprise when she'd gotten sick and passed. But it had still been a shock, one that Marsh suspected none of them, his dad nor his brothers, had fully recovered from. He was pretty sure he hadn't. And maybe that was why he was so reluctant to get in a relationship.

"I'm happy, though, that Hope is thrilled to be back at school," Becca said. "As an only child myself, I always loved being in school."

"Or at the ranch with us," Collin reminded her.

"Sadie said you were heading out to the ranch this morning," Taye said to Marsh.

He nodded. "Yes, and thank you for saving some cinnamon rolls and muffins for me. They were delicious."

"There were more?" Baker asked, his light brown eyes wide with shock.

Taye chuckled and nodded. "Of course there were more."

"I should have known," Baker said. "My fiancée cooks enough for an army."

"She pretty much *is* cooking for an army, one of Havens and Cassidys," Cash said with a chuckle. Then he turned toward

Marsh. "So, why were you out at the ranch, Sheriff? Were you cautioning our grandmother about disturbing the peace, too? Or about her matchmaking?"

"That would disturb my peace," Marsh muttered beneath his breath.

Cash and Collin heard his comment because they both laughed. Even Sarah glanced at him, and heat climbed into his face.

"The first time that you guys came out to the ranch, we warned you about her," Baker reminded the Cassidys. "She loves playing matchmaker."

"I don't think it's turned out too badly for any of us," Collin said as he pulled Genevieve a little closer.

"It's still meddling," an older woman said. Marsh recognized her from the hospital and from prior visits to Genevieve's house. She was a nurse. "And my saying so is as well, which is my cue to leave."

"Me, too," Sarah said, her face flushed.

"I'll walk both of you out," Genevieve said as they started toward the door.

Knowing he was blocking them in, Marsh started out, too, with an, "I'll need to—"

But Cash caught his shoulder. "So, who is Sadie trying to set you up with?"

Collin's gaze followed Sarah out the door, and he wriggled his eyebrows.

Marsh shook his head. "No..."

"Sadie casts a wide net when she sets couples up," Baker said. "She found Dusty's wife when he couldn't. So it might not be Sarah."

"Dad loves Sarah and Mikey," Collin said.

"Dad won't let Sadie push Marsh into a relationship," Cash said.

Marsh was getting irritated with how they were talking around him like this was going to happen, so he spoke of himself in the third person, too. "*Marsh* isn't going to let anyone push him into a relationship."

He needed to make it clear to them because he wasn't sure

whether Sadie had enlisted his brothers to help her scheme or maybe even his dad. But it didn't matter who she had helping her; her plan wasn't going to work. Especially if Sarah was the match she intended for him. She'd slipped away from Genevieve and Sue and rushed right to her car as if she couldn't wait to get away from him. She was obviously not interested in getting to know him any better, or maybe she didn't want *him* getting to know *her* any better.

GENEVIEVE HADN'T MISSED how quickly Sarah had rushed off, either. But she wasn't sure if that was because of the Cassidy brothers' teasing or for another reason. After waving at the young nurse who was already in her vehicle, she turned back to the older one. "Sue, I know the reason you gave for not applying for the job at the school, but you're great with kids. You'd be great as the school nurse. You were very sweet to encourage Sarah to go for it instead." She'd probably realized that Sarah's job was about to end; JJ was doing so well.

"I'm not great with kids," Sue said. "Bailey Ann isn't really a kid."

Collin came up behind Genevieve where they were standing in the doorway and chuckled. "No, she's Grandma Sadie in a child's body."

Becca and Cash, who were also on their way out, laughed. "Hope is, too. Sadie's getting to all of them, so we should be glad they're back in school."

"I think she's getting to all of you, too, with the meddling," Marsh said. He had already walked past them, but he turned back now to ask, "Why are you all encouraging Sarah to apply for a job at the school? Is it just because of Bailey Ann?"

Genevieve nodded. But clearly the sheriff was suspicious of their motives and worried that they were matchmaking, too.

"Will she?" he asked.

Genevieve shrugged. "I don't know. She seemed interested but apprehensive."

"Apprehensive?"

She shrugged again. "I can't say for sure. I don't know her very well."

"Nobody does…" he murmured as he turned back to where the young woman sat in her vehicle, which his sheriff's department SUV had blocked into the driveway. Then he started toward the street, but as he approached her car, his steps slowed. He was clearly going to stop and talk to her.

And Genevieve had a feeling he was going to try to get to know Sarah better. But after insisting that he wanted no part of Sadie's matchmaking, why would he? Because he was interested in her as a man, or as a lawman?

## CHAPTER FIVE

So FAR, school wasn't as bad as Mikey had thought it would be. It was nothing like his last school. Nobody called him names. And when they talked to him, they were pretty nice. Hope was the nicest, though.

At recess, she didn't run off to meet up with Bailey Ann, who waved at her from the swing set; she stayed with him. "Grandpa JJ said you took really good care of that stray kitty from the Cassidy ranch," she said. "You left her so much food that she was able to take care of her kitties until me and Cash found her in the loft."

"She's okay?" he asked, remembering how she'd rubbed against him and purred. Her fur was so soft, and even though she was gray, the pattern of it had reminded him of a tiger or a leopard or some big cat. And when she'd stalked the mice in the barn, she'd looked like a big cat.

She nodded. "And she has the cutest kittens. I want to keep every one of them, but my mom says it's not fair to keep them all to myself. That we really need to share them with other people who would love to have one of them as a friend."

A friend. The mama cat had been his friend. Both she and Miss Darlene's mare had kept him company on the ranch. He missed them. He missed the ranch.

But it was his fault that it was gone. It must have been his fault...

He closed his eyes for a minute at that awful thought and the rush of guilt it brought him.

"Are you okay?" It was Bailey Ann who asked the question. She must have rushed up from the swings when he'd closed his eyes.

He opened them to stare at her.

"You look like I did before I got my new heart," she said, her voice all serious.

"What?" he asked uneasily.

"Really tired," she said. "I was tired all the time." She was breathing a little heavy now, like that short run from the swing set to where he and Hope stood by the slide had worn her out. She touched her chest. "But my new heart fixed me. Do you need a new heart?"

Did he need a new heart? Was there something wrong with his old one? It seemed to hurt a lot, especially when he thought about the fire. Or his old life at his old school...

Or his dad.

"I dunno," he replied.

"My daddy is a heart doctor," Bailey Ann said. "He can find out."

"He doesn't need a new heart," Hope said almost defensively. "He needs a friend."

Bailey Ann nodded. "Everybody needs friends."

He'd never really had any before, though. He wasn't sure how to be a friend.

"And everybody needs a best friend," Hope said. "Like my mom and Cash were best friends all through school."

"Aren't you going to be *my* best friend?" Bailey Ann asked.

Hope nodded. "Yeah, but I think maybe you can have more than one best friend. Like how Caleb has Ian and that horse that Dusty Chaps won."

Bailey Ann laughed. "Which one of us is the horse?"

He liked the sound of her laugh. It made him smile. "I want a cat," he said. He'd loved Miss Darlene's horse, but she hadn't purred and snuggled like that cat had.

"Come to my house after school," Hope said. "And you can pick one out."

"I want one, too," Bailey Ann said.

"You both have to ask your moms," Hope said. "I know my mom will be really happy to have some of the kitties go to other homes."

Would his mom let him have a cat? She'd never let him have any animals before, but that was because they were always moving, just staying with people for a little while until they were better.

Mr. JJ was better now. Were they going to have to leave again soon?

If they were, Mikey would need that cat even more than Bailey Ann would. Because she would have Hope, and he would have nobody once again.

Nobody but his mom. For as long as he could remember, it had only been the two of them. Hopefully, she would let him get a cat.

SARAH'S STOMACH MUSCLES had knotted the second she'd seen the sheriff's department SUV parked behind her car, blocking her from leaving. She'd felt trapped in that house with all the Havens and Cassidys joking around.

But she still wasn't able to escape. Instead of going back inside, she got in her vehicle and waited. He would probably be leaving soon. But when he stepped out of the house, he stopped to talk with the others who were slowly departing. And she closed her eyes and lowered her head a bit, not wanting to get caught staring at him like she'd probably been staring at him inside the house.

All of the Haven and Cassidy men were good-looking, but she'd never been tempted to stare at any of them the way she'd stared at Marsh. But he had more than an attractive appearance; he had a presence, too, one that drew her attention.

And after he'd comforted her last night, she couldn't stop thinking about him. And staring at him…

She closed her eyes more tightly, trying to shut him out of her mind as well as her sight. But then a tap on the glass startled her, and she jumped and whirled toward it to find him leaning down so that their faces were level with only that glass separating them.

He tapped again, and she rolled it down and leaned back a bit so that he wasn't too close.

"I'm sorry I startled you again," he said, his voice deep with what sounded like genuine remorse. "And I'm sorry I blocked you in."

Not wanting him to feel bad, she smiled and said, "I didn't mind having a minute to…" Try not to think about him. But she couldn't say that, so she just trailed off.

He smiled and glanced back at the people standing outside the house. "My family can be overwhelming, and this is probably only about half of them."

"I know," she said. "I met them all at Ranch Haven." That had definitely been overwhelming for her and for Mikey. He'd clung to her hand. Like her, he'd never seen that many family members in one place. Even before she'd been disowned, she'd just had a dad and mom, with no siblings. Like Mikey.

Like Hope. But unlike Hope, who seemed eager to go to school to be around other kids, Mikey was always reluctant to go. Like she was reluctant to leave now. But the morning was slipping away. "I should really get back to your dad's," she said.

"You don't have to rush off. He's probably still at Ranch Haven," Marsh said.

JJ hadn't asked her to go along with him. He didn't need her anymore; unlike Bailey Ann, he had no problem taking his medications correctly. And he always made sure to get his rest and try not to do too much too soon.

Except for the fire.

He could have died in it, trying to find her son. And that would have been her fault because she should have known where her child was.

"If you'd like to stay and visit with the others, you should," he said.

She shook her head. "No, I really need to get some things done around the house." Since she and Mikey lived with them, she insisted on doing most of the housework and cooking to cover their room and board, especially now that JJ was so healthy he didn't need her medical help. At least she could do something for him. But she owed him more than housework, especially if...

"The house is spotless, Sarah," he said, and his dark eyes narrowed a bit as he studied her face, which was too close to his with how he was crouched down next to her car. Maybe he suspected she just wanted to get away from him.

He wasn't wrong.

"I need to figure out what to make for dinner, so I have to get back," she said.

"It's not even lunch time yet," he pointed out with a slight grin, like he knew she was looking for an excuse to get away from him.

"Still, I have work to do," she said. She should probably get her resume together just in case that job did open up at the school.

"I understand that," he said. "I need to head to the sheriff's office, too." But he seemed reluctant to head to his SUV. Then he asked, "How was Mikey this morning about going to school?"

Her heart softened a bit with his concern. "Nervous. I had to keep reminding him that he knew some kids already, the kids in your family."

"So he knows a lot of kids then," Marsh said with a smile. "My head's still whirling from how we went from being a family of all bachelors with Mikey as the only kid in our orbit to all of these little Havens and Bailey Ann and Hope now, too."

"They're all very sweet kids," she said with a smile, thinking again of how kind and welcoming Hope had been toward her son.

He nodded. "I don't know a lot about kids, but they seem like really good ones. Like yours..."

Was she just being paranoid or did he not sound quite as certain of Mikey's goodness? Did he know about Mikey's father?

Then he added, "Would it be okay for me to ask Mikey some questions about the fire?"

And her stomach dropped as fear gripped her. "Why?" she asked.

"I'd just like to question him about what he remembers about it, about things that had been happening around the ranch around that time..."

She nearly shivered at his mention of questioning her son, like he was a criminal, like the child was like his dad. The sheriff definitely wasn't convinced yet that her kid was as good as his relatives.

She shook her head. "That's not necessary." And it wasn't going to happen. "He was in the barn when the fire started, and he was always in the barn. He wouldn't have seen anything around that time that wasn't in the barn." She drew in a shaky breath, trying to steady her voice before she continued, "Can you please move your vehicle? Now."

He stood there for a moment, still leaning over to meet her gaze, before he finally nodded and started walking toward the street.

She held her breath until he started his SUV and backed up. She held that breath until she was able to back out and speed away from him.

But she wouldn't be able to escape him for long. They lived in the same house. With her son.

Her son whom a sheriff wanted to question about a fire.

She had been concerned last night that Marsh suspected her son might have had something to do with it. Now she was terrified that he did and that maybe he had a good reason to be suspicious.

She had to talk to her son before the sheriff did. She had to make sure that, when she'd found him in the loft, he had only been apologizing for scaring her and not for...anything else.

WHEN MARSH BACKED up his SUV, Sarah wasn't the only one who exited the driveway. Collin drove off, too, and Cash and Becca as well. Yet Sarah was the one he was tempted to follow; she'd gotten too defensive over his questions. Both last night and just now, like she was hiding something.

Like he'd pointed out to Genevieve, nobody really knew that much about her. And that seemed pretty remiss of him and his brothers since she'd been hired to care for their sick and vulnerable father. Surely one of them must have checked her references or ran an employment check on her.

So despite needing to get to the office, he followed someone out of the driveway, but it wasn't her.

When he pulled in behind Collin's car in the hospital parking lot, his brother stepped out and asked, "Was I speeding, officer?"

"I don't think you could in that old hybrid," Marsh admitted.

Collin almost lovingly patted the roof of the vehicle with its faded paint and assorted dings. "She carried me through college and med school and my residency and fellowships," he said. "She's been faithful."

Collin was faithful as well, to his career and to his patients and especially to his family. Although he'd never admitted it aloud, it was pretty clear that Collin had become a cardiologist because he'd wanted to help their father. Surely he would have had Sarah checked out before hiring her to care for him.

"Speaking of faithful," Marsh said, "there's something I should have asked you a while ago about Dad. Actually, it's not so much about Dad as about someone close to him, maybe too close to him…"

Collin's brow furrowed. "I know Dad kept some secrets from us, some major ones, but he's still faithful to Mom's memory even though she's been gone nearly twenty years."

"What are you talking about?" Marsh asked.

"Dad dating," Collin said. "Isn't that what you wanted to ask me about?"

"No," he said. But he actually wished his father would find someone, especially now that Darlene was moving on and starting a life of her own. Not that she didn't deserve it. She'd helped them all so much with Dad and with the ranch. They would never be able to repay her for all she'd done for them and for all she'd sacrificed. "But if that's what you thought, I guess I worded that awkwardly."

"Thinking of Dad dating anyone is awkward," Collin agreed. "But it is overdue. Cash thinks he might be interested in Dusty's mother-in-law, Juliet."

Juliet was also the mother of Cash's half sister; they shared the same father. Poor Juliet had been through a lot thanks to her philandering husband. Marsh wasn't sure she would take a chance on romance again. Or that Dad would either, for that matter.

The only thing he knew for certain was that *he* wasn't about to take a chance on romance, no matter how much scheming Sadie did.

"I didn't follow you here to talk about Dad's love life," he said. Or his own. "I have some questions about his health care."

Collin's brow furrowed again. "He's doing well. Actually, with the transplant putting his lupus into remission, he's thriving. The transplant surgeon and his cardiologist are the best in their fields."

"What about his home health nurse?" Marsh asked.

"Sarah's an excellent nurse," Collin said, and he sounded a bit defensive. "She's taken exceptional care of our father. If he hadn't had her helping him before the transplant, I'm not sure he would have made it until his new heart became available."

Marsh sucked in a breath. He knew she was a good nurse, but he hadn't realized that she might have actually saved his father's life. He owed her his gratitude. But instead of thanking her, he'd upset her. However, he also had to know the truth.

"So you knew her before you hired her?" Marsh asked. "You worked with her or something?"

Collin shook his head. "I didn't know her, and I wasn't the one who hired her. Darlene did."

He nodded. "Okay, so she probably ran a background check on her. Hopefully, she'll know more about her."

"And now you're going to grill Darlene?" Collin asked. "Why?"

"You don't think we should know more about this woman who's been living with our dad?" Marsh asked. And he felt foolish that he hadn't thought about that when Sarah and her son had first moved to the ranch. But with his job, he hadn't gotten out there as much as he should have. And he'd just assumed Collin knew her.

"Darlene lived with our dad a lot longer, and we never knew she was our aunt," Collin pointed out. "She took care of him and us. That's all that matters. Just like Sarah has been taking care of Dad."

"I know, but..." He felt like there was more to Sarah Reynolds, like his dad wasn't the only one who'd been keeping secrets. Sarah was, too. But what kind of secrets?

"Instead of interrogating Darlene, why don't you just ask Sarah about Sarah?" Collin asked. "You seem very interested in her all of a sudden."

It wasn't all of a sudden, but he wasn't about to admit that to his brother. Until now, he'd been able to ignore his interest, until he'd started investigating the fire.

"And what does it matter now?" Collin asked. "Dad doesn't actually require help anymore; I just think he doesn't want Sarah or her son to go. I also think she's aware he doesn't need her anymore, so if she applies for the job at the school, which I hope she does, the school will thoroughly vet her before hiring her."

That was true, but it didn't negate the fact that they should have known more about her before letting her move in with their father and Darlene. While she was a good nurse, it didn't mean that she was a good person. Yet, he could hardly bring himself to think that with how sweet and compassionate she always was.

But she seemed defensive and a little secretive, too, now that he'd started asking her questions. Like she had something to hide...

And he was determined to find out what that was and, however unlikely, whether it had anything to do with the fire at the ranch. But he didn't know if his motivation was just to protect his father or to protect himself.

# CHAPTER SIX

EVER SINCE LEAVING Ranch Haven, Jessup had had a smile on his face. As he drove back into the city limits of Willow Creek, he kept thinking of Juliet fawning over her grandbabies and of how happy and vivacious she was.

And beautiful.

He had a granddaughter now himself since Collin was adopting Bailey Ann. He already loved that little girl so much, and he probably understood her better than anyone else did since they'd both had their health struggles and heart transplants. Now Hope was joining their family as well; just seeing her reminded him so much of her mother, of how Becca had spent every moment she could at the ranch with them. She'd always loved animals and his son. She already felt like his daughter.

So he had every reason to be happy. But all the changes made him uneasy as well. Darlene was leaving. When he pulled into the driveway next to the two-story brick traditional, he saw the boxes loaded into her vehicle. Not that she had much to move. She'd lost everything in the fire like he had. Well, they'd lost everything but what really mattered: family.

In fact, the fire had inadvertently reconnected them with all of their family. But Darlene wasn't moving to the ranch with her sons; instead, she was going to be working for Jessup's oldest son, Cash, and his partner at Willow Creek Veterinarian Services.

He parked his vehicle, stepped out and asked, "Do you need any help?"

She closed the back door of her little SUV and shook her head. "No. That was pretty much the last of it. I feel bad, though, like I'm booting Cash out of his home."

Jessup snorted. "His home is with Becca. The studio apartment connected to the barn of the veterinarian practice isn't his home."

"Yes, and I could have waited until he and Becca were married before moving into it," Darlene said.

But Jessup doubted that; he knew she'd been looking for a job and a place of her own since shortly after they'd moved to Willow Creek from Moss Valley. After reconciling with her sons, she had a new lease on life, like he did with his heart, and clearly she wanted to live it to its fullest.

"Instead, Cash moved out for me," Darlene continued, "and he's staying in the house with Dr. Miner until his and Becca's wedding."

"That's because he's going to marry Becca as quickly as he can," Jessup said. "Something he should have done years ago."

Darlene smiled. "You're starting to sound like your mother."

"Bite your tongue," Jessup teased.

She laughed.

That wasn't a sound he'd heard often from her. Eighteen years ago, she'd shown up at the Cassidy ranch as broken as a person could be and still survive—as broken as he'd been. And without her, he wasn't sure he would have survived. He'd needed her, and she'd needed to be needed.

"Sounding like Sadie isn't a bad thing," she said. "I idolize your mother."

That was why Darlene had tracked him down, to bring him back home to Sadie after his brother had died. But he'd been in no shape to reconcile with his mother then. He hadn't thought he would survive much longer, and he hadn't wanted to put her through the death of another child.

But he had survived. So now he had to figure out what to do with this second chance of his.

Darlene had already figured out hers. She'd gotten a job that he had no doubt she was going to love. And with the look that came over her face whenever she talked about Dr. Miner, Jessup wondered if she might come to love more than the job.

"I wish I could be more like her," Darlene said.

"You are," Jessup assured her. "If you're talking about her strength. As for the meddling, you don't have it in you."

"I don't dare meddle with my children," Darlene said. "I just want to be part of their lives again."

"What about mine?" Jessup asked.

"Of course I want to be part of my nephews' lives, too," she said.

"You are. They adore you," he assured her. "I meant about the meddling. Would you help meddle with mine?"

"Sadie hasn't asked me to," she said.

"What if I asked you to?"

She narrowed her hazel eyes and stared at him like he'd lost his mind.

Maybe he had. Maybe spending so much time with his mother was making him think like Sadie. Or maybe just seeing his other kids so happy made him want that happiness for all of them—for Marsh, too.

"What are you talking about?" she asked. "Colton is engaged. Collin is already married and Cash will be married soon. And Marsh...oh..." Her mouth dropped open slightly as she must have concluded what he had.

"Marsh deserves to be happy, too," he said.

She nodded. "I know..."

"And Sarah..."

"Sarah?" The sound of a car drew their attention to where the nurse was parking at the curb outside the house. Darlene smiled and nodded. "Yes, Sarah and Mikey deserve happiness."

"Want to help me help them find it?" he asked.

She shook her head. "I don't want to meddle."

He knew how much Darlene had suffered over thinking that anyone was unhappy or resentful of her. For years, she'd thought her own children, and Sadie, had hated her after her husband's death. She wouldn't risk being resented again.

But Jessup figured Marsh's happiness was worth the risk.

WHEN SARAH STEPPED out of her car and walked up to the house, she caught the look that JJ and Darlene exchanged before they turned toward her. The bright smiles they flashed made her even more uneasy. "Everything all right?" she asked.

They both nodded quickly. "Yes, of course," JJ said.

"How did the school drop-off go this morning?" Darlene asked.

"There was a lot of anxiety," Sarah admitted.

"Yours and Mikey's?" Darlene asked with a gentle smile. As a mother herself, she undoubtedly understood.

Sarah nodded. "And Collin's and Genevieve's and Taye's," she said. "I think the only one who wasn't worried about their child was Becca Calder." Sarah envied her that. Becca was a single mother like she was, but she'd instilled confidence and kindness in her child while Sarah must have instilled shyness and insecurity in hers.

"Hope is Becca's mini-me, so I'm not surprised she loves school, just like her mother did," JJ said. "I can understand why Taye might be concerned with the boys returning to school for the first time since the accident. But why were Collin and Genevieve anxious?"

"Because of Bailey Ann," Sarah said. "They don't think the current school nurse understood the schedule or the importance of her anti-rejection meds."

JJ gasped. "That is a concern."

"Collin is going to check on her throughout the day," Sarah assured the new grandfather. "He's also hoping that the nurse will retire soon and someone else might apply..." She saw the sudden widening of his dark eyes, and the slight easing of the tension in his body.

"You?" he asked.

And her heart sank a bit. He didn't need her anymore, and he had pretty much just confirmed it. She forced a smile and nodded. "I was second choice to Sue, but she didn't want it."

"Do you?" Darlene asked.

She glanced over at the older woman and noticed the boxes in her vehicle. She was moving out. She was moving on. Sarah needed to do that, too. But she'd never met anyone as kind as the Cassidys and Darlene. Tears pricked her eyes at the thought of leaving them, but she quickly blinked them away and forced a smile. "I think I might—" she turned back to JJ "—if you don't think you need me anymore."

JJ smiled back at her. "At my last follow-up, Dr. Bixby said I'm doing so well that he couldn't believe this isn't my original heart." He touched his knuckles to his chest, where she knew all too well he bore a big scar. "He thinks I'm doing really well."

Meaning that he didn't need her anymore, and he probably hadn't for a while. But being as sweet as he was, JJ hadn't had the heart to dismiss her.

"Then I think I will apply for that job," she said. "It would be good for me to be close to Mikey during the day, too, after having homeschooled him for a while now." She'd done that because other kids had been bullying him just as their parents had been bullying her. If she could get this job, she might be able to make sure that didn't happen again.

If they gave her the chance.

JJ's head bobbed. She didn't think he was eager to get rid of her, but it was clear he'd known before she had that it was time for her to move on. "That would be good for both of you," he said. "And I hope you know that you can stay here as long as you'd like."

She glanced again at those boxes in Darlene's vehicle. Then she heard the rumble of an engine and turned toward the street, where the sheriff's SUV was pulling up to the curb behind her car. Was he going to block her in again?

That was why she couldn't stay here. Marsh was everywhere lately. And she needed some distance between them for Mikey's sake and for hers. He was entirely too good-looking for her peace of mind.

"I appreciate that," she told JJ. But she had no intention of staying here any longer than necessary; she just had to find another place to live.

Becca Calder was a real estate agent. Hopefully, she also handled rental properties and could help her find another place for her and Mikey.

A place far away from the sheriff.

*SHE PROBABLY THINKS I'm stalking her.* That was Marsh's thought when he saw the paleness of Sarah's face and the widening of her dark eyes as he walked up from where he'd parked his vehicle behind hers. He probably should have driven past when he saw her car parked at the curb, but then that might have looked more suspicious, like he was just checking up on her.

Which was exactly what he was doing, but he didn't want her to know that. So he just spared her a nod, which was all he'd ever given her until that conversation the night before, and he turned toward Darlene. "You're moving already? Do you need some help?"

She shook her head. "Like I told your dad, I'm all loaded up already."

"Do you need help unloading? I can follow you back to your new digs at the veterinarian practice," Marsh offered. Thinking of that reminded him of the night before, and he found himself adding, "You probably shouldn't have told Mikey you're going to live in a barn. Last night, he was trying to convince Sarah to let him go to work with you rather than go to school."

Darlene and JJ glanced from him to Sarah. Sarah's face flushed, her cheeks pink. Was she embarrassed to admit they'd been talking?

The way JJ and Darlene looked at each other next, with slight smiles and bright eyes, had him flushing a little, too. Did they think he and Sarah had done more than talk last night? Or were they just surprised they'd talked at all?

Marsh had certainly not made any effort to talk to her before last night. Maybe that was why he was embarrassed, because he felt bad he hadn't at least thanked her for all she'd done for his father. As Collin had pointed out, he might not have survived until his heart transplant without her medical care.

But instead of thanking her, Marsh had interrogated her. While he felt bad about that, he also needed to find out what really happened with the fire so he could protect his family. Ever since he was a kid, that was all he had ever wanted to do, but he hadn't been able to protect them from bad health and accidents.

Hopefully that was all the fire had been. He couldn't imagine anyone wanting to purposely burn down the place.

Sarah cleared her throat and said, "Yes, it's Mikey's dream to live in a barn."

Darlene chuckled. "It was mine, too. I've always loved animals just like Mikey and apparently Becca and Hope, too."

"And Cash," Marsh added.

"That's how Marsh persuaded Mikey that he needs to go to school," Sarah said. "So that he can become a vet like Cash."

"I'd love to introduce him to Dr. Miner, too," Darlene said, and there was a slight catch to her voice when she mentioned Cash's partner's name. Then her face flushed. "He's funny and great with the animals."

"How is he with you, Darlene?" Marsh asked. He wasn't sure if he should be concerned or not, but after everything his aunt had done for them, he felt awfully protective of her. He had felt that way even before he'd learned how much she'd already lost in her life.

Darlene's face flushed a deeper pink. "Dr. Miner is very professional or, at least, as professional as he probably knows how to be."

Marsh's dad looked at her with concern then, too. "You know you can continue to live here, right? You can work for the veterinarian practice without living there."

She shrugged and sent a furtive glance at Sarah, as if trying to signal to Marsh and his father that they shouldn't talk about moving in front of her, and maybe they shouldn't. Then she smiled. "It's past time for me to be a part of the real world again," she said. "I think I was hiding from it out at the Cassidy ranch."

"So selling it was a good thing," JJ said. "For both of us. We needed to leave there."

"The fire wasn't a good thing, though," Marsh said, thinking again of how he, his father and Collin had been injured. It could have been so much worse. Sarah could have lost her son, too, if he'd actually been in the house instead of the barn that day. His heart ached at the thought of that little boy losing his life before it had even really started.

As if she was thinking the same thing, the color drained from Sarah's face.

"Of course it wasn't," his father said. "We lost so much. The photographs of your mother and all of you kids. Your school awards and yearbooks. And the ribbons and souvenirs from your mother's days of traveling with the rodeo." He touched his heart then as if it hurt at the thought of what they'd lost.

Or maybe of her, his late wife.

Sarah cleared her throat. "I'm sorry... I just remembered I forgot to pick up a prescription..." And she turned and almost ran to her vehicle, as if desperate to get away from them.

Or to get away from him?

Or talk of the fire?

## CHAPTER SEVEN

SARAH HADN'T FORGOTTEN a prescription. She wished, however, that she could forget all about the fire, but Marsh seemed determined to keep bringing it up for some reason. She could guess what that reason was.

He thought someone was responsible for it. And with the way he was suddenly focusing on her and Mikey, she could guess who he thought that was.

Nerves fluttered in her stomach, making her feel ill and anxious. She had to move out of that house. Maybe even out of Willow Creek.

But she would need a job to support herself and Mikey, and if the school would consider hiring her, and Mikey was already making a friend in Hope and maybe the other Havens and Bailey Ann, then it would be better for him if they stayed in Willow Creek. While they could stay here, they couldn't stay in the house anymore with the sheriff and JJ.

JJ didn't need her, and with Darlene leaving, it would be even more awkward than it had already become since the night before. Since Marsh had started talking to her.

Or interrogating her?

She had to find a place of their own for her and Mikey. And she had to do it as soon as possible. Since she had no need to stop at the pharmacy for something she hadn't forgotten, she headed to Becca Calder's real estate office instead.

With the money she'd saved, she could pay rent and take care of her and Mikey for a while. Then, if she couldn't get another job, they could leave town. Of course, she would rather buy a house, but she knew it wasn't smart to count on anything or anyone.

She had to take care of herself and her son on her own, like she always had. She found a spot near the real estate office, parked and then headed toward the building. At the morning drop-off, Becca had been dressed like she was going to work, so hopefully she was here now and not busy.

Sarah pushed open the door, and an older woman looked up and greeted her with a warm smile. "Hello there, my name's Phyllis Calder," she said.

With her dark hair and eyes, she looked a lot like Becca, so she was probably her mother. Sarah smiled back at her. "Hi, I'm—"

"Sarah!" Becca said as she stepped out of a doorway that must have led into her private office. "I'm so glad you stopped by. Mom, this Sarah Reynolds, who's been taking such wonderful care of JJ Cassidy."

Sarah smiled and shook her head a bit. "He really doesn't need *anyone* taking care of him anymore. He's doing so well."

"That's good," Mrs. Calder said. "He's always been such a kind man. He never minded how much my daughter hung around his ranch."

"He's a sweetheart," Becca agreed. "And was always like a second father to me."

"And he will be that officially as soon as we can get this wedding together," Phyllis said as she waved her hand over the bridal magazines spread across her desk.

"If we just did the city hall thing, there would be nothing to get together," Becca said.

Her mother gasped as if appalled. "My only daughter getting married—"

"I know, I know," Becca said. "We'll have a wedding, but it's going to be on my ranch, Mom. Low-key and casual."

Sarah had done the city hall thing with Michael, with no family present, because nobody had approved of their marriage. She hadn't realized until it was too late that they'd had good reason not to approve.

"Just don't muck out the stalls in your wedding gown," Phyllis said, and she winked at Sarah to show she was teasing.

Sarah laughed.

Then Phyllis Calder sighed. "The sad part is that she probably will."

"I'm sure Sarah isn't here to talk about weddings," Becca said. "Unless Sadie is already working on you..."

Sarah shuddered. "Oh, no. I'm not here about weddings," she said. After being so wrong about a man she'd known since they were kids, she didn't trust her judgement enough to date anyone else, let alone marry them, especially while Mikey was so young and impressionable yet.

"Are you here about kittens?" Becca asked.

Sarah looked around, wondering where they were and why they would be at the office. "Kittens?"

Phyllis Calder laughed. "Becca is fostering the mama kitty from the Cassidy ranch, and she has a bunch of babies that Hope would love to keep."

"But those babies will grow up, and my house and my ranch will be overrun with cats," Becca said. "They should be ready to go to their new homes in a couple weeks."

"I need a home first," Sarah said. "JJ—Mr. Cassidy really doesn't need me anymore."

"Do you want to buy?" Becca asked.

Sarah sighed. "I would love to, but I'm not sure where I will find my next job."

"Hopefully at the school," Becca said. "I think Collin and Genevieve would feel a lot better about Bailey Ann being away from them if you were there to make sure she got her medication correctly."

A little jab of fear struck Sarah's heart at the thought of that sweet girl having a medical emergency while at school. She'd seemed so excited to be there that morning, unlike Mikey. "Collin said he was going to check on her," she said, as much to re-assure herself as to reassure Becca.

"Yes, but he's also busy at the hospital," Becca said. "And if you don't get the school job, I'm sure you could work there, too."

So she had options in Willow Creek as long as no one found out about her past and started judging her and Mikey as harshly as they had in their old hometown. As interested as the sheriff suddenly seemed in her and Mikey, it was probably only a matter of time before he found out, which meant that she should probably just tell him herself.

Sarah shrugged. "I would hate to buy a house and then have another opportunity come up..." Or so many opportunities taken away that she had to leave.

"I hope that you'll stay in town," Becca said. "My daughter seems to really like Mikey."

Her son having a friend meant so much to Sarah. She smiled. "Hope is so sweet."

Becca smiled, too. "Yes, she is."

Phyllis sniffled even though she smiled, too. "She's a beautiful girl inside and out."

Sarah nodded in wholehearted agreement. Because Hope was so kind, maybe it wouldn't matter to her if people started talking about Mikey's father. Maybe she would still be his friend no matter what.

"Although, in this market, it will probably be easier to find you a place to rent rather than purchase. There's just not much for sale right now," Becca said.

"It's probably easier to find a good man than a good house," Phyllis said with a laugh. "At least, it seems that way with all the bachelor cowboys finally settling down."

"Thanks to Sadie," Becca said with a laugh of her own.

"It was probably the only way her grandsons would have settled down," Phyllis said. "And if I remember right, there's one left single, isn't there? The sheriff?" She gave Sarah a significant look, like she was implying...

Sarah nearly shuddered again. "I'm sure Sadie isn't going to try to match me up with one of her grandsons." Especially if she knew about the mistake Sarah had made all those years ago. "And even if she did, I'm only interested in a house. Not a man." Good, bad or otherwise.

Becca gestured for Sarah to come into her office. "Let's get some specifics and get away from my mother, who's been spending too much time with Sadie."

"I'm sorry," Phyllis said. "I'm so happy that Becca is finally marrying her best friend that I just want everybody else to be that happy."

Becca and Cash were happy. Sarah had seen it herself at Genevieve and Collin's that morning. The lawyer and the cardiologist were also very happy. And Taye Cooper and Baker Haven as well. If she hadn't seen it for herself, she might not have believed it was possible. But even though she'd seen the love between those people, she didn't believe a love like that was possible for her.

"I'll be happy with a nice place for me and my son to live," Sarah said. That was all she wanted. Security for her little boy. She turned then and followed Becca into her office, where she filled out a rental application.

"You have more than enough money for a down payment," Becca said as she read what Sarah had filled in as her bank account balance. "If I can find a suitable house for sale, you really wouldn't be interested? You'll have more freedom in a house that you own. You won't have to abide by the landlord's rules."

"Like the no-pet one some of them have," Phyllis Calder called out through the open door. "Becca really wants to get rid of a kitten."

Despite going into Becca's office, they really didn't have much more privacy than they'd had in the reception area.

"A kitten or two," Becca called back to her mother. "Unless you want them all, Mom."

"I can't hear you," Phyllis said.

"Sorry about that," Becca said to Sarah. "We get a little carried away around here. Ignore us. Let's focus on what you want."

"Well, I'd just feel safer renting," Sarah said. Like she had an escape plan in case she needed it.

Becca nodded. "I understand. Then the landlord is responsible for maintenance and repairs. Unfortunately, there isn't much more available for rent than there is for sale."

Panic gripped Sarah again. What if she couldn't find somewhere for her and Mikey to live? Of course JJ had said they could stay as long as they wanted. But with Marsh there, too, Sarah couldn't wait to leave.

"I really don't care what it is," she said. "I don't mind sleeping on a couch if there's only one bedroom."

"We'll find you something," Becca promised. "Some landlords have gotten really picky. But I'll do my best to find someplace that allows pets."

Sarah laughed at her persistence. "Like I said, I really don't care what it is as long as it's a safe place for me and my son."

"I think pretty much everywhere in Willow Creek is safe," Becca assured her with a smile.

But Sarah didn't smile back at her. She didn't feel safe staying with JJ anymore because of the sudden interest his son, the sheriff, had taken in her and in Mikey. About the fire…

"Are you okay?" Becca asked, her voice a whisper now as she leaned across her desk.

Sarah nodded.

"I don't know what your situation is…" Becca said, and she glanced at Sarah's bare ring finger. "But I've been a single mom, too. I was fortunate enough to have a lot of support from my parents and my best friend. But even then, it wasn't easy. If you ever need anything, let me know."

Emotion rushed up the back of Sarah's throat. She hadn't had the support that Becca had; her parents hadn't been there for her. And the person she'd thought was her best friend had let her down more than anyone else.

But to have Becca make the offer she had, to know there were people here who genuinely cared about her and her son, moved Sarah to tears.

She furiously blinked them back and forced that smile. "Thank you."

Would she have this care and support though if she told the truth? Since JJ's doctors had so highly recommended her, he and Darlene probably hadn't dug any deeper into her past. But with the sheriff asking his questions, it would probably come out, either through him or through the in-depth background check a school or hospital might run. So she needed to tell everyone the truth.

But first, she had to talk to her son. Or at least get him to talk to her before she or he talked to anyone else, especially the sheriff.

"SHE DIDN'T REALLY forget a prescription, did she?" Marsh asked as he looked at all the pill bottles on the kitchen counter.

His dad looked at the bottles and shook his head. "Nope. They're all here."

So she probably was worried Marsh was stalking her or, at least, that he had some suspicions. And those suspicions were obviously spooking her. Would she react that way if she didn't have something to hide?

"What were the two of you talking about last night?" Darlene asked. Even though her vehicle was all packed, she hadn't left yet for her new place. Maybe because she'd realized it was lunch time. She flipped a sandwich on the griddle, and melted cheese oozed out between the grilled slices while steam and the scents of tomato and basil rose from a pot of soup simmering on the back burner.

Marsh shrugged. "Not much. Just Mikey…the first day of school…" The fire. But for some, reason he didn't want to broach the subject yet with his dad and Darlene. He didn't want to worry them if there was nothing to worry about, if the fire had truly been an accident. And no matter what or who had caused it, he really believed that it hadn't been intentional.

His dad narrowed his dark eyes and studied his face. "That was all?" Being that he was a man who'd kept secrets of his own, maybe he had an uncanny ability to detect when someone else was keeping secrets.

Marsh shrugged again. "I might have asked her about the fire."

JJ tensed. "Why?"

"I'm just trying to figure out everything that happened that day."

JJ snorted. "You and the insurance company. Even though the fire inspector ruled it an accident, they're still dragging their feet on the final payout, but maybe that's because I'm not going to rebuild. I'm just trying to close the sale with Dusty, but the title company won't sign off on the final sale with an open claim on the property."

"So what did happen that day?" Marsh persisted.

"We were all out in the barn when we noticed the smoke coming from the house," Darlene said. "Sarah and I ran inside to see what it was and get the oxygen tanks out. And then once we were outside, we realized we didn't know where Mikey was. She tried going back in, but by then, the fire was going strong, flames everywhere..." Her voice cracked as emotion overwhelmed her.

"And you ran inside to look for him," Marsh said to his dad, his stomach sinking as he thought of how close his father had come to dying. Again.

"We should have realized he was in the barn," Darlene said.

"But you were just out there and hadn't seen him," Marsh pointed out.

"We were by the mare," she said. "Mikey was in the loft with that cat."

Marsh nodded. And maybe it was as innocent as that. But why was the insurance adjuster so convinced that there was more to it?

And why was Sarah so reluctant to talk to him?

"What do you know about Sarah?" he asked.

"That she's an incredibly sweet, compassionate person," JJ said.

Marsh smiled. "I understand why you're a fan." For what she'd done for his dad, he was, too. "But I mean, what do you really know about her?"

"What are you asking about?" JJ asked, and again, he stared at Marsh as if he suspected he had ulterior motives for his questions.

"I mean like where she came from, if she has a record, that kind of thing."

"Record? Like police?" JJ asked, horrified. "That's ridiculous."

Marsh turned back to Darlene, who was flipping the grilled cheese sandwiches onto plates. "You ran a background check on her before you hired her, right?"

Darlene laughed. "I wouldn't know how to run a background check on anyone. No. I take that back. If I needed one run, I would ask you."

"Why didn't you?" he asked.

She shrugged. "The cardiologist highly recommended her. She had great references, too, from other patients and doctors. And when we met her..." She smiled.

"She just clicked," JJ finished for his sister-in-law. "She felt like family, her and Mikey. He's such a sweet kid, and he loved the ranch."

"She never told you about his dad?" Marsh asked.

"What about him?" JJ asked.

"Like why he's not involved," Marsh said. "Like why it's just her and her son and nobody's come to visit them and they've not gone to visit anyone."

"Some people aren't as lucky as we are to have so much family," JJ pointed out.

"Even more than we realized we had," Marsh shot back at him. But he grinned. He'd forgiven Dad long ago for the secrets he'd kept. His health and his happiness were much more important.

JJ grinned back at him. "And some people we meet become family to us," he said. "Sarah and her son seemed like a great fit for us."

"As your in-home nursing care," Marsh said.

JJ shrugged. "Maybe not just that." He winked. "Maybe she would be a great fit for someone else in our family. Like the last bachelor..."

Marsh groaned. "Has everyone caught Sadie's matchmaking bug?"

His dad chuckled. "You can't dispute that your brothers are happy."

No. He couldn't. "But that's them. They have more time for romance than I do. I have an election coming up," he said. "The last thing I have time for is dating."

But dating would be a good way to get to know Sarah and Mikey better. Maybe once he knew what she was hiding and everything they knew about the fire, he wouldn't be so fascinated with her anymore.

SADIE HAD PLANNED on meeting her husband for lunch today, so Taye had packed her a picnic basket before she'd left that morning to take the kids to school. Lem would appreciate that Taye had prepared it and not her. He certainly hadn't married Sadie for her cooking skills; maybe he had married her for Taye's, though.

But when she carried the basket into his office at city hall, he reached for her first instead of it. He closed his arms around her in a warm hug. "Hello, my blushing bride," he greeted her with a grin and love sparkling in his blue eyes.

She was certainly too old to be called that, but the strange thing was that her husband could make her blush like she was a young girl again. He made her feel like a young girl again.

"Hello, my…" Sadie wasn't good at endearments, especially with Lem. She'd called him an old fool longer than he'd actually been old. But he was always so sweet to her even when she hadn't deserved his sweetness. "…my heart," she finished, her voice a little gruff with emotion. Because that was what he was to her: her heart, her soul—her sanity, sometimes.

Tears glistened in his blue eyes until he blinked them away. "You're my heart, too, Sadie March Haven-Lemmon."

Tears rushed to her eyes. She waved them away with a shaky hand and swung the picnic basket onto his desk with her other one. "You are going to need to retire soon," she told him. Because at their ages, they couldn't waste any of the time they had left.

"I agree," he said. "I've already told Ben he needs another running mate for the next election."

"Who's he thinking of asking?" she wondered aloud.

"I think Genevieve."

His new cousin-in-law was a lawyer who'd worked in DC for a while. "She's perfect," Sadie said. "Did your grandson Brett contact her?"

Lem shrugged. "I'm trying to stay out of it," he said. "How about your meetings this morning? Is that what you were told?"

She shook her head. "Surprisingly not. I think Jessup might actually appreciate my meddling. And Marsh...he had something else on his mind."

"What?"

"The fire."

"What about the fire?" Lem asked, his brow furrowing beneath a lock of white hair that had fallen across his forehead.

She brushed it back, marveling at how soft it was. "He says the insurance company thinks that it may have been deliberately set."

"By whom?" Lem asked, clearly appalled.

She sighed. "I don't know. But Marsh doesn't want his father getting upset when he's finally doing so well." The way Jessup had been looking at Juliet that morning had Sadie hopeful that he was ready to enjoy the second chance at life his new heart had given him.

"We'll make sure that doesn't happen," Lem assured her. "Should we hire a private investigator? Or have Ben talk to the insurance company as Jessup's lawyer?"

Sadie smiled at how quickly he'd come up with solutions to their families' problems. "I am so lucky to have you," she said.

"And I am so lucky to have you," he said.

"I don't think we need to do anything yet," she said. "Marsh is working on it." She had faith in her grandson, or she wouldn't have instigated his becoming the interim sheriff of Willow Creek. She had to make sure that he secured that position in the next election. "But we'll keep an eye on the situation and step in when we need to," she added. "Just like with your grandsons."

Lem smiled. "Yes. We will do whatever we need to..."

"To ensure the happiness of our family," Sadie finished for him.

"Ohhh," a deep voice murmured. "I just got chills."

She turned to find Ben standing in the open doorway to her husband's office. She smiled at her grandson.

"It's like I stumbled into a secret meeting of a crime family."

Sadie chuckled at his silliness even as she felt a little uneasy. Surely that fire had not been a crime. "We are just a family," she said.

"A family you two will apparently do anything for," he said. "Why does that scare me?"

"You don't need to be scared," Sadie assured him. Ben was happy. Settled. "Before this year is over, you're going to win the next election and marry your perfect mate." Just like she'd married hers.

"Yes, you have all of us partnered off now except for our sheriff," Ben said, and his dark eyes narrowed. "So Marsh is the one who needs to be scared?"

After their meeting that morning, Sadie was pretty sure her last single grandson was already scared, but it wasn't over her matchmaking. He was worried about their family, too.

## CHAPTER EIGHT

SARAH PACED NERVOUSLY on the sidewalk in front of the house. She should have picked up Mikey from school. Letting him ride the bus home on his first day had been foolish. Drivers were too busy focusing on the road and their stops to notice all the bullying that took place on buses, so they wouldn't be able to stop it.

But after lunch, the school had sent out a mass email addressing the traffic congestion from that morning and advising that all children on bus routes would be sent home on buses that afternoon unless there were extenuating circumstances that prevented them from riding.

Sarah's fear and overprotectiveness probably weren't valid extenuating circumstances. Not like a doctor's appointment or a sudden illness. She felt sick with anxiety, though, as she waited outside for the bus to appear.

It was later than the time that had been indicated in the registration packet she'd received after she'd signed him up for school. Due to their proximity to the school, Mikey didn't have a long ride, which was good. But their address was going to change soon.

It had to; Becca had to find them someplace else to live, someplace far away from the sheriff. But not the school.

Was that possible?

Was it even possible for her and Mikey to stay in Willow

Creek? If Mikey liked the school, if he was making friends, she would get another job here; she would stay if he was happy. He hadn't been happy in so long.

Before she saw it, she heard the loud engine of the bus and the soft squeak of air brakes as it slowed to turn onto their street. Sunshine glinted off the yellow paint and the glass windows. Then its lights blinked as it stopped right outside the house. The doors opened, releasing a rumble of voices and laughter and, finally, a little boy. He skipped down the steps, but instead of walking up to her, he turned around and waved at all those windows as the bus moved, driving off down their street.

He was waving?

Sarah stared at her son through wide eyes, shocked at his friendliness. Then he turned toward her with a bright smile. "Hey, Mom…"

"How was your first day?" she asked.

"Good. Can we go to Hope's house now?" he asked.

"What?"

"Hope asked me to come over after school and see the mama cat I took care of at the…" His smile slipped away then, and he stopped as if unable to even bring himself to say the word *ranch*.

"That was nice of her," Sarah said.

"She is really nice," Mikey said. "She told me I can pick out a kitten to take home when it's ready to leave its mama. Can I have a kitty, Mom?"

She wanted to say yes, especially because she'd had to deny him the last thing he'd wanted, to go to work with Darlene instead of going to school. But after her conversation with Becca just a short while ago, she wasn't sure that would be possible. "There are a lot of things up in the air right now, Mikey. And I'm not really sure that we'll be able to take care of a cat."

And themselves, if she didn't find a place and a job to support them so her savings didn't run out. But she didn't know how to explain that to her son without potentially frightening him about their future. She wanted him to feel secure and as happy as he'd looked when he'd first gotten off the bus.

There was no hint of a smile on his face now. Instead, his lips had pulled down into a frown, and he wouldn't meet her gaze.

But she could still see the hint of tears in his eyes, and pain gripped her. "Oh, Mikey, I wish I could say yes..." She wanted so badly to get him everything he wanted, but she didn't want to be another parent who made promises they didn't keep. "I'm sorry..."

As she said that, she remembered him saying those words over and over when she'd found him in the loft the day of the fire. Since he was already upset, she forged ahead, desperate to get answers to questions that she knew the sheriff was going to eventually ask. "Mikey, we need to talk about some things."

He shook his head and turned toward the house. But before he could open the front door, she stepped in front of it. Then she drew in a deep breath, determined to have this talk with him.

"I told you school was good," he said, but he was mumbling, his head down.

"Good," she said. "I'm glad. And I hope you can keep going to that school, but we're not going to be able to stay here."

He glanced up at her then, his eyes wide.

"Mr. JJ doesn't need me as a nurse anymore," she said.

"He's all better now."

She nodded. "So we have to find a new place to live, and I'm not sure they'll let us have a cat."

He released a shaky sigh, and tears pooled in his eyes.

"I'm sorry," she said again. "I know you really love animals, like Miss Darlene's horse and the cat from the ranch."

He gasped at the mention of the ranch.

"What happened at the ranch?" she asked softly like he was that wild barn cat he'd befriended. "Why don't you want to go back there? Why have you been so quiet since the fire?"

He shrugged his shoulders then and stared down at the front steps. And a tear dropped from his face onto the concrete.

Her heart ached for upsetting him, and she crouched down to try to meet his gaze. "Is there something you need to tell me about that day?" she asked.

He shook his head.

"Mikey, you can tell me anything," she promised, and she started to close her arms around him.

But he dodged her hug and darted around her. Then he pushed

open the front door and ran into the house. And she didn't know if he was upset about the move or the kitten or about the fire.

Instead of getting answers, she just had more questions.

ONCE HE FINALLY got into the sheriff's office, Marsh did what he should have done before she moved into the ranch with his father and Darlene and ran that background check on Sarah Reynolds. It took a while to get enough information to discern which Sarah Reynolds she was of the several women with the same name. But by tracing her through her nursing license and her son's birth certificate, he found the right one.

He was also right to think she was keeping secrets. But he understood why she would. And instead of feeling more suspicion about her, he felt sympathy and respect.

She'd fought hard to support herself and her son. She probably could have chosen a different career, one that wouldn't have required as much education or as long hours. But clearly she hadn't wanted to just help herself and her son; she'd wanted to help other people as well.

Like his dad.

And she had. According to Collin, who would know, JJ might not have made it if not for her care.

Guilt gripped Marsh, bowing his shoulders slightly. He shouldn't have been so intrusive into her personal life. He already knew she was a good nurse, so there had been no reason for him to run that background check on her. Sure, he'd been concerned that she had a secret. And after all the secrets kept in his family, he had no patience for them anymore. But, with the way she'd taken such great care of his dad, he was more curious than concerned about her.

She intrigued him as no one ever had. And now, after finding out what he had, he was even more intrigued and impressed. Sarah Reynolds was a strong woman and an incredibly fierce mother.

And now he owed her his gratitude and an apology for prying into her life. But if he showed up at the house again, she might take off like she had earlier.

Obviously, she didn't want to be around him anymore. Maybe

that was the best way he could apologize, by going back to ignoring her like he had been. He just wasn't certain that he could do that anymore, not after talking to her and, last night, holding her.

He wanted to hold her again, especially after what he'd just learned about her. And he wasn't sure that he would be able to stay away from her.

Maybe Darlene shouldn't be the only one moving out; maybe he should as well.

He released a heavy sigh and leaned back in his desk chair. It creaked beneath his weight and another creak echoed as the door to his office opened.

"Marsh, Mrs. Little let me come back," his dad said. "I hope that was all right."

Marsh nodded. "Yes, of course." Then he quickly signed off of his computer, not wanting his father to see what he'd done, that he'd run that background check on Sarah. When he turned his attention from the black screen to his father's face, he noticed the tension in it and in his shoulders. And he jumped up from his chair. "Dad, what's wrong? Are you all right?"

Had something horrible happened?

Again?

JESSUP WANTED TO smile and reassure his son, but he was too upset to do that now. Marsh had always been the strongest of his children, the one with the widest shoulders to help carry Jessup's burdens. He knew that hadn't been fair when Marsh was young. That he'd probably done that parentification thing to him that caused so many issues for people even after they grew up and left home. That caused so much resentment, too.

But Marsh had never seemed to resent him then or now. He'd jumped up from his chair so quickly that it had bumped into the wall behind him. "Dad? Are you all right?"

Jessup nodded. "Yes, physically, I'm fine." Emotionally, he was kind of a wreck right now. He was just so mad and frustrated and confused.

"What's going on? What's happened?" Marsh asked. "Is everyone all right?"

Jessup released a shaky sigh and reminded himself while answering his son, "Yes, everyone's fine. After we talked about the fire again, I called the insurance company to find out why they haven't settled yet. I hate that they're holding up the sale with Dusty because the property is still in escrow. I also borrowed money from Darlene, from the sale of her mare, and I want to pay her back. She shouldn't have to stay in a barn."

Marsh smiled slightly. "You know she prefers that. And I have some money you can have."

"You can't have much," Jessup said, "because you've helped me out so much already. I'll be fine with the sale of the ranch. But the insurance adjuster said they've asked the fire inspector to reopen their investigation. They don't believe the fire was an accident."

And that was what really upset him.

But Marsh had no visible reaction. He didn't even blink, just like he'd reacted when Jessup had revealed that Cash wasn't biologically his son. Marsh had already known that somehow, just as he seemed to already know this.

"You're not surprised," he concluded.

"My old boss gave me a head's up last night," Marsh said. "I knew the insurance company has concerns, but I didn't want to worry you if nothing came of it."

"But why would they have concerns?" Jessup asked. "There was no one in the house at the time the fire started. It had to be an accident."

"You and Darlene and Sarah were out in the barn?"

"Yes, Sarah would still hover when I'd walk around on my own in those days. She didn't want me to overdo it."

"And moments later, you ran into a burning house."

"To find a child," Jessup said, and he shuddered as he remembered that horror of thinking the little boy could be inside the smoke-and-flame-filled structure.

"Why would you think he was inside?" Marsh asked.

"We just didn't know where he was," Jessup said. "And the smart thing to do was to make sure that the house was empty."

"The smart thing to do was wait for the fire department to show up."

Jessup chuckled. "Something you didn't do, either."

"You were inside," Marsh said. "Collin and I weren't going to risk losing you..."

"Again," Jessup finished for him. They'd nearly lost him so many times. "I'm sorry for putting you through that scare. And I'm sorry for coming here to dump this on you." He wasn't even sure why he had except that *he* was scared now. "If they manage to blame someone for starting this fire, it's going to be me, isn't it?"

Marsh tensed. "What do you mean?"

"Well, I'm the only one who would have something to gain," he said. "Which is stupid, really, because I would gain more if the sale were to go through than whatever they were going to pay me for our destroyed personal property and a run-down building that nobody intends to replace. Dusty only cares about the land and the barn."

"And you've given him free reign of the property already," Marsh said. "He's not going to back out of the sale. And I am sure Darlene isn't worried about getting that money back. And I will give you everything I have—"

"No!" Jessup said, his pride smarting as well as his conscience. "I've already taken too much from you. I feel like I've always relied too much on you."

"I'm glad that you did," Marsh said. "I was happy to help out however I could. And I want to help you now."

And that was why he'd come to Marsh. "Whatever you can do to convince them that it was just an accident..."

Marsh nodded. "I'm working on it..."

"What do you mean?" Jessup asked. "Were you already looking into it?"

"I told you, my old boss already called me," Marsh said. "Don't worry about this, Dad. I'll take care of it. I'll take care of you."

And that guilt Jessup had been feeling intensified even more. "You reminded me earlier today that you're too busy to date because there is an election coming up."

Marsh's head bobbed in a nod so quick that the brim of his hat slipped down a bit over his face. "That's different, though."

"Not really. If you're too busy to date, you're too busy to take on any more of my problems. You need to focus on your future. You need to win to keep this job that I think you love. I don't want you to risk losing it because of me."

His boys had already sacrificed and suffered too much because of him. He didn't want to cost them anything else. He wanted them to be happy, even if that cost him…

## CHAPTER NINE

ONCE SARAH HAD followed Mikey into the house, she hadn't immediately looked for him. Instead, she'd checked on JJ, who'd just been wrapping up a phone call in the kitchen. He'd looked pale after putting his cell away. And before she'd even been able to ask him what was wrong, he'd rushed away from her like her son had.

Knowing how Mikey shut down when he was upset, Sarah gave him some space. But she wasn't sure why he was upset. Because she'd asked him about the fire? Or was he just tired after his late night and early morning? Or did he really want that kitten?

She felt like an ogre for not taking him to Hope's ranch to pick out a little furry friend. Or at least check on the cat he'd cared for at the Cassidy ranch.

But if she did that, it would be even harder to deny him a kitten—if he saw all of them. It would be hard for her not to take one as well. Mikey wasn't the only one who wanted a pet. She had always wanted one, too, but with how often she'd moved in with patients while caring for them, she hadn't thought it appropriate to ask them to house an animal as well as her and her son.

That was another reason they needed their own place now; she didn't want to move in with strangers again. Not that JJ and Darlene had ever felt like strangers; they'd felt like family. But

Darlene moving out was the signal to Sarah that it was time for her to do the same. Then there was Marsh and his sudden interest in her...

She had to leave, and until she knew if her new landlord would allow pets, she didn't want to get Mikey's hopes up about having one. So there was no sense in going to Hope's home, but maybe they could have the little girl over here to play or meet her at the park.

She wanted Mikey to have friends—human friends. And he seemed to be off to a good start with Hope. She wanted him excited to go back to school tomorrow. So after giving him some time alone, she fixed a snack plate of apple slices, cheese and pretzel sticks and called out to him.

"Mikey?" Her voice seemed to echo in the empty house that had gone almost eerily quiet since JJ had left.

Darlene had already been gone when Sarah had returned from the real estate office. She'd texted that she was coming back later this afternoon to talk to Mikey about his first day of school and to show him where she was going to work and live at the veterinarian practice.

Darlene and Mikey had formed a bond over their shared love of animals. Sarah was so grateful that the older woman was going to continue to nurture that bond even after moving out. He had no family besides Sarah. His maternal grandparents had disowned Sarah years before he was born, and his paternal grandparents hadn't been there for their own son, so they'd had no interest in his child, either.

"Mikey?" she called out again. "I have some snacks for you. Do you want me to put it out on the table on the deck?"

Was that where he'd gone after running inside? Outside again? That was usually what he did. He loved the swing set in the backyard. So did she.

She walked through the dining area of the big kitchen and pushed open the sliding door. But the chairs on the deck were empty, and the swings were completely still with not even a breeze to sway them.

"Mikey?" she called out again as she looked up at the window above the portico. "Mikey?"

The curtains didn't move this time like they had the night before. If he was in his room, he wasn't near the window. So maybe he couldn't hear her. She brought the plate back into the kitchen and set it on the white quartz counter. Then she headed upstairs.

A knock at his door went unanswered. She opened it and looked inside, but the bed was made like it had been that morning. He wasn't in it or on the chair in the corner near that window. He wasn't anywhere in the room.

"Mikey?" She turned and headed back out to check the bathroom. The door was open, the room empty. Her heart was beating harder and faster now. Where had he gone?

She hadn't heard the front door open except for when JJ left. Had Mikey slipped out with him? But JJ would have checked with her before letting her son leave with him. He had to be somewhere in the house yet since the fenced backyard had been empty.

"Mikey?"

The living room was empty as was the formal dining room. She ran back upstairs and checked all of the bedrooms up there again before returning to the main floor and the one room she hadn't checked.

The den.

It was where *he* slept. So she never went in there, not even to clean. On one of the few occasions he'd done more than nod when they'd crossed paths, Marsh had made it clear she didn't need to go in there. He hadn't done it in a rude way. In fact, he'd been very sweet. "You already have too much you're doing around here. You don't need to clean up after me," he'd said. "I take care of myself."

And while it had been sweet that he'd acknowledged how much she did and hadn't wanted her to put herself out on his behalf, it had also been sad somehow. That he was used to taking care of himself because nobody else had.

She could relate to that. She'd had to take care of herself and Mikey for so long on her own. Yet in moments like last night, when she'd thought she was alone on the deck, she could admit how alone she felt and that sometimes she yearned for more.

For someone to be there for her.

She lifted a shaky hand and knocked on that door, not that she thought Marsh was home. Even if she didn't see him, she could always sense when he was in the house, like she became more aware of everything around her, more alive.

It was weird. And another good reason to move out.

Nobody answered the knock, so she reached for the knob now. Was it locked? She wouldn't have even tried it if she hadn't knocked first to no answer. That meant Marsh wasn't in the den, but that didn't mean that Mikey wasn't.

He was clearly not acknowledging her calling out to him. And he had to be able to hear her, right? He had to be somewhere inside the house yet.

"Mikey?" She turned the knob and pushed open the door, but there was no sign of him. There was no sign that anyone was even staying in the room.

The brown leather couch, which was a pullout bed, was neatly put back together. And the bedding and the clothes must have been stowed away in the built-in, dark wood cabinets that surrounded the TV.

Marsh wasn't wrong that he could take care of himself. Clearly he could because the room was probably the tidiest one in the house. And because it was so tidy, she doubted that a six-year-old boy could find anywhere to hide in here. While the built-ins had several doors and drawers, they would be a tight fit for a body to hide in, so they wouldn't be neatly closed with everything tucked away behind them.

But still, she thought about checking one of them. It felt like an invasion of privacy, though. Of the sheriff's privacy...

"Mikey?" she called out again, hoping against hope that this time he would answer her.

But nothing stirred inside the room except her bangs when she let out a shaky sigh. Then she turned and nearly collided with him. So much for always knowing when he was in the house.

She hadn't felt him or even heard his SUV or the front door, and she let out another squeak of surprise over his sudden appearance. Then she pressed one of her hands against her madly pounding heart.

"Sorry for startling you again," he said. "I know I promised I would stop doing that, but I didn't expect to find you in here."

Heat rushed to her face as he stared at her like he probably would a suspect across the table in an interrogation room. "I…"

"Were you looking for me?" he asked.

She shook her head. "No. I can't find Mikey, and…" She was starting to panic like she had that day of the fire. Not that anything was burning now, but she was worried.

"He's home from school?"

She nodded.

"When did you see him last?"

"About…" She glanced at her watch and gasped again at how much time had passed with her looking for him. "…forty-five minutes ago, getting off the school bus," she said. "And then he ran inside…"

"Rough first day?" he asked with sympathy in his deep voice.

She shook her head. "No. Just the opposite. He was so happy and then…"

"What happened?" Marsh asked.

She sighed. "He wanted to go to Hope's, and I didn't take him."

Marsh tensed a bit. "You don't want him hanging out with Hope?"

"I would love for him to hang out with Hope. I just don't want him picking out a kitten," she said.

"Oh…"

She sighed again, but it was shaky. "I really would love to let him have a pet, but I just can't make him any promises right now."

"I want to ask why," he said. "But let's focus right now on finding your son. Where have you looked?"

"Everywhere," she said. "In the backyard, every single room in the house…"

"Could he have gotten outside the house or yard?"

"The latch on the gate on the fence is too hard for him to open on his own, and the only time I heard a door open was when your dad left." She hadn't heard Marsh come inside, though, so it was possible that Mikey had left as quietly as Marsh had entered. And the thought of her little boy running around Willow Creek on his own had her knees going weak for a moment as she started to shake.

Marsh reached out like he had last night, closing his big hands around her arms as if to steady or comfort her. "I'll text Becca to see if he showed up there."

"He doesn't know where she lives."

But he released her to send that text. Then he shook his head. "He's not there."

"He has to be here," she said but that was because it was what she wanted to believe.

"Well, let's search everywhere again," he said. "Just to make sure that you didn't miss his hiding place."

"And if he isn't here?"

"We'll look *everywhere else* until we find him," he assured her. "We will find him."

She wanted to admonish him for making a promise he had no way of knowing if he could keep. Kids disappeared all the time, never to be seen again. Probably not in Willow Creek. But it happened in other places, so it could happen here. But as much as she didn't want another man making her empty promises, she wanted to believe him even more.

They had to find her son. She couldn't even consider the alternative, not without losing her mind and her heart.

MARSH HAD UNDERSTOOD why his dad had gone back into the burning house all those weeks ago. With there being a possibility that Mikey was inside, JJ had had to do everything he could to save him.

Marsh wasn't sure this was a life-and-death situation like that one could have been, had the boy been inside the house. But he still understood the urgency to find him, to make sure that he was okay. As much for Mikey's sake as for the boy's distraught mother.

Sarah's eyes were bright with the tears she kept blinking away. She was scared.

Marsh had to find her son. He had to keep that promise he'd made to her. Marsh wasn't one to make promises lightly, and he hadn't in this case. But he should have known there were things beyond his control, especially after living so much of his life with no control over his parents' health or their financial struggles.

Another sweep of the house and yard hadn't turned up the boy. Was he hiding?

Or was he just gone?

Marsh called Darlene, who was already on her way back to the house. She promised to help look. "The last time I was out at Ranch Haven, I played hide-and-seek with my grandsons. Kids that age are very good at hiding. You need to look everywhere," she advised.

Marsh had his cell on speaker so that Sarah could hear, too. "I think we did look everywhere," Marsh said. And his next call after Darlene was probably going to be to dispatch to send some deputies out looking for the boy.

"I didn't look for him like we're playing hide-and-seek," she said. "I probably should have checked in all the cabinets and the back of the closets..."

Marsh hadn't either, but he hadn't thought that was necessary since they'd been calling for the kid. Even if he'd been intentionally hiding, wouldn't he have come out after a while and declared himself the winner?

Marsh and his brothers had never waited that long for whoever was "it" to find them when they were kids. They'd been too impatient to stay hidden, unless they'd fallen asleep. "Ooh..." he murmured as he clicked off his cell phone.

Remembering his childhood antics gave him a clue to where Mikey might be hiding, and he rushed back up to the kid's room. Sarah was right behind him. While she opened the closet door, Marsh dropped down to his knees to look under the bed. After lifting up the ruffle that hung down to the floor, he peered underneath and found a little blond-haired boy instead of dust bunnies. The kid was small enough that he'd managed to curl up in a ball under the box spring. And his chest moved slightly as he slept.

"Mikey," Marsh said, and his voice cracked a bit from the relief rushing through him. Thank God the kid was all right. "Mikey, wake up…"

The boy's blue eyes popped open wide, and he uttered a gasp as the color drained from his face. Marsh had startled him just like he kept startling the boy's mother. But Mikey had scared Sarah a lot more than Marsh had.

"You found him!" she exclaimed, and her voice cracked, too, with tears. And then she was on the floor next to Marsh, peering under the bed. "What are you doing under there?"

Mikey rubbed his eyes and blinked, trying to clear his vision—maybe because he didn't quite believe what he was seeing. Marsh and his mother, shoulder to shoulder, on the floor by his bed. "I must've fell asleep," he said.

"But why under the bed instead of on it?" she asked.

"It's dark under here," he said. "And quiet…" And he had obviously wanted to hide. From his mother? Or from Marsh? He kept shooting nervous glances at him. "Did you call the police on me, Mommy?" he asked.

"No, no," Marsh assured him. "She was scared, though, when she couldn't find you. Like that day at the ranch…"

Tears welled in the child's blue eyes now, and he murmured, "I'm sorry. So sorry…"

"It's okay," Sarah said. "You fell asleep. It was an accident."

And Marsh couldn't help but wonder if they were talking about today or that other day he'd gone missing, the day of the fire. Had that been an accident or a malfunction due to poor maintenance or…arson? He still couldn't believe it was arson; there was no motive for it, nothing to gain and only more to lose than they'd already lost.

"Come on," Sarah said. "Let's get you out of there. You must be hungry." She reached for him, taking his hands in hers to tug him out. But as she did, she flinched and jerked back. "Ouch. What's in your hand?"

"Are you okay?" Marsh asked them both, and then he reached under the bed and helped the little boy shimmy out without hitting his head on the box spring or the wooden side rail.

When the little boy lay between them on the floor, he opened his hand, and something shiny gleamed in the late afternoon sunshine pouring through his window. "I found this," he said. "I didn't take it."

He sounded a little defensive, and that might have been because of who Marsh was, a sheriff, or because of who the boy's father was. If the kid even knew...

"What is it?" Sarah asked.

"An earring," Marsh surmised. The post must have jabbed her when she'd closed her hand over her son's. "Is it yours?" There were hoops dangling from the post that were either purposely intertwined or had gotten tangled up together.

Sarah shook her head. "No. I don't wear jewelry." And she sounded a little defensive, like her son had.

And he had a pretty good idea why.

She stared at him, and her dark eyes widened like her son's had when he'd woken up to Marsh peering in at him. He hadn't done anything to startle her this time, but maybe he'd given something away with how he'd looked at her.

Like what he knew.

"Maybe it belongs to the lady that used to sleep here," Mikey said. "I found her charm bracelet in here, too."

"Livvy?" Marsh asked.

The little boy nodded. "Colton said she was really happy I found her bracelet. Her mom gave it to her."

Livvy's mom had passed away from breast cancer, just like Marsh and his brothers' mom had. "Yes, it's really special to her," Marsh said. "You did a good job finding that."

And he started to wonder what else the little boy might have found...

Like out at the Cassidy ranch.

HE'D DONE IT AGAIN. He'd scared his mom so much that he'd made her cry. Just like *that* day, that horrible, horrible day.

No wonder she wouldn't let him have a kitten. He was kind of surprised that she'd even let Miss Darlene take him back to the barn where she was going to live, especially since she hadn't let him go to Hope's ranch.

He wanted to see the kitties and mama kitty, but mostly,

he wanted to see Hope. To see if she was still as nice as she'd been at school.

If she was really his friend.

If she was, maybe he could tell her about that day. That horrible day...

He knew he should tell Mom, especially since she kept asking him about it, but he didn't want to make her cry again. He'd already made her cry too much. And he felt really bad that he'd crawled under his bed to hide because he'd been so upset. And not just because Mom told him no about the kitten, but because he'd lied to her again.

"Hey, you okay?" Miss Darlene asked. "We don't have to do this today, if you're still tired."

He shook his head. "No. I'm not tired." But he was worried that he was something else, something that people always said his dad was: bad.

Miss Darlene pointed out the window. "You didn't even notice that we're here...at the veterinarian office."

He unbuckled the booster seat and scrambled out of the vehicle. But when he saw the barn, he stopped for a minute, remembering another barn. On the Cassidy ranch...

At least it hadn't burned down. At least something he'd tried to do had worked out right.

If only...

"Come on," Miss Darlene said. "Doc CC, who is Marsh's brother Cash, just brought a baby into the world a few days ago. A baby miniature horse." She took his hand and led him toward the open doors of the barn.

He rushed along beside her, eager to see this mini animal. But the barn seemed dark after the brightness of the sunshine, and he held her hand a little tighter.

"Ah, now I see why I don't have a chance with you," a deep voice remarked. "You've already given your heart to another."

Darlene smiled. "Yes, I have, Dr. Miner. This is my special friend, Mikey Reynolds. He loves animals as much as we do."

A man with gray hair and dark eyes walked up to him. He had some lines around his eyes and mouth like he smiled a lot, like he was smiling now. "That's good news. I'm going to need another partner in this practice. Doc CC isn't pulling his weight anymore now that he's in love."

"Hey, I heard that," another man said.

Mikey recognized him because he'd been coming around the house lately; he was a new kid of Mr. JJ's. Really an old kid that hadn't been around for a long time.

"I'm not denying it," the man continued. "Just letting you know I heard you."

They all laughed. This looked like it would be a real fun place to work. "I want to be a vet, too," Mikey said.

"Ah, gunning for my job," Doc CC said. "Just like my soon-to-be daughter, Hope."

"Hope is your daughter?" he asked, awed.

"You know Hope?"

"She's in my class," Mikey said. "She's really nice."

"Yes, she's pretty special," the man agreed.

Mikey felt a pang of regret that his mom didn't bring him over to her house to play and see the kittens. But the barn was full of animals that Darlene was showing him, like that mini-mini horse.

"She might be the cutest thing I've ever seen...next to you..." Darlene said, and her arms, which were holding him on the top rung of the stall fence, tightened around him in a hug.

She was so nice to him. Everyone here in Willow Creek was. But then, they didn't know the truth...

# CHAPTER TEN

SARAH WAS STILL shaken over not being able to find her son. And she was even more shaken over what he'd said when they had found him, over how he'd apologized again. She wanted to be reassured that when he'd been so apologetic the day of the fire, it was just because he'd upset her like he had today. But she still couldn't be certain.

And she'd seen the way the sheriff had been watching him, like he had some suspicions of his own.

That was why she'd been so quick to let Darlene take him to her new job and living quarters. She hadn't wanted the sheriff to ask Mikey any more questions, not until she got the answers out of him herself. She needed to figure out how to do that, though, without having him shut down even more than he already had.

"I'm very sorry about that," Sarah said once she joined Marsh on the back deck, where he was already sitting in a chair. She'd had to take some time alone in the bathroom to pull herself together. She'd been so scared when she wasn't able to find Mikey. "You must think I'm a horrible mother, never knowing where her son is."

"I don't think that at all, Sarah," Marsh said. "In fact, I think you're a wonderful mother. You obviously love your son very much."

"With all my heart," she said. "He's the best thing that ever happened to me." He was the good that had come of all the bad.

"So, naturally, you would be concerned about him when you couldn't find him," he said. "You're a great mother."

Tears stung her eyes, and she squeezed them shut, trying to keep the tears from leaking out again. She'd just washed off the last ones she'd shed; she really didn't want to cry again. "I don't know about that," she said. "Half the time, I don't know if I'm doing the right thing or not." But she always tried to do the right thing. "No matter how much I try."

Marsh sighed. "Yeah, doing the right thing isn't as easy as it sounds."

She smiled at him sitting there in his white hat with the gold badge pinned to the pocket of his Western shirt. "Somehow, I don't think you have a problem knowing what the right thing to do is."

She usually didn't either. "I took him out of his last school and started homeschooling because he was being bullied."

"Then that was the right thing to do," he said as if it was that simple.

"But then he got even shyer than he used to be." And after the fire, he'd withdrawn even more.

"Why was he being bullied?" Marsh asked.

This was it: her opening to come clean about the past. Her knees shook a little with nerves, so she dropped onto the chair across from him. "Through no fault of his own," she said. "He was going to the same elementary school that I went to, the same one his father went to in my hometown."

"You met your ex-husband in elementary school?" he asked.

She tensed for a moment. "How do you know he's my ex-husband?"

He pointed across the table at her bare hand. "You don't wear a ring."

"That doesn't mean I ever did," she said, wondering how much of her history Marsh already knew. Had he checked her out?

He was a lawman, so he probably had.

She sighed. "But I did. We married out of high school, but

not because we had to. We thought we were in love. We were just so young and naive." Her more so than he'd been. "I even put myself through college." With no help from her parents and, despite what some people had accused her of, with no help from her ex, either.

"Impressive," Marsh said.

She was pretty sure he'd done the same. JJ had obviously been in bad health for a while, and the ranch had been in disrepair, too.

She shrugged. "I thought my ex was working hard, too, but apparently he was stealing," she said. She sneaked a glance across the table at Marsh, but he didn't look surprised. "I swear I didn't know. And when he was arrested, I filed for divorce." Michael had been so upset about that, that she wouldn't stand by him. But how could she have trusted him again? He wasn't the man she'd thought he was. He wasn't even the boy she'd once known. "But people in small towns don't get over things like that."

"And they took it out on a little boy?" he asked, his voice gruff with emotion.

She nodded. "Yes, he was bullied over what his father did."

Marsh grimaced. "That's harsh. I have a feeling he's not the only one who suffered. You must have, too."

She nodded. "It was hard to find jobs. So I started doing the traveling nurse thing, trying to get away from where we grew up, where everything went so wrong." Heat rushed to her face, and she hastily added, "Except Mikey. He truly is the best thing that has happened to me. And I know he wouldn't be here without the bad." She sighed. "So it is what it is." She shrugged. "I just want to protect him from going through all that again. That's why I'm worried about applying for that job at the school. I'm worried about people finding out about Mikey's dad being in jail and calling him the horrible things that they used to." Emotion choked her as she remembered how upset he used to get at school. How he used to get off the bus crying, not like he had today, waving at the windows as it pulled away.

She wanted to stay here, wanted him to be happy and secure, but she wasn't sure how to make that happen. And like the night before, her frustration turned to tears again. Embarrassed, she buried her face in her hands.

MARSH FELT GUILTY all over again for running that check on her. He also felt guilty that she was crying again, like he'd brought on her tears with his questions. And maybe his suspicions.

He had a knack for getting suspects to talk. He'd honed the talent with his brothers, always making them confess to whatever dumb thing they'd done. Even recently, it had worked on his younger brother, making Colton confess to finding the lighter. And, usually, all it required was his silence and a look.

So he held himself responsible for her having to relive that pain and embarrassment she'd suffered. "I'm sorry, Sarah." He rose from his chair, came around the table to kneel in front of her and placed his hands on her shoulders. "I'm sorry."

"What...why?" she asked as she lifted her face from her hands.

"I keep upsetting you, and I'm sorry about that," he said.

"That's why Mikey apologized, too," she said with a tremulous smile. "He hates upsetting me."

"He's a good kid then. And he clearly loves you as much as you love him."

"Thank you," she said.

"It's the truth," he said.

She smiled. "No. Thank you again for helping me find him today and that day of the fire." Her smile slid away as if the mention of the fire upset her.

The lawman in him wanted to push, wanted to ask her more questions about it. But she'd had a long day, and he didn't want to upset her again. "I'm the one who should be thanking you," he said.

Her brow furrowed beneath her wispy bangs. "For what? I don't understand."

"For my dad, for taking such great care of him," Marsh said.

"He doesn't need me anymore," she said. "That's why I'm going to have to apply to that job at the school."

He could have told her that she didn't need to worry about the background check they might run on her. A routine employment one wouldn't turn up what he had. She had nothing on her record. But her ex-husband…

He was going to be in jail for a while. The detectives who'd caught him had investigated his wife as well but concluded that she'd had no idea what he'd been doing, just like she'd said. But the detective's notes were in records that the general public couldn't easily access.

Maybe they should be more easily accessible; then it could have been made clear in her old hometown that she and her son had had no knowledge of or involvement in her husband's crimes. Instead, she'd been denied work, and her son had been bullied.

But she'd found a way to support them and protect her son. "I'm sure you'll get the job," he said. He would make sure that she got a lot of letters of recommendation. "What I'm trying to thank you for is how you kept my dad alive and in good enough health that he made it until his heart transplant. Even though my brother couldn't treat Dad, Collin, the cardiologist, made it clear to me that you saved his life."

She shook her head. "No. I didn't do anything but follow his doctor's instructions for his care."

"You need to take credit for what you did," he insisted. "For how…amazing you are…"

Her eyes, still wet with tears, widened in surprise.

"Shoot, I did it again," he remarked. "I startled you." He found it sad that a compliment would startle a woman like her, a woman who deserved a lot of compliments for her hard work and her compassion.

She smiled at him. "I just didn't expect you to…"

"Be nice?" he finished when she trailed off.

Her face flushed. "Not that. I know you're a nice man. You're so good to your dad and brothers and Darlene."

"But you didn't expect me to be nice to you," he concluded.

She shrugged. "I just… We haven't talked much…"

"Until last night when I found you out here."

She ran her hands over her face, brushing away her tears. "Doing what I'm doing now. You must think I'm an overly emotional wreck."

"I think you're a single mother with a lot of responsibility," he said.

"I think you know what that's like," she said as she met his gaze again.

He smiled slightly. "I'm not a single mother."

"I think you've always had a lot of responsibility," she clarified. "Because your parents were sick, I think you probably had to grow up really fast and learn to take care of yourself and your brothers."

Now he was the one who was surprised, his mouth dropping open a little with his shock that she saw him so clearly, that even though she hadn't been at the ranch then, she knew how he'd grown up. Fast.

For the first time in a long time, he felt seen as more than the sheriff or a son or a brother. He felt seen as a man. And the sensation was a little overwhelming.

He leaned closer to her then, so tempted to kiss her, with gratitude and with attraction. She was so beautiful and not just on the outside. She was beautiful on the inside, too.

But when he leaned forward, she jerked back. And he found himself saying, "I'm sorry. I'm so sorry—"

But she wasn't looking at him; she was looking over his shoulder, toward the patio door they'd left open. They weren't alone.

He turned around to find his grandmother standing behind him. And she was looking entirely too happy.

SADIE BARELY RESISTED the urge to slap her hands together with glee. Maybe this was going to be even easier than she'd thought because, clearly, she'd walked in on a special moment between her grandson and her son's nurse. If Sarah hadn't noticed her standing there, he might have kissed her.

"Grandma," he said. "This isn't what you think. Sarah and I were just talking." His face was flushed, though, and she wasn't sure if that was with embarrassment over getting caught nearly kissing the young woman, or if it was because he'd nearly kissed the young woman.

Sarah jumped up from her chair, and her face was flushed,

too. "Mrs. Haven-Lemmon, I'm going to leave you two alone to talk."

"You don't have to rush off on my account," Sadie said as the young woman drew closer to where she stood in the doorway.

"I really need to get dinner started," Sarah said. "It's already past time that I should have, but Darlene took Mikey to check out the veterinarian practice. They should be back soon, and JJ...he should be here soon, too." She was clearly anxious, either to start dinner or to get away from them. When she stepped even closer, Sadie saw that her face wasn't just flushed, it was tear stained.

Not wanting to embarrass her any further, she moved aside and let the young woman pass her. But when Marsh started forward, as if he intended to follow, Sadie stepped in front of him, blocking him from entering the house. Then she joined him, pulling the door closed behind her. "What's going on between you two?" she asked.

"Like I said, it's not what you think," Marsh insisted.

But at the moment, she wasn't sure what she thought. "Why is she so upset?" Sadie asked. She loved her grandson, but she was very fond of Jessup's nurse as well.

"She had a little scare with Mikey earlier," Marsh said. "She couldn't find him."

"Oh…" She had to press her hand to her heart as pain jabbed it. She knew all too well how frightening and emotional it was not to know where your child was. For too many years, she hadn't known where Jessup was or even if he was still alive. "But she did find him. She said he's with Darlene."

Marsh nodded. "He's fine. He's safe."

There was something about the way he said it, with a fierceness and a protectiveness, that implied he intended to keep it that way. Sadie smiled. Things were going according to plan then—at least, her plan.

"What about you?" she asked. "Are you fine?" He might have been irritated with her for interrupting what might have been a kiss. Or maybe he was irritated with himself for almost kissing Sarah. Or maybe it was something else entirely…

But usually Marsh was the calm one, the unflappable one. Like his uncle that she'd lost much too soon.

"Dad knows what's going on with the ranch," Marsh replied. "He knows that the insurance company asked the fire inspector to reopen the investigation."

She sucked in a breath. "I guess we should have expected that."

Marsh sighed. "I'm surprised they let him know since they obviously consider him a suspect since he's the only one with something to gain."

Sadie had had a feeling she needed to check on Jessup even though she'd seen him that morning. Or maybe it was just that she'd gone so long without seeing him that she wanted to see him every chance she got now.

"I have to figure out what really happened, Grandma, or I'm afraid, like Dad is, that the insurance company is going to try to pin this on him." he said.

And now Sadie was frightened, too.

# CHAPTER ELEVEN

SARAH WISHED SHE could rewind the entire day. No. She wished she could rewind even further, to the night before, so when Marsh joined her on the deck, she just got up and walked away from him.

Because now she felt exposed and vulnerable in a way that she hadn't since Michael got arrested. Since his whole secret life was exposed.

She hated secrets because people usually kept them to protect only themselves. But in rare cases, like the Cassidy family, people kept secrets to protect the ones they loved. Once the secrets had come out, JJ and Darlene had filled her in on the history despite her protests that it was none of her business. They'd been telling her for a while now they considered her family.

But she wasn't really. And she felt guilty for overhearing Marsh's conversation with his grandmother. But they'd started talking the minute she'd stepped inside, and as she'd told them, she was making dinner, in the kitchen right next to where they were talking. While Sadie had closed the slider, a window was open, so she heard everything.

Now she understood why Marsh was asking questions about the fire. The insurance company must suspect arson. And his father?

Not JJ. While he was happy everyone had survived, he was

upset he and his sons had lost the pictures and mementoes of his wife, their mother. He had also already accepted an offer on the property, the sale he needed to pay off all his medical debt. He hadn't needed to burn down the house for money.

And even if he had needed money, he wouldn't have committed arson. She knew he hadn't started that fire. But she wasn't sure that someone else hadn't.

"Mommy!" Mikey exclaimed as he ran into the kitchen and threw his arms around her waist. He hugged her tight before pulling back. "You should see the baby horse at Miss Darlene's work. It's so small. I never saw a horse that small before. Even the mama is small and she's old."

Sadie pushed open the slider and stepped into the kitchen with them. And Mikey's eyes went wide. "You know," she said, "my doctor tells me that when we get older, we start shrinking."

In her boots, the older woman had to be over six feet tall, nearly as tall as her grandson who stepped into the kitchen behind her.

Mikey stared up at her, and his mouth dropped open with shock. "You used to be taller?" he asked.

She nodded. "At least an inch or so."

"Wow…" he murmured in awe.

Sadie smiled at him so warmly, and then she smiled at Sarah the same way. Instead of smiling back, Sarah had the urge to cry again at the guilt that rushed over her. But she really couldn't let herself think that Mikey had had anything to do with that fire, at least not intentionally. That wasn't why he'd apologized so emotionally that day. It wasn't.

But what if she was in denial? What if she was wrong? And now there was an investigation?

She glanced at the sheriff standing behind Sadie Haven. Apparently there were two investigations. The fire inspector's and his.

Was that why he'd been so nice to her? So interested in her and Mikey?

Heat rushed to her face again with the embarrassment over his grandmother catching them nearly kissing. Because if that was what he'd been about to do, Sarah would have welcomed his kiss. He was so good-looking. But more than that, he was a good man.

And no matter what his reasons, he had helped her find her son today. But now she didn't want the boy in the same room with him, at least not until she could talk to Mikey again and actually get answers out of him. "Hey, you better go wash up since you were playing with all those animals," Sarah said to him. And then she managed to smile for Sadie and Marsh. "Will you both be staying for dinner?"

"No," Sadie said. "I'm on my way out. I will catch up with my son another day."

"I'm leaving, too," Marsh said.

And something about his tone chilled her. Leaving to do what? Investigate her some more? Because she had a feeling that he hadn't been too surprised at what she'd told him. But he had been sweet about it.

"Is everybody leaving?" Darlene asked as she walked into the kitchen just as Sadie and Marsh were walking out.

"Yes, dear," Sadie said, but she paused to hug her. "We'll have to catch up another time."

Marsh just nodded at her as he followed his grandmother out.

Darlene tousled Mikey's hair. "Your turn to wash up," she told him.

Sarah smiled at her. Darlene was so kind and so nurturing and not just with Mikey. The little boy rushed off, probably more because Darlene had told him to wash up than because Sarah had. But she didn't care. She was beginning to realize she needed help with him.

"Are you going to stay for dinner?" she asked Darlene.

She nodded. "Yes, I promised Mikey that I would."

"He's going to miss you," Sarah said.

"Even though I moved out, I'll be over visiting a lot. I promise," Darlene said.

"Good, because I'm going to miss you, too," she said. "But I'm not sure how long I will be around." Especially if…

"You're not going to leave Willow Creek!"

"I don't want to," she admitted. "But I do need to find another job."

"JJ would love for you and Mikey to stay here," Darlene said.

Sarah would love that, too, but she already felt like she'd taken advantage of him. Then there was Marsh, and Sarah didn't trust herself around him for a few reasons now. She'd shared too much with him, and she felt vulnerable in a way that she hadn't in so long.

"JJ is very sweet," Sarah said. That was why she also had to make sure he didn't get blamed for something he didn't do. But she couldn't do that unless she learned what really happened. "How was Mikey?" she asked.

Darlene grinned. "So excited to be in a barn again. He loved all the animals."

Sarah felt another pang of guilt that she'd had to deny him a kitten. She really wanted him to have one. "I know how he feels about them," she said. "I just wish I knew how he felt about other things."

"What other things?" Darlene asked. "School? He seemed to enjoy it today. Sounds like he made friends with Hope."

Sarah gestured for Darlene to come closer, and she lowered her voice so that Mikey wouldn't overhear them like she'd overheard Marsh and his grandmother. "I know, and I'm happy that this situation might be better than our old one..."

"But what?" Darlene whispered back. "What's wrong, Sarah?"

"I don't know if I screwed up with the homeschooling and moving him around or if I should have done it sooner because of the bullying in his old school."

Darlene hugged her. "Take it from someone who royally screwed up as a mother: You're doing a great job with him. Stop beating yourself up."

Sarah held on to her for a moment before taking a deep breath and stepping back.

"If you want some of the answers to your questions, you could have him talk to someone," Darlene suggested. "My grandsons have a counselor who's been helping them deal with their grief over losing both their parents so suddenly."

Like everyone else living in Willow Creek, Sarah knew the tragic story of how Dale and Jenny Haven had died in a car crash. Their children had been in the vehicle with them, and fortunately, they'd survived. But the trauma they must have suffered…

She shuddered. "I'm so sorry that happened." Dale was Darlene's son, and she'd never even had the chance to meet his wife.

"Bad things happen," Darlene said fatalistically. "That's why we have to hang on extra hard to the good." She touched Sarah's chin when she said it, like she was saying that Sarah was the good.

Tears stung her eyes. The Cassidys and Havens had been so sweet and supportive of her, totally unlike her own family.

"Mrs. Lancaster works at the school," Darlene continued. "She's the school psychologist, so it would be easy for you to get her to speak with Mikey."

Sarah nodded. "I will keep that in mind. But with how shy he is with strangers, I'm not sure he would open up to her."

"He was talking very easily with Cash and Forrest…" Her face flushed a bit. "Dr. Miner. But then we were talking about animals, and that's his favorite subject."

It was. Sarah knew that about her son. She should know how to get him talking. "I think I'm going to try to get him to open up a bit more with me first, before I reach out to Mrs. Lancaster," she said.

Darlene nodded. "You'll know what's best. I'm the last one who should be giving parental advice. I'm very fortunate my kids are talking to me again."

She'd shared her history with Sarah. The tragic loss of her husband, for which she blamed herself and thought her children blamed her, too. Trying to find JJ to bring him back to his mother only to find him so close to death…

"The only advice I do feel confident giving is not to let things go too long," Darlene said. "Make sure you clear up any misunderstandings or confusion so that you don't have all the regrets that I have."

It was too late. There was already so much that Sarah regretted. And the most recent one was that almost kiss with Marsh. But she wasn't sure if she regretted that it almost happened or that it hadn't.

MARSH COULDN'T BELIEVE he'd almost kissed Sarah Reynolds and, unbeknownst to him, in front of his grandmother. He was losing his mind and maybe his perspective, too.

He needed distance to regroup and some counsel he could trust. While he loved his brothers, he was always the one who'd advised them.

And even though he'd already sought out his grandmother, he didn't entirely trust that she didn't have ulterior motives with all her advice. Obviously, she wanted him to get coupled up like all her other grandsons were.

The only one who'd effectively handled her, by turning her matchmaking on her, was Ben. Ben was more than his cousin; as the mayor of Willow Creek, he was essentially Marsh's boss as well.

He was also a lawyer.

Marsh regretted not going to him first. A quick text exchange let Marsh know where to find him, at his office at city hall. But when he walked into it, he found that Ben was not alone.

His fiancée and he were scrolling through something on a tablet she held.

"I'm sorry," he said. "I don't want to intrude."

Emily smiled at him. "You're not intruding. You're saving Ben from wedding planning stuff."

"Hey, I'm as into this wedding as you are," Ben said. "I just wish it would happen sooner."

They'd decided on a Christmas wedding. Marsh had already received a save the date. He couldn't help but wonder where he would be then. He couldn't continue to live with Dad, not at his age, and if he lost the election for sheriff, would he even stay in Willow Creek?

But no matter what he was doing or where he was living, he wouldn't miss his cousin's wedding. It was strange that, despite how short a time they'd known each other, Marsh felt so connected to all of his cousins, but especially to Ben.

"We agreed that it would be better to do it after the election, and so that we could honeymoon during my Christmas break from school," Emily said. She was an elementary teacher.

"And what if I don't win the election? Will you still want to marry me?" Ben asked.

She shrugged. "I don't know. But with Sadie campaigning for you, I don't think you can lose."

"If you'll still marry me, I'll win either way," Ben said.

She laughed. "I don't think you have to worry about losing."

"That makes one of us," Marsh said.

"Sadie will be campaigning for you, too," Ben said, "and so will I. You've really implemented some great things as sheriff."

"Like the retired deputy in the school," Emily said. "That makes us all feel safer."

"And you're enforcing the parking limits, which our downtown business owners appreciate very much," Ben said. "You won't have any issue winning an election. But I'm happy to help with your campaign."

"Thank you," Marsh said with great appreciation. "I could use your advice." He sighed, ready to get into the real reason for his visit. "And not just with the election."

Ben chuckled. "I figured as much. I overheard Lem and Sadie scheming earlier today. Is she already working the angle with you that she tried with me? That it would help my reelection campaign if I was married?"

"Married?" Marsh shuddered. "What does that have to do with politics?"

"A lot with small-town politics," Ben admitted.

"Is that why you're marrying me?" Emily asked, but she was smiling, so obviously she had no doubts about why he was marrying her.

Ben replied, "I'm marrying you because you asked me to, and I didn't want to turn you down and embarrass you in front of our audience."

She elbowed him, but it must have been lightly because Ben didn't even flinch.

He laughed instead, then he wrapped his arm around her and pulled her against his side. "And I am hopelessly besotted and in love with you," he added.

"That's how he's going to win the election," Emily said. "That ability for sweet-talking."

Marsh didn't have that ability or a wife. If that was what was necessary to win an election, though, he would rather lose. But as he saw how happy his brothers and cousins were, he couldn't help but feel a little like he'd already lost. Especially since he hadn't even gotten to kiss Sarah today.

"Two trips out here in one day?"

Jessup glanced up at his mother's question. He was sitting in the formal living room that was rarely used, rocking a sleeping infant, when Sadie walked into the house at Ranch Haven.

Until just a short time ago, Juliet had been sitting in the chair next to his, rocking her grandson. Jessup held the little girl, and his great-niece was already wrapping him around her little finger.

"Yes," he said. "Am I wearing out my welcome?"

She snorted. "You know I would love for you to move in here. But I don't want you putting yourself at risk health wise."

"Health wise, I'm doing great," he said. It was everything else he was worried about, and if not for that, he might consider taking the risk of living farther from town. When once, as a rebellious teenager, he couldn't wait to leave his mother's house, now he couldn't stay away.

But that probably had less to do with the house than the people. He glanced down at his sleeping great-niece, but it wasn't just her who'd wrapped him around her little finger. He was quickly falling for someone else. But he had less to offer her now than he had before. So he probably should have stayed away.

His mom dropped into the rocking chair next to his. "Are you not doing great with other things?" she asked.

He sighed. "I wasn't going to tell you. I didn't want to worry you…" And he hadn't wanted to admit to his situation with Juliet, either. "But then I realized that nothing good came of all the secrets I'd kept, so I don't want to do that anymore. I don't want to hurt anyone I care about."

Sadie reached across and grasped his arm. "I talked to Marsh."

"Yes, this morning—"

"And again this afternoon at your house," she said.

"So you know?"

She nodded.

"Can you believe that they would think I would burn down my own house? My memories, like that?"

"I don't know what they believe," she said. "And neither do you, so you're the one who shouldn't be worrying."

"But I am worried," he admitted.

"Marsh was already on it," she said. "He will take care of it."

"I already rely too much on Marsh."

"Because he's strong," Sadie said, "and can handle it and so can I."

For so long, Jessup hadn't been strong. He'd been so weak physically and maybe emotionally as well. But his new heart had given him a strength he'd never had before. "I can, too," he said. "We'll be okay."

"We'll be better than okay," his mom said as she squeezed his arm again.

He looked up at Juliet as she descended the front stairwell into the foyer. Everything had to work out. He'd already lost one woman he'd loved. And even though the situation was completely different, he didn't want to lose another.

He didn't want to lose his son, either. And he wasn't sure how much of his burden he could keep expecting Marsh to carry for him. He needed to take care of himself now and make sure that Marsh had someone to take care of him for once.

Someone like Sarah.

## CHAPTER TWELVE

SARAH WASN'T SURE if she should be relieved or upset that she hadn't seen much of Marsh since that day he'd nearly kissed her on the back deck. Of course, she'd been busy, too, over the past few days, polishing up her resume and getting letters of recommendation so that she could apply for that position at the school. An email had gone out to parents about the current nurse retiring, and then the job had been posted on the school website.

Sarah had filled out what she could online, and she'd been asked to stop by the office to pick up another document that needed to be completed before she would be interviewed. So she was driving Mikey to school.

He'd grumbled about wanting to take the bus instead, but she needed to be at the school before it opened, and she hadn't wanted to ask JJ to wait for the bus with him to make sure that he got safely on it.

So he rode in the back seat of her car, his lips pursed in a slight pout. Now probably wasn't the time to try to talk to him, but she had tried a few other times during the past week, unfortunately at bedtime. So he'd closed his eyes and shaken his head as if he just wanted to block it out. Or maybe he wanted to block her out. Then he'd pretended to fall asleep.

"Mikey, I really want to talk to you about what happened at the ranch. You've been so quiet since then—"

"I'm always quiet."

That was too true.

"But if something's bothering you about it, I hope you know you can tell me what it is…" She glanced in the rearview mirror to see him shaking his head again, just like he had at bedtime.

So which was it? Nothing was bothering him? Or he didn't think he could talk to her about it? While she was in the office, picking up whatever paper the principal wanted her to complete with her application, maybe she would ask about Mrs. Lancaster. Even if Mikey didn't want to talk to the psychologist, Sarah could, and maybe a professional could help her figure out how to talk to her own child because she couldn't.

"I love you," she said, and she glanced in the rearview mirror again.

A smile replaced his pout, and in the mirror, he met her gaze. "I love you, too, Mommy."

She steered into a parking space in the school lot and turned fully around in her seat to say, "I'm so proud of you. You're doing so well in school." The teacher had been sending her emails praising how well he was doing with the work, which made Sarah feel better about having homeschooled him the previous year.

"I like it here," he said as he reached for his belt to release himself from his booster seat.

"You're such a good kid," she added because she knew that he needed to hear that most of all.

But his hand stilled for a moment on the clasp he had yet to release, and his smile slipped away. Then he lowered his head and murmured, "But I make you cry…"

"Oh, honey, that's not your fault," she assured him. "There's just a lot going on right now. Mr. JJ is all better, which is a good thing, but it means that I need to find another job. That's why I'm here at the school, applying for the nurse job here. Is that okay with you?"

He shrugged. "If it means we'll stay in Willow Creek…"

"We will," she said.

Because if she didn't get this job, she would apply at the hospital and every doctor's office in Willow Creek. But Becca also had to find them a place to rent, and all she'd found so far were small apartments with no yards. Of course, JJ tried to convince her every day to just stay with him, that the house was too big for him and Marsh alone.

But because of Marsh, she couldn't stay. Since their almost kiss, she'd been spending most of her time in her room working on her resume and…avoiding Marsh.

Mikey stopped avoiding her gaze and met her eyes now, and his were hopeful. "We'll stay?"

She nodded.

And he unclasped his belt and pushed open the back door. When she stepped out to join him, he threw his arms around her and tightly hugged her.

So happy to see him happy, she leaned over and kissed his forehead. "And maybe you'll even be able to get a kitten, if Hope's mom can convince a landlord to let us have a pet." Given how badly Becca wanted to get rid of those kittens, she would probably try very hard to find an accommodating landlord for them. But even though the apartments allowed them, Sarah knew Mikey needed a yard, so hopefully Becca could find them a small house or condo with one.

His blue eyes lit up with that hopefulness she hadn't seen in him in so long. Maybe he was okay. Maybe she was worried about nothing.

Having to wait until the bell rang before he could go inside, he ran out to the playground to wait for the other students to arrive. He waved at her as she walked toward the front door. She had to wait, too, after she buzzed for the door to be opened. "I'm Sarah Reynolds," she said as she walked into the office. "I have to drop off some paperwork and pick up something."

"This is what the school district requires all applicants to have done before they are even interviewed," the receptionist said as she passed a paper across her desk to Sarah.

Sarah glanced down and saw what it was: a request to be fingerprinted.

"You can have it done right at the sheriff's office," the receptionist said, as if being helpful.

But that wasn't helpful to Sarah because it undid everything she'd been working so hard to do all week: avoid seeing Marsh.

MARSH SHOULD HAVE been happy that he hadn't run into Sarah the past few days. But he wasn't happy. Maybe that was because of everything else going on with the fire investigation, with not knowing what the Moss Valley Sheriff's Office might find.

But Sarah was on his mind more than anything else. And it wasn't because he thought she had any more secrets. It was because he hadn't had the chance to kiss her, and now he was stuck wondering what it might have been like.

But she might have pulled back even if Sadie hadn't appeared. She probably wasn't interested in him. As she'd pointed out, she had a lot of responsibilities.

And so did he.

He sighed as he leaned back in his desk chair. He needed to talk to his old boss and the fire inspector and see if they had found any reason to change their original finding of poor maintenance to arson. For some reason, the insurance company, probably to get out of paying the claim, was pushing that agenda. But if there was no evidence of arson, he and his brothers and now his dad could be worried about nothing.

At least, concerning the fire.

Marsh was worried about Sarah, though, and why he couldn't get her out of his mind. Even now, through his open door, he imagined he could hear someone saying her name.

"Sarah Reynolds?"

"Yes."

That was definitely her voice answering Mrs. Little. The sound of it jolted his body out of his chair, and he rushed out to the reception desk. A window of glass and a door separated Mrs. Little from the public reception area. Sarah stood on the other side of that glass.

Her hair was down today and curled around her heart-shaped face. Instead of scrubs, she wore a pastel-patterned dress that wrapped around and tied at her waist. She looked so beautiful that, for a moment, he lost his breath.

"Uh, what's she doing here?" he asked Mrs. Little.

The older woman glanced at him over her shoulder. "The elementary school requested that she be fingerprinted and have a background check run on her."

He'd already run the in-depth background check that the school needed, but he hadn't fingerprinted her yet, which they would also require, like many other companies, for the safety and security of their other employees and students. "I can take care of that," he offered.

Mrs. Little lowered her eyebrows and stared at him. "It's not a problem for me—"

"I know Sarah," he interrupted. "She works for my dad."

A smile spread across Mrs. Little's lips. "Ah… Sadie strikes again?"

Heat flushed his face, and he shook his head. "It's not like that."

Sadie had had nothing to do with Sarah's hiring. She hadn't even known that her son was still alive at that point. He opened the door. "Sarah, come on back. I can help you."

She hesitated for a moment before walking through the door he held open for her. He could see how stiffly she held herself, as if making sure that she didn't even accidentally touch him. He'd already suspected she'd been avoiding him the past few days, and the way she was acting now pretty much confirmed that suspicion.

"I have a fingerprint scanner in my office," he said. And he escorted her down the hall and through the open door. Not wanting Mrs. Little to eavesdrop, he closed that door.

And Sarah tensed.

"I'm sorry," he said. "I should have already apologized before now. Obviously, I'm making you uncomfortable, and I don't want you to feel that way in your home or here." He reached for the knob to open the door again, but before he could turn it, her hand covered his.

"What are you talking about?" she asked.

"I think you've been avoiding me the past few days, and I am pretty sure that I know why," he said, and his face felt even hotter than it had in the reception area. "And I owe you an apology for making you feel uneasy. I'm really sorry that I almost kissed you—"

"Why?" she asked.

He tensed. "Why am I sorry? Or why did I almost kiss you?"

Her lips curved into a slight smile. "Both."

"I don't want you to feel unsafe in your home—"

"It's not my home."

"It's not mine, either, and I can leave if that would put you more at ease—"

"I'm not uneasy," she said.

He pushed back his hat and arched an eyebrow to show his skepticism.

And she smiled. "Well, maybe a little."

"About the kiss?" he asked. Or his questions...

"What kiss?" she asked. "Nothing happened."

"And it wouldn't have without your consent," he assured her. "And if just the fact that I wanted to kiss you makes you uncomfortable—"

She moved her hand to his face, and she pressed her fingers across his lips. "Stop," she said. "Stop apologizing for something that didn't happen."

But he wished that it had and spent entirely too much time imagining what it would have been like.

"But if it makes you uneasy, we need to clear the air about this," he said.

"Then tell me why you wanted to kiss me," she said. "Was it out of pity?"

He snorted. "Pity? Why would I pity you? For being strong and resilient? For being compassionate and beautiful?"

Her lips parted on a soft gasp.

And he wanted to kiss her again. So badly. But she'd avoided him for days after his last clumsy attempt, so he wasn't about to risk it again.

Then she wrapped her hand around the nape of his neck and pulled his head down while she rose up on tiptoe and pressed her mouth to his. The shock of her silky lips brushing across his caught him off guard, and he tensed instead of doing what he really wanted to do: wrap his arms around her and kiss her back.

She jerked away before he could react, though. Then she pressed her hand over her mouth and murmured, "Oh, no. I'm so sorry..."

"Please, don't be," he said. "I'm not." But he was unsettled. Just that slight brush of her mouth across his had affected him. "I've been wondering what it would be like..."

Her face was so flushed, but her eyes widened in surprise, as if she'd been wondering the same thing.

But knowing just made him want to kiss her again, which was crazy. He had no time for anything but his family and the election. But he wanted to make time for her and found himself asking, "Would you go out with me?"

And her dark eyes widened even more.

"It doesn't have to be a date," he said. He hadn't been on one in so long, he wasn't even sure what a date was anymore. "It can just be a thank-you for all you've done for my dad. And Mikey can come along."

While it wasn't his motivation for asking her, it occurred to him now that maybe outside of the house, in a relaxed environment, they could talk more freely about the day of the fire. Maybe one of them would remember something that could help prove it was the poor maintenance the fire inspector had concluded was the cause. At least, that was the excuse he gave himself for asking and for pressing when he could see her hesitation. "We can take him for ice cream or something. Just a thank-you, Sarah, for taking care of my dad all these months. For keeping him alive."

She shook her head. "That's a big overstatement of what I did."

"He's alive," Marsh said. "And I think you're a large part of the reason for that. And that's not my opinion alone. That's Collin's, too, and he's a cardiologist."

"It's not necessary," she said.

"It's just ice cream, Sarah."

She nodded then.

For some reason, he felt like she'd agreed to be his date for prom—he felt like a teenager again. But this wasn't a real date, and he would have to remind himself of that. It was just ice cream. And they would have a six-year-old chaperone along, so there would be no more kisses.

As happy as he was to spend some time with her and her son, he felt a pang of regret that there wouldn't be another kiss. But he should have been relieved. As he kept telling everyone else, he had no time for romance.

DESPITE NOT GETTING to ride the bus that morning, Mikey was having a good day. And his favorite part of the day was recess, when he got to play with not just his class but with kids from other classes and grades, like Miller, Ian and Caleb.

"Do you want to play cops and robbers?" Caleb asked. They'd just been playing rodeo riders on the spring animals on the playground. Caleb wanted to be a rodeo rider like his uncle Dusty Chaps.

Mikey thought Hope was the better rider, though. She didn't even slip in her "saddle," no matter how much her "horse" was bucking.

But Caleb's question made Mikey nervous, and he slid off the spring animal to walk over near the fence. But the others followed him.

"We can play over here," Caleb said. "We just gotta figure out who's the cops and who's the robbers. But you probably know who you wanna be, Mikey."

Did they already know? Had kids from his old school talked? He couldn't even look at them, so he stared down at the asphalt and asked, "Why do you say that?"

"You know why," Ian replied for his best friend. He and Caleb were more than cousins; they were super close.

Mikey felt sick, his stomach bucking up and down like the horses Dusty Chaps used to ride in the rodeo. "No. I don't. Why?" he asked again.

Bailey Ann sighed then and said, like he should have known, "Because the sheriff is going to marry your mom."

"What…" he murmured. He knew they'd talked a few times, but he hadn't even seen the sheriff over the past few days.

"Ew…" Caleb said with a grimace. "No more lovey-dovey talk for me. I'm heading over to the monkey bars. Come over if you wanna play." He headed off across the playground with Ian right behind him, while Hope, Bailey Ann and Miller stuck around the fence with Mikey.

Maybe they knew he felt funny all of sudden, kind of dizzy like they'd been spinning on an old merry-go-round instead of riding the spring animals. "The sheriff and my mom?" he asked. "Getting married?"

"They're the only ones left," Hope said. "All Uncle Marsh's brothers and cousins are either married or getting married like Cash is going to marry my mom soon."

"And Daddy already married Mommy," Bailey Ann added in with a big smile. "Uncle Marsh is gonna be next, and your mommy is the only one close to his age." Her forehead scrunched up. "At least, I think they're close in age."

"Yeah, they are," Miller Haven chimed in. "Marsh is cousins with my dad and uncles."

"So if your mom marries Uncle Marsh, we'll all be cousins," Bailey Ann said.

"The family will be even bigger," Hope said, and she was smiling so big that Mikey found himself smiling back a little. Then her smile fell away, and she suddenly looked really sad.

And Hope never looked sad, so Mikey quickly asked, "Are you okay?"

She nodded. "Yeah, it's just that…for so many years, it was just me and my mom. Uncle Cash was around, but he was just Uncle Cash then…and now I have all kinds of family…" She blinked and smiled again. "And friends…"

Family and friends. That was something Mikey had never had. Just like Hope, for so many years, for all his life, it had just been him and his mom. But then they'd moved into the Cassidy ranch and had Miss Darlene and Mr. JJ and the others.

"So do you want to play cops and robbers, so you can be the sheriff?" Miller asked.

He shook his head. "I like to play vet and fix animals."

"They're no animals here," Bailey Ann said.

"Yes, there are." Hope giggled and pointed to Caleb and Ian, who were hanging off the monkey bars making monkey noises.

Miller snorted but laughed, too.

And a strange noise slipped out of Mikey: a giggle of his own. He was happy, and the thought of being part of a family, of having cousins and uncles and aunts and a...dad...filled him with warmth.

But then that warmth reminded him of the fire and how it had burned down the one place he'd felt safe and happy.

And he doubted that he would ever have any family or even any friends if the truth came out...

## CHAPTER THIRTEEN

FROM THE OTHER side of the fence separating the playground from the parking lot, Sarah heard her son's giggle. A sound she hadn't heard in so long, and tears rushed to her eyes.

He was doing well. He was going to be okay.

She just wished that she knew if she would be okay. Or had she lost all her common sense along with her self-control? That was the only explanation for why she'd kissed the sheriff. But he'd been saying such sweet, sincere-sounding things to her.

And it had been so long since someone had looked at her the way that he did, like he really believed she was beautiful, and he made her believe it, too. He made her believe a lot of things were possible that just weren't.

Now she wished she hadn't accepted his invitation. But it was just ice cream, and Mikey would be along with them. It wasn't anything romantic.

Because she didn't have time for romance.

She might actually have a job, though. The principal had already called her for an interview, and she wasn't even sure that he would have received the results of her background check yet.

So, once again, she found herself buzzing to be let in the door, and then she was in the principal's office. He seemed like a very kind, older man. "I didn't expect to hear from you so soon," she admitted.

He smiled. "Well, our current nurse would really like to retire as soon as possible. She and one of our parents are really not comfortable with the level of care one of the students needs."

Bailey Ann. But the principal probably couldn't release the child's name or medical condition.

Then he continued, "And you have so much experience with someone with those needs. You also come highly recommended from several of our Willow Creek citizens."

She'd dropped off some letters of recommendation, but those had been from doctors and patients she'd worked with in other areas. "From Willow Creek?" she asked.

"Yes, one of our teachers and several of our parents recommended you, as well as Sadie Haven herself."

Sarah bit her lip, uncertain if she should protest or not. She wanted this position, but she wanted it on her own merits. "I didn't ask any of them to do that," she said. "I want to get this job because I deserve it, not because someone asked you to give it to me."

He grinned. "They didn't ask, but there was some mention of how foolish I would be if I didn't hire you immediately."

Sarah's face flushed like it had after she'd kissed Marsh Cassidy.

"But I already determined that myself from the glowing letters of recommendation from every patient you've ever had and from every doctor you've ever worked with. They also share in those letters that you're not just a great nurse, but you're also a great mother."

"To be totally honest with you, I am a good nurse," she said. She knew that; she knew how to treat patients and doctors. "But I'm not always so sure about how great a mother I am," she admitted. "I was actually going to ask to speak to Mrs. Lancaster."

"That's what makes you a great mother," he said. "Knowing when to ask for help."

She'd never had anyone she could ask before, not until she'd started working at the Cassidy ranch. Then Darlene and JJ had stepped in like surrogate grandparents to her son. And the rest of the family was amazing, too.

But instead of thinking of all of them, she thought of only one, of a cowboy lawman in a white hat.

MARSH COULD NOT remember the last time he'd been on a date. Not that this was really a date.

It was just ice cream with his father's nurse and her kid, as a thank-you for how well she'd cared for him. "Pretty lame thank-you," he muttered to himself as he sat in his truck at the curb outside the house.

He should have taken her to dinner and a movie or something even fancier. Maybe to Sheridan to a fancy restaurant and a show or something.

But that would definitely be a date and one that they couldn't include Mikey on. So Sarah probably would have refused to go out with him then. And he wanted to talk to the boy, not just about the ranch, but about school and his interest in animals. He wanted Mikey to feel comfortable around him, but that was probably asking a lot when kids were never comfortable around him.

He really had no business trying to date a woman with a child, especially given how busy he was. Not that it was a date. It didn't sound like Sarah would have accepted if she'd thought it was anything more than ice cream.

But she had kissed him. His lips still tingled from that all-too-brief contact. After she'd done that, he'd asked her out. So it felt like a date to him.

He felt as nervous as if it was one. He wasn't even sure if he should just walk into the house or if he should ring the doorbell for her to answer.

And that was ridiculous, acting like a teenager showing up for the first time at his girlfriend's house, afraid to meet her father. After all, the man in this house was *his* father, who was probably going to be pretty confused if Marsh rang the doorbell.

He was probably going to be pretty confused by Marsh taking out his nurse and her son anyway. And he was probably going to be pretty pleased, too.

JJ would definitely get the wrong idea, just like Sadie had

the other night when she'd interrupted their almost kiss. But she hadn't been there to stop Sarah that afternoon.

Why had she kissed him? She'd apologized, but she hadn't explained why she'd actually done it. Though he was really glad that she had.

Staring at the house as he was, he noticed curtains moving in the living room. Was she in there, watching him and wondering if he'd changed his mind?

If he'd chickened out?

He faced danger a lot in his job, and he never hesitated to rush in, to rush to the rescue. But Sarah didn't need anyone to rescue her. She was the one who took care of everyone else, her patients, her son.

Maybe it was Mikey looking out the window. Hopefully, the kid was eager to go out for ice cream with him. Hopefully, Marsh didn't intimidate him too much as he tended to do to other kids. He got out of his truck and headed up to the front door, and he hesitated for a moment, uncertain again if he should knock before letting himself in. But he shook his head at the silliness of that and opened the door to step inside.

Then he glanced through the foyer into the living room. But it wasn't Mikey and Sarah who'd been watching him through the window; his dad stood there.

"What's wrong?" JJ asked. "You were sitting in your truck for a long time."

"I was…" He couldn't admit that he was scared, not to his dad, who always relied on him to be strong. "I was finishing up some emails on my phone." Now he was the one lying.

His dad snorted. "You were staring at the house the whole time."

"I…just have a lot on my mind," he admitted.

"I'm sorry," JJ said. "I know I dump all my troubles on you—"

"Dad," Marsh interrupted him. "I wasn't thinking about you."

Heels clicked against the hardwood floor, and they both turned to where Sarah was walking in from the kitchen. She was still wearing that pretty dress with sandals that she'd been wearing earlier.

She blushed when he met her gaze. "I can change," she said.

"No!" he said a little too forcefully. "I mean...you look..." Beautiful.

"It's just ice cream," she said.

"Ice cream?" JJ asked, and he was watching them with a smile on his face and twinkling in his dark eyes.

"Yeah, I'm taking Sarah and Mikey out for ice cream," Marsh said.

"To celebrate her new job?" JJ asked.

Marsh turned back to Sarah. "You got it?"

She smiled, and her whole face glowed with happiness. And something shifted inside Marsh, making his breath catch for a moment in his aching chest.

She was so beautiful.

"That's great," he said. "Congratulations."

"So you didn't know before you invited her and Mikey for ice cream," JJ said, musing aloud.

"I'm taking Sarah out to thank her for taking care of my ornery old father all these months," Marsh remarked. "How she ever managed to put up with the curmudgeon, I'll never understand."

JJ laughed, and so did Sarah. And that bright, happy laugh affected Marsh even more than her smile but not as much as her kiss.

Mikey must have heard the laughter because he appeared on the stairs. But he didn't run down them like the Haven children did; they always sounded like a herd of stampeding mustangs when they came downstairs. Mikey was quiet, as he always was, but he was smiling as he stared at his mother. "What's funny, Mom?" he asked.

"Mr. Marsh was teasing his dad," she said.

Mikey glanced at him then quickly looked away again.

"Ready for some ice cream?" Marsh asked.

Mikey hesitated. And Marsh didn't know if it was because he was shy or if he just didn't like him.

"Or he can stay here with me if he'd like," JJ offered.

Marsh shot his meddling father a glance. Was his dad offering that for Mikey's sake or for another reason, like matchmaking? "Are you Sadie?"

"That's why you ate all your vegetables, so you could have a hot fudge sundae," Sarah said, as if to remind her son that he had agreed to this. She also sounded a bit desperate, like she really wanted him to come, or maybe she just didn't want to be alone with Marsh.

"Hot fudge," Marsh said. "My favorite. I'd sure like to eat one with you, Mikey. Will you come along with us?"

Finally, the little boy nodded, making his blond curls bounce on his head, and he offered Marsh a shy smile.

And like when Sarah smiled or laughed, it affected Marsh, making him smile, too. He was glad the little boy was coming along with them and not because he wanted to ask him questions, but because he genuinely wanted to spend time with him.

"Are we going to walk to the ice cream place?" Sarah asked. "Because I should probably change my shoes." Her sandals were heels, though they weren't very high. "And my dress…"

"I can drive," Marsh offered because he really didn't want her to change. She looked so pretty.

"But they're having that movie in the park thing," Sarah said. "So it might be hard to find a place to park. I don't mind changing so we can walk."

"You look nice, Mom," Mikey said. "That dress is prettier than your work clothes."

Marsh liked the dress, too. With her out of her work clothes, he didn't feel quite as weird about taking out his father's nurse. Not that JJ needed her anymore. And now she had a job.

Sarah sighed, but she did it with a smile. "Okay, I'll leave the dress on and just slip into some flats." She had a pair by the door, and once they were on, she reached for the door handle.

But Marsh was also reaching for it, and their hands touched. He felt a jolt pass through him. And he was doubly glad that Mikey was coming along with them. Or he might want another kiss.

And this wasn't supposed to be a real date. It was just a thank-you and now a celebration of her getting the job at the school.

Marsh had also considered asking them more about the ranch,

but he felt guilty even thinking about it for some reason. Like he was betraying them both—and maybe even himself—by not focusing only on them. But maybe that was the betrayal, to start something he really didn't have time for.

JESSUP WANTED TO tell himself that he kept going out to the ranch just because he'd missed it all the years he'd been away. But it was more than that.

It was Juliet.

It was also his mother. And all the other people around the ranch. It felt like it was in his blood more now than it had been even when he was a kid. Maybe that was his new heart. The heart he suspected had belonged to his nephew who'd died earlier that year.

Dale had loved the farm so much that he'd been the ranch foreman with his older brother Jake as the overall manager. Jessup didn't want to step into either of those roles. He hadn't managed the Cassidy ranch well enough to keep it going. Of course, his health had limited his capabilities then. Ranch Haven was so big now, so much bigger than when he'd grown up on it, that they had a big staff. They probably didn't need help, but he would love to pitch in where he could.

At the moment, he enjoyed helping with the babies. He enjoyed helping Juliet, seeing her, talking to her.

Like Marsh with Sarah today.

The look on his face when she'd laughed...

It was probably the same look on his when Juliet smiled at him when he walked into the kitchen at Ranch Haven a short while after Marsh, Sarah and Mikey had left for ice cream. She was at the sink, cleaning up the dishes from the dinner they must have just finished. It looked like everyone else was already gone but for his mother and stepfather, who sat yet at the long table.

"Hey there, stranger," Juliet greeted him.

This was his first visit to the ranch today. Had she missed him like he'd missed her?

Sadie, sitting at the end of the long table, snorted. "Stranger? He's been hanging around here every day lately. You might as well move in," she said, and that twinkle was in her dark eyes.

Lem, sitting next to her, chuckled around a bite of cobbler he'd just spooned into his mouth. "You'd love that," he said, and he squeezed her hand.

It had been strange at first not just to see his mother with another man besides his father but that that man was Lem Lemmon, her old archrival. But they made such sense that he couldn't help but smile at them.

"Lem, I really do feel like your son's house is too big for me now," he admitted. "What with first Collin and now Darlene moving out…"

"And Sarah got the job at the school," Sadie said, "so I'm sure she and Mikey will get a place of their own."

He chuckled. "How do you know that she got the job? Or should I even ask?"

"You already know the answer," Lem said with a conspiratorial wink.

No doubt she knew it because, like most things, she had probably made it happen, just as she'd gotten Colton moved from the Moss Valley Fire Department to the Willow Creek one. And how Marsh somehow wound up taking the interim job of sheriff after the previous one suddenly retired.

It was good that she knew about the issue with the fire at the ranch. He had no doubt that she would probably somehow take care of that as well. After some sleepless nights, he'd figured out that there was nothing he could do. And since he knew he'd done nothing wrong, he wasn't going to worry about it.

That was money and property, and he'd learned a long time ago that people were what mattered most.

The people you loved.

Maybe he should move into the ranch. While Collin had wanted him closer to town in case there were issues with the transplant, Jessup wasn't as concerned about that as he had been. And Baker, who'd taken his brother Dale's place as ranch foreman, was a paramedic. He'd saved Sadie's life when her heart had stopped, ironically the same day as the fire, probably because she'd heard about it and she'd worried she'd lost him all over again.

But he was here. And he wanted to make up for all the years they'd missed being together.

"You should have brought Mikey and Sarah along with you today so we could celebrate her new job," Sadie said.

Jessup grinned at her. "Actually, she has a date."

Sadie's dark eyes went wide. "A date?" The twinkle was back. "With Marsh?"

"They're both determined not to call it a date," Jessup warned her. "And they insisted on bringing Mikey along with them. Maybe as a buffer, so that they won't fall for each other."

Sadie laughed. "Having kids around doesn't prevent love. In fact, I think our little guys at Ranch Haven have been the reason some have fallen in love. Bailey Ann, too."

Jessup chuckled at that and over the look he'd seen on his son's face, and not just when he'd looked at Sarah but when he'd looked at Mikey, too. "Marsh doesn't stand a chance."

# CHAPTER FOURTEEN

SARAH WASN'T SURE what she expected since this wasn't supposed to be a date. Marsh claimed it was just his way of thanking her for what she'd done for his dad. She wanted to say it was the same as she'd done for every other patient she'd had, but JJ wasn't just a patient to her. He was family. And tears stung her eyes at the thought of moving out and away from him.

JJ would be fine without her. She wasn't sure that she would be fine without him, though.

"Hey, this is supposed to be a celebration," Marsh said softly as he leaned closer to her where they sat on one side of the outdoor picnic table at the ice cream parlor. Mikey sat on the other side, shoveling his sundae into his mouth.

Of course Marsh wouldn't have missed the hint of tears in her eyes. She doubted he missed much being as observant as he was. He was probably a very good lawman.

"Are you okay?" he asked.

She nodded. "Yes. I am going to miss your dad, though."

"He's sincere about you staying with him," Marsh said. "He will really miss you and Mikey, too."

She doubted that Marsh would miss them, though. Until this week, he hadn't ever paid them that much attention. And she couldn't help but wonder why he seemed so interested in them now. Or was it the fire that he was interested in?

When she'd overheard Sadie and Marsh talking about it, Marsh had already known about the insurance company asking the fire inspector to reopen their investigation.

"We really need a place of our own," she said. For her and Mikey. She wanted to give him a home and roots, a sense of security that neither of them had had for a long time.

"And can we get a kitty for our new place?" Mikey asked hopefully.

"Miss Becca, Hope's mom, is going to try to find a landlord that will let us have a pet," Sarah said.

So far, Becca hadn't found anything, but she was stepping up the search for houses, warning that the rent and deposits would be higher. Now that Sarah had the job at the school, she was willing to pay more so that Mikey could have a yard and a kitten.

"There's Miss Becca now," Mikey said, his voice rising with excitement. "And Hope and Doc CC!" He jumped up from the bench and ran across the grass to meet them.

Marsh emitted a low groan and grimaced slightly. Obviously, he wasn't thrilled about running into his brother. Was he ashamed of being caught on an outing with Sarah and her son?

Maybe he should be concerned about that, though. A single mother whose ex-husband was in prison wasn't the best company for a sheriff up for election to be keeping.

"It's okay," she said. "We can tell them we just ran into each other."

"What?"

"You don't have to tell them that you asked us to come here with you," she said. "You can say you just ran into us."

He sighed. "It's not that I don't want to be seen with you and Mikey," he said as if he'd read her mind. "It's just that my family all have matchmaking on their minds right now, and they think everybody they know needs to couple up."

"And you're the last man standing," she said. She'd heard JJ and his brothers teasing him about that.

He nodded. "That's why they are all so determined to meddle in my life," he said. "But I don't have time for that, not right now."

Because he had so many other things to deal with. Like the fire...

Sarah wondered if that was why he asked them out for ice cream, to interrogate them over sundaes. But he hadn't asked about it yet, and with his brother, Becca and Hope walking up to them now, hopefully he would not have the chance.

Because she didn't want him talking to Mikey about it until she had the chance to find out what really happened.

"WELL, WELL, WELL..." Cash murmured as he walked up to the picnic table where Marsh sat yet with Sarah.

Marsh swallowed the groan burning the back of his throat, not wanting to offend her again like he seemed to have with his first one. Like she thought he was ashamed to be seen with her or something. Maybe that was because of how people had treated her after her ex-husband's arrest, like she was a criminal, too. The only thing she'd done was trust someone she loved.

Maybe that was why Marsh was so opposed to marriage, because he wasn't sure he would be able to trust someone like that. And it wasn't just because of his job but because of all the secrets their dad had kept from them.

Like Cash's paternity. His brother, with his blond hair, most of which was under his brown cowboy hat, and his blue eyes, looked more like little Mikey than he did Marsh or Colton or Collin.

"Well, well, well," Marsh replied back to his brother. "What brings you here?"

"Family outing," Cash said. "Becca and Hope and I are going to watch the movie in the park." He glanced at his watch. "But we have a little time to kill before it starts and decided to get some ice cream. Seems like you had the same idea..."

*Family outing.* That was probably what people thought of him, Sarah and Mikey all getting ice cream together. That they were a family.

He waited for the panic he usually felt when he thought of having a family of his own. But it didn't come. Maybe because he didn't have time with Mikey and Hope running up to join them. Then the little girl said to her new friend, "See, I told you that Uncle Marsh is going to marry your mom."

Sarah gasped before he could, even though he felt like he'd been sucker punched. "What?" Sarah asked, her face flushed a bright red. "Where did you get that idea?"

"Hope," Becca said, and the slight sharpness of her tone was an admonishment of its own. "You are not scheming with Grandma Sadie again, are you?"

Hope shook her head. "No. Bailey Ann said it first, that Uncle Marsh and Miss Sarah are the only ones left that aren't married or engaged yet. So they have to get together." She clapped her hands. "And here they are." She bumped her shoulder against Mikey's. "Told ya."

Mikey's face flushed, too, as if he was embarrassed.

"We're just here for ice cream to celebrate Miss Sarah getting a job at the school," Marsh said. That was easier to explain to the kids than that it was a thank-you for taking care of his dad.

But he wondered if maybe he should have gone with that when his older brother pushed back his brown cowboy hat and arched an eyebrow at him.

Becca cheered. "That's wonderful, Sarah. Congratulations! I'm sure Collin will be so happy that you'll be there to take as good care of Bailey Ann as you did JJ. That is cause for celebration for all of us. And maybe a kitten for you guys."

"I should wait," Sarah said, "until you find us a place to rent that allows pets."

"Of course," Becca said. "I actually might have a lead on the kind of place you need, with the yard and…" She glanced from Sarah to Marsh. "But I'm not sure yet if it will pan out."

Did Becca also think he was going to wind up with Sarah? Why? Just because they were the last singles their age in their group of acquaintances? He was sure there were plenty of other singles their age in Willow Creek. Probably teachers at the school. Would Sarah meet one of them now that she was working there?

That would be a safer bet for a spouse for her, someone with the same schedule and interests.

Marsh really had nothing to offer her but very limited time.

And yet, he didn't want the night to end, even though they had all finished their ice cream.

"Are you going to watch the movie, too?" Hope asked Mikey. "It's supposed to be scary."

"A scary movie for family movie night?" Marsh teased his brother.

"It's *Fantasia*," Becca said. "The 1940 animated version."

"What's that?" Mikey asked.

"Mickey Mouse," Marsh answered him. "We watched that when we were kids. When my dad or mom was sick and it was too late for me and my brothers to go outside, we would watch movies with the volume really low."

Cash's eyes glistened for a minute. "I remember that, too. Watch it with us."

"We didn't bring chairs or anything," Marsh said.

"We have extra blankets, and we can all sit on those," Becca said.

"We really couldn't impose," Sarah said.

And he wasn't sure who she was worried about imposing on, Becca and Cash or him, because she glanced nervously at him.

"Please, Mom," Mikey asked. "Can we watch it?"

"I'm sure the sheriff is busy—"

"No, I'd like to watch it again," he said. Especially with the brother who'd been missing from his life for so long. "Unless you need to get back to the house, Sarah."

"Your dad left just as we did," Sarah said. "So I don't think he'll need me tonight."

"He's probably heading out to the ranch again," Cash said. "I definitely think he has a crush on Melanie's mom."

So even his father was coupling up. Then Marsh would definitely be the last man standing. But he had to stay that way; he had too many responsibilities already to take on a wife and a child, too. He wouldn't be able to give them the time or the attention they deserved.

He didn't mind taking the time for ice cream and now for this movie. Once they made it to the park and found an area big enough for them all to sit together, the movie started to roll across the screen of the amphitheater in the center of the park.

Somehow, Marsh wound up sitting between Mikey and Sarah. At first, the kid leaned away from him, closer to Hope, who sat on his other side. Like his mother leaned away, too, as if unwilling to touch Marsh.

But then as the movie continued to play out with all its animated drama, Mikey edged closer and closer to him. And so did Sarah.

At one point, when the evil monster appeared on the screen, the little boy gasped and reached for Marsh's hand. And instead of taking just his hand, Marsh slid his arm around the little boy's slightly shaking shoulders. "I've got you," he said. "You're safe."

That was what he used to tell Collin and Colton when they'd get scared during that part. But he hadn't been able to keep them safe. Their mother had died, and they'd nearly lost their dad so many times. This little boy had suffered, too. In a sense, he'd lost his dad, and he'd been bullied because of what his father had done. Marsh didn't want him to suffer anymore.

Sarah leaned closer to him, her hand sliding over his, and she whispered in his ear. "Thank you."

He wasn't sure what she was thanking him for...

He was the one who was supposed to be thanking her. Now he wished he'd done that with something other than ice cream. He wished he'd done it with a kiss.

Or that this was a real date because then he could look forward to maybe kissing her at the end of it. But it wasn't a date. Like he'd had to keep reminding his family.

And himself...

"So," Lem said when he closed the door to their suite. "What part did you play in *all* of this?"

All of this was Jessup agreeing to spend the night instead of driving back so late. It was Sarah getting that job at the school. And it was Sarah and Marsh...

Sadie smiled at her husband, who knew her so well. "Actually, not as much as you might think..."

But she was so pleased with how everything was going, and with a big smile, she took a seat in the rocker recliner in the sitting area of their suite.

Once Lem settled into the easy chair next to hers, Feisty jumped up and claimed her seat on his lap. That little dog loved him.

Everybody did. No one more than Sadie herself.

She couldn't believe that herself sometimes. But it had worked out that way, entirely unlike what she would have chosen for herself, and maybe that was what was happening with Marsh right now.

Despite how determined he was to stay single, he'd taken Sarah and her son out for something. No matter that they both claimed it wasn't a date, it sure looked and sounded like one.

She glanced down at the screen of her cell phone now to look at the picture Cash had texted to her a short while ago. Marsh sat in the middle of a blanket on the grass with Mikey pressed up against him on one side and Sarah on the other, while the light of the screen played across their rapt faces.

But they weren't staring at the screen; they were looking at each other. Marsh at Sarah and Mikey at Marsh and Sarah at them both. And they looked like a family...and as she could tell her stubborn grandson, family was *everything*. It was more important than anything else.

And because they were family, they would figure out the rest of it like the fire...

# CHAPTER FIFTEEN

SARAH WAS SCARED and not because of the animated film they'd watched that was probably going to give Mikey a nightmare tonight. She was scared because of how sweet Marsh had been with him, how he'd comforted and protected him.

Even now, he was carrying him home. What had started out like a piggyback ride was now Mikey asleep on Marsh's shoulder, his arms draped around his neck from behind him. Every time she looked at them, she smiled and her heart ached with a yearning sense that this was what she wanted for her son.

A strong male role model. Someone who would love and protect him and never ever hurt him. And while Marsh looked like he fit the part now, she knew it wasn't a role he wanted. He'd said several times now that he was too busy, had too much on his plate, and now another burden weighed on his shoulders: her child.

"I can carry him the rest of the way," she offered. Again. But like the times she'd offered before, he shook his head.

"I've got him," he said. "And look…"

They were nearly in front of the house. The porch light illuminated the front of the traditional brick two-story house. It even had a white picket fence around it. This was what Sarah wanted, too.

"Did JJ leave the light on for us?" she asked. She didn't see his vehicle in the driveway, though.

"I left it on," Marsh said.

Because, as a lawman, he would think of things like that, like security. Which was what she wanted more than anything else for her son. But she was going to have to be the one who provided it for him. She couldn't count on anyone else. Not even Marsh Cassidy.

"I'll get the door," she said as she rushed ahead of him to punch in the code for the digital lock. Because so many people had been staying at the house, it had been smarter to install this than make copies of keys for everyone.

But while the house had once seemed full of people, now it was eerily empty. Collin was gone. Darlene had moved out, too, and tonight, even JJ was gone.

"I wonder where your father is," she murmured with concern.

"He's at Ranch Haven," Marsh replied, his voice a low whisper. "Cash got a text from Sadie while the movie was playing. It got late, and he didn't want to make the drive in the dark."

Or he wanted to give them some time alone like he'd tried to do when he'd offered to watch Mikey for them. Part of her wished that JJ had watched the little boy.

She didn't want her son to believe what Bailey Ann and Hope were saying, that she and Marsh would wind up getting married. That wasn't going to happen.

Marsh had the election to think of and that fire. While she was attracted to him—or she wouldn't have foolishly kissed him like she had—she wasn't the right choice to be the wife of a public official. She'd seen too many campaigns where opponents went after the spouses and family of the candidate more than the candidate themselves, and she was not about to put her son through a nightmare like that.

It would be worse than the one he was probably going to have tonight after that movie. But at least the nightmare he had tonight he would be able to wake up from.

A vicious campaign would ruin more than one night for them. It would ruin the life they were building in Willow Creek. He had friends. And she had a new job.

And hopefully, they would have a place of their own soon. But it wasn't soon enough now, with the prospect of her being alone in the house with Marsh. Because she was worried that she would be tempted to kiss him again.

"Don't worry," he said. "If you're nervous about him not being here, I'll sleep at the office tonight. I have some things I need to take care of anyways."

Of course he would notice her uneasiness. He didn't miss anything.

But Sarah couldn't help but wonder if she had missed something at the ranch that day of the fire, when Mikey had gone missing...

She reached out for her son. "I can bring him upstairs and tuck him in."

"I've got him," Marsh said, and he started up the stairs with her son dangling off his back.

She followed them up, sticking close in case Mikey slipped. But Marsh had one hand behind his back, holding him securely. Keeping him safe from a fall.

But who was going to protect her from one? Because she could feel herself starting to fall for this man with his white hat and white-knight manner of taking care of everyone around him, like he'd probably been doing since he was a boy himself.

Once in Mikey's room, she helped him remove the little boy from his back and settle him into his bed. She probably should have woken him up, but he was so limp with exhaustion that she didn't have the heart. He hadn't been sleeping well for weeks now; he needed his rest. She pulled the blankets up to his chin and stepped back from the bed and brushed up against Marsh, who stood behind her.

She tensed with nerves and awareness.

"We should go out in the hall," Marsh whispered close to her ear, and his warm breath made her shiver a little. "So we don't wake him up." He stepped back then, the floorboards creaking beneath his weight as he moved into the hall.

Sarah followed him, but just so she wouldn't wake up Mikey. She pulled the door partially closed behind them, so that Mikey wouldn't hear them.

"You don't have to leave tonight," she said. She didn't want to make him leave his own home. "I'm going to stay in Mikey's room, in case he has a nightmare."

"I'm sorry," Marsh said. "I should have thought of that. That movie used to scare the twins when they were even older than Mikey is."

"Not you?"

He shook his head.

He was so tall and broad, so muscular and strong, not just physically but emotionally, too. While his brothers had had their bouts of getting upset over their dad's health or with their dad for the secrets he'd kept, Marsh had always been calm and patient.

"Does anything scare you?" she wondered aloud.

Marsh stepped a little closer to her and stared intently down into her face. So intently that Sarah couldn't breathe for a moment; she couldn't swallow. She could only stand there. And she kind of wished she'd kept her heels on so she wouldn't feel so small and vulnerable in front of him. And maybe so that she could reach him again like she had in his office, so that she could kiss him.

But then she didn't have to because he leaned down. Their lips met, both of them coming together. The kiss was a jolt that went through her, that made her feel alive in a way she hadn't for a long time.

If ever...

But before she could wrap her arms around him, he pulled back, and his gruff voice finally answered her question. "You, Sarah. You scare me."

MARSH WAS SURPRISED he hadn't fallen down the steps when he walked away from Sarah. But he'd had to leave so that they wouldn't be alone in the house. He didn't want Sarah to feel at all threatened or intimidated.

Like he felt.

He'd once stared down the barrel of a carjacker's gun at what he'd thought was a routine traffic stop and hadn't felt as scared as he had in the hallway with Sarah, kissing her. That was why he'd gotten out of there as fast as he could.

He hadn't run away from the carjacker, though. He'd actually managed to talk the guy into giving him the gun. But he couldn't talk to Sarah, not without wanting to kiss her. And that was why he was definitely safer back at the sheriff's office. So he wouldn't do something stupid, like start falling for her.

Sarah deserved more. She was so compassionate and caring, and she'd already handled so much on her own that she deserved to have someone who could dote on her and Mikey, who could give them all their time and attention and who would never put them through any more pain and loss. Because what if the next carjacker couldn't be talked out of using his weapon?

Marsh had a dangerous job where he couldn't be distracted. And he'd already let his interest in Sarah distract him too much, from the upcoming election and from the fire at the ranch.

When he got back to the office, he found a note dispatch had left on his desk. The Moss Valley sheriff had returned his call requesting the meeting, and his old boss's reply was that they needed to talk as soon as possible. He had some vital information for him but was going out of town for the weekend, for a fishing trip where there was no cell reception. They would have to wait until Monday to meet up.

Marsh would have to wait until Monday to find out what this vital information regarding the fire was. Had the fire inspector changed their initial determination? If so, maybe Colton could find out since he'd worked for the Moss Valley FD before getting transferred to Willow Creek.

Marsh had to find out if the fire was going to be ruled arson. But he couldn't imagine anyone intentionally wanting to burn down that decrepit old farmhouse. It had to have just been an accident.

A horrible accident like how he was messing up with Sarah. He had to be sending her mixed signals, saying one minute that he was too busy to get involved with anyone, but kissing her the next.

And while he hadn't intended this evening to be a date, it definitely felt like one to him. It must have to her, too. So his only excuse for the mixed signals was that he was mixed up himself. While he kept saying that he had no time for anything but family and his job, he wanted to make time for Sarah and Mikey. But Marsh was used to putting other people first, like his mom and his dad and his brothers. And putting Sarah and Mikey first meant understanding they deserved more than he could give them.

MIKEY HADN'T BEEN sleeping like they thought he'd been. Because as tired as he was, he was also really excited. Not the nervous stomach excited like the night before school, but like the night before Christmas excited.

Hope was right. The sheriff taking his mom and him out had to have been a date. Hope insisted that because they'd eaten and watched a movie, it was. And once Mom and the sheriff dated for a little bit, then they would get married.

Or maybe they would just get married like Bailey Ann's parents did. They weren't exactly sure how it worked when people were older like Mom and the sheriff. Hope just knew that once they started kissing, they got married.

And tonight, through the crack in his door, Mikey was pretty sure he saw them kissing. But he hadn't wanted them to hear him, so he'd been super careful to move really quietly and not get too close.

It was weird seeing his mom with anyone. Mikey didn't even remember his dad; he'd been in jail so long. Mom offered to take him there to see him if he wanted, but Mikey didn't want to go to jail.

He really didn't want to wind up there like his dad, like the kids at his old school said he would. And he'd been so careful… had tried so hard to be good…

Like tonight. He'd worked hard to be good so that the sheriff wouldn't get upset with him. He'd tried to be big, but that movie had been so full of loud music and creepy cartoon monsters…

And Mikey had gotten scared.

But not about the sheriff. He wasn't as scary as Mikey had thought he was. He was actually really nice and really strong. And Mikey felt safe with him…until he thought about the fire.

Then he got scared again because he knew it was just a matter of time before the sheriff or someone else figured out that it was all his fault.

# CHAPTER SIXTEEN

SARAH HAD SPENT a restless night in Mikey's room, sleeping on an air mattress next to his bed. He hadn't had a nightmare, but she had. In her dream, Marsh was slapping cuffs around her son's thin wrists, and Mikey was crying and screaming for her to stop him.

To save him...

She awoke with tears running down her face and Mikey patting her hair. "Mommy, it's just a dream. It's just a dream. You're okay."

But she wasn't.

Thankfully, Darlene had shown up that Saturday morning with a "job" for Mikey to help her at the vet barn. Otherwise, Sarah might have smothered him with hugs and kisses and freaked him out with her overprotectiveness.

It was just a dream. It wasn't going to happen. Her son had done nothing wrong. But then why had he apologized that day?

She knew she needed to find out. But she also needed to get out of the house where Marsh lived. With Darlene gone and JJ spending more time out at Ranch Haven than with them, it would look to others like she and Marsh were living together.

And while it wasn't like that, it would probably start rumors that could affect his election. Mostly, it just unsettled Sarah too much for her to stay.

So once Mikey left with Darlene, she left for Becca's office. The realtor had mentioned, while they were at the movie the night before, that she would be at her office in the morning.

And now Sarah was there, too, pushing open the door to the empty reception area. Phyllis Calder wasn't at the desk. "Hello?" Sarah called out.

"I'm in my office," Becca called back.

Sarah walked through the open door to join her. Becca was at her desk, studying the screen of her computer. But she wasn't dressed in her usual business suit work attire. Instead, she wore jeans and a button-down shirt, and her usually perfect dark hair was mussed.

"Don't mind me," Becca said. "I mucked out the stalls this morning before popping in here to go over some documents for a closing next week. I figured what was the point in changing since I'm going to head right back to the barn after this."

Sarah smiled. "Makes sense. And I have a feeling that you like ranching more than real estate."

Becca shook her head. "No. I really enjoy both," she said. "I've always loved animals, but I also love helping people find their homes."

"You found me one?" Sarah asked hopefully. "You mentioned last night that you had a lead?" Because she really, really needed more space from Marsh, or she had no doubt that she would fall for him, especially when he was so sweet and affectionate with her son.

She couldn't risk Mikey getting attached to him any more than she could risk herself getting attached to him. And she was getting worried that it might be a little too late for her.

"Is that why you're here?" Becca asked. "Or is it about my daughter putting ideas in your son's head? I'm really sorry about her talking about you getting married. I'd blame Sadie for putting the ideas in *her* head, but I think she would have come up with them on her own. Cash and I are pretty sure she's a mini-Sadie."

"She looks like a mini-you," Sarah said.

"Acts like me a lot, too, according to Cash," Becca said. "But

I would be the last one to meddle in anyone else's love life. I didn't do so well with my own."

"But you and Cash are engaged," Sarah said. "Isn't that what you want?"

"Yes," she said. "I wanted it for twenty years, and I wish I'd told him earlier how I felt about him. But I was afraid that I would lose him and his friendship if he knew how I felt."

"Sometimes we outgrow those childhood crushes, though," Sarah said. "So maybe it's best not to act on them until we're older and wiser."

"Speaking from experience?"

Sarah nodded. "Unfortunately, yes. But I got Mikey out of it, and he's the best thing that ever happened to me."

"Same with Hope," Becca said. "I chose to have her on my own because I wanted so badly to be a mother. There's nothing better than having a child."

"Or scarier," Sarah said. She was so worried that she was doing the wrong thing with Mikey and that she was going to mess up his life and lose him.

"Love is pretty scary, too," Becca said.

Sarah stepped closer. "Are you sure you and Cash are okay?"

Becca smiled. "Definitely. But it was really scary letting him know how I felt about him, letting him know the mistakes I made over the years in not being totally honest with him. Cash has a thing about secrets. He hates them. But he forgave me for keeping some big ones from him. I was so afraid that he wouldn't."

Secrets.

Sarah had kept her share, but she'd told Marsh about her past. She just hadn't told him about her suspicions about the fire.

"But," Becca continued. "He understood that sometimes we keep secrets to protect the people we love."

Like Mikey.

That was what Sarah needed to do more than anything else. Protect him. "So about that place you might have found for me?" she asked. "How soon will it be ready? Today?"

Becca chuckled. "I can't believe JJ is kicking you and Mikey out."

"No, of course not." JJ was too sweet to do that. "He would like us to stay, but I told him that we needed to find our own place." Like Darlene and Collin had found places of their own already.

"Any reason you're so eager to leave?" Becca asked.

"It just doesn't feel right to take advantage of JJ's hospitality," Sarah said.

Becca narrowed her dark eyes and studied Sarah's face with obvious skepticism. "Is this about not taking advantage of JJ or is this because of JJ's son who still lives in that house?" she asked.

Sarah sucked in a breath, surprised at how astute the real estate agent was.

"You and Marsh seemed to be getting along last night," Becca said.

"I thought you didn't put those ideas in Hope's head," Sarah teased.

Becca held up her hands. "I swear. No meddling. I just haven't seen Marsh out with anyone in a long time."

So had he really asked them out for ice cream just as a thank-you, or had he intended to interrogate them? She couldn't imagine, with him as busy as he kept saying he was, that he was actually interested in dating her.

"I wondered if he actually took us out to ask about the fire again," Sarah admitted.

"Fire? At the Cassidy ranch?"

Sarah nodded. "Mikey and I were there that day."

"Of course you would have been," Becca said. "That must have been so scary."

"It was," she said. "I couldn't find Mikey for a while. That's how JJ and Marsh and Collin all got hurt, going back inside to look for him." She shuddered as she relived those horrifying moments.

Becca jumped up from her desk and came around to hug her. "I'm so sorry." She pulled back. "About the fire and about Marsh asking those questions." She shuddered now. "He interrogated me once about that fire."

"Why?" Sarah asked in surprise.

Becca sighed. "Apparently, after it was out, Colton found Cash's lighter in the cellar. I guess, because Cash was gone so long, his brothers were worried that he might have started the fire out of spite. Marsh was asking me if I let Cash onto the property, in the house."

"Darlene and JJ filled me in on what happened with Cash, why he was estranged from his family for so long."

"He was never estranged from me," Becca said. "And so Marsh thought I would know what happened. Cash stayed away more out of guilt than anger. He would never have risked hurting his family any more than he felt he already had."

"But the lighter…"

Becca shrugged. "I don't think it had anything to do with it. But it is a mystery how it got into the house since Cash never set foot inside. He suspects he lost it in the barn when he was checking out Darlene's mare a couple weeks before the fire."

The barn. A lighter. The house.

The words swirled through Sarah's mind like that nightmare she'd had. She shuddered again. "I—I should let you get back to your paperwork," she said, and she took a step back. "And I should go check on Mikey. He's with Darlene at Willow Creek Veterinarian."

"Hope is there with Cash today," Becca said. "They're going to have so much fun."

Sarah didn't want to take Mikey away from that, away from his friend. She would have to wait to ask him the questions she needed to ask him. But she needed answers. Soon. So she knew what and whom she had to protect him from.

The outer door creaked open, and a deep voice called out, "Hello?"

Her heart seemed to jump in her chest, and her pulse quickened. And Sarah wondered who was going to protect *her* from *him*.

MARSH HADN'T EXPECTED to find Sarah in Becca's office. And, clearly, she hadn't expected to see him, either. All the color left her face, making her eyes look even darker and bigger and more unfathomable.

"I—I was just on my way out," she said, almost defensively.

As if she expected him to argue with her. Then she turned sideways and tried to squeeze through the doorway without touching him. But her body brushed against his, and he sucked in a breath at the jolt of attraction that rushed through him.

And he heard her breath catch as well. Maybe that was why she was so eager to get away from him; this attraction between them unsettled her as much as it did him.

"I'll let you know when I hear back from the landlord," Becca called after her.

But the outer door was already closing behind Sarah, who'd gone back to being as skittish around him as that bronco Dusty had already moved out to the Cassidy ranch because nobody trusted it around the kids at Ranch Haven.

Marsh had no doubt that Sarah could be trusted around kids, or he wouldn't have offered his own letter of recommendation for the school to hire her. But he wasn't sure that he could trust her around him.

Or, at least, around his heart. He was determined to protect that, to not trust it to anyone, but he was afraid that if he wasn't careful, she might just steal it from him.

"What'd you do last night?" Becca asked him.

Heat rushed to his face. "What do you mean?"

"Well, she couldn't get out of here fast enough," she said, pointing toward the door that had just closed behind her.

"Maybe that was your fault," Marsh said defensively. "Maybe your daughter got those ideas about marriage from you, not Sadie."

Instead of being offended or defensive, Becca laughed. That was what he'd always liked about her, how straightforward she'd always been. Except, apparently, with Cash. Marsh hadn't realized how she'd really loved her best friend all these years. Maybe he wasn't as observant as he'd prided himself on being.

"Are you here to interrogate me about meddling?" Becca asked. "Or do you have another reason for this visit?"

"I heard you say last night that you were coming in this morning," he said.

"Yeah, that's *how* you knew *I* would be here," she said. "But that doesn't explain *why you're* here."

That was the other thing he really liked about her; she was smart. He chuckled. "I'm here for you to find me a place," he said. "I think it's about time." He couldn't spend another night in his office.

"Yeah, it is about time," Becca agreed. "Your dad texted me last night, and he's going to tell you this today. He wants me to find someone else to sublease the house he's renting from Bob Lemmon."

Marsh sucked in a breath. "I know he was saying that it was too big, but he also offered to let Sarah and Mikey stay as long as they want."

"Yeah, and that could be the end game for them to stay in the house, unless you want to sublease it. Your dad is going to ask you first."

Of course he would. But Marsh shook his head. "It's too big for me." It was really too big for Sarah and Mikey, too…unless she found someone. She was young and beautiful; surely she would get married again and maybe grow her family. He should have been happy for her and her possible future happiness, but instead, he felt sick.

"I'm not sure Sarah will want it, either. She wants something right away. And you're still living there—"

"I can crash with Colton for a while at his place until you find me something," he said.

Becca nodded. "That could work," she said. "Then when he and Livvy get married, and he moves into her grandpa Lem's old place with her, you can take over Colton's lease."

Marsh nodded. "Yeah, that sounds good." It also sounded really lonely for some reason.

"Unless…" Becca murmured.

"Unless what?"

"Unless you plan on getting married soon yourself."

Marsh laughed, but he had to force it, and it echoed almost hollowly in her office. "You're listening to your daughter's schoolyard tales, too?"

She smiled and shrugged. "I don't know…you and Sarah are the last ones…"

"That's hardly a good reason to get together," he pointed out.

"No, but you were out with her and Mikey last night," she said. "Why?"

And now she looked at him like she was the one interrogating him. He backed out of her office.

"I'll leave you to get back to work," he said. "Sounds like I don't need your help at all." He doubted Colton would turn down his request to crash at his place for a while. As a paramedic and firefighter, the guy spent a lot of time at the firehouse.

Becca laughed and clucked her tongue, making chicken noises at him. "You probably have more help than you even realize yet."

Sadie. She was warning him or mocking him about Sadie and her matchmaking. But her meddling wasn't going to work this time.

Not with him.

ONCE JESSUP HADN'T been able to get away from the ranch and his mother fast enough, now he couldn't wait to get back.

But not just to her…

Not that he was going to be staying in the house. He was going to use the foreman's cottage that nobody was using anymore because the kids loved everybody being in the big house together. After they'd lost their parents, making Miller, Ian and Little Jake feel secure and happy was the priority. As it should be.

But having not been around any kids except Mikey for a while, Jessup figured he needed to get used to the constant commotion in the big house. And maybe he needed a place to rest away from it. Not every kid was as sweet and quiet as Mikey was. In fact, he was worried about the boy, which was why he'd rather leave the house and have Sarah and Mikey stay in it. Permanently.

He hesitated for a moment as he threw clothes into a duffel bag on his bed. Maybe he shouldn't leave Mikey and Sarah yet, not until he was sure they were all right, that Sarah would be able to afford to rent on her own. Not that Bob Lemmon was charging much, but it was probably a special offer to Jessup since they were stepsiblings now with their parents married.

"Where are you going?" a deep voice asked.

Jessup looked up to find Marsh standing in his open doorway.

"Becca just told me you were giving up the lease, but I didn't realize you were going to take off right away," Marsh said. "Where are you going?"

"I'm sorry," Jessup said. "It was a sudden decision. But I intended to tell you and Sarah and Mikey."

Marsh shrugged. "It's fine. I understand that the house is a lot for you. Where are you going, though?"

"The ranch."

"But Collin said that will be too far away if something happens…"

"If my new heart rejects me?" Jessup assumed that was what his son meant and couldn't bring himself to say, like voicing his worst fear aloud would superstitiously make it come true.

"I'm not worried about this heart rejecting me," he assured his son.

He was worried about someone else's heart rejecting him, though. Juliet had been treated so badly by her ex-husband that she probably wouldn't be willing to risk her heart again on anyone, least of all someone with his health issues and his penchant for secrecy. But he was leaving that all behind him now.

"Baker might have given up his paramedic job, but he knows what he's doing," Jessup said. "He saved Sadie before, and he constantly monitors her. I'll be safe out there."

"But why move out right away? Is this about the insurance money?" Marsh asked.

Jessup shook his head. "I really don't need the insurance money. Dusty insists on buying the ranch, and the insurance company can't indefinitely hold up the sale when it doesn't affect them. Sadie already has Ben and Genevieve working on that."

Marsh grinned. "Of course she does." His grin slipped away. "But you once planned on buying this place when the ranch sale went through. Why did you change your mind? Are you afraid something's going to happen?"

"No." He was hopeful that Juliet might take a chance on him, but he didn't want to share with Marsh that he was probably about to really be the last bachelor in the Haven/Cassidy family. "Are *you* afraid of something happening?"

Marsh shook his head. "No. I'm sure everything is going to be all right. The fire investigator would have to have some evidence to change their determination from accidental to arson."

Jessup had just about forgotten about the fire. But if that wasn't what Marsh was afraid of, was his real fear of something happening between him and Sarah?

# CHAPTER SEVENTEEN

AFTER A LONG weekend spent avoiding the house and Marsh, Sarah was happy with how fast her first week on the job at the school was going. Bailey Ann wasn't the only child who needed to take medication throughout the day, nor the only one Sarah needed to monitor to make sure she was doing okay. Despite the health issues and behavioral issues some were being treated for, the kids were well-adjusted and happy. Maybe happier because of the treatments, because the parents made sure their children got the help they needed.

Which made Sarah feel even more like she'd failed her own child. So she'd made an appointment with Mrs. Lancaster for herself first. She settled onto one of the small chairs around the table in the brightly painted office of the school counselor. The other chairs around that table were occupied by stuffed animals and dolls, making Sarah feel like Alice in Wonderland.

But Mrs. Lancaster wasn't the Mad Hatter. She was an older woman with gray hair and warm blue eyes. "Call me Beth, please, Sarah," she said. "I'm so happy you've joined us on staff at the school."

"Thank you," Sarah said. "Everyone's been so kind and welcoming." But she wondered if that would have been the case if they'd known about her ex-husband. For the older woman to help her son, though, she would have to tell her the truth.

And she couldn't help but worry that the rumors would start to spread then.

"You're already doing a great job," Mrs. Lancaster said. "You haven't called me once this week to help you with any of the students."

Sarah furrowed her brow with confusion. "What? Help me with what?"

"Some of the children need to be convinced to take their medications," she said.

Sarah shook her head. "No. They were great. And I checked to make sure that they really swallowed them."

Mrs. Lancaster smiled. "Yes, hiding them under their tongues is unfortunately something children do all too often."

"Not just children," Sarah said. "I've had my share of adult patients who have done the same."

"But I have a feeling you're not here to talk about the patients," Beth said.

"No," Sarah said. "I want to talk to you about my son. I'm concerned about him."

Mrs. Lancaster's brow furrowed now. "His teachers haven't shared any concerns. And from the times I've seen him around the school, he seems to be settling in well."

Sarah's anxiety eased some.

But then Mrs. Lancaster added, "He just seems to be quite shy."

"I have concerns about that," she said. And about the fire. "After homeschooling him, I was worried he would have trouble with socialization."

"He has friends," Mrs. Lancaster assured her. "I've seen him on the playground with all the Haven and Cassidy children and, of course, Hope Calder."

Would they still be his friends if they knew the truth? Marsh knew it, but maybe he hadn't shared it with anyone yet.

"I need to tell you some things that I'm concerned might make that situation change," Sarah said. For both of them.

"Whatever you say to me is confidential," Mrs. Lancaster assured her.

So Sarah shared her history with the older woman, who responded much the same way Marsh had, with little surprise and more sympathy and respect.

"I can understand why you have concerns about him," Mrs. Lancaster said. "But he seems to be doing so well."

"Will you talk to him?" Sarah asked. "Just to make sure? I've tried to get him to talk, but he just shuts down every time."

The older woman's blue eyes narrowed. "Is there something you specifically want to know?"

Sarah nodded. "Yes, he's been even more quiet and withdrawn than usual since the fire at the Cassidy ranch. I want to know why."

"It must have been quite frightening for him," Mrs. Lancaster said.

"For me, too," Sarah admitted. "And maybe I just freaked him out. Or…"

"Or what?"

"Or maybe he had something to do with it starting," Sarah admitted, dread gripping her. But ever since Becca had told her about the lighter—about the shiny lighter—Sarah's suspicions had increased. "I need to know…" So that she could help him, so that she could protect him.

MARSH'S MEETING WITH his old boss gave him more questions than answers. So he sought out his new roommate for his opinion. But, as he'd predicted, Colton was rarely at the apartment they shared now, so he had to track him down at the Willow Creek Fire Department.

"Man, you keep turning up everywhere I am," Colton joked when Marsh walked through the open garage door of the bay housing a shiny red firetruck. "I might have to report to the sheriff that I have a stalker."

Marsh snorted. "Yeah, right. I have to track you down here because I haven't seen you since I moved in. You sure you live there?"

"Sometimes it feels like I live here," Colton said. "Or at the hospital. But that's not such a bad thing." Because he got to see his fiancée at the hospital. Livvy was an ER doctor.

"Well, I'm glad you have so many places to live," Marsh remarked.

"I'll give you my place as soon as I can get my beautiful fiancée to the altar," Colton promised. "But I don't want to rush her."

Livvy's former fiancé had been a controlling narcissist, so it was good that Colton was giving her time. His brother was a smart man and a good judge of character.

"So why'd you track me down?" Colton asked.

"I had a meeting with my old boss today," Marsh said. "Did you get a chance to talk to yours?" After the message from Sheriff Poelman, Marsh had called Colton to get him to reach out to his former fire captain.

Colton groaned. "Stupid insurance adjuster is putting pressure on the inspector to take another look at the scene. But there were no signs of arson."

"But you found that lighter," Marsh reminded him.

"I wish I'd never seen it," Colton admitted.

"Even if you hadn't, this wouldn't be over," Marsh said. "That insurance adjuster is also pushing the Moss Valley sheriff to pull some people in for questioning."

Colton groaned again. "Dad?"

Marsh nodded.

"Is he going to do it?"

"No," Marsh said. "Sheriff Poelman isn't going to question anyone about poor maintenance, or he'd have to question himself." Marsh chuckled like his boss had during their meeting when he'd shared this *vital* information with him. "But if the inspector changes his report..."

"He'll have to bring Dad in," Colton finished for him, and now he released a shaky sigh.

"And Darlene and Sarah and Mikey." That scared him even more than his dad being questioned. Mikey was such a shy little boy, and Sarah was so worried about them being judged because of what her ex-husband had done. After the bullying they'd both suffered, she had reason to worry.

Someone might judge them because of that.

Marsh would hope that his former boss wouldn't, but from working with the man, he knew that the Moss Valley sheriff was a pretty cynical guy from all his years in law enforcement. And he did tend to rush to judgement. Like if one member of a person's family had committed a crime, he tended to believe the whole family were criminals. That had been the case with some of the families in Moss Valley.

But it wasn't the case everywhere else. He hadn't been able to convince his boss of that, though. That was another reason he was so happy to have his job in Willow Creek. He was definitely in a more positive environment, and he was the one who set the example for his deputies to be open-minded and fair.

Unlike his former boss.

Marsh didn't want him talking to Sarah and Mikey; he didn't want him judging them unfairly. And he most certainly didn't want them getting hurt.

They'd already been through too much. They deserved happiness and security. Hopefully, even though he couldn't offer that to her, Sarah would find that in Willow Creek. But the thought of her finding that with anyone else made him feel sick again.

"You okay?" Colton asked with concern. "You look a little pale."

Marsh nodded. "Yeah, I'm fine."

"I'm not sure I am," Colton admitted. "It doesn't sound like the issues with the fire are going away."

"Not until we prove what really happened," Marsh said.

*What had really happened?*

"IT WAS MY FAULT," Mikey said. And when he said it, he felt like a balloon that someone had popped with a very sharp pin. Like all the air left him...and he was just deflated and a little relieved, too.

Mrs. Lancaster didn't look shocked and upset with him like he was sure his mom would. She smiled at him across the table, where he sat like he was having a tea party with all her stuffed animals.

He wasn't sure why an old lady like her had all the toys. He didn't even like toys that much, especially not stuffed ones. He'd rather have real animals than pretend ones.

Like that cat in the barn and Miss Darlene's horse. And he'd just been trying to keep them safe.

"I don't understand," Mrs. Lancaster said.

And he felt even more deflated.

She'd promised that they could talk about anything and everything and that she would help him understand stuff. And he'd been so hopeful that things would get better. That it would all make sense.

But if she didn't know what happened, how could he explain it?

He wasn't even sure now what had happened. It had all gone so wrong so fast.

"What do you think is your fault, Mikey?" Mrs. Lancaster asked.

"The fire," he said. "It's all my fault…"

# *CHAPTER EIGHTEEN*

MIKEY'S FIRST MEETING with Mrs. Lancaster was right after school on Friday. Sarah didn't get the chance to ask either of them what they'd talked about, though. When she opened her mouth to ask the school psychologist, Mrs. Lancaster just shook her head then explained, "Mikey will fill you in when he's ready."

Then Sarah noticed how despondent Mikey looked. His head was down, and he wouldn't even meet her gaze when she called his name. Her stomach knotted with dread. But Mrs. Lancaster reached out for her hand and gave it a reassuring squeeze.

"It's not going to be as bad as either of you think," Mrs. Lancaster said. "We're all going to be fine."

And the pressure on Sarah's chest eased a bit, but Mikey didn't look up and his shoulders stayed bowed, as if he was carrying some weight on them. She wanted to cheer him up, and thanks to the voicemail Becca had left her a short while ago, Sarah might be able to do that.

So once they were safely buckled up in her car, she started up the engine and headed away from the school. But she didn't turn toward town.

"We know for sure that we can have a pet at our new place," Sarah told her son.

Ironically, she didn't know for sure yet where that new place was. Becca's voicemail had reminded her that she didn't care as long as it was safe and Mikey could have an animal. But she promised her more details soon and invited them to come out to the ranch to pick out a kitten before they were all gone.

She glanced into the rearview mirror, but Mikey was still looking down, physically and figuratively. "Did you hear me?" she asked.

"What?"

"We can go pick out a kitty," she said.

He didn't say anything.

"Don't you want one?"

"I… I do…but…"

"But what?" she asked.

"If I can't take care of it, will you?"

"You took good care of the mother cat at the Cassidy ranch, and you helped Miss Darlene take care of her mare," she reminded him. "You'll be great with your new furry friend."

"Mommy?" he asked, and there was some urgency in his voice. And this time, he met her gaze in the mirror. "Will you?"

"Of course I'll help you," she said. "I will always do everything in my power to help you, my sweet boy."

He let out a breath, like he'd been holding it, and he finally seemed to relax a bit.

She really needed to talk to Mrs. Lancaster, or maybe she just needed to talk to her son. Really talk to him…about everything. But Mrs. Lancaster's words seemed to caution Sarah against pushing him; she'd said he would tell her when he was ready.

Becca's ranch wasn't far, so Sarah didn't have the chance to get anything else out of him. She was glad that she hadn't tried and upset him when she saw all the other vehicles in Becca's driveway. A truck with Willow Creek Veterinarian Services was parked behind Becca's SUV. A truck with a light on the roof was parked behind that; it must belong to the firefighter, Colton. And then the sheriff's SUV was parked behind that.

The only Cassidy brother not present was the doctor, unless he'd ridden with one of the others. Sarah thought about backing up and turning around to drive off, but before she could shift her car, Hope was running up to the vehicle. So she turned off the ignition and unlocked the door that Hope then opened for Mikey.

"You came!" she exclaimed. And she sounded so happy to see him even though they'd been together just a short while ago at school. "I want to show you my horse and Mama's horse, and Cash has one here now, too, that's really big. Do you like big horses like Caleb likes that rodeo bronco?"

Sarah held her breath while she waited to see if Mikey would answer his friend or if he'd entirely shut down.

"I like Miss Darlene's mare," he said. "But I don't like it when animals are too wild."

Hope chuckled. "My horse is really calm. But some of the kitties are pretty wild. They were climbing all the curtains, so Mom made me move them out to the barn. The mama kitty is out here, too." She took Mikey's hand in hers. "It's right this way."

"He probably could have figured that out for himself," Becca said as she appeared beside Sarah.

Sarah knew Becca wasn't the only one who'd walked up to her. She could feel Marsh there, too, because her skin was tingling slightly. And there were several shadows on the asphalt around her vehicle. But she was focused on watching the kids run off toward the barn which wasn't that far from the house.

"She's like you were with me when we were that age," Cash said. "Bossy."

"You better run out there with them," she told him.

And he laughed. "Some things never change." He started after the kids, but she ran up and kissed him. And he laughed again. "And some things do."

"You're whipped," Colton, the firefighter, teased his brother as he followed Cash toward the barn.

"And you're not?" Cash teased.

Colton shrugged. "I'm not saying it's a bad thing. I'm not like Marsh, who swears he's staying single. But you know, I do remember saying that myself…until I met Livvy. Love changes everything." He turned back and stared at someone standing behind Sarah.

"Some things never change," Marsh said pointedly. "Becca's still bossy, and you're still a pain in the butt, little brother."

"If I'm so bossy, what are you doing standing here instead of going out to the barn with your brothers?" Becca asked.

"I didn't hear you tell me to," he said.

She jerked her thumb in the direction of the other Cassidys. "Sarah and I have some business to discuss. And as you pointed out, you didn't need me to find you a place to live."

"You found another place to live?" Sarah asked him. That explained why she hadn't seen him the past several days. She figured he'd just been avoiding her like she'd been avoiding him after that last kiss.

He nodded. "I'm crashing with Colton for now, until he gets married. Then I'll take over his place."

"His bachelor pad," Becca said. "I wonder why that sounds so sad…"

Marsh grunted. "Because Sadie has brainwashed you."

"Nothing wrong with thinking like Sadie Haven. She knows how to fix things and get things done," Becca defended her future grandmother-in-law. "She's brilliant. I wish I thought like her."

Sarah did, too. Maybe she could figure out how to protect her child while still doing the right thing.

MARSH WAS UNCOMFORTABLE leaving Sarah alone with Becca, especially since it seemed that his future sister-in-law was all in with Sadie's matchmaking. Even her daughter was all about marrying off whoever was still single.

But he had to agree with Becca, that bachelor pad now sounded sad to him, too. Lonely.

And Colton's place, with him gone so much for work or with Livvy, was a lonely place without Sarah fussing over everyone and Mikey quietly playing. He missed them more than he missed his dad.

"There he is again," Colton said when Marsh joined him and Cash in the barn. "He's following me all around. It's kind of sad…"

There was that word again. The word that had never been

applied to Marsh before. Now, Mikey—that little boy looked sad way too often. Except now.

Now, he and Hope played with the kittens that Becca had confined to one of the empty horse stalls. Or, at least, she'd tried to. They climbed up the door, their nails sinking into the wood. Hope giggled while Mikey kept catching them before they went over the top. His little forehead was furrowed with concern as he worked hard to make sure that none of them fell.

"You followed me," Marsh reminded him. He was the one who'd wanted to talk to Cash again about the lighter.

"But I beat you here," Colton pointed out.

"And I should give you a ticket for speeding," Marsh said. "You were driving too fast."

"Occupational hazard," Colton said.

"You are a hazard."

Cash laughed. "I would say I missed this, but..." His grin slipped away. "No, I did miss this. A lot. I really missed you guys."

Marsh's throat filled with emotion that he had to swallow down. He'd missed his older brother so much. The twins had always had each other; he'd felt the closest to Cash. Then he was gone not long after Mom passed away.

That pain and loss echoed inside his heart, making it feel hollow and empty. But it was safer to leave it like that than to give it to someone, someone that he might lose like he lost Mom and Cash and nearly Dad so many times.

He couldn't lose him over this, over a fire that wasn't his fault. That was probably nobody's fault, or so Marsh hoped. He guided Cash a bit farther from the kids, out of their earshot. They were busy with the kittens in the stall, so they were safe.

Marsh wanted to keep them that way. "Hey, I wanted to ask you about your lighter again."

Cash groaned. "I've already told you I don't know how many times. I wasn't in the house. I don't know how it even got there."

"You still carried that thing with you always?" Marsh asked with some surprise.

Cash nodded. "Yeah, since I'm not a smoker, I just carried it as a good luck charm."

"Like a rabbit's foot," Marsh remarked.

"Yeah, but my luck actually got better after I lost it," Cash said. "That was when I finally realized I was in love with Becca, probably my whole life."

"Maybe you should lose the thing, too," Colton suggested. "Maybe your luck would improve, too, Marsh."

Marsh wished he could lose it. But it was potentially evidence, so he couldn't, in all good conscience, destroy it. But he worried that if he didn't, he might wind up destroying someone's life.

SADIE'S CELL BUZZED, vibrating on the table next to her easy chair. She glanced down at the screen, but she didn't recognize the number.

"Are you going to answer that?" Lem asked. His eyes were closed; she'd thought he'd fallen asleep watching his news. But he hadn't, and he hadn't lost his hearing yet, either.

She wasn't sure who it was, but with everything going on in their lives, she didn't dare miss a call. So she swiped to accept. "Hello?"

"Mrs. Haven-Lemmon?"

"Yes, who is this?" she asked. Hopefully not a telemarketer.

"Uh, this is Sarah. Sarah Reynolds, Mrs. Lemmon."

"Sarah!" Sadie exclaimed. "I'm so happy that you called." She hadn't even realized the young woman had her number, but she was so glad that she did.

"I... I..."

Alarm shot through Sadie, and she sat up straighter in her chair. Attuned to her, Lem sat up straighter, too, and Feisty growled in protest of his movement. "Is everything all right, Sarah?" she asked with concern.

"I'm... I'm not sure."

"Jessup is here," Sadie said. "He seems fine..."

"He is," Sarah said.

"So this isn't about Jessup?"

"No," Sarah said. "I just need some advice. And you..."

"I would be happy to help you," Sadie said.

Lem chuckled. "Try thrilled," he muttered.

"Please, come out tomorrow. It's Saturday, so we can make a day of it." A party even.

"I just need a few minutes of your time—"

"I have all the time in the world for you," Sadie said. "And bring Mikey with you. Two o'clock."

"Thank you," Sarah said.

"You're welcome," Sadie said. "I can't wait to see you both." And she disconnected the call before the young woman could reconsider her request or realize what Sadie was up to.

But Lem knew. "Is she walking right into your web, my dear?"

"Did you just call me a spider?"

"It's better than the things you used to call me," he reminded her.

Better and probably pretty apt. She was weaving a web, but she wasn't trying to catch Sarah Reynolds for herself. She was trying to catch her for Marsh.

But she suspected Sarah's call for advice had nothing to do with Sadie's grandson. And suddenly, her blood chilled and she shivered.

Lem immediately lifted her blanket from her lap to her shoulders, making sure she was warm. Taking care of her.

He really was the sweetest man. But he couldn't chase away this chill. Because Sadie had a bad feeling that things weren't going to go exactly as she planned.

All she could hope for now was that nobody got hurt.

## CHAPTER NINETEEN

SINCE SHE'D MOVED to Willow Creek, Sarah had heard all about Sadie Haven. The woman was a legend for how she protected her ranch and her family and had even used a crowbar to rescue a dog from a hot car. She didn't hesitate to step up and do the right thing.

That was what Sarah needed to do. So she'd taken Becca's advice and reached out to ask Sadie for advice. She was less fearful about talking to this fearsome woman than she was her own son.

The trip to Becca's ranch had cheered up Mikey yesterday, so Sarah hadn't wanted to bring him back down by asking him about his meeting with the school counselor the previous day. She waited until the drive out to the ranch the next day before she asked, "What did you and Mrs. Lancaster talk about?"

Silence was his reply. She glanced into the rearview mirror to see if he'd fallen asleep. Even though his eyes were closed, his small body was stiff with tension. He wasn't sleeping. He was avoiding her question, like he'd avoided having a real conversation with her since the fire.

"I can pull over, and we can talk," she offered.

"No," he said.

She swallowed a groan. How had Mrs. Lancaster gotten him

to spill to her during one session and Sarah couldn't get him to talk to her at all?

"Mikey, you've been shutting me out since the fire," she said. "And I want to know why."

"I don't want you to hate me," he said.

And now she knew what she'd suspected for a while. "Mikey, I could never, ever hate you," she vowed. "I love you so very much."

His breath caught. "No matter what I do?"

"No matter what," she assured him. And it was true. He was her son. Her heart. And she knew him so well that she knew whatever he'd done hadn't been on purpose; it hadn't been malicious, which was why she'd made this appointment with Sadie. She wanted the older woman's advice on how to protect her family like Sadie always protected hers. "I love you so much, Mikey."

"But it was all my fault," he said, sobs making his voice shake like Sarah was starting to shake.

She tightened her hands around the steering wheel. "What, Mikey? What are you talking about?"

"The fire…" he murmured, his voice choked now as the sobs overwhelmed him.

"You apologized to me that day," she said. "But that was because I didn't know where you were, because you were in the barn…" She glanced in the rearview again, and he was shaking his head.

"I think I started it…"

"What?"

"I didn't mean to," he said.

"I know that. Of course you wouldn't mean to…"

"I found this old lighter in the barn," he said.

The lighter that Cash had lost. Of course Mikey would have found it; he always found things, especially if they were shiny, like Livvy Lemmon's charm bracelet and that earring.

The little boy continued, "And I didn't want it to start a fire out there with all the hay and Miss Darlene's horse and the cat…"

He would have been concerned about the animals because they had been his only friends out there.

"So you brought it into the house?" she asked when he trailed off. And she saw him nod in the mirror. "What happened then?"

"I dunno…" he murmured. "There was smoke."

"Where did the smoke come from?" she asked.

"I dunno," he said. "I didn't see the fire, but it must have started it. I touched it, Mommy. I touched the lighter. I must've started it."

She wanted to pull over now; she ached to hold him, to comfort him. "Whatever happened, it was an accident, Mikey," she said. "It wasn't your fault."

"The sheriff won't arrest me?"

"No," she said. She would make certain Marsh understood it was an accident.

"Will he still marry you?" he asked. "Will he be my daddy even though I'm bad like my daddy?"

"Mikey!" she exclaimed, and now she had to defend her son from himself. "You are a good kid. You are such a good kid. You are so sweet to every living thing in this world. You would never intentionally hurt anyone." But people had intentionally and unintentionally hurt him.

"I didn't mean it," he said. "I didn't mean for anybody to get hurt."

"I know," she assured him. She pulled her gaze from his in the rearview mirror and peered through the windshield at the sign for Ranch Haven. She was here. For a second, she considered turning around and going home, packing up and leaving. But that wouldn't protect her son.

And that was what she had to do above anything else. She had to make sure that Mikey was safe and that he could forgive himself for what happened. She was pretty sure that everyone else would.

As she neared the house at the end of the long drive, she noticed all the other vehicles parked near it. There were even more here than there had been at Becca's house. All the Havens and the Cassidys were here.

So she was probably about to find out if she was right, if they would really forgive them for the fire.

SADIE HAD SUMMONED everyone to the ranch this Saturday. Marsh figured it was to celebrate her oldest son finally moving back home. But then he saw Sarah's vehicle pull into the driveway, and he wondered.

Sure, Sarah was close to his dad; she could have been invited to the celebration. But was that his grandmother's real reason for inviting her, or was she playing matchmaker again? And why didn't that possibility annoy him like it once would have?

He still didn't have time for her games. He probably had less time than he had before. With the fire investigation, with the election coming up. But he was thinking less about them lately than he was about Sarah and her son.

So he stepped out of his SUV and headed toward her vehicle. She jumped out of the driver's door and jerked open the back door, and then Mikey was in her arms. The way they were clinging to each other had alarm shooting through Marsh.

He ran toward them. "What's wrong? Did something happen?"

Mikey wriggled loose from his mother, and he stared up at him with wide blue eyes full of fear.

"What's wrong?" he asked again.

"Nothing," Sarah said. "Nothing that you need to be concerned about…"

But he was concerned, very concerned. "I…care about you two," he admitted. "I want to make sure that you're okay…"

She nodded. "We're fine." She squeezed her son's shoulders. "Everything's going to be fine." But she sounded as if she was trying to convince herself of that as much as she was her son or Marsh.

"You're here!" Hope yelled as she ran toward them. Bailey Ann was close behind her, and then the rest of the boys followed, their white cowboy hats bobbing on their heads. "We were just going to go for a ride around the ranch. This place is so much bigger than ours. Come with us."

Mikey turned back toward his mother, and that fearful look was back on his tense face. "Can I?"

"Of course," she said. "As long as there's enough supervision."

"There will be," Baker said as he walked up behind the kids. His oldest brother, Big Jake, was right behind him. Baker turned toward Marsh. "You still know how to ride, Sheriff?"

Marsh grinned. "I might be a little rusty, but I still know how."

"Want to help keep these little cowboys and cowgirls in line?" Baker asked.

"They might be better at keeping me in line," Marsh said. "But yeah, I'll go." He wanted to keep an eye on Mikey, make sure that he was really okay. But before he could follow the others off toward the barn, Sarah grabbed his arm.

"Can I... Can I ask you something?" she asked.

He nodded. "Of course. What?"

"Did... Did a lighter start the fire in the house?"

He tensed with dread because now he had a pretty good idea why she and Mikey had been so upset. "I'm not sure what started it," he replied honestly.

"You asked Becca about Cash's lighter," she said.

"Yes, because it was found in the house." And he suspected she knew how it had gotten there. "But the Moss Valley fire inspector originally ruled that poor maintenance caused it."

"But they reopened the investigation," she said. "I heard you and Sadie talking about that."

He nodded. "But that—"

"Sheriff!" Baker yelled out. "You coming?"

"Sarah—"

"Go," she said. "I would appreciate you looking out for Mikey."

"Of course," he said. "I will. I'll make sure that nothing bad happens to him." And not just during the ride around the ranch.

Tears glistened in her eyes as she stared up at him. "Thank you, Marsh."

He wanted to kiss her then, so badly, to comfort her. But he'd already made her a promise that he might not be able to keep.

JESSUP STUDIED JULIET'S FACE, which was flushed either from running around after the kids or from the oven she'd just closed. She was working in the kitchen with Taye.

Miller, his seven-year-old great-nephew had been cooking with them until Caleb had pleaded for everyone to go for a ride around the ranch. Big Jake, named for his grandfather, Jessup's father, had caved in first to his stepson's plea, and Baker had been right behind him with the nephews he and Taye were going to legally adopt. Then the girls, Hope and Bailey Ann, had wanted to go, too. Baker and Jake claimed they could handle all the kids, but Colton and Cash said they were going, too. Since Collin, Genevieve, Becca and Livvy had been busy in town, Cash and Colton were responsible for taking care of both girls.

But now, they stepped back into the kitchen. "What?" he asked his sons. "You guys forget how to ride?"

They both chuckled. "No, we're going to see if Marsh did, though."

"What? Marsh is here?"

"He just drove up, or maybe he was just sitting in his SUV until Sarah got here."

"Sarah's here, too?" Sadie asked the question from where she sipped a cup of coffee near the hearth.

"Like you didn't know, Grandma," Cash scoffed.

Jessup's heart warmed hearing him call her that. He glanced at Juliet, who was smiling, too. Cash could have been a living example to her of her husband's infidelity, but she was so forgiving and kind that she looked at him as family. Period. And so did Sadie.

Jessup was so fortunate to have so many strong and loving women in his life, like his late wife. She'd felt so bad when she'd found out that Cash's father was married; she'd had no idea. But Jessup felt now that she was at peace knowing that her family was reunited and that Juliet wasn't bitter and resentful.

"Did you get a chance to meet Sarah the last time she was here?" he asked Juliet.

She nodded. "We didn't talk much, though. She was very quiet. Her son, too. But having all the Havens in one place can be a bit overwhelming for people who aren't used to all of you at once."

"You're a Haven now, too," Sadie said.

She wasn't yet, but Jessup wondered if she would consider becoming one.

Then Sadie added, "I think Sarah and Mikey had a situation much like you and Melanie had with Shep." Melanie and Dusty were upstairs with their newborns.

Juliet sighed. "Where the man she married wasn't who she thought he was…"

"You know?" Sarah asked. She'd slipped into the kitchen behind Colton and Cash, and since they were so big, they'd blocked her from everyone's sight. "You all know about my ex-husband?"

"Know what?" Colton asked.

"Sarah," Jessup said, and he didn't want to hurt her feelings or offend her, but he probably should have already told her this. "One of the nurses in the cardiologist's office told me and Darlene about your ex-husband before we hired you."

She grimaced. "Told you or warned you?"

He shrugged. "Maybe she thought she was warning us. I think she was just jealous because you're so much better at your job. Darlene and I knew, but we didn't tell anyone." He glanced at his mother. "I'm not sure how she knows."

"How she knows everything…" Lem remarked. He was at her side as usual, but he was bouncing Little Jake on his lap. With that long, snowy white beard and his bright blue eyes, he looked so much like Santa Claus that it was no wonder the toddler was so drawn to him.

Sadie had always been drawn to him, too, even when she'd thought she hated him. And probably the only reason she'd thought she hated him was because he knew her so well; he'd seen her in a way that nobody else had.

And that made a person feel vulnerable, like Sarah clearly felt vulnerable now.

"So you were keeping more secrets," Cash remarked.

Jessup tensed, worried that his son was going to be angry with him again.

But Cash smiled. "To protect someone…"

"But Sarah doesn't need protection from that," Sadie said, and she stared at the younger woman, her dark eyes intense. "Nobody should judge you because of what your ex-husband did."

"Nobody should, but they do," Sarah said. "And Cash is right about not keeping secrets. I should have told everybody already about my ex-husband. He is in jail for robbery. Apparently, he'd been robbing places for years. I thought he was working construction out of town. I had no idea."

"Of course not," Sadie said.

"Does Marsh know?" Cash asked. "Have you told him?"

Sarah nodded quickly, but her face flushed. "I think, like his grandmother, he already knew, though." Then she focused on Sadie. "I didn't realize that everybody would be here."

And, clearly, she felt ambushed and was starting to back up into the hall. "We can talk another time…"

Sadie jumped up from the table, and despite her age, she moved quickly, pushing through her grandsons to take the young woman's hands in hers. "I'm sorry, Sarah. We can go into my suite and talk privately."

Jessup considered stepping in to save Sarah from his mother. But he wondered now which of them had instigated this meeting. Before he could intervene, Sadie had whisked Sarah down the hall toward her private rooms.

Cash and Colton stared after them as if they wondered if they should rescue the young woman, too. "Poor Sarah…" Cash murmured.

"Because of her ex or because she's now alone with Grandma?" Colton asked with a chuckle.

Cash laughed, too. "Both. Maybe we should go catch up with the others on their ride." And his sons walked away, leaving Jessup, Lem and Juliet alone in the kitchen. The other Havens who were home were probably upstairs helping with the twins, who he could hear almost half-heartedly crying.

"I think Sadie is going to have her work cut out for her getting Sarah and Marsh together," Juliet mused quietly.

"Why?" Jessup asked and then bristled slightly. "He won't judge her for what her ex-husband did."

"He doesn't have to," Juliet said. "She's the one judging herself. And after being married to a man who turned out to be bad, she might not be willing to take that chance, to risk her heart, again."

"Even on a good man?" Jessup asked. And he wondered if Juliet was talking about Marsh and Sarah or about them. Not that he had always been a good man. But Marsh certainly was. He definitely wouldn't judge Sarah for her ex; he would respect her even more for how she was raising her son alone.

Jessup didn't want her to be alone any longer, though. And he realized he didn't want to be alone any longer, either.

# CHAPTER TWENTY

SO MANY EMOTIONS pummeled Sarah. Shock and fear over what Mikey had confessed to her. And then Marsh…

He'd been so sweet, so protective, so much the white knight rushing to her rescue. But that was just who he was; she couldn't take it personally. And once he knew the truth, he would have to follow the law no matter what promises he'd made her. She didn't expect him to keep them.

She'd also felt disappointment and humiliation walking into the kitchen and hearing them talking about her and about her mistakes. And she'd just made another one. Instead of following Sadie into her private suite, she should have run out of the house. But she couldn't leave without her son. And she had no idea where he was riding on the ranch with the others. But she did know that Marsh would make sure he didn't get physically hurt. That promise he would keep.

But the others…

"This was a mistake," she said aloud.

"I'm the one who made the mistake," Sadie said. "I shouldn't have invited everybody else out. I just thought this was a great opportunity—"

"To meddle." She should have been furious, but it was somewhat heartening to realize that Sadie knew about her past but still wanted to match her up with her lawman grandson.

Sadie gestured toward the chair next to hers. "Please, Sarah, sit down. Let's talk."

She shook her head and stayed near the closed door, ready to make her escape. But to where? To sit and wait in her car until Mikey returned from the ride?

"Sarah, I am very sorry," Mrs. Haven-Lemmon said. "I did take advantage of your request to talk to me to set up this little get-together in the hopes of bringing you and Marsh together as well."

"You wasted your time," Sarah said. "Your grandson will never want a relationship with me. Not once he knows…"

"You said that he knows about your ex-husband."

She nodded. "I told him that, though, like you and JJ, I think he already knew." She shouldn't have been surprised that Dr. Stanley's nurse would have "warned" them about her. Glenda was a gossip.

"Then what could he learn that would make him not want to date you?" his grandmother asked.

Sarah shook her head. "I can't tell you. This was a mistake." When she'd asked Mrs. Haven-Lemmon for her advice, she'd only had a suspicion, but now she knew.

"We all make mistakes, Sarah," Mrs. Haven-Lemmon said. "I made a big one today with you, by inviting the others to come out, too. And I am very sorry that I did that and didn't warn you."

Sadie had apologized many times, so Sarah found herself softening. "I appreciate that," she murmured. "And I should be flattered that you want to set me up with your grandson even though you know about my past."

"It's not your past," Mrs. Haven-Lemmon said. "It's your ex-husband's past. None of that was your fault, Sarah. And Marsh knows that."

"Voters might not," Sarah pointed out. "You shouldn't want me for Marsh. I would only hurt him. While you and your family don't judge me, other people do, like the nurse at the cardiologist's office. And the parents of the kids at Mikey's old school. Being involved with me in any way could hurt Marsh's

chances of getting elected." And she didn't want him sacrific-
ing a career he obviously loved.

"Sarah, that's—"

"It's the truth," she interrupted to insist. "But it doesn't matter. I don't have time for anything but my son. I have to figure
out how to protect him. And that's why I came to you for advice, because you try so hard to protect the people you love."

Mrs. Haven-Lemmon smiled. "They don't always appreciate that," she said. "And it doesn't always work."

"But you try."

The older woman nodded. "So try me, Sarah. Ask me whatever you want."

Sarah bit her bottom lip. Once it was out, she wouldn't be able
to take it back. "This might be one of those secrets that need
to be kept." That was probably the best way to protect her son.

"You took care of my son when I couldn't," Mrs. Haven-
Lemmon said, and her deep voice was even gruffer with emotion while tears glistened in her dark eyes. "You helped him
survive until his transplant, and you took care of him when he
was recovering from the transplant. You gave him back to me,
and after everything and everyone I've lost, it was the greatest
gift anyone could have given me."

She glanced down at her hand and the tattoo on her finger.
"Well, besides finding the love of my life right under my nose.
But Jessup coming back into my life was a miracle that I never
expected. You gave me that miracle, Sarah."

Sarah shook her head. "No, doctors and surgeons and probably JJ's nephew's heart were responsible for that miracle,"
she said.

The tears in Sadie's dark eyes spilled over and slipped down
her face. "None of that would have mattered if he hadn't made
it, if he hadn't been healthy enough for the transplant. You are
part of the miracle, too, Sarah. And the least I can do after everything you've done for my son and my family is give you my
loyalty, Sarah. You have it. You can trust me and know that I
will always be here for you. I will always give you my support
and protection."

The sincerity in the older woman's voice and on her face

overwhelmed Sarah. And tears rushed to her eyes. "When I married my high school sweetheart, my parents disowned me... even before I had Mikey. So I didn't dare go to them after his father's arrest. I know they would have just said that they'd told me so. And they had..."

"So you had no one," Sadie said.

Sarah nodded. "It was always just me and Mikey." That was why she was so afraid that she was going to screw up and screw him up. Had she? "Having support means so much to me."

Despite her age, Sadie easily jumped up from her chair then and pulled Sarah into a tight hug. And her big body shook slightly in Sarah's embrace.

"What's wrong?" she asked, worried about the older woman's health. Mrs. Haven-Lemmon had her own heart issues.

"You just..." She pulled back and stared at Sarah. "The way you look, your sweetness and now your situation with your family...you remind me so much of Jenny."

"Who?"

"Jenny is...was...my first granddaughter-in-law," Sadie explained. "She died in the crash with her husband, Dale."

Sarah sucked in a breath. Poor Jenny. She'd lost more than her life; she'd lost the chance to mother her sons. "Leaving those three boys orphaned..."

"Orphaned but not alone," Mrs. Haven-Lemmon said. "And you're not alone now, either, Sarah. Whatever you need, I will help you."

"I'm not sure how you can help," Sarah admitted. "I don't know what I expect you to do except maybe just listen and not..."

"Judge," Sadie finished for her. "I hate how alone you've been for so long, Sarah."

"I wasn't alone," she said. "I have Mikey. And I can't lose him."

"You won't," Sadie promised. "We'll figure this out. We'll make everything all right."

Just like her grandson had, this woman was making Sarah promises she probably wouldn't be able to keep. But she was so desperate that she wanted to believe them. And she really didn't have any other options.

So she told Sadie the truth and hoped that she wasn't making a terrible mistake.

MARSH HAD MADE a terrible mistake. He should have kissed Sarah when he had the chance, every chance he'd had. But that wasn't the only mistake he'd made.

He should have spent more time with Mikey while the boy and his mom had lived at the Cassidy ranch. The kid loved horses, but he didn't have any idea how to ride. So Marsh helped him on the horse and taught him the basics before they started off on their ride.

Then, on the return trip toward the big red barn they could see in the distance, when the sun beat down on Mikey's blond hair, Marsh took off his hat and put it on the little boy's head, but it slid down over his whole face.

The other boys laughed at him.

"You have a white hat like ours now," Caleb said.

"But it's too big," Miller said. "Here, use mine." He threw his hat like a Frisbee toward Mikey. But there was no way the kid could see it coming; he couldn't see anything with Marsh's hat covering his entire head.

But he instinctively took one hand off his reins and reached out for it, nearly sliding out of the saddle. Marsh was riding close enough that he was able to grab him and steady him.

"That looks fun!" Caleb said, and he threw his hat, too. Ian, of course, followed suit. The hats landed near Miller's in the mud along the trail.

It was good that they were heading back to the barn now because Mikey was probably going to be sore and maybe a little sunburned from the ride. Marsh hadn't done a good job taking care of him like he'd promised his mom he would. Marsh stopped both their horses and dismounted to pick up the hats.

Jake and Baker were in front of him, trying to keep up with Hope and Bailey Ann. Bailey Ann rode on the same saddle with Hope, her arms around her while the little girl galloped toward the barn. Hope rode like her mom, like she was born in the saddle. Caleb, hatless, put his horse into a gallop to try to catch up with the girls.

"Hey," Jake said. "You need to get your hat." He sighed. "I'll catch up with them." And he urged his horse, a tan quarter horse, to a gallop, too.

Marsh was trying to pick up all of the hats while holding his horse and Mikey's steady. Then Baker, who'd turned back to help, came up beside the horses to steady them.

"Maybe white wasn't the best color to pick for them," Marsh mused as he hit each hat against his leg and tried to get the mud off them.

"Jake got the boys those hats for his and Katie's wedding," Baker said. "But now they wear them every chance they get, not just for weddings, although we've had quite a few of those, too." Baker reached out and tried to raise Marsh's hat above Mikey's face. "This guy could use the same milliner we had fit the boys."

Marsh would buy Mikey a hat the first chance he got; the boy should have one of his own, especially if he kept hanging out with Hope. And Marsh had a feeling that he would. She'd already promised to teach him to ride. But Bailey Ann had insisted on being taught first, so she'd ridden with Hope instead of Mikey.

Mikey should have a lot of things, like a dad he could count on, one who would be there for him like Marsh wished he could. But with his job and his family, he wouldn't be able to give Mikey the time and attention the little boy deserved.

That the boy's mother deserved.

He plucked his hat from Mikey's head and put it back on his own, then he put Miller's on Mikey. The little boy smiled shyly at him, and something shifted in Marsh's heart, making him gasp at the intensity of it. This kid deserved so much, but he didn't expect it, and whatever attention he got, he seemed to appreciate so much.

"You're doing great," Marsh told him. "You're a natural rider."

"Really?" he asked. "Like Hope?"

The fact that he recognized how good Hope was proved he would be good, too.

Marsh nodded. "Yup, you'll be riding right with her in no time."

Instead of being pleased, the little boy's smile slipped away, and Marsh had that feeling he'd had when he'd first approached Sarah and Mikey by her car. Something had happened. Something emotionally traumatic for them both. He wanted to help, but he wasn't sure that she would let him.

That she would let anyone help her. She was so fiercely independent and protective of her son. And with good reason: they'd both been hurt.

Mikey followed the rules that Marsh had taught him, hanging on with his legs while tugging gently on the reins, and he rode along to the barn.

Baker took Caleb's and Ian's hats from Marsh so that he could climb back onto his horse. "Your brothers were wrong about you."

"What?" Marsh asked. "Did they think I forgot how to ride?" It had been too long, though. He missed it.

"They thought you might not be able to handle all the kids," Baker said. "But you're a natural."

Marsh chuckled and shook his head. "No. They were right about that. I've never been good with kids."

"I used to be uncomfortable around them, too," his cousin confessed, which was ironic since he was adopting his three orphaned nephews, and they clearly all already looked at him as a father figure rather than just an uncle now.

"I was the one who made them uncomfortable," Marsh admitted.

"Mikey's a shy kid," Baker said. "But he looks pretty comfortable with you."

"That's new," Marsh said. But that was because he was making an effort, one that he should have made sooner. But Sarah had made him uncomfortable, Sarah and all the feelings she'd inspired in him—the ones Marsh had been trying so hard to ignore. The attraction, the fascination...the warm fluttering in his stomach and his heart.

"Something's weighing on the kid," Baker said.

Marsh shouldn't have been surprised that Baker had noticed; Mikey's shoulders sagged as if the weight was almost literal.

"I saw that same weight on Miller after Dale and Jenny died," Baker said. "He blamed himself for his parents' accident."

Marsh sucked in a breath. "That's horrible."

"Yeah, guilt is a horrible weight to bear," Baker said.

And Marsh suspected his youngest cousin had carried that weight himself. Baker had been the first on the scene of that horrific accident.

"I can't imagine..."

Baker stared at him for a long moment. His eyes were a lighter brown than his brothers' or cousins', like topaz. "I think you can..."

Marsh had felt guilty that he hadn't done more for his parents, for his brothers, that he hadn't been able to do more, to help more with their medical issues and the ranch.

"That's too much weight for a kid to bear," Baker said.

Mikey needed help. And Marsh really wanted to be the one to help him. But he wasn't sure how he could or if he would just make it worse.

By the time he and Baker got back to the barn, Mikey was gone. Marsh rushed out of the barn to see Sarah driving away with her son, as if she'd just been waiting for him so she could leave.

And he had a moment's panic that they might not just be leaving Ranch Haven. They might be leaving town, and he wouldn't get the chance to see either of them again. A sense of loss rushed over him, overwhelming in its intensity, reminding him of how he'd felt when his mom died and when Cash left, reminding him of why he was so determined to stay single, so that nobody could hurt him again.

But he had a horrible feeling that it was too late this time. Sarah and her son had gotten to him.

SADIE HAD HAD Cash and Colton watching for their brother. And the moment he got back from the ride, they took him to her suite.

"Grandma, I don't have time for this," he protested.

"You told me you took the morning off work," she reminded him.

"It's not work," he said.

"It's Sarah," she surmised.

His face flushed, but he shrugged. "It's a lot of things."

"The fire," she said. "I know you're worried about that, about what the fire inspector is going to rule. I can tell you what it was."

He tensed. "What?"

"Arson," she said.

He sucked in a breath. "You think someone purposely burned down the ranch?" Because clearly he didn't think that was the case. He knew it was an accident.

So did she. But she had promised her protection. So she said, "Yes, I know it."

"Grandma…"

"And I know who did it."

He groaned and closed his eyes. "I don't think I want to know…"

She had a pretty good idea that was because he suspected, and probably had for a while, who was responsible.

She sucked in a breath, bracing herself before revealing, "It was me."

"What?" he asked, his dark eyes open and full of disbelief.

"It was me," she insisted almost defiantly. Lem was probably going to divorce her over this. But she'd made a promise. "I burned down the ranch."

## CHAPTER TWENTY-ONE

SARAH AND MIKEY came home to a little bundle in a basket inside the door. Someone must have given Becca the code to the digital lock. And now Sarah knew why the real estate agent hadn't been at Ranch Haven with Cash and Hope. She'd been out making deliveries.

Sarah was glad Becca had when she saw how happy Mikey was when they opened the door to the kitten chewing on the basket. "I forgot which one you picked that day," she said. Marsh had been there, so she'd been distracted.

"She picked me," Mikey said as he dropped down onto the floor next to the kitty. It had the tiger markings of its gray tabby mother, but its hair was longer and fluffier. "Hope and I sat on the floor, and she came over to me first and climbed right up." As if on cue, the kitty did it again, climbing up his chest to settle onto his shoulder like a parrot. It rubbed its face against his. And Sarah could hear it purring.

"She loves you already," she said as she eased down onto the floor next to them.

Mikey reached up to hold the kitten against his face. "I love her."

"And I love you so very much," Sarah said.

"Still?"

"Always," she promised.

"No matter what?" he asked.

"Definitely," she said. "But you know what happened…"

"The fire," he said, and there was the catch of tears in his voice. One slid down his cheek, and the kitten chased it with her paw.

"It wasn't your fault."

"It was."

"It was an accident," she said. "You didn't do it on purpose. You won't get in trouble for an accident."

He turned toward her. "I won't?"

With Sadie vowing her support and protection, she didn't think anything would happen to a six-year-old who'd accidentally started a fire. But remembering the destruction and the injuries because of it, Sarah felt sick. "We should tell the truth, though," she said.

Mikey released a shaky sigh and nodded. "I felt better just telling Mrs. Lancaster."

And she mentally kicked herself for not getting him help earlier.

"She said it was an accident, too," he said. "And it really was, Mommy. I just didn't want that lighter in the barn with the animals…and I brought it in the house to give it to you. But you and Mr. JJ and Miss Darlene weren't inside. And then there was the smoke, and I didn't know what to do."

He'd said the same thing in the car, but Sarah wasn't driving now and could focus more on what he was saying. "I think the sheriff has the lighter now," Sarah said.

"Good. He'll make sure it doesn't start any more fires." Mikey shuddered, and the kitten cuddled closer to him.

"We should tell him, too, about what happened," she said.

Mikey tensed. "He'll arrest me…like my daddy."

"Marsh didn't arrest your daddy," she said. "And your daddy did the things he did on purpose. What you did was an accident. You're a good kid, Mikey. The sheriff won't arrest you." She wasn't exactly sure what he would do to him.

How much trouble could a six-year-old get in for an accident?

Sarah drew in a deep breath, acknowledging that it was time to find out.

"Bailey Ann says her family has a rule," Mikey said.

"What kind of rule?"

"That they always have to be open and honest," he said. "No secrets. No lies."

Sarah sighed. "That's a good rule."

"Yes," he agreed. "We can go tell the sheriff what happened."

She had a feeling that he already knew.

SADIE HAD TRIED to talk Marsh into taking her into the office, where she could write out her confession. He'd told her she was full of it and that he wasn't taking a false confession. He didn't bother pointing out that the fire wasn't even in his jurisdiction because he hadn't wanted her to confess to his old boss, who might have taken it. And she'd told him he would be hearing from her lawyer. He figured it was Ben. But a couple of hours later, it was the deputy mayor who walked into his office, not the mayor.

He hadn't intended to work this Saturday, but it had been pretty obvious that his grandmother wasn't going to let this rest. "What are you doing here?" Marsh asked his step-grandfather after the receptionist escorted him back.

Lem held out his hands over Marsh's cluttered desk. "Arrest me."

"For what?" Marsh asked. "Did you strangle your stubborn bride out of frustration? The woman is infuriating." And wonderful, too.

Lem shook his head. "No. I'm here to confess that I was the one who started the fire, not my wife."

"Of course," Marsh said. The old man loved his wife so much that he would probably take a bullet for her, and apparently even a prison sentence for arson.

Lem wiggled his hands. "So, are you going to slap the cuffs on me?"

"No."

"What about your grandmother?"

"I'm not going to slap them on her, either," Marsh assured him. "I don't believe either of you started the fire."

"You don't?"

"Why would you?" Marsh asked the question that his grand-mother hadn't been able to answer, either. "What would the two of you gain by starting that fire?"

"Uh…maybe to get Jessup to move home?"

"He could have died going into that burning house," Marsh said. "There is no way she would have risked that. Grandma nearly died when she heard about the fire. She was at Ranch Haven in front of witnesses." As he'd pointed out to her.

"But *I* still could have done it," Lem persisted.

"But you didn't," Marsh said. "I don't know why you two are spontaneously confessing." But he had a pretty good idea. "I am not arresting either of you or letting you make any more false confessions. The only thing I will do is walk you out." He stood up and escorted Lem to the door between the back and the public reception area.

"There are other people here to see you, Sheriff," the receptionist said.

And he groaned, imagining that his entire family was standing in the public reception area. But when he opened the door, he didn't see any Havens or Cassidys. He saw Reynoldses: Sarah and Mikey. This wasn't a confession he wanted to take, either, but this might be the only honest one.

"Sarah," Lem said. "Sadie told you that she would take care of this. You shouldn't be here."

So Lem knew and Sadie knew. It was time that Marsh knew, too.

"Thank her," Sarah said. "But Mikey and I have talked about this, and he wants to tell the sheriff everything."

Marsh knelt down in front of the little boy, who was staring at the floor. "I appreciate this, Mikey. You are very brave and very honest."

The boy's chin quivered a little, but he nodded.

Then Marsh looked up at Lem. "Tell Grandma everything will be fine." There was no way he was letting a six-year-old carry any weight of guilt. Just like Baker had said, it was too much for him to bear.

He reached out to take Mikey's hand in his. "Everything will be fine," he assured the child, and he gently squeezed his small hand. It was so small.

Then he looked up at the boy's mother, and he was glad he was on his knees or his legs might have given out. The look on her beautiful face, the mix of gratitude and fear and fierce love for her child...

She'd never been more beautiful or more vulnerable. And Marsh had never been as affected by anyone...ever...

He managed to get to his feet and guide her and Mikey down the hall to his office. Then he shut the door behind them, and he went around his desk to fall into his chair before his legs actually gave out. "Sarah, if this is about what I think it is, I want to remind you that it's not my jurisdiction, but I will still have certain legal obligations to share what I learn."

She nodded. "We understand. But it was an accident. And maybe you can help us explain that to the right people."

He nodded now. "I will do everything within my power..." But he didn't have as much power as she or his grandmother thought.

She held his gaze for a moment, as if trying to determine if he was telling the truth. Then she nodded. "Okay, Mikey, you can tell Sheriff Cassidy what you told me and Mrs. Lancaster."

"Mrs. Lancaster?"

"She works at the school, and she's been helping Miller, Ian and Little Jake, too."

"Good," he said. If Mikey was going to tell him what he thought, the little boy was going to need some counseling. "Okay, Mikey, you can tell me."

"You won't put me in jail?"

"Of course not," Marsh said. "And whatever happened, I believe your mom, that it was just an accident."

Mikey nodded, sucked in a breath and then released it and a long, run-on sentence of an explanation of what had happened. He'd talked so fast that Marsh had to rewind the conversation in his head, and then he started asking questions to clarify what had happened.

"So you found the lighter in the barn?"

Mikey nodded.

"And you didn't want it starting the barn on fire?"

"I didn't want the kitty or Miss Darlene's horse to get hurt," he said.

"So you brought it in the house?" Marsh asked.

Mikey nodded.

"He was going to give it to me or JJ or Darlene," Sarah rushed in to explain, "but we were already outside then."

"You didn't see them going out to the barn to see Miss Darlene's horse?" he asked.

"I always ran around to the back of the house because I didn't want to wake up Mr. JJ if he was sleeping in the front room."

Marsh's heart warmed with the boy's consideration for others. He really was a sweet kid.

"We must have just missed each other," Sarah said. "He must have been going in the back when we were coming out the front. The front was easier for your dad when going down to the barn."

None of the steps had been in very good condition. The house had gotten really run down.

"Then what happened?" Marsh asked.

"I started the house on fire," Mikey said, and tears pooled in his blue eyes.

"How?" Marsh asked.

"With the lighter, in the kitchen."

Colton had found the lighter in the cellar because the kitchen floor had collapsed into it. Most of the house had collapsed into the cellar because it had been so structurally unstable even before the fire.

Marsh opened his middle drawer and lifted out the bag with the lighter inside it. Ever since he'd talked to Cash, a thought had been niggling at him. "How?" Marsh asked. And he came around his desk, opened the bag and handed the lighter to the little boy. "Show me."

"Marsh!" Sarah exclaimed.

"Show me how it works," Marsh said.

The little boy stared at it. "I dunno…"

"How did you even know it was a lighter? Did you see a flame come out of it?"

He shook his head. "Mr. JJ showed me a picture of it once.

Doc CC was holding it, but he looked a lot younger than he does now."

So Dad had still had a picture of Cash despite Marsh trying to hide them all after his brother had run away. He smiled. "So you don't even know how it works?"

"No, Mr. JJ told me that they're really dangerous, though, and to give them to an adult."

"You didn't try to use it?"

The little boy's face flushed. "I tried, but it hurt me, and I started coughing. There was so much smoke."

"Try to use it now," Marsh said. He pointed toward the wheel. "You push that down with your thumb."

Mikey bit his bottom lip and pressed on the wheel, but then he jerked and dropped it onto the floor next to Marsh. "Watch for the smoke now."

"There's no smoke," Marsh said. "And there's no fire." He picked it up and tried to spin the igniter with his thumb. A metal burr jabbed him. "Ouch," he said with a grunt. But he kept the pressure on it, trying to turn it. It was frozen in place. Cash had carried it like a rabbit's foot, but he hadn't actually used it. So nobody had realized it didn't even work.

"No way," Marsh murmured. And then, thinking of all the weeks he and his brothers had obsessed over this stupid lighter, he started laughing.

MIKEY TENSED. He'd been so scared coming here. Sure, Mom said that the sheriff wouldn't arrest him, but he hadn't really believed her. He'd started a house on fire, so of course he would go to jail.

He was bad.

But the sheriff wasn't arresting him. He was laughing at him.

"What is it?" Sarah asked. "Why are you laughing?"

Mikey was glad she'd asked because he wanted to know but was too afraid to ask.

The sheriff was actually crying now, or at least, wiping away a tear. "The lighter doesn't work."

"What?" Sarah asked.

He tried to push his thumb down that little wheel thing and grimaced.

Mikey knew why; it had hurt his thumb, too. "It's like it bites."

"Yeah, it is," the sheriff agreed. "I'm so sorry, Mikey, that you thought you started it this whole time."

"I did."

"But you couldn't have started it with the lighter," he said. "It doesn't work."

"Oh…" Confusion pounded at his head. "But there was smoke…"

"Are you sure it was after the lighter, or was there smoke when you walked into the house?"

He shrugged.

"Try to remember."

He'd tried so hard to forget that day, to forget what happened. But because the sheriff told him to, he thought hard about it. "It smelled funny when I walked in the house. The back door opens into the kitchen, though, and sometimes Miss Darlene burns stuff."

Marsh chuckled. "Yes, sometimes she does."

"She had made lunch that day," his mom said, "because I was doing the laundry."

"A stove left on or a dryer," Marsh said. "I'm pretty sure one of those things started it, not any of the people who confessed."

"Who else confessed?" his mom asked.

"My grandmother, Sadie, confessed earlier today, and the deputy mayor just confessed, too," Marsh said. "That's what he was doing here when you two came in."

"The guy who looks like Santa Claus?" Mikey asked. "He burned down the ranch?"

"No. He didn't, and neither did my grandma and neither did you," Marsh said. "I am really sorry that you thought all this time that you did."

"It was bad," Mikey said. "I felt so bad."

"You should have told somebody," Marsh said.

"Open and honest," Mikey repeated. Bailey Ann was even smarter than he thought.

"Why weren't you?" Marsh asked, and he glanced at Mikey's mom, like maybe he thought that she told him not to.

"I didn't tell nobody," Mikey said. "Because I didn't want to get in trouble. I didn't want everybody to think I'm bad like they did at my old school."

"Those people were wrong," the sheriff said. "And they shouldn't have called you that. You are a very good kid. Your only mistake was in not telling somebody, at least your mom, about what happened. What will you do if something like this happens again?"

"I'll do the right thing," Mikey replied. "That's why we're here, that's what Mommy says we have to do."

"Your mommy is very smart," Marsh said with a smile. "And very pretty."

Mikey felt little butterflies in his stomach, happy ones, though, that made him feel excited, not scared. Maybe Hope was right. Maybe the sheriff would marry his mommy, and then they would all be family. A big family.

"Your father is here," a woman said as she opened the door to Marsh's office. "Sorry," she said, "but he insisted on seeing you right away."

Marsh started laughing again as he turned to look at Mr. JJ standing in the doorway. "Let me guess—you're here to confess, too."

"Yeah, it was me," Mr. JJ said. "Don't listen to what Mikey is telling you."

"Mikey is the only one telling me the truth," Marsh said. "And because of that, we figured out that nobody started the fire, especially not with a lighter that doesn't even work."

"It doesn't work?" Mr. JJ asked.

Marsh nodded.

And then Mr. JJ started laughing until tears ran down his face like they had the sheriff's a little while ago.

Mikey wasn't sure what was so funny. Mom wasn't laughing, either. But there were tears running down her face. He wanted to reach for her, but then Marsh turned back to Mikey and held out his hand.

Mikey didn't know what he wanted, but then Marsh took

Mikey's hand and shook it. "Thank you, sir," he said to Mikey. "You helped me figure out a big mystery. You were so helpful. I should probably make you a deputy."

"Probably," Mikey agreed.

Then the sheriff pulled him into a hug. And Mikey linked his arms around his neck and held on. He liked the sheriff's hugs. Mom's were nice, too; she was soft and warm.

But the sheriff was so big, and that made Mikey feel safe like he hadn't felt in a long time. But then, over the sheriff's wide shoulder, he saw his mom's face.

And there was such a funny look on it, like she was the one who was afraid now. Did she think he was still in trouble? Or did she think she was in trouble?

## CHAPTER TWENTY-TWO

SARAH SHOULD HAVE been relieved. And part of her was. But another part of her was angry with herself for not questioning Mikey earlier and for not questioning his confession like Marsh had.

Poor Mikey had spent all these weeks blaming himself and feeling guilty. And Sarah felt guilty about that. But, in addition to the relief and the anger and the guilt, she felt something else.

Something she had no business feeling. But when Marsh was so sweet with her son and enfolded him in that bear hug, she fell for him. Hard.

Still, part of her couldn't help thinking that this was all he had really wanted from them: the truth about the fire. And that was fine, but suddenly Sarah wanted more from him.

But that wouldn't be right or fair. Not when she knew how a relationship with her might hurt him. Or, at least, his chances in the upcoming election. She closed her eyes, shutting out the image of Marsh holding her son, comforting him in a way that she hadn't been able to no matter how much she'd tried.

Because she hadn't been able to prove to him that he'd done nothing wrong. And that was what mattered most to Mikey, that he wasn't bad, that he did the right thing.

Now Sarah had to do the right thing. "Uh, Mikey, we should

let the sheriff get back to work," she said. "And we should get back to your new kitty."

"You have a new kitty?" Marsh asked.

"Yes, Becca dropped it off while we were at Ranch Haven," Sarah said. "I hope that's okay," she added to JJ.

He grinned. "Of course. I know she worked it all out with Bob Lemmon."

"Good," Sarah said. "But we should get going…" If she could pry Mikey away from the sheriff.

"Dad, can you take Mikey out to the reception area? I know Mrs. Little keeps some candy in the bottom drawer of her desk that she shares with really good kids."

"And we have a really, really good kid here," JJ said, and he reached for Mikey, swinging him up in his arms.

The nurse in her worried for a second that lifting the boy wasn't good for her heart transplant patient, but Mikey was light, and JJ was so much stronger than he'd been for probably a very long time. She wished she was as strong as he was…emotionally. She had to get away from Marsh. "I'll walk out with you both," she said, but when she started forward, the sheriff encircled her wrist with his hand.

"Please, talk to me for a minute," Marsh said.

She wanted to do more than talk; she wanted to hug him like he'd hugged her son. But it wouldn't be fair to either of them if she acted on her feelings.

"We really should get back to that kitten." She'd put her in the laundry room with food and water and a litter box. But she still didn't want to leave her alone for long.

Marsh's hand on her wrist held her long enough for Mikey and JJ to slip out of the office and close the door behind them. But the minute the door shut, he released her. "I just want to apologize, Sarah."

"Then I was right…" she muttered more to herself than to him since sobs were rushing up the back of her throat.

"Right?"

"You were just being nice to me and Mikey because you thought he had something to do with the fire," she said, and she was still whispering because she didn't want her son to hear that.

Marsh didn't immediately deny it, which she actually appreciated. Instead, his face flushed a bit. "I never thought he started it on purpose or that anyone did," he insisted. "The fire wasn't the reason I wanted to spend time with the two of you…"

She narrowed her eyes even as her pulse quickened. She wasn't sure she believed him, but she wanted to. Then, reminding herself and him, she said, "It doesn't matter, Marsh. It doesn't matter." Because it didn't change anything; she was still not good for him, not when he had an election coming up.

"Sarah—"

"Thank you," she interrupted him. "Thank you for helping him figure out that it wasn't his fault at all. He was carrying that guilt way too long." Her heart broke over that, over letting her son suffer. "I'm glad you got what you wanted, Marsh."

Then she stepped around him, opened the door and rushed out. And she couldn't help but feel like she was leaving behind what she wanted.

MARSH CALLED A meeting in Moss Valley with his old boss and with the fire inspector. They met in the sheriff's office in Moss Valley. Marsh dropped the bag with the lighter in it onto his desk. "This was found in the cellar of what was left of the house."

"So it was arson," the sheriff said.

"No," the fire inspector and Marsh said at the same time.

Marsh unsealed the bag and dropped the lighter onto the surface of the desk. "Try it," he said. "It doesn't work."

"Then why did you bring it to me?" the sheriff asked. "And why didn't you already turn this in?"

"While this was found in the house, it didn't start the fire," he said. "The fire was not intentionally set. Two witnesses there that day confirmed to me that an oven was used earlier that day and the dryer was on."

"That tracks with my first report," the inspector said. "The fire was caused by poor maintenance. Either the dryer vent had never been cleaned out or maybe the wind jammed it open and birds or mice made a nest in it, but I am certain the fire started there. The damage to the dryer indicated from the beginning that the fire originated there."

"Why doesn't the insurance company believe that?" the sheriff asked.

"Because that adjuster is notorious for pushing for arson charges so that he can deny claims," the inspector said. "He gets a bonus for every claim he denies or a percentage or something."

"So he's the one you should be investigating," Marsh told his old boss. "I know if he tries this in my jurisdiction that I will make sure it gets handled correctly, so that people who've already suffered a loss don't have to suffer more."

Suffering made him think of Sarah and Mikey, of the suffering they'd endured. The bullying, the judgement…and the way she'd turned on him in his office earlier this afternoon had him feeling like a judgmental bully himself.

He wasn't sure how he could make that up to her, to them, but telling her that the police investigation was closed was a start. And with the sheriff and the fire inspector closing the official investigation, the insurance company wouldn't be able to keep it open, either.

JESSUP COULDN'T BELIEVE the turn his day had taken. When he'd left Ranch Haven, he'd intended to turn himself in for something he hadn't done. He was pretty sure that Marsh wouldn't have actually arrested him, but Juliet hadn't been as confident. And when he'd left the house, she'd sent him off with a kiss and the promise to bake him a cake with a file in it.

He smiled just thinking about her, about that kiss, about how alive he felt. But he'd refrained from rushing back to her because he was concerned about Sarah. Even though she had proof that her son had done nothing wrong, she was still upset. And Jessup was worried that maybe *his* son had done something wrong.

He followed Sarah and Mikey back to the house to retrieve the kitty, and they'd all gone to Willow Creek Veterinarian Services to fill Darlene in on what happened and to have Dr. Miner check out the kitten.

Not that Cash hadn't probably already done that. But Mikey

was nervous about making sure that she was big enough to be away from her mommy.

Dr. Miner took the little boy to his office to evaluate the feline while he and Sarah talked to Darlene. Her hazel eyes filled with tears. "That poor little boy," she said, "thinking he'd caused it..."

Sarah's breath hitched as she nodded, her eyes filled with tears, too. "I was worried that he had something to do with it with the way he kept apologizing when we found him in the loft. He was so sorry."

Darlene nodded. "I know. I wondered about that, too."

Jessup had been in an ambulance at that time, so he hadn't seen Mikey's reaction to the fire. But he'd been so quiet after it. The boy was always quiet, though, so Jessup hadn't been too concerned about him. "I really just thought it was poor maintenance or, like Marsh pointed out, that the oven or the dryer caused it."

Darlene's face paled. "The oven. I was baking something before we went outside. Did I leave the oven on?"

"I was drying clothes," Sarah said. "It might have been that..."

Jessup winced as he tried to remember the last time he'd cleaned out the vent. He would have had to get out a ladder to do it, so he doubted that he had. And he'd always forgotten to ask the boys to do it when they'd come for a visit.

"No matter what caused the fire," he said, "it was an accident. No one is at fault."

Sarah nodded.

"Why aren't you happier?" he asked.

She shrugged. "I just feel so bad for doubting my son..."

"What about my son?" Jessup asked.

She tensed. "What about him?"

"You seem upset with him," Jessup said.

She shrugged. "I appreciate how he handled the situation with Mikey."

"What about you?" Jessup asked.

She shrugged again. "That's it. The sheriff got what he wanted. The truth. That's all he wanted."

"Are you sure?" Darlene asked the question now.

Sarah nodded.

"I'm not sure that's the case," Jessup said. He saw the way Marsh was with Sarah and Mikey. "I think he's really interested in you."

She shook her head. "He was just interested in how the fire started. He's told me many times that he's too busy to date, and he has the election coming up. Being involved with me wouldn't help him win that."

"Sarah," Darlene began, "I hope you know how beautiful you are, how deserving of love you are. Marsh would be lucky to have you in his life."

Sarah blinked several times as if trying to clear away tears.

"She's right," Jessup said.

Sarah smiled. "My son loves me, and I love him. It's more than enough." And she walked away from them, heading toward where Dr. Miner had taken Mikey and the kitten.

"Oh, Sarah…" Darlene sighed. "I wish she would realize how amazing she is."

"Ditto," Jessup said.

"What?"

"You," he said. "You have no idea how amazing you are, Darlene."

She blinked like Sarah had, like she was fighting tears. He didn't want to make her cry. Darlene had cried too many tears over the years. She'd lost too much.

He noticed Dr. Miner walking out with Sarah and Mikey, the kitten cuddled against him. The way the veterinarian was watching them brought a smile to Jessup's lips. Someone had realized how amazing Darlene was even though she hadn't. Apparently, he considered Jessup a threat, which was funny. Darlene was his sister, his best friend, his savior for years.

"Hey, little man," Dr. Miner said to Mikey. "Your kitty is in great health. So, do you still want to be a vet?"

Mikey tensed and turned toward the older man. "I…uh… I might have changed my mind."

"Really?" Dr. Miner asked. "What do you want to be now?"

"Maybe a sheriff."

Jessup laughed and so did Darlene, but Sarah was curiously quiet. Jessup loved that the little boy was idolizing Marsh. Marsh deserved it. He deserved Sarah, and she deserved him. But they weren't the only ones who deserved some happiness.

Dr. Miner sighed. "So I've lost another one," he said. He turned toward Darlene. "I hope *you* still love me."

Her face flushed, and her eyes glittered. "I tolerate you," she said.

Jessup laughed because he knew she more than tolerated him. She wouldn't have taken this job—wouldn't have moved into the barn—if she wasn't excited about her future.

Like he was excited about his.

His only concern was Marsh and Sarah. He wanted them to find their happiness, too.

# CHAPTER TWENTY-THREE

SARAH WAS LIVING out of boxes, waiting for Becca to set her up in her new place, which Becca had promised would be ready soon and that she would love. And even though both JJ and Mr. Lemmon had assured her it was fine, she felt strange staying in the house that JJ had rented.

Sure, he and Darlene had been as sweet as they could be, so supportive and kind. But she knew now that they wanted her to wind up with Marsh. But that was for her sake, not for his. They didn't consider what was best for him. So she had to.

She knew that *she* was not what was best for him.

And that was what she told him when she opened the door a few days after that eventful Saturday. "You shouldn't be here," she told him, but she stepped back and let him walk past her into the house.

Maybe he'd forgotten something when he'd moved in with his brother.

Everybody was gone but her and Mikey. And they would be gone soon, too, once Becca told her where they were moving. She should have pressed the realtor for more information, but she'd been busy with her new job and with her happy son and his new kitten. She'd started packing up some of their stuff so they would be ready to move as soon as the new place was ready.

She wondered now, as Marsh walked into the house, if she

should have moved away from Willow Creek just so she could get away from the sheriff and the feelings she had for him. But Mikey was happy here. He loved the school and even the bus and most especially his friends. He loved this house with its big backyard, so she wasn't in a hurry to move him out of it.

"Why shouldn't I be here?" Marsh asked.

"People shouldn't see you hanging out with me," she warned him. Too many people knew about her ex-husband for the gossip not to have started, not that anyone had started treating her any differently. Yet.

"What people and why not?" Marsh asked.

"Voters shouldn't see us together," she clarified. "If they think I'm as big a thief as my ex was, they'll never trust you, either."

"Sarah…"

"What?"

"Is that why you've been avoiding me?" he asked. "For my benefit?"

"I haven't had to avoid you much since you got what you wanted," she pointed out with a pang of hurt striking her chest.

"What did I want?"

"To find out what happened with the fire, and now that you know that Mikey had nothing do with it, you've been leaving us alone." It hadn't been that long since she'd seen him, but it felt like it had been.

"I know that Mikey had nothing to do with it," Marsh said. "But you don't know what caused it."

Her stomach tensed because she knew that he knew. "What was it?"

"The dryer."

"So it was my fault." Horror washed over her. JJ, Marsh and Collin had gotten hurt because of her.

"No, it was the fault of me and my brothers, who didn't keep up on maintenance at the ranch," he said. "We didn't clean out the vent. Or maybe it was the fault of the birds or the mice who put a nest in it. It was not your fault, Sarah."

She loved him for saying that. And just plain loved him. She knew that now without a doubt. He was such a sweet man. Such a champion for everyone he cared about. He took responsibility for everyone else, whereas her ex-husband refused to even take responsibility for himself.

"Marsh…" she murmured.

"Sarah," he murmured back. "I missed you."

"It's only been a few days since I've seen you," she reminded him. But it had felt like forever. It had felt like so much longer than it had actually been.

He stepped closer, and her mouth dried out as attraction overwhelmed her. "Why are you here, Sheriff?" she asked.

"To tell you what happened and that the insurance company has to settle. It's over, Sarah."

"Yes, Marsh, it's over," she agreed.

"Are you mad at me?" he asked.

She wished she was mad at him. It would make it easier for her to resist him, to ignore her feelings for him. But it was because she loved him that she had to resist him.

"I don't think you were completely honest with us, even though you wanted us to be honest with you," she pointed out. "I think you only started paying attention to us because of the fire."

"I honestly think that Mikey is an amazing kid. He's sweet and considerate and empathetic. He's such a good boy. And you…"

She didn't want to ask, but she didn't stop him, either.

He continued, "And you're amazing. You're beautiful and smart and compassionate. You're a loving mother and life-saving nurse."

"Marsh…" She wanted to tell him how amazing he was, too. He was righteous and kind.

"Go out with me again, Sarah," he said. "Just you and me, a real date."

She shook her head.

"Why not?" he asked.

"For your sake, I can't," she said. "You shouldn't be seen with me."

"Why not?" he repeated.

"I just explained to you that I could hurt your campaign

for sheriff," she said. "Even your own family had questions about me."

"Who?" he asked.

She shook her head. "It doesn't matter." She cared about him too much to allow him to risk his future for them. "Go, Marsh. You've said a million times that you don't have time for a relationship, that you can't give anyone outside your career the time and the attention they deserve."

He opened his mouth, but he didn't say anything. Obviously, he couldn't argue with her. But she didn't give him the chance. She left him standing in the foyer and ran upstairs, desperate to get away from him before she did something stupid and selfish.

Before she told him that she loved him.

MARSH WATCHED HER run away from him, and he didn't know what to do. He didn't want to run after her and put pressure on her to give him a chance. He wanted her to be with him because it was what she wanted, not because it was what he wanted.

He wanted a relationship with her and Mikey so very much, though. But he stood helplessly at the bottom of the stairs, staring after her.

"Hey..." a little voice murmured.

And he turned to find Mikey walking in the front door behind him.

"Did you just get home from school?"

Mikey nodded. "Mom lets me ride the bus now."

"Of course, she would," Marsh said. "You're very responsible." He'd brought a gift for Mikey. Sarah hadn't noticed the box, but Mikey did, his eyes wide. "This is for you."

Mikey stared at the box Marsh handed him.

"Open it," he urged him.

Mikey glanced around as if waiting for his mom to stop him or give him approval to open it. But then the temptation must have overwhelmed him because he took the top off the box and pulled out the white cowboy hat Marsh had had made. "For me?" he asked, and his voice quavered a bit.

"Yes," he said. "See if it fits."

And Mikey put it on his head. It fit perfectly, like Miller's hat had.

"It's white like yours," Mikey said.

"Yes. Do you like it?"

"I love it," Mikey said. Then he threw his arms around Marsh's waist and hugged him. "I love you, too."

"And I love you, Mikey," Marsh said. He loved the boy's mother as well.

But he didn't know how to make her believe it. And, even more, he didn't know how to get her to give him a chance, to love him back.

WHEN MARSH WALKED into her suite, Sadie held out her wrists. "Are you here to arrest me, Sheriff?" she asked. She knew that he wasn't here for that, but she did wonder why he was here.

He chuckled. "No," he said. "I'm not here to arrest you. Didn't you already figure out what caused the fire?"

"Me," she said. She would much rather take the rap than have a child be put through any more trauma than he'd already endured.

"Are you a stuffed-up dryer vent?" Marsh asked. "Because that's what the fire investigator determined right after the fire happened and again after the insurance company urged him to take a second look."

"Really?" Sadie asked with surprise. "It was a dryer vent that caused it?"

"Yes, it hadn't been cleaned out for a while or a bird or mice made a nest in it. Either way, the vent was clogged, and it caused the dryer to catch on fire," he said.

"Then why hasn't the claim been settled yet?" she asked with quiet fury.

"Because the insurance adjuster gets bonuses for every claim he denies."

"We'll see about that," Sadie said. She had to make certain that didn't happen again.

"I suspect he might not have a job after you're done with him," Marsh said.

"I don't want him putting any other family through this,"

Sadie said, justifying what she was about to do, what she had to do, so that her grandson didn't think she was just being vindictive, no matter how much that would have been justified as well. The adjuster had put a recent heart transplant patient through an unnecessary investigation. "I want to make sure that nobody else has been hurt because of his greed. And I want to make sure that he doesn't hurt anyone else."

"That's why I love you," Marsh said.

A smile twitched her lips even as warmth flooded her heart. "Why do you love me?"

"Because you use your powers for good," he said, and his lips were twitching, too, as if he was trying not to laugh.

She smiled and then sighed. "That's what I've been telling you." That was really all she wanted for her family. She just wanted them all to be as happy as she and Lem were now.

"That's why I'm here," Marsh said.

"It's not to arrest me?"

"Or Lem," he said.

"Lem?"

"He confessed, too, and Dad tried as well."

She smiled, so impressed with the men she loved. "But that's not why you're here," she said. "Why are you?"

"Because I need your help, Grandma."

# CHAPTER TWENTY-FOUR

THIS WAS THE day that Sarah would finally get to check out where she and Mikey were going to be living. So she should have been excited, but she felt listless instead. Mikey was excited, but he'd begged off going with her to check it out so that he could stay at Becca's ranch with Hope. Cash was going to supervise Hope teaching him to ride. She stared through the windshield at them as Becca backed her SUV, in which Sarah was a passenger, out of her driveway.

Mikey was all ready for the outing with that adorable white hat on his head. He looked like a little cowboy with that and the boots she'd bought him. Her eyes misted with how fast he was growing up.

And now he was happy and bubbly. He loved school, and he loved all his friends, though he'd admitted to Sarah on the way to Becca's that he wished they could be family, too.

He wanted more than just her and him and their new kitty. But she couldn't give it to him, at least not with Marsh. She couldn't risk affecting his career. Yet, she wasn't interested in dating anyone else, not even the nice male teacher who'd asked her out for coffee. She wasn't interested in dating anyone who wasn't Marsh.

"You're quiet," Becca said, and she glanced over the console of her SUV at Sarah. "Don't worry about Mikey. Cash and Hope will both make sure he doesn't get hurt."

"I'm not worried about Mikey," she said. And that was a strange new sensation, to not be worried that she was going to screw him up, that she was failing as a parent.

"And don't worry about your new place," Becca said. "You're going to love it."

Sarah nodded. She wasn't sure about that. "Aren't you driving away from town? I thought it was still in town?"

"It is," Becca said. "I have to take a bit of a detour. Road construction or something. You know..."

There was always some project going on in Willow Creek. It was being revitalized and reenergized. Sarah hoped the same would happen to her. Maybe the new place would help. But she loved where she lived right now. She loved that deck off the big kitchen and the fenced backyard with the swing set for Mikey and for her, where they had their nightly competition to see who could swing higher, high enough to touch the stars.

She loved that place. Maybe that was why she hadn't packed up much of their stuff yet. Not that they had much. They'd been nomads for so long. "Maybe I should buy..." she muttered.

"This place has an option to do that," Becca said. "I have a feeling when you see it, you'll want to stay."

Sarah didn't feel like they were ever going to get there, though. Becca seemed to drive around the entire perimeter of the town before she finally turned and started heading through it. Then she turned onto a familiar street. And Sarah leaned forward in the passenger's seat. "It's right in the same neighborhood?"

"I know you and Mikey are happy here." And then she pulled into the driveway of the house that JJ had been renting from Bob Lemmon, the house where she'd been living since the fire.

"I can't afford this, though," Sarah protested.

"The rent is on the low end of what you said you could afford. And as for purchasing, you have enough for a down payment as well. The payments wouldn't be much higher than the rent," Becca said. "You could handle this on your own. But you don't have to be alone anymore."

"What do you mean?" Sarah asked. "I can't take money from anyone." But she could pick up shifts at the hospital; Sue had already reached out to ask her to help out when they were short-staffed. She had always made certain to have a sizeable emergency savings fund, just in case something happened and she had trouble getting another job. That fund had accumulated quite a bit. She could do this, and Mikey would be so happy. She turned toward Becca and narrowed her eyes. "Does Mikey already know?"

"My daughter has a big mouth."

"She must get that from her mother. Because how else would Hope have heard?" Sarah asked, but she was smiling.

Instead of being offended, Becca laughed. "I'm tired of keeping secrets. It's better to be open and honest, but I did want to surprise you."

"I am surprised."

"Come on," Becca said, as she reached for her door handle. "Get out. Let's check out your new place."

"I just left here…" Longer ago than she'd realized when she glanced at her watch. "I know what it looks like."

"But then it wasn't yours," Becca said. "It's yours now. And somehow I don't think the house is the only thing that's yours."

"What are you talking about?"

But Becca had already hopped out of the vehicle and shut her door. So Sarah got out, too. Becca was fast; she'd already rushed into the house. Sarah followed slowly, hesitantly, as if she needed to be cautious. She felt a little like she was being ambushed again, like she'd felt at Ranch Haven a week ago.

But the house was as empty as she'd left it when she and Mikey had headed to Becca's ranch. Even Becca was nowhere to be seen.

She called for the realtor. "Where are you?" She glanced up the stairwell, but she didn't hear any footsteps overhead.

"Out here," Becca said. "What a gorgeous backyard."

It really was. JJ had liked it so much, too, that Sarah was surprised he'd left it. But he was home now, where he'd grown up, from where he'd run away. Where he belonged.

And maybe this was where Sarah and Mikey belonged. In Willow Creek. In this house.

But then other images flashed through her mind, of Marsh holding her son, comforting and protecting him. Of Marsh holding her, comforting and protecting her, and then the kisses they'd shared.

She released a shaky breath before walking through the kitchen and then through the patio door Becca had left open. She stepped out onto the deck to a profusion of flowers and balloons and even more twinkling lights than had already dangled off the pergola over the deck.

"Surprise!" a chorus of voices rang out.

One of those was her son's, and Mikey ran up to her, his white hat bobbing on his head. The other boys were there with their white hats. And he really did look like one of them, like he was a Haven. But that wasn't possible.

"Mommy, are you surprised?" he asked.

"Yes, very surprised."

"I'm sorry I wasn't open and honest, but Hope said that this was a good secret to keep."

Bailey Ann pursed her lips. "But—"

"I know, Bailey Ann," Hope interrupted her before she could start. They were more like sisters than cousins or friends. But she and Mikey were definitely best friends. She looped her arm around his shoulders so companionably. Though they were the same age, she was almost a head taller than him.

Like Sadie and Lem. They were there, standing behind the kids. And JJ was there, with his arm around Melanie Haven's mother, Juliet.

And Darlene was there with Dr. Miner, too, sneaking glances at him as if she couldn't look away from him. He was doing the same with her.

Everyone was coupled up but Marsh, who walked through the crowd alone. He wore his white hat and a deep green shirt. The badge wasn't pinned to his pocket today. He wasn't on duty, but his brothers teased him about responding to a call about disturbing the peace.

The only peace disturbed was Sarah's.

Everyone stepped back as he walked, letting him make his way to the deck. To her. But once he got there, he dropped down to one knee. And Sarah's heart dropped.

"What are you doing?" she asked, panic clawing at her, making her voice squeaky. "You need to get up…" Everybody was staring at them, and heat rushed to her face.

"Sarah, I know this might seem sudden, but I finally understand what my whole family has been blathering about," he said.

His family chuckled.

"When you know, you know," he said. "And I know that you and I and Mikey would have a beautiful life together. You've made me realize what matters most in the world. Love. I love you, Sarah, and I would be so honored and humbled and happy if you would accept my proposal."

She gasped and shook her head. "No. This is crazy. We barely know each other."

"I know that you are the most beautiful woman I've ever met. Inside and out. You care so much about all people and the most about people you love. You would sacrifice anything for the happiness of the people you love, even your own happiness. You don't have to do that, Sarah. If you would be happy with me, please say yes."

There were no chuckles now, but a few people sniffled. Sarah was one of them. Tears spilled out of her eyes. She wanted so badly to say yes. Because, despite what she'd said, she did know him. She knew he was such a good man, maybe the best man she would ever meet. And she wanted to accept his proposal for herself and for her son, who clearly already worshipped the man.

But could she be that selfish?

"Marsh, I don't want to hurt you…" she whispered.

"You'll only hurt me if you say no," he said.

MARSH FELT AS if he'd been down on one knee for a while. And she still hadn't said yes. But she hadn't said no, either.

He should have done this in private, though, he realized now. He'd taken some bad advice from his grandmother on this one.

But then Mikey walked up and put his arm around Marsh's

neck. "Mommy, please say yes," he pleaded. "I want this family to be our family."

"It is," Marsh assured the little boy. "Even if your mother doesn't want to marry me."

"I do," she said.

And everyone gasped.

But she didn't look happy about it, with those tears trailing down her beautiful face.

He couldn't stay on his knee any longer. He jumped up and cupped her face in his hands, brushing away those tears. "Don't cry, Sarah, don't cry. I don't want to make you sad. I want to make you happy."

"I just don't want to hurt you," she said.

"And like I said, the only way you'll hurt me is if you say no," he reminded her.

"But the election..."

"If people won't vote for me because of something that has nothing to do with you or me or Mikey, then I don't want their votes." He stepped slightly aside, so that she could see the backyard full of people. "Besides, with all the votes I have right here, there is little doubt that I will win. But I don't care about losing the election. I just don't want to lose you, Sarah. You and Mikey mean more to me than anything else."

She stared up at him then, with such wonder and awe, like she couldn't believe what he was saying. Like she couldn't believe he loved her. But then she must have seen it in his face because she wrapped her arms around his shoulders and hugged him tightly. "Yes, then, Marsh, yes, I will marry you."

He leaned down and pressed his lips to hers, sealing the proposal with a kiss. And his head buzzed as happiness and love overwhelmed him. He'd never loved anyone so much, and he knew he'd never been as loved.

She'd been willing to sacrifice her happiness for his. She was the most selfless, beautiful soul.

"Hey, cheapskate, where's the ring?" Cash called out.

And laughter followed.

Marsh patted his pocket, and panic flashed through him.

"I got it," Mikey said.

"Of course you do," Marsh said. And he stepped back so that the little boy could squeeze between them.

He opened the box and held it up to his mother. "Isn't it pretty, Mommy? I helped Marsh pick it out."

"Mikey has great taste in jewelry," Livvy Lemmon said with a smile. The little boy had found some items she'd lost in the room that had once been hers and would now be his for a long time to come, until he went off to college.

"It's beautiful," Sarah said, but she wasn't even looking at the ring. She was looking at her son and Marsh.

Marsh plucked it from the box that Mikey held, and he slid the ring with a sparkling oval diamond onto her finger. It fit perfectly. Just like they did.

"I love you," Sarah said.

"I love you."

"You two should get married right now," Mikey said. "Right here."

Marsh chuckled. "Well, we have to get a license first. But I do think this would be a beautiful place for a wedding." In what would be their own backyard.

"Caleb is eating all the cookies!" Hope called out to Mikey. "We have to go get some." Then she reached between them and pulled Mikey away.

Marsh laughed. "She is so much like her mother."

"She's already stealing my son," Sarah said, but she was laughing.

"Are you sure?" he asked her. "I know I sprang this on you…"

"Somehow, I think this was someone else's idea…" She pointed toward his smiling grandmother.

"She helped me get everyone together and work out the timing," he said. "But it was my idea. I can't imagine my life without you and Mikey in it. And I do want to get married as soon as possible."

"Me, too," she said. "I love you."

"I love you."

People rushed up to congratulate them then. They oohed over the ring and slapped his back. And then some teased his grandmother. "What will you do now, Grandma?" Ben asked her. "Take up knitting?"

She laughed, and it was an unsettling laugh. And Marsh had no doubt that she was already scheming.

As MIKEY LOOKED around the backyard full of people, he remembered the first time he'd met all the Havens and Cassidys in one place, at Ranch Haven. He'd been so scared, not of them, though. He'd been so scared that someone would find out he'd set the fire. But he hadn't set the fire.

He'd just been trying to stop one. He wasn't bad. He was good, really good, like the man who was going to be his daddy. Marsh.

"So I hear you're switching to being a lawman now," Uncle Cash said to him, and he touched the white hat that Mikey was wearing.

He nodded. "Yup."

"I'm still going to be a vet," Hope assured him. "Bailey Ann doesn't know yet if she's going to be a doctor or a lawyer."

"She has a lot of time to figure it out," Uncle Collin said with a really big smile.

Mikey loved this family. They were all so cool. But the coolest was probably Grandma Sadie. She'd told him to call her that, and that snickerdoodles were the best cookies. Hope thought so, too, but Mikey wasn't as convinced. He might have to have a few more before he made his final decision.

As he neared the table with all the food on it, he heard Grandma Sadie talking to Grandpa Lem. Something about how all the Havens and Cassidys were happy now, so they could focus on the lemons.

He grimaced at the thought of lemons. He'd rather have the cookies. But if they were focusing on lemons, that would leave more cookies for him.

Unless Caleb ate them all first...

\* \* \* \* \*

# WESTERN

*Rugged men looking for love...*

## Available Next Month

**The Maverick's Promise** Melissa Senate
**Big Sky Bachelor** Joanna Sims

........................................................................

**Faking It With A Fortune** Michelle Major
**Her New Year's Wish List** Makenna Lee

........................................................................

LOVE INSPIRED

**Forgiving The Cowboy** Tabitha Bouldin
**A Protector For Her Baby** April Arrington

brand new stories each month

# WESTERN

*Rugged men looking for love...*

MILLS & BOON

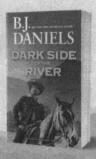

# ubscribe and ll in love with Mills & Boon eries today!

u'll be among the first read stories delivered your door monthly d enjoy great savings.

WE
SIMPLY
LOVE
ROMANCE

# MILLS & BOON